Nerves of the Heart

Nerves of the Heart

A NOVEL

Lucy Ferriss

THE UNIVERSITY OF TENNESSEE PRESS / Knoxville

Copyright © 2002 by The University of Tennessee Press / Knoxville.
All Rights Reserved. Manufactured in the United States of America.
First Edition.

Lines from "Mustang Sally" by Bonny Rice reprinted
by permission of Fourteenth Hour Music Inc.

Lines from "Ode to Billy Joe" by Bobbie Gentry reprinted
by permission of Universal-MCA Music Publishing.

This book is printed on acid-free paper.

Library of Congress Cataloging-in-Publication Data

Ferriss, Lucy, 1954–
    Nerves of the heart: a novel/Lucy Ferriss.— 1st ed.
    p. cm.
ISBN 1-57233-185-2 (cl.: alk. paper))

1. Heart—Transplantation—Patients—Fiction.
2. Children—Death—Fiction.
3. Mother and child—Fiction.
4. Roanoke (Va.)—Fiction.
5. Grief—Fiction.
I. Title.
PS3556.E754 N47 2002
813'.54—dc21   2001006533

For Daniel and Luke Couzens

♥

It is absolutely necessary to conclude that the blood in the animal body is impelled in a circle, and is in a state of ceaseless motion, . . . and that it is the sole and only end of the motion and contraction of the heart.

—William Harvey, *De Motu Cordis*

But I will wear my heart upon my sleeve for daws to peck at.

—Shakespeare, *Othello*, Act I, Scene 1

Acknowledgments

Thanks to Matt Hogan and the research librarians at Hamilton College for help in unearthing both the metaphors and workings of the human heart. My son Dan's knowledge of basketball was invaluable. Jerri Gavalchin of Syracuse University was generous with her time and insights into the life of an oncology researcher. For editorial support and guidance, thanks go to Mark Couzens, Bill Cobb, Eric Goodman, Rose Ann Miller, Josip Novakovich, Geri Thoma, Kip Kotzen, Barbara Phillips, Rod Stein, Jennifer Siler, Jeanne Leiby, Cary Holladay, and others too numerous to mention. Among dozens of sources consulted, the following were especially useful on heart transplantation and the medical history regarding the role of the heart: Robert A. Erickson, *The Language of the Heart 1600-1750* (Philadelphia: University of Pennsylvania Press, 1997); Gweneth Whitteridge, *William Harvey and the Circulation of the Blood* (New York: American Elsevier, 1971); Charles Siebert, "Carol Palumbo Waits for Her Heart," *New York Times*, June 13, 1997; O. H. Frazier, *Support and Replacement of the Failing Heart* (New York: Lippincott, 1996); Ira Parness and Alexander Madas, "Cardiac Transplantation in Children," *Pediatrics in Review* 10, no. 4 (October 1988); Kathy Lawrence and Jay Fricker, "Pediatric Heart Transplantation: Quality of Life," *Journal of Heart Transplantation* 6 (1987); Karen Uzark and Dennis Crowley, "Family Stresses after Pediatric Heart Transplantation," *Progress in Cardiovascular Nursing* (New York: Lippincott, 1986); Larry Gold et al., "Psychosocial Issues in Pediatric Organ Transplantation: The Parents' Perspective," *Pediatrics* 77, no. 5 (May 1986).

Nerves of the Heart

Waiting for her dad to get home from the garage, Brooke Hunter sat on the white boulder overlooking the road and the hill, and she thought about Charlie. A month ago Charlie had finally come to Granite Falls to visit, her brother Charlie, and he'd danced with her the way kids used to dance in the 1950s, whipping each other around by the arms like salt-water taffy. He was an awesome dancer, and she wanted him to stay and see her in Afro-Haitian, but her mama said no, he had to get back to Nashville, and Charlie said, "Sis, I am persona non grata," which sounded like a disease she didn't like to catch.

When she got older, Brooke was going to run away from home and find Charlie in Nashville. He hadn't ever, not once, told her she was pretty or a genius, but she loved him like crazy anyhow. How his hair flopped over his eyes so he had to push it out of the way. How he shut his whole face down when he played his saxophone, and she thought a boy must look like that when he lay down with a girl and started touching her. She didn't want to marry Charlie, nothing like that. Only to hitchhike to Nashville and arrive at his apartment with the clothes on her back—she'd wear her Save the Whales T-shirt and her cargo pants because they held plenty—and maybe her Cherokee loom stuck in a backpack, and he wouldn't expect anything of her. "This is my little sis," he'd tell his friends, and they'd all play music, and she'd just get lost in it.

Then her dad was coming up the road. She could hear the cycle a half-mile off. It scared her to death, the way ambulance sirens and planes taking off scared her. She didn't admit this to her dad. He'd just look at her with his mouth in an O between his mustache and his peppery beard, and he'd say, "Not *my* girl," as if suddenly she was someone's else's chickeny girl, and he was about to brag on the real daughter he had. Her mama was scared of these noises too, but they never talked about it. It was like that story about the boy with his finger in the dike. If they talked about being scared, it would be like they'd both taken their fingers out of the dike, and the sea would come washing in.

"Hey, Daddy," she said when he'd shut the motor down. He lifted the black helmet off his head, and he was human-sized again; he even looked sort of pin-headed. "Did you get the muffler fixed?"

"You heard her purring, didn't you?"

"Yeah. Not *so* loud."

He nodded fast, like she'd already guessed five right answers. "Eight times seven," he said, coming to sit next to her on the boulder, "minus four, times two, divide by four, add one, divide by three, multiply by eight, minus sixty-four."

"Right where you started," she said. She was leaning into his denim jacket, trying to sniff the smell. "Eight."

"My genius Brooke."

"You smell like wood."

"That's Eli's shop. Stopped by there on the way back. He's making wooden boats, you know, toy boats but big ones, the kind you can really sail. They sail them in the Tuileries."

"In Paris."

"There's my smart girl. When I take you there, you'll see."

"I don't want to go to Paris yet."

"Course not. You're not ready yet." He put his arm around her, and she liked his smell now, the oily tinge of the motorcycle shop and the sweet brack of the lake where he took her fishing.

"School starts in two weeks."

"*School.*" He gave her shoulder a squeeze. "The last thing a girl like you needs."

She knew better than to say she liked school. Her heart always beat a little faster around her dad, partly because he did all the exciting stuff but partly because everything was a test. "Ma's inside."

"Good. I love this time of day. Don't you?"

"Yeah," she said, and it was true—the sun was at a comfortable slant above Sawtooth Mountain, the birds were having a busy time, the cool air was just starting to slither up from the valley—but it was early yet, still afternoon, you hadn't given up the day. Right now Charlie was maybe coming home from his secretary job, stopping off to get some noodles and cheese for dinner with his friends. She couldn't picture the way light fell in Nashville.

"I'll go give Linsey a kiss, and we'll have us a little ride. Maybe I'll take you by Eli's shop; you can start imagining Paris."

"We didn't buy me no helmet yet."

"*Any* helmet."

"We didn't buy one."

"You've got the purple one, don't you?"

"Yeah. I guess."

"Then I'll go tell Linsey."

"Mama, you mean." He wanted Brooke to call her mama by her Christian name, but she didn't like that.

"Hssh." He put his rough index finger on her lips, the finger that got callused splitting wood toward winter. "We are the safety patrol," he said.

"Well, *I* am. In the fall."

"*School,*" he said again, his lip curling underneath his face hair. "We'll just do Dogwood Hill. You remind me to turn at the shop. C'mon now." He slid off the boulder and stood on the grass. He put his arms under her shoulders and lifted her, spinning her a little, her legs loose then snapping back. "Get your helmet and meet me at the cycle. Don't come in the house, okay? Or you'll get Linsey wheedling at you. We'll wave at her in the window, okay?"

"Daddy," she said, and she put her arms around his tight waist, his brass belt buckle at her nose. For a second her eyes filled with tears, and if she'd had to say why, she'd have said she missed her mama, but that was silly; she'd just helped her mama warp the loom. It was Mama who'd shooed her on outside; she had a cakewalk pattern to finish, her mama said, for a wedding order. Brooke didn't know why she cried so much. Her grandma in Wardleysville said it was her despond, which sounded like a growing-up thing.

"Let's get going, now. You got dance lesson in an hour."

He walked quickly to the house, whistling "King of the Road." Her bike helmet was on her handlebar, in the shed. She'd run fetch it in a second, and the wind pants she kept on a peg there; she'd be perfectly ready—*surprise!*—when he loped back out. For now, though, while he didn't look back, she stretched her neck this way and that, stepping into the driveway and round the other side of the apple tree. She strained after a glimpse of her mama's face in the kitchen or by the loom. She would give her a little air-kiss, to let her know she wouldn't just take off, even with Daddy on the cycle, without waving good-bye.

Chapter 1

*T*hey trained you, in the waiting period, to think of the heart as working tissue. They told you the terrible story of the first attempt at pediatric transplant. The donor, they told you, was a baby born with no brain, its heart a dumb muscle bound to die within minutes, hours at most, and the surgeon ready to harvest, to save a different baby, a sick baby who had a brain. But the law said no, they told you, the law back then, the law that said a beating heart meant life. Shutting his eyes by his son Toby's hospital bed, Nicholas Ames used to picture the surgeon's assistant standing behind the donor—*no brain*, not even a skull really, only a pinched dead little face like a dried-apple doll, with a cloth over it—ready to stop the knife if the surgeon began while the muscle still contracted.

But the law had changed now, they told you. Brain death was the rule of thumb. The organs came healthier.

They trained you, in other words, not to care what the heart had been doing before it arrived in the picnic cooler. Not to feel shy about scanning the headlines for news of a fatal crash, a sniper attack, a freak fall. "We're not adopting a *child*," Susannah Ames took to telling people, when they dared to ask after the heart's origin. True, this was the same heart Linsey Hunter had heard, a decade ago, on the sonogram pressed to her belly. But they trained you to think of it as useful, a young heart still beating for a child whose brain was alive.

Nonetheless you were grateful. Not just to the healthy heart, but to the person who'd signed, who'd said go ahead, take it, take it still beating. So when Life Givers had sent the form, the square box to check if the donor family could contact, Susannah had marked Yes. Let them contact. Please. She hoped they would, to receive this burden of gratitude, now that Toby could smile again, walk again under the sharp, waning sun of last year's autumn in the Blue Ridge. What could it be like, to refuse? You'd lie awake in the night, your child breathing deeply in the next room. You'd have notified someone's grieving mother, we want you in parts but never whole. Don't come 'round here.

A person couldn't say that. Oh yes, a person could, Nick had countered last fall. It was a simple word, No. He was grateful, but he could say No. Susannah could say it, too. If she'd try, she'd see how simple.

By spring, the spring Linsey Hunter sought them out in Roanoke, Virginia, Nick and Susannah had started to emerge like chrysalides from the white cocoon of hospital sheets and lab print-outs and pain. Toby was theirs again. He was not going immediately to die. It had all been very swift in the end, the violent mechanics of transplant. And so the slow artlessness of the natural world astonished them—leaves tight-budded, moss creeping on rocks. For their own separate reasons, they did not quite trust what was afoot. It seemed that the timing might miss, the roots miscode the dots and dashes hurtling through trunk and stem, the sunlight fail to quicken the chlorophyll.

Early in the spring mornings, while the robins were building their nest in the tree near her study window, Susannah wondered what this Linsey Hunter had wanted, to go to such trouble. First Mrs. Hunter had had to pester Life Givers, which told her they didn't set up phone contact, even with families who'd checked the box. They would forward letters, was all, with the name and address of the sender scratched out; they would forward responses back to her. Forewarned, she must have sat down with lined paper and her loopy scrawl. "I have been laying awake nights worrying over my girl's heart," was what she'd written. Nick hadn't wanted to write back; Life Givers didn't advise responding, especially not now when Toby was on a normal schedule at last. Then he'd said okay, but tell her how thankful we are and be done with it.

We would love to meet you someday, was what Susannah had written. And had received back a photo of the little girl who had died, along with a note that Mrs. Hunter was thinking of moving. "My memory pains me here," she wrote; "I may go on back to where I was born." Good, said Nick; she sounds like a sensible woman. Let's keep in touch, Susannah had written, including phone number and address.

And so, like an aunt from a forgotten branch of the family, Linsey had appeared shipwrecked on their shores, where they had dry towels and new clothes all waiting.

For Linsey Hunter, hesitant spring guaranteed only one thing: fall. Dry death, the skitterings of leaves. For now she preferred winter, that locked-up season, icy like the first day she'd met Toby Ames who carried her daughter Brooke's heart around in his chest.

That had been February. On impulse, Susannah's letter clutched in her hand, Linsey had driven north and from the Blue Ridge Motel, out by the parkway, had with shaking fingers dialed the number on the rose-colored stationery. She'd never been to Virginia before; never been out of the Carolinas. These were just mountain people, she told herself, who spoke in tighter voices. Still, she'd felt like one of those adventuresome heroines in the old fairy tales, who go out to the cold forbidden regions and face seven trials to rescue—

Well, all right girl, she instructed herself. Finish it out. To rescue a loved one captured by the Death Queen. But she wasn't after that, not that at all. She followed Nick's Yankee-accented directions to their cul-de-sac neighborhood with its frozen bluegrass lawns and wraparound porches. She let Toby take her hand and show her his hidden meadow across the street where crocus broke through icy mud. Back in the big, hickory-beamed house, she greeted their dog, a black Lab with the uninspired name of Coal, who smelled the woods on her and sneezed. She accepted hot chocolate from Susannah and followed Toby up to his room with his sports card collection and the Wilt Chamberlain card he'd picked out to give her. He knew, Toby said, that she wouldn't care about the card, but if she married again and had a little boy, he would want her to give it. He stared at her a lot that day. When she got in her car to leave he asked—as if he'd been holding it in—if Brooke had looked like her. No, she'd said. Brooke was stronger than me. Bigger boned, like her daddy.

I knew it, he said. I guessed that one.

That had been February. By March 30, when Linsey moved from Granite Falls, outside Greensboro, to Roanoke, spring had arrived punctually in Virginia, the dogwood opening into flower, the icy breezes changing without fanfare to cool puffs with balm in their backsides. Now summer was ready to pick up the baton and run with it until the first few hundred leaves turned and fell on the night of the autumnal equinox. In all seasons, wherever Nick and Susannah looked, mountains regarded them, the changes mere coats of color on their dromedarian humps. But they rarely spoke of this cycle, of the precision of the seasons. They ran the danger of saying, both at once, "This time last year—" and then gaping like drowned fishes at what they'd unleashed.

This time last year, Linsey told Susannah on Memorial Day, her husband John had just finished the hot tub, but they agreed not to use it until the first frost, which came too late.

This time last year—Susannah began; but then she got confused. It all swims together, she said, like those minnows you can't catch.

Though later she remembered distinctly the puke-green Laz-E-Boy on which she'd spent the night this time last year, relieving Nick by Toby's bedside at the hospital downtown, waiting for word from the Duke Transplant Center. For a while at this time—late spring it was, yes, the iris forming purple hearts on the hospital lawn—Toby was on a respirator, dreaming beneath a blue mask. Susannah pictured the bloated heart inside her son's chest like Marlon Brando in *The Godfather*, monstrously slow, torpid in his movements but a killer just the same.

Sometimes, this year, very late at night, Nick Ames held his wife's full body and wept against her neck. Sometimes, from her new house on the new, winding drive up the back of Tinker Mountain, Linsey Hunter walked all the way to Carvin's Cove and studied the water there, the stars crowded into its inky surface. Even with the leaves filling the trees, you could hear Interstate 81 from both their houses, the continuous rumble of combustion engines and radial tires echoing off the hills.

By spring's end they were friends. New friends, whose Sunday barbecues and offers of help descended from gratitude and need. But were they less genuinely friends, Susannah wondered, for having nothing in common beyond a dead girl's pound of flesh? Rising early with the advancing light, she left Nick's warm and seed-scented body to slip down the back stairs of the old Tudor they'd bought the year of Toby's first illness. Brewing a pot of espresso, she thought of Linsey Hunter waking alone, of the photo by Linsey's futon, and her own heart ached. More than once, as the steam gathered and hissed, she recalled a story Toby's doctor, Ben Lieberman, had told, of a girl who was persuaded to give a kidney to her brother. Waiting for the anesthesiologist, the child had asked her mom, "When do I start to die?" Every time she heard that girl's voice, now, Susannah imagined she heard Brooke. Oh, she thought, to stroke that forehead and say, like any mother, "No, darling! This won't *kill* you."

But that, in Brooke's case, would be lying.

For her part, Linsey knew the contours and edges of the situation. When she thought of herself in a bad light, as a weak-minded mother who had stalked her daughter's heart to Roanoke, she reminded herself of her cousin Rose who'd gone Jehovah's Witness. When she'd made bold enough to ask Rose what she was up to, bothering people in their homes on Sunday afternoons, Rose had smiled like she knew this one was coming. "You think I don't know I bother people?" Rose had asked. "You think I would do it if something greater didn't compel me?"

And so it was. Linsey was compelled. And still she never dropped by the Ames's house unannounced, never asked for their time. It was enough, to be nearby. But they invited her. They wanted her to approve the basketball hoop Nick had raised up for Toby, the goldfish pond he'd sunk into the back yard; they wanted her to join them for picnics at Bluegrass Lake. At first she knew only that they were better than she had expected. True, they ate meat, and they shopped at Kroger; but they were big on books and classical music so they didn't junk their child's mind up. They weren't Jews or Christians—they were like John that way; you couldn't say what he was. Nick and Susannah didn't come from money the way John had, but they didn't care about it either, except for affording Toby's medicines. At first she knew only these things, and that she could remain in harmony with them, for Brooke's sake.

And then she started, little by little, to care. To listen for Toby's step on her walk; to worry when Susannah worked through the weekend. To mention them in what, if she'd still been religious, she would have called her prayers.

Nick was glad for Linsey to be his wife's friend. Certainly Susannah needed friends. But he did not consider that he had anything in common with Linsey Hunter, and he spent as little time thinking about her as possible. About Brooke who had died, he tried not to think at all. He did sometimes, on a long afternoon in the toy-soldier shop he ran downtown, put on Dink Johnson's "Stella Blues," which he had once played. Listening to the delicate, descending triplets, he sat behind his counter and considered love's shrapnel, which was insanity. He did stop, now and then, to gauge the distance he, like Linsey Hunter, would cross for his child's sake, which was infinite.

In the afternoons, when his mom was still at work and his dad had ordered him to take a break from shooting hoops, Toby put on rock radio in his room and had conversations with Brooke. He described to her the dreams he used to have when they first put him on meds. He thought she ought to know about the galloping dream horse and how he'd had to cling to its mane as it tore down narrow paths between gnarly, bunched-up trees. She wasn't as frightened as he'd expected. She'd been through stuff like that. She wasn't a bad person to have for a heart. And sometimes, when his parents and the rest of them had made him so mad he could've killed somebody, he went to his room again and put on Third Eye Blind and just hung on to Brooke, hung on so hard he could let go of Toby and be Brooke, and it was like a kind of flying.

Chapter 2

*J*une had arrived suddenly, the dogwood in full fleshy bloom. On the asphalt, Toby did the reverse lay up. The ball kissed the backboard and went in. He and Nick, over by the new goldfish pond, exchanged thumbs-up. Coal barked from the deck. Setting down her iced tea, Susannah gave a low whistle.

"Hasn't he played twenty minutes yet?" asked Linsey, who had brought the tea.

Susannah checked her watch, already marking its pale tattoo on her bronzed wrist. "Fifteen," she reported. "But the twenty's just a guideline. I let him go a half-hour this morning."

"Your husband said it was the limit."

"Yeah, well." Susannah scratched Coal behind his warm, thin Labrador ears. "Nick won't have any truck with risk."

"I'd say that's a good thing."

"Oh, sure. It's a great thing. Only he can get—I don't know. Preachy."

Linsey lifted her sunglasses and squinted her pale eyes. "He don't look the part," she said.

Nick was lifting large rocks, gripping one edge with his good hand and balancing the other on the palm of his damaged one, then setting them in place by the pond. The part he looked, loose-limbed and long-muscled, was of the self-made adventurer he'd left behind a decade ago. What he preached now was seatbelts, bicycle helmets, Walk signs, a leash on the dog, twenty minutes on basketball. Play by the book, finish the book, he said like a commercial. No matter that it took fifteen minutes to get Toby's heart rate up; the doctors said to quit at twenty, and at twenty the boy would quit. Rakishly, Susannah foiled his precautions, at least for

Toby. Wasn't she a doctor, or almost? Firmly she stood between her son and the cliff.

"All Toby wants from life," she said, gesturing as the next ball swished, "is to make the basketball team next fall. Which in theory he can do. He's *allowed* to do. Has to build for it, is all."

"They wanted Brooke on the soccer team," said Linsey. "Last spring. She was a good kicker. But John, he wasn't happy with the competitive side of it. She took Afro-Haitian dance instead. You saw that photo of her."

Susannah nodded. "She looks to have been a robust little girl."

"John said—John said she was born to be a dancer." Linsey's lip quivered; she sipped tea. "Even her organs were robust, did they tell you that? Viable, the harvest team called them. I looked it up. *Able to live.*"

Susannah leaned over. Linsey's hand—long-fingered, weathered on the knuckles—trembled on the arm of the director's chair. Gently she took the fingers in her own. Toby's basketball clanged off the backboard. "I guess you donated everything, didn't you?" she said after a while.

"'Cept her appendix. She'd had that out, two years back." Linsey stared thoughtfully out at the goldfish pond.

"Appendicitis?" said Susannah. When Linsey nodded, she said, "My brother had that. Died of it."

The back yard seemed full of sound—the roar of a lawnmower next door, a petulant gurgle running into the goldfish pond, a radio somewhere. She ought, Susannah thought, to have driven up to the lab this morning, that quiet unpeopled place.

"They say no one needs an appendix anyway," said Linsey, "so I don't guess my daughter's would have done anyone good."

"Research," Susannah said, as gently as she could. She rubbed Linsey's damp knuckles.

"I wouldn't let them have my child's organ for that," Linsey said, giving a swipe at her cheeks with her free hand. "They can use monkeys."

Chahld, she pronounced it. *Munkehs*. Dogwood petals floated down in the lazy breeze.

This time last year, Susannah had been talking about Toby as if he, too, were a potpourri of parts, oxygenation and atrial fibrillation, the ventricular pump, arterial scars. Now, squeezing Linsey's hand, letting go, she watched her son on the asphalt. Since the last time he could shoot hoops, sixteen months ago, Toby had grown four inches. Before, he'd been a wiry little shooter, all long legs and baggy red shorts, his skinny butt hiked out like the Jungle Boy learning to tiger-walk. Now the steroids had fattened him; he moved as if through water.

"You know what I heard the other day?" Linsey said. She'd sat up, tipping her thin face into the sun. "Some fellow on death row had a daughter needed new lungs and he tried to give his to her. I guess there wasn't any other match. And you know what? The state wouldn't let him. They were bound and determined to kill him in their own way. That didn't seem right to me."

"Time," Nick called out to Toby—*tiym*, the tight *I* of New York—as he carried pipe joints back from the corner of the yard by the fence. He bent his wrist so that his watch faced Susannah, though she couldn't read it in the sun. He was wearing a tennis visor perched like a white terry diadem on his broad forehead.

"Me either," said Susannah. The ball boinged off the basket. Linsey swirled her glass and the ice cubes clinked. "You want a refill on that?"

"Thanks, hon. I'll be on my way. I know you've got work."

"I can come help paint later."

"Thanks. I finished the ceiling."

"Black?"

"I had to, with red upholstery."

"*Feng shui*," said Susannah. "You're a kick, Linsey."

"We aim to please."

"One minute, Tobe!" called Nick from the storage area below the deck. Susannah and Linsey stood up together as Coal, anticipating, barked.

Toby heard his dad's voice, *time*, like some excited fan shouting from the bleachers. Still five minutes left in the quarter, and two time-outs for the Knicks. The new asphalt he was playing on gleamed black as Coal's coat in the hot spring sun. They'd put the asphalt down when he was in the hospital, and then when he got home, they wouldn't let him play on it, not for months. But now he had his Kobe Bryant ball, and his team was in the second game of the playoffs. His dad could wait. His mom usually waited, though she whined and worried at him after, and made him sit for blood pressure and pulse and all that and then told him over and over,

You're fine, you're fine, as if that was some kind of miracle. But you could bend her a little. With his dad you played the odds. Like maybe his dad would forget about *time* because something was going wrong with his new goldfish pond, and then you could just play until he remembered he was supposed to be in charge of you.

Toby used to do a lot better. His arms used to react faster. He could feint right, then whirl and hurl the ball up from the left, almost as far out as the three-point line. He used to pull off—this was his record—thirteen free throws in a row. Now his arms were pale and padded-looking like that fat new kid in school, and his legs were jerky, like a wind-up action figure. The reverse lay up his dad taught him that morning was a good shot, but he couldn't pull it off fast enough to use it in a real game.

Toby dribbled a figure-eight, passed to Allan Houston, easy lay up. His dad had gone into the basement from under the deck. Maybe time was down. That was what he used to say, when he was little and playing with blocks or something and his mom told him time was up. "No no," he used to yell, "time's *down.*" That was when he was cute and not sick and everything was easy. Last week, when they did Community Projects in school, his mom asked him on the way home whether he wanted to grow up to live in the city or the country. He'd had to explain to her about the NBA, how you needed to live near your home stadium, how you traveled eight months out of the year to other cities where you lived in hotels. He could tell she didn't believe him. He could tell she didn't even think he'd live long enough to be in the draft pick, much less actually play in the league. She knew his statistics, just like he knew the Knicks'.

That was when he decided it was better not to talk to her—to either of them—about what he'd do when he and Brooke's heart grew up.

One minute, Tobe! There came that shout again, from the bleachers. Hair tossed back from his face, Toby took a free throw. Maybe this wasn't the playoff game. Maybe it was one-on-one, Houston on Eddie Jones. He liked playing that, and he could quit easier. Houston could make the three-pointers, while Jones went down to the post. Last time he'd left them at sixteen-thirteen, Houston. Now he was up to speed, and they were back. Jones got the ball, and without looking at the basket, he spun around and lofted the easy shot. Houston tried to drive, thinking he had a lay up, but Jones blocked. Mouth open, Toby breathed heavily. He could hear the grownups talking. His dad coming out from the kitchen onto the deck, the clink of Coal's metal collar. Houston shot, swished. Steps on the wooden stairs, his dad on the asphalt.

"Not *yet*," said Toby. He did the figure-eight dribble; his dad couldn't steal from him.

"Yes, yet," said his dad. "You've been at this for twenty minutes. That's your limit. Stop right now, and I'll let you watch the NBA draft tonight on TV."

Jones, unbelievably, made a three-pointer. The orange ball dropped from blue sky through hoop, leaving the white net trembling. "Dja see that, Linsey?" Toby called.

"Sure," said Brooke's mom. Up on the deck she wore a smile like a rabbit caught in the headlights, trying to be a statue.

"Dad said time, Tobe," his mom called.

"I just warmed up!"

"And now"—his dad stood cross-armed by the post—"it's time to cool down."

"C'mon, Dad. Score's twenty-one to eighteen. I'm just playing to twenty-five."

"You mean twenty-one *plus* eighteen. *You've* made all those shots."

"So? I'm playing till twenty-five."

"You've shot total, let me see—"

"Thirty-nine. And not all today. I'm not scoring that way, anyhow." Houston shot from the right corner: a brick.

"You're done, champ," Toby's dad said. "Draft pick tonight. Come on." Catching the ball single-handed off the hoop, he started back toward the deck.

"You said one more shot!" Toby cried.

"So? You took it. I didn't say one more *basket*."

Toby's legs twitched. "I am still *playing*," he cried. His eyes burned. He looked for his mom, on the deck. In a second his dad would tell him that it was all in his head. That what was happening here, on the drive-way, was a boy with a new heart overstaying his time instead of taking his meds. That if playing basketball was going to mean quarrels about time, then Toby-loby wouldn't play basketball.

His dad stopped; he dribbled the ball a couple of times. When Toby tried to steal it his dad held it high. Toby hopped around him. He kicked at his shin, and missed. Then, just as his dad reached the steps to the deck, Toby scooped a handful of the gray gravel at the edge of the asphalt, and flung it at his dad's back.

Not a smart move, Tobe. His dad examined the Kobe ball, as if he were checking it for leaks. "You will not behave this way," he said when he'd finished. Toby knew the voice his dad was using. It was a patient voice, but ready for action, like Indiana Jones. His dad tossed the ball onto the deck, where Toby's mom stood with her eyes in cross-hatches. Toby started up the stairs, but his dad caught him from behind, under his arms. "Michael Jordan behave like that to his father?" he asked.

Toby rolled his eyes. "Dennis Rodman would," he said, talking away from his dad.

"My point exactly." Lifting Toby down from the steps, his dad crouched down next to him, on the gravel. Up close, the skin of his dad's face had a mottled, worn look, with snail-tracks of sweat running down from his close-cropped sideburns. When he smiled at Toby, a long dimple puckered his right cheek; his mom said Toby had the same dimple, but he couldn't see it. "I'm stopping you for your own good, and you know it, Tobe," he said quietly. "Now you have twenty minutes of rest, okay? And if you jump the gun, I'll have to make it a half-hour. Are we straight on that?

Toby jerked his head away. His mom had pushed back from the deck rail. She was starting down the steps, Coal behind her with his tail wagging. She was going to agree with his dad, sort of anyway. Like you could just pack up Houston and Jones again and again and then bring them out. Like who could do that? Who ever made it to the pros by packing it in all the time? Who?

His mom had her mouth open. Nick, she was saying, Nick please. Toby drew in his breath. He had things to say, but they wouldn't come out; thick saliva had gathered in the back of his mouth. He didn't look at his mom, coming down the steps. Trying to breathe, he coughed, spat. Spat right on his dad's forehead.

"Jesus Christ!" said his dad. He stood up, got out a Kleenex, wiped a little line of spit from his eyebrow. "Got a little mess here," he said. Toby thought he saw the dimple, just for a second, but it wasn't meant to last. His dad folded the Kleenex, tucked it back in his pocket. Just as Toby turned—to retrieve the basketball from the deck, you didn't leave a good ball in the sun like that—his dad grabbed the back of his T-shirt. "Hey,

Master Rodman," he said. "You can forget about the draft pick tonight, and you can forget about playing any more basketball this afternoon."

"What? The draft pick?" Toby turned. No no no. This wasn't the way. "Dad! Jeez! What'd I *do*?"

"You spat at me and threw rocks at me and tried to *kick* me, that's what."

"I what? You liar! I did not!"

"Toby, you *spat* at me!"

"That was an accident!"

Up on the porch, Linsey was started to talk. There shouldn't be a discussion, she was saying. Rules. His mom was shaking her head, like this had something to do with her. "Toby, let's go," she was calling.

"I am *going*," Toby said, "where you two can't *find* me." He glanced up to the deck; no chance to retrieve the ball. He started walking fast, across the muddy lawn, toward the edge of the fence and the woods beyond.

It was hard to say when the moment went wrong, or when they realized it was going wrong, or if going wrong and realizing happened at the same time. Nick had Toby under his arm like a football, hauling him back from the woods to the house, and Toby's arms were flailing, and his face had gone red, way red, too red. With a sick dagger in her stomach, Susannah saw the scene from that morning, the scene she'd tucked behind a scrim. It had been the last pill of the morning, the Minipress, the one Toby hated most, the brown pill big enough for a horse, the pill that tasted like castor oil and gave Toby sweats. The pill that tamped down his heart. "C'mon, Tobe," she'd said, "down the hatch," and he'd nodded and tipped the Minipress toward his mouth—and then, as she'd turned away, he'd slipped the thing into his pants pocket and swallowed water.

Half-life of forty-eight hours, she had told herself. Dosage up to 120 pounds, and Toby weighed 85. So obedient, the kid had been, and patient, and God the meds were awful, Ben Lieberman overdid them, everyone said he did. She could always watch Toby's pulse, she could make him pop the thing later in the day. Between her son and the cliff she stood.

"Nick," she said now with Toby's face red, and Toby gave a sudden convulsion, and a thick stream of tawny mucus shot from his mouth.

"Christ almighty," said Nick. He set Toby down. Toby's skin was going from hot pink to alabaster and back again. He was coughing, choking.

Susannah crouched in front of him on the asphalt. With a tissue she wiped his mouth. She got a hard look then, and she heard herself telling Nick he didn't look good, not good at all, his pupils were dilated.

"Straighten up, Tobe," said Nick—his voice scared even though he didn't know about the horse pill, he didn't see what Susannah saw. "Let me have a look at your eyes."

"I can't!" Toby coughed; phlegm on the asphalt, with the other mess. Coal moved in to lick it up. Toby's voice was high, a cat's mew. "I'm dizzy. Something's ringing in my ears."

"It's called being tired, champ. I tried to tell you—"

"Something *more*. Like I'm in a cave, I can't *hear* you."

"I'll get him in the house," said Nick.

"No, not you! *Mom* get me in. Or *Linsey*."

Not Linsey, Susannah had time to think. Then his arms went over her shoulders, his sweating neck against her face. With her lips she felt his beating artery. One two three, she cut her eyes down to her watch—first thing they teach you in med school, always wear a watch—and figured a hundred fifteen a minute. Sinking a hip onto the asphalt, she cradled Toby's head in the crook of her arm. His face was putty, his lips the color of eggplant. Oh Kobe Bryant, she thought, Latrell Sprewell. As if those guys were Toby's patron saints, standing with her, blocking the cliff. "Pressure sleeve," she said to Nick, and he was off, and then there was Linsey, crouched next to her, a Botticelli mask of worry, what could she do, send her for the pill, the brown pill, the pulse in Toby's wrist like a humming-bird now, and Linsey gone, the dog gone, Nick back with the gray sleeve, wrapping it expertly one-handed around Toby's arm, pumping the ball with thumb and index, pinky on the cool metal disk, asking is it okay for him to take two of those pills before dinner, and now was the time to tell him, to let it out *This is only one pill, he skipped the other I saw him.*

"It's what they tell you to do," said Susannah.

She kept her eyes on Toby. Racing heart happened. Ben had warned them of it. Even with Minipress on the clock, it happened. Freaking Toby out, the way Nick did, that couldn't have helped. No, no, she couldn't blame Nick; she wanted to, but she was the one who'd done it, who'd seen the pill slip into the pocket; she was the one between Toby and the cliff, and the cliff was too broad, and she should have known.

"And call the doctor," she said, her voice a dry tube. "Tell them to send an ambulance."

Chapter 3

Money the great green demon, the destroyer of peace. Behind everything Susannah did hung a knot of worry over money. In a green spiral notebook on her desk at home, she recorded the amounts for the drugs, the hospital stays, the consultations, therapies, more drugs. Equipment—wheelchair, IV pole, blood-pressure sleeve, beeper for Toby, cell phone for the car. Not recorded was the drop in income last year, when she took unpaid leave from the lab. Back then they'd still been within the insurance cap, and Nick flush with a series of estate sales, tiny priceless miniatures dug out of attics and auctioned through the catalog he designed as if for a museum, nubby paper and a backdrop of Maxwell Brady daguerreotypes. Back then Toby had been ensconced in a bright yellow room at the Duke Transplant Center, two hundred miles from Roanoke. Money was not among their priorities. Toby was Status One.

He slept the way he was sleeping now, with the hospital bed propped up. Then, the Durham team wanted to keep blood from pooling in the chambers of his sick heart. Now he just liked the hospital bed that way. He looked as if he'd fallen asleep reading a book, his perfectly shaped head with its mop of peanut-colored hair dropped to one side. They were bringing his heart rate down. Yesterday Ben Lieberman had catheterized him, running that awful tube up the artery from his leg to tap at Brooke's heart. Three times an hour since he'd come out of recovery, a nurse came to check his pulse. Over in Durham the team had been alerted; they were ready as relay racers to run the next lap if Ben ran out of ideas.

Last fall, when Nick and Susannah took turns on the Laz-E-Boy in Durham, a kid named Shawn slept on the other side of the blue curtain. This time, they had Toby in a private room—but he'll be in and out so quick, Ben said, your insurance won't even blink. Fine-tuning meds, was what this little crisis was all about. Susannah had spent the night on a mat of blankets on the floor. "He's still sleeping," she told Nick when he called.

"Come on home then," he said. "The kid's a veteran."

But they wouldn't make love if she went home, and she didn't want to shower. "I'll be fine," she whispered and rang off.

If they could make love, she thought, peeking through the heavy shades of the hospital room, the money knot would loosen a little. Outside, dawn was just beginning, red streaks behind the extinguished Star on Roanoke Mountain. If they could make love, she would tell Nick about the horse pill slipping into Toby's pocket. Nick would say it made no difference. He'd say, like Ben Lieberman, that it was time to ratchet things up a bit anyhow. If if if. She stumbled down to the cafeteria, drank watery coffee, ate a bitter orange. When she came back, Toby was stirring.

"Did I miss the draft?" he asked. He rubbed his eyes, and the IV tube wiggled.

"What draft?" ————————

"The NBA pick. On TV, last night."

"The medicine made you sleepy."

"It's all Dad's fault." He glanced at her, then glared dramatically ahead.

"I'm not biting."

"Well, it is. One fucking basket."

"You say fucking again and I leave the room."

"One freaking basket." A whisper of a grin hovered over the left corner of Toby's mouth. Everything's pretend with him, Nick once complained. Maybe you'd pretend too, she'd said, if you'd spent three months on Status One. No, Nick said, he was like that before.

"It was not your dad's fault," she said now to Toby. "It was my fault."

"I didn't skip a pill yesterday!"

"*Toby.*"

He started to sit up, then turned pale. "How come"—he licked his lips—"I feel so weird?"

"Weird like how?"

"Weird like I used to. Before I got Brooke's heart."

"Must be the meds, honey." Susannah plumped the pillow, added another, and eased him back. "To keep the beat from getting too fast."

"Can't I ever have the heart"—he licked his lips again; the lower one was cracked—"without the meds?"

"You know you can't."

Toby reached out a white hand, clammy and unsteady. "Love you, Mom."

"You too, Tobe."

"Can you find out about the draft for me? I want to know if Obatu Johnson went to the Knicks."

"Sure, Tiger."

But he didn't hear her; he'd dropped off. He slept like a petal floating on the creek, light and swift. Bright sun flooded the cheap lace curtains. Susannah swiped her son's lips with Chapstick; he flinched and turned away. Gently she held his wrist. How comforting it was, this steady signal of the blood. At last she let go, and turned to the telephone. Time to dial Linsey, to let her know her daughter's heart had come through again.

Linsey's house lay in a new development up Tinker Mountain, the other side of the city from Nick and Susannah but not far from Susannah's lab. She'd bought it over the course of one weekend in April. She hadn't cared what sort of ceilings or furnace she lived with; had wanted only the creek at the back of the property and Brooke's heart within reach. Slowly—in part, Susannah liked to think, through their friendship, through sudden crying jags and a few white-wine evenings and Toby—she had come back to caring. Had started to move furniture around, to open up doorways to create good *ba-gua* in the house, to repaint walls in *feng shui* tones of harmony and wholeness.

Best of all, for Toby, Linsey would pick him up from school and bring him up the mountain. There he'd take his afternoon meds and watch her paint; he'd help plant and weed the vegetable garden in back until Susannah or Nick could pick him up. Three days after the SVT episode—Ben had promised a blink, and delivered a blink—Toby was back at school and back at Linsey's. When Susannah drove over from the lab, she found him, as always, studying the photos.

There was one of the extended family, John's parents well-dressed and sleepy-eyed, Linsey with her head turned, Brooke at perhaps five in the folds of her mother's homespun skirt. There were snapshots of the hills around Granite Falls where they lived on ten acres; of the house John had built himself, with its weaving studio and lookout deck. Susannah liked John, from his pictures. He had a way of looking sideways at the camera, as if he'd caught the photographer in the act and not vice versa. A compact, muscular man, with springy facial hair and a long jaw. He'd grown up in Charlotte, Linsey explained once, where his father was a math professor. She stroked the picture lightly. The kids at Brooke's school adored him. Linsey had met him a dozen years ago, at a party given by her yoga teacher; that night, she had driven out to John's place and climbed through his bedroom window. "Well, it was a farm, you know," she told Susannah when she could tell she'd shocked her. "I didn't want to set off the dogs and the rooster. He said to me, 'Hang on, let me get some clothes on,' and I said, 'I've just climbed in your bed and you want to put clothes *on?*'"

She and Charlie, Linsey said, moved out to the farm the next week. Charlie was Linsey's son. He did not, Linsey claimed, have a father. That's biologically impossible, Nick said when he heard this. It's a figure of speech, said Susannah. There were a couple of pictures of Charlie on Linsey's shelves—a tall, wispy-looking young man with a shock of lemon hair. He had large hands that seemed, even in the still photos, to be fidgeting; in one shot he held a cigarette between his fingers, which were fanned back with his arm up to keep the smoke away. He was living in Nashville, Linsey said, trying to make it on the music scene. In one photo he was playing a clarinet while a baby Brooke sat splay-legged on the floor.

Even in the baby photos, Brooke dared the camera to catch her. She stood feet planted on the beach, with her tongue stuck out and thumbs in her ears, waggling her fingers. She turned to dash, the camera hopeless in the chase. She swung from a tree and aimed the soles of her feet at the lens. A tanned, plump-cheeked girl. Brilliant, was what Linsey called her. She had been going to skip fifth grade. She composed music; at her service, John's sister had played one of Brooke's pieces on the flute.

Me, Linsey said the first time Susannah and Toby came up to the ranch house, I was never any good at school. John was the first guy I really knew who finished college. I had my talents—arts and crafts, you know, and I could model clothes—but it's not like brains.

Now Toby picked up the pictures as if they were old friends looking back at him. Susannah slipped on a smock—one of John's old shirts, actually, though they never mentioned that—and opened a paint can. She was just taking a break from the lab, she'd explained to Linsey; Nick would pick Toby up when she had to head back. As Linsey was blending carrot juice in the kitchen, Toby tucked the photo from the beach into his pocket. Susannah knelt down to the baseboard. They had started painting over Memorial Day, the bright rich colors that came from Linsey's *feng shui* catalog, guaranteed to spiritualize any house. Only baseboards and the kitchen were left.

"I'm going out to the garden," Toby said, and Susannah nodded, not wanting to look up. She had told Linsey the last time, when Toby took Brooke's gymnastics photo, and Linsey had just winked and said, "That is exactly the idea."

He kept the photos under his mattress at home. He used to ask Linsey questions about Brooke—what were her favorite foods? did she know anything about basketball? had she grown out of watching cartoons?—but he'd stopped. They didn't have TV at their house outside Greensboro, Linsey had said. They were all vegetarians. Brooke's favorite sport was Ultimate Frisbee because it was so beautiful and her daddy played it.

Susannah stirred the thick green, dipped the brush, stroked. Linsey came and stood in the doorway. "That looks great," she said. "You paint so smooth."

"It's good paint," said Susannah. "I would never think of it. I mean, leaf green like this, all around the room? The black ceiling?"

"But it's peaceful, isn't it?"

Susannah sat back on her haunches. Her eyes went from the green to the black and back again. Under her ribs, her diaphragm seemed to relax and flatten. "I wish I could pull this off in my house," she said.

"We'll do some *feng shui* in your house." Linsey crouched, and with a rag wiped a feathery line of green that had escaped the masking tape. "Just you wait." She nodded toward the back door. "He acts tame," she said.

"Tired, more like," said Susannah. "Twenty-four hours in the hospital always punches him a little. Do you want me to paint the doorframe?"

"Leave it for now. I got to check my chart. What did you call it? What happened, I mean. Sounded like a sports car."

Susannah straightened and stretched her back. Paint stained John's shirt. She shook out her fine hair; she should have pulled it back. "SVTs. Subventricular tachycardia. Racing heart. You and I have a nerve—it's called the paripathetic vagal nerve—to control our heartbeats. Toby doesn't have that. He has medication instead."

"I'd think they'd just hook that nerve back up."

Laughing, Susannah moved to the kitchen. When she'd rinsed her hands, she knotted the unruly hair and poked a chopstick through it. From the window, she could see Toby moving through Linsey's back yard. It was a lousy day out, for early June; he had on his gray fleece pull-over, hands stuck in the pockets. "It's like if you broke your neck, Linse," she said. "The sympathetic nerves aren't strings you tie back together. But it's fine, if he stays on his med."

"You said that medicine made his heart beat ninety times a minute!"

"So?"

"Well," said Linsey, lifting a potted plant to swipe the table with her sock, "what's yours?"

"Sixty-five, at rest. But mine's not an allograft."

"Hm."

Linsey moved through the kitchen with the paint and set it down noisily in a small closet. Emerging with a white sock on her right hand, she lifted objects and wiped underneath them. Funny, Susannah thought; for a woman with such stillness in her, Linsey never quite stopped moving. "Why is it medical folks won't speak plain English?" Linsey said.

"Allograft," came Nick's baritone. Susannah turned; he'd slipped in through the side door. He was like that, a cat on soft feet. He wore a khaki shirt open at the throat; his glasses seemed a prop, like Harrison Ford's wire-rims. "A transplant," he explained, helping himself to a glass of carrot juice, "from your own species."

"All right, showoff." Linsey came back into the kitchen and made a playful swat at Nick with the dusty sock. "That still don't explain ninety beats a minute. Her heart is working too hard!"

"Under other circumstances," Nick said mildly, setting down the glass to cross his arms over his chest, "her heart would not be working at all."

"Nick," Susannah warned. But Linsey only removed the dusting sock from her hand—delicately, with thumb and finger, as if it were a calfskin glove—and fixed her gaze on Nick. Susannah watched her rude husband color up. She imagined cutting the air between them, like slicing a nerve.

"So what went wrong with Toby," Linsey said carefully, "had to do with his medicine."

"It's not too likely to happen again," Susannah said quickly. She stepped to the back door and opened it. "Come on, Toby!" she called. "Dad's here, time to go!"

It was a relief, stepping outside. Glancing back in, she saw Nick and Linsey leaning against opposite counters, ready for the next round. Something happened when they were in a room together; she wasn't quite sure what. It had everything to do with Toby's heart, and at the same time nothing to do with it. They were both like cats, she thought, the way cats circle. "Come on, Tobe," she said again.

Then as she started down the back steps, Susannah's own heart jumped. There was Toby, not plucking weeds from the vegetables, but sprawled on the damp lawn in what had turned from mist to drizzle. Sprawled flat. She opened her mouth to yell. But no, take it back. He had his chin propped on elbows, one sneakered toe tapping the grass. Alive, alive. When would she stop melting in gratitude at this mere fact of his life? "Toby-loby," she sang out, "get off that wet mattress before you catch pneumonia! What're you doing?"

"Mealworms," he said, not turning his head. In the light drizzle, his fleeced back glowed and shimmered, like a centipede's fuzzy envelope. "Teaching 'em," he said when she drew close.

"Teaching them what? What are mealworms?"

"Geez, Mom. You're a *scientist*."

"I'm not an entomologist. Did these come from the garden?"

"No, dummy. They came from my backpack. You signed the slip, Mom."

She probably did. She always signed slips. Next to him, she crouched down. All over the square back lawn Linsey had thick grass growing, like a dense green sponge. "So these guys came from school?"

"*Yes*. You *signed* for them."

"Don't be impatient with me, Toby. We went to the hospital, and I forgot a lot of what was going on here. These'll turn into—"

"Beetles. I'm teaching 'em to play basketball." Toby's finger traced the plastic straw he'd stuck in the grass next to the shallow styrene tub filled with oatmeal, two thin slices of potato, and what looked like a half-dozen gigantic maggots. At the top of the straw, with a twist tie, he'd fastened the metal ring from a soda can. "Couldn't find a net," he said.

"You don't really need a net. Who's the best so far?"

"Obatu Johnson."

"Which one's that?"

"Jeez, Mom, can't you tell?" Toby pushed a bit of oatmeal aside, and an ivory-colored mealworm swayed blindly. "He's playing for the Knicks," he said.

"I thought you told me the Jazz got him."

"Not *this* Obatu Johnson." With a blade of grass he stroked the mealworm's head.

"And I guess that pea's the ball."

"It's a little big for them, but it fits through the hoop. Watch."

"Dad's waiting, honey. And I have to go back to work."

"All right."

It was true; he was tamer. Susannah wasn't sure she liked him this way, but it worked for Nick and for Linsey, and he was taking his meds. Three mornings in a row she'd picked the new pills out of their boxes, laid them in a row, and watched Toby swallow them, his round green eyes on her. When he paused, she looked from the next pill to his water glass, then back to the pill, until his hand moved to take the next dose.

If they could make love, she thought again, she would tell Nick about the horse pill. Or if he quit the profession of being right all the time. *If you let Coal off the leash, he'll run off. Let the caterpillars live, and they will eat the garden. Let Toby skip meds, and he will die.* He was right about these things, and she was wrong. Head versus heart. When, he would ask if she told him about the pill, will you learn to play the heavy?

Now, she would tell him. *Starting right now.*

"Susannah!" Nick called from inside.

"C'mon," said Toby, as if it were his mother who was dawdling. Sitting up, he clamped a transparent top with punctured holes over his mealworms. The pole and basket he uprooted and stuck in his shorts pocket. Working so carefully, competently, he looked younger than his years, like a precocious five-year-old. Maybe it was the pudginess the meds put on. Or maybe it was his emotional nakedness, making him younger. Susannah could look at any square inch of her son—his ears now healthy pink, his sharp chin, the left nipple on his chest, narrow muscles around it, the astounding scar below—and see into his soul. Other fourth-graders, the ones staring when Toby came back to school in February, had put on a veneer during his absence. Arms crossed over their chests, they guarded themselves; to Susannah their eyes gave away nothing.

Outside, in Linsey's driveway, Nick hung on the door of Susannah's car. "You think this is all insurance payout?" he asked.

"All what?"

"This house, the lifestyle. She says she hasn't sold the place in North Carolina. I don't hear her talk about getting a job."

"They both bought good policies, she said. I guess John's brother's in insurance."

"Jesus."

Nick pushed shut her door, but kept his hands on the open window. She wanted to touch the maimed right hand, the stubs of fingers he'd lost years back, in his adventuring days. Instead, she contented herself with a stroke of her index against his wrist, where the coarse hairs began. "Jesus what?" she asked.

"I don't know." He ran his good hand through his hair. "Look, even the one night in the hospital wasn't a blink, money-wise. We're over the limit; we've got one card left that isn't maxed out. And she's painting her kitchen. . . ." He leaned farther down, elbows on the car door. "Why the hell *is* she painting the kitchen? She had the whole backyard landscaped, right? Couldn't she afford painters?"

Susannah smiled. "It was an excuse," she whispered back, "to spend time with us."

"Well, she has a lot of disposable income."

"And we have a family. Want to trade?" Susannah started the engine. "That was a rude thing you said to her."

"I don't recall."

"She lost her *daughter*, Nick. I've never *known* you to be so cold."

Nick hung his head. He passed his thumb over the stumps of what had been his fingers. "She confuses me," he said at last.

He pushed away from the hood, permission for Susannah to go. Backing up, she remembered the last time she'd come here, a warm May day that Toby had used up with a nap. She'd taken a break from painting and stood over her son. One two three, she'd counted—three heartbeats, more or less, to a breath. Whatever dream he'd been having had made his lips shudder slightly. Then Linsey had come up behind her, counting as well, and put her thin arm around Susannah's waist. There was a clean edge to her, like a nurse, even in painting overalls and a thin pink T-shirt. She was taller than Susannah; her small breast grazed the back of Susannah's shoulder. Susannah had felt Linsey's breath on her hair, smelled the clean stench of paint on her hands. Okay, Linsey had said at last, let's finish up that kitchen.

Now Linsey's face appeared at the picture window, alert as a cat. Susannah clicked the wipers on, and between their blades waved good-bye, first to her son, then to her friend.

Chapter 4

*A*fter running through a half-dozen *asans*, Linsey usually found her yoga mind in the Bow. Hands clenched to ankles, she extended her back like a lobster's tail and rocked against the mat. Her muscles arched from her breastbone all the way under her hips out to her knees. She could feel the flat balloon of her stomach, the fibroid in her uterus. Mound of Venus, they called the bone she rocked on. Her teacher Priya Roy, back in Greensboro, had taught her to empty her mind in this position by reciting the word *alone*.

Back in Greensboro, swimming in the lake used to empty her mind. A mile it was, over and back. Stroke, stroke, breathe; stroke, stroke, breathe. If her mind wandered—if she thought of John, for instance, how she'd disappointed him when his friends came by, those sparkling people—she lost the rhythm of the stroke. She smacked the wave, or caught at water weeds. So she emptied her mind into the water rising, the hot sun on her back, the slick of the warm patches.

Weaving too, or mostly. Barley Corn Weave, with its heavy tabby and silk glaze. Wide basket stripes, all thicks and thins like the pattern you get with strobe light on a dance floor. Rose of Sharon, *M* and *O*s. The old four-harness loom that she'd crated up here from Greensboro had belonged to her great-great grand-mother Eustacie. Packed in the cedar chest in Linsey's new bedroom was the white Cakewalk tablecloth Eustacie'd woven for Gramsie's mother's wedding. See here, Gramsie had said when Linsey turned twelve. See this tooth break crackle pattern? Africa, it comes from. Born a slave, was your old Eustacie.

Which had sort of shocked Linsey who still went by Lynette, back in Wardleysville, where she stood naked in front of the long narrow mirror behind Mama's bedroom door. She checked out the straight hair, the freckles, the pale tiny breasts. Only the full lips, to suggest. Fat lips, her mama called them. To prove it didn't show, she slept with three of the most popular boys and told them afterwards that she might be part nigger. They had a good laugh. Around school the only rumor that flew was that Lynette was crazy.

Still, even as she moved away from Wardleysville and made the craft-fair circuit and came to Greensboro where all she had to hide was her hick accent, Linsey meditated on the pattern, on the Cakewalk. John thought it was sexy, how she meditated. He thought an ounce of black blood was sexy. He didn't know. He came from money. Going downhill—rich to poor, white to black—didn't take so much concentration.

Stretched, repackaged, powerful, Linsey came out of the Bow into the Lotus. She was building energy, *gi*. Energy she could store up to use the next time something went wrong with Brooke's heart, the next time signals of distress failed to reach Toby because the nerves had been cut. *Toby-loby*, she tried chanting, but the name stopped her breath. *Alone.*

When the doctors talked about harvesting organs, she saw in her mind a field of wheat, a tablecloth spread with gourds like in pictures of the Pilgrims. Brooke had been a bushel of corn still on the stalk, facing the reapers. The year before, they'd all signed those cards, donor cards. Some tall, strict-looking woman came door-to-door. Think about it, the woman had said. What would you be needing with your eyes, your lungs, your spleen? Linsey didn't even know what the spleen did. *Bone marrow*, the form listed, and she thought of soup. She signed for herself and Brooke; she took one for John and he signed that night. Same week he got the Yamaha and the jacket to go with. Half the women in southern India, John told her when they were undressing for bed, go around with only one kidney. They get a thousand bucks for the one they sell, and the middleman gets ten thousand, and the patient at the other end has to scrape together fifteen. But the thousand is enough to feed the donor's family for a year. If there wasn't that scar on the one side, he'd said, they'd probably go out and sell the other.

John had been to India. To Afghanistan, to Tibet. He talked about taking Brooke there, maybe when she was twelve. Just Brooke. That bother you? Susannah had asked when Linsey told her, and Linsey'd said she couldn't have kept up, it would have been better just John and Brooke. Susannah's mouth had curled downward at that, but she didn't understand. How you love a man who loves your daughter, how your cup overflows.

Lifting her hips up into a shoulder stand against the fresh-painted wall of her narrow, carpeted living room, Linsey slipped from the yoga path. In the black ceiling she saw the doctors' eyes when they gave the news. They needed to move quickly, they said. Their eyes shone like John's when he went fishing in the big river, when he had a trout on the line and no longer fighting in the deep water, and he could taste what a meal this one would make. With John, there'd been just the lungs, which weren't in such great shape, and the eyes. Crushed pelvis, where all the other organs lived. Oh please don't take his eyes, she'd whispered when the doctors came to her in the waiting room. They had flecks of gold in the blue. A tiny red stain at the lower outside of the left one—an arrow tip, when he was five. Large eyes; his lids covered them sleekly, like a zippered purse. You don't transplant lids—no, of course not. She whispered, but they didn't hear her. They took the eyes. Offered glass ones in their place, if she wanted an open casket. Stupid!

She thought about that story she'd heard—it had been the landscaper telling her, a large slope-shouldered man who looked, himself, like an ex-con—about the condemned father giving his lungs. John would have done that for Brooke. What bothered her a little was that Brooke, in her turn, would have done it for John. Well, they'd both done it now, for strangers, and only she, Linsey, was left whole.

Down she eased from the shoulders: blades, vertebrae, rump, onto the mustard shag. Caution, that was John's motto. He wasn't going to take Brooke on the Yamaha at all, and then he was just going to take her up and down their little road. Then to the health-food store. And now she saw them, over and over while she started to lean into the Lotus. Hell for leather down Dogwood Hill. Around the curve they came, toward the narrow driveway of the woodworking studio, where the delivery truck filled with pinie cut left at the same time. The truck driver hadn't noticed the blinker, thought they would roar on past, and there was all that loose gravel spilled out from the driveway into the road. On and on it goes, the motorcycle skidding, the high blast of the truck horn. When they shot under, the truck chassis tore John right open, but Brooke flew out, like some kind of stunt, into the oak tree. A bike helmet'll do her fine, that was what John had said. Psychedelic designs on the side, and it had cracked like an egg.

The tape rewound. They were coming down the hill again. Going fifty, the coroner had estimated, slowing maybe to thirty-five for the driveway. The truck charged with wrongful left turn. Why so fast? A last-minute decision to drop in on his friend Eli, show off his cycle and his brave girl who rode shotgun. Brooke the brave telling him faster faster. A problem with brakes—no, that was ruled out, though how anybody looking at the mangled bike could know was past Linsey's understanding. Something else on his mind maybe, his mind always so full and restless. Over and over he takes the road like there's a fire. He comes down Dogwood all in black doing fifty and Brooke with her purple helmet like fireworks clinging to her head, and the truck comes the truck comes.

Alone, she recited. *Alone, alone.*

Normally you weren't supposed to know who got what. A child in Oregon needs a new pancreas, and they fly the thing in overnight. Somewhere else the liver arrives. The organ procurement organization was called "Life Givers," but it still sounded like a debt collector. What happened was mostly fine with Linsey. They'd signed the cards. Except John's eyes and Brooke's heart because life support kept it still beating. *Robust; viable.* A compliment, as her mama would say, and you ought to say thank you. But she didn't. They'd passed a law, the doctor said, about brain death. In order for the heart not to go to waste.

Heart disease, John had said once, pointing to a chart in the newspaper, is plain bad habits. The habits of a wealthy greedy nation. Life Givers said they screened recipients, but Linsey didn't believe it. She pictured some fat heart-diseased McDonald's monster, like her brother Bobby's porky kids who loved TV, Nintendo, and Little Caesar's best of all. Brooke's heart—she'd tried telling one of the younger residents, a plain fellow with a receding chin and stores of patience—could never beat for a child like that. The heart's a pump, he'd said; it doesn't pass judgment. Like a genie, she said. No, he repeated, like a pump.

She made the Plow, head between knees. From here she could see the blow-up doll, called "Safe-T-Man" on the box, that Mama had sent her for protection when she moved to this city. Drinking wine with Susannah and putting him together, that was the first time she'd laughed out loud since the accident. Garter belt, Susannah had demanded, holding out her hand like a surgeon's for the scalpel, and Linsey had handed her the lacy red elastic from her wedding. They'd put a bra on him too, the cups wrinkled against the smooth vinyl chest, and then one of John's old sweaters and a pair of jeans. Anatomically incomplete, Susannah had said with a tongue-cluck. Linsey'd known what she meant by the way she directed her eyes.

Alone, alone. She hadn't ever lived alone. That was maybe why Mama had sent her this silly doll, this Safe-T-Man. There'd been one guy after another on her way out of Wardleysville, and then Charlie had come along, and they'd made themselves a family until John drew them in. Decide what *you* want, John used to tell her. So kindly he looked at her, that light in his eyes, priest of desire. She pulled a big fat blank. She'd wanted to be out of Wardleysville, and she was out. She wasn't Lynette any more. After that there were all these more important questions, like what did *John* want. What did Charlie want, what did Brooke. Linsey wasn't even here, in Virginia, because she wanted to be. That was the fact. Brooke had died and given her heart to this boy, and so Linsey had come to be near him.

What did she want?

A piece of something.

Piece of what?

Brooke, now. There was a girl who knew what she wanted. Sit down at the piano and belt out one of the tunes John had sheet music for— Chopin, Kabalevsky, Jelly Roll Morton. John would sit behind Brooke, his big hands resting either side of her small ones, and they'd make the music fancier. Or Oomani's Afro-Haitian class at Spider Ridge Alternative, where she waggled her hips and thrust her shoulders out and down one after the other. That's her African great-great-grandma in her, John whispered to Linsey, who nodded—but really it was all her, it was just Brooke.

A low buzz. The day she moved in here, she'd put out her string of bells, brass chimes on a strip of leather, but no one ever used them. They went for the lighted button to the right of the screen door. Buzz like a growl. Linsey arched, straightened, padded across the waving mustard.

"Nicholas," she said, opening.

"Toby left his mealworms."

"His medicine, you mean."

"No no. Mealworms. Maggoty things. Here they are," he said, and strode past her to the bench near the floor loom. "School project. Cute, aren't they?"

The plastic tub held a dozen blind white shrimps in a nest of oatmeal. "God's creatures," Linsey said, sounding like her own mother. "He didn't forget any medicine, then?"

"Not this time." Nick was studying the tub.

"When you said 'mealworms,' I thought you said the other. The name of that pill I fetched for him."

"Minipress."

"That's the one. Big brown tablet. Slows the heart."

The standing lamp lent an amber cast to Susannah's husband's well-tooled face. About his joints there was a looseness that didn't quite fit with Susannah's wiry hair and quick, round step. His right hand, at first glance, looked fisted; only when you looked close did you see he was missing all digits but the thumb. A rafting accident, Susannah had said; luckily Nick was left-handed.

"They say you can immerse a person in ice water," said Linsey. "Slow the heart with the shock."

"Well." Not *Wayul*, the way her people said it, but *Wull*, like some kind of cleaning agent. "That would require sympathetic nerves."

"Susannah talked about those."

"Did she?" Nick made a snipping motion. "Then you know they've been cut."

"I guess they don't grow back, do they?"

Leaning against an arm of the couch, Nick held up his right hand, which made her think of a fingerless glove. "There are a lot of things," he said, a tug at his mouth, "a person can't grow back."

"Right." She colored up. Her eyes fixed on his collarbone, sunburnt and tendoned under the khaki collar, fine as the pterodactyl wings John had sculpted once for Brooke. "Can't help taking it funny," she said.

"What?" He lifted her jade turtle from the coffee table.

"Toby with his sympathy nerves or whatever, or I mean without. With them gone from his heart so he can't react, and meanwhile they say folks with missing parts are always feeling something there. Twinges. That happen to you?"

"The pinky itches sometimes," Nick said, his left hand demonstrating, scratching at thin air. "Phantom itch, they call it. I used to dream I had a cast on my hand."

"How'd it happen?"

"Susannah hasn't told you?"

"We've had a lot else on the agenda."

"I thought you were her new best friend."

She sat on the edge of a folding chair. "How did you lose your fingers?"

"I rolled the dice," Nick said, "and I lost."

"Well now, that's a real informative statement."

"I flipped a raft in whitewater, and a boulder shifted and rolled onto my hand. My buddy had to cut me loose."

"That's awful."

"Drowning's worse." He flexed the stubs of the joints.

"I heard you can stitch fingers back."

"Not if they're under three feet of rushing water and a half-ton rock, you can't."

"I am sorry," said Linsey.

She felt a little out of breath. They both studied the carpet, its polyester shine and creeping baldness. So smooth the stumps of Nick's fingers were, and nailless, like the unfinished hands you see on fetuses. Linsey pictured his long body stretched downstream, clamped like a dishtowel. "I didn't just come here," Nick said when he'd pushed the shag this way and that with his toe, "for the mealworms. I mean, he did leave them here. But. . . . " He drew a pair of wire-rimmed glasses out of his shirt pocket and put them on. "I'm—ah—sorry for what I said today. About your daughter."

"You had your reasons."

He looked up, studying her.

"You're concerned for your boy's heart," Linsey said. "Makes you a mite caustic."

Carefully he picked up the miniature basket of worry dolls from the coffee table, turned them this way and that. "I wanted to ask for your help," he said.

"All right."

"That Minipress you mentioned. He's supposed to take it every day. Along with about eight others. And then the afternoon ones, that you've overseen, and then more at night."

"Hey, I looked in that cabinet in your kitchen. I never seen so many pills in my life. You sure those doctors aren't ripping you off?"

"They lose money," said Nick, "on people like us."

He was back to the jade turtle, holding it up to the light. Standing, she opened the drawer of the coffee table, pulled out her dust cloth, started to wipe things. "So doesn't Toby take the Minipress?"

"When you make him, sure."

"So you make him, right?"

"*I* do. When it's my turn. I don't know about my—about Susannah."

"Susannah! Why, she's a *doctor*."

"She's a research oncologist. She works with cells."

"But why wouldn't she give him his pills? That's silly, Nicholas."

She swiped at the sideboard with its antique chiming clock, at the dusty rose lampshade on the standing lamp that always made her think of her Aunt Eilda on May Day. Perched on the couch arm, Susannah's husband laced his good fingers into the stumps of his right hand. She called him *Nicholas*, though she could tell by the way he shifted in his seat that it irritated him. *Nick* seemed more like a tag, like *Mac* or *Doc*, than a name. He used to fly planes, Susannah had said. To float balloons. Now he kept feet on ground. Had a shop downtown, *Soldiers on a Shelf*. No wonder he liked touching her little whatnots. "The pills have side effects," he was saying. "It's hard to give a kid something that you know is going to make him sick to his stomach, that's going to make him fat and sluggish."

"Fat and sluggish and *alive*."

"That's why I'm asking for your help." Such a sharp *r* on *your*, like turning a page.

Linsey finished the sideboard and went to the bookshelves, mostly empty except for stacks of picture frames and old *Mother Jones*. From outside the spring peepers had started up, drowning out even the highway noise. This time last year, six weeks before the accident, her son Charlie had driven from Nashville to visit them all in Granite Falls. He'd got her to leave John and Brooke behind to walk in the fields with him, and for the first time since her marriage she'd cried in front of her boy. "I don't think you've ever seen Brooke," she said.

"I think I have," said Nicholas.

"I don't think so." She rummaged through the frames waiting to go onto the wall. "This one. Here's my little girl."

He didn't want to take it, but he pretended to look interested in the broad-cheeked girl holding the fish, the sun glinting equally off its scales and her hair. "Very nice." He handed it back. "You fish?"

"John used to take her. Here's another."

"This looks posed."

"John had this photographer friend, took a few shots. He thought she could maybe model, you know, or go into acting. Natural, wholesome kids, they say they get the best parts, and John, he—" She stopped, her hand reaching over the photo. Gently he handed it back to her.

"I'm sorry."

"You think she's totally dead and gone, don't you? You think her whole soul was in her brain."

"I—" With his good hand he rubbed his chin, which needed a shave. He was wishing he hadn't driven up the hill, into these winding developments with their prefab houses. "I guess I don't think you can be a little bit dead," he said.

"That's what I thought you'd think." Linsey propped the photo up on the sideboard, the grinning kid in spaghetti straps, thumbs hitched enticingly into belt loops. She paced the room, over to the four-harness loom at the other end, still strung for the rug she'd started this time last year. "I am not a crazy person," she said over her shoulder. He'd got up and followed her. She hated that about carpet: you could never hear anyone coming.

"I've never thought that. You've been through a lot."

"But you didn't want me to come to Roanoke."

"I was scared to have you come here. I am still scared. We're pretty much a house of straw, as you might have noticed."

"I noticed you still have your son. And I'm glad he's fine. I am."

Nick approached the loom. With his one hand he caressed the woven pattern, a combed cotton herringbone in burnt red and charcoal. "Look," he said, "what you've been through and what we've been through are two completely different things. You didn't come in like a sacrificing angel and cure Toby. Statistically, he was going to get a heart. And getting a heart just means a person is sick in a different way. Not a terminal way, like before, but chronic. He is a boy with a transplanted, denervated heart. If I ever decide I want a relationship with you—if I ever decide anything about my wife's relationship with you—it won't be based on a shared muscle. I say this with all due respect."

Linsey tossed her head. She didn't like him at all. She wanted John here, big-chested and bulldoggy, to bully Nicholas Ames out of the house. All she had was a big blow-up dummy in the kitchen. But she kept her chin high, her chin like Brooke's. "I got some meditating to do," she said. "I expect you can find your way out."

"Please," he said. He touched her arm. "About the meds."

"If I keep Susannah in line with your rules—"

"Not my rules. Medical rules. Doctor's orders."

"If I do that to keep my daughter's heart beating for your boy, then I believe we have us a relationship."

But he let the bait lie. He spent a moment pinching the cloth laid on the loom, the tight weft of the herringbone, the silky glaze on the cotton. "Well, look. I needed to fetch the mealworms, anyhow," he said. He threw a look at the kitchen door. "I'll let you get back to your guest."

Once Nick's car had pulled out from the gravel drive, Linsey lit a bayberry candle and took it to the kitchen. The Ameses are crazy people, she told Safe-T-Man. They don't know where their hearts belong.

So pack it in. Go stay with Charlie awhile.

But they've got my girl.

She had noticed it the other day, how Toby had started to furrow his eyebrows toward the center, but with the right brow lifting a bit, like Brooke. But a heart can't tell you what to do with your facial muscles. It must be Linsey did it herself. Brooke copied her, now Toby copied her. All children are mirrors.

The candle sputtered on an air bubble. She wet her fingers and pinched it out, a tiny bit of machismo.

You can't tell me, she said in the dark to Safe-T-Man, that heart won't love me still. You cannot say that for sure.

What do you want? he asked. A piece of what?

Linsey knew what Priya Roy would say: We should want to be rid of wanting. But then she saw Nicholas's high forehead, his good hand rubbing the jade lady, his hoarse voice asking for help. Asking Linsey to police his wife. Already she had a piece of a piece. It wouldn't be human, not to want more.

Chapter 5

G liding down Tinker Mountain, Nick put the van in neutral and worked the brake. The vague unease with which he'd set out from the house had spawned a kind of vertigo, as if he were falling off the mountain and could hope only to land on the wheels, or on his feet, some position from which he could negotiate.

He had expected—what? That he would tell his story, and this Linsey character—who had no reason to be fond of him, who knew mostly that he hadn't wanted to answer her letter—would fight at his side? She didn't even believe him about the Minipress, and who would? Toby's heart had raced. The Minipress was a morning med. Early that morning, fog rising through the hills, Nick had been on his way to the catalog printer. Had kissed Susannah goodbye and yes, she'd said, yes she could stay home and fix Tobe breakfast, administer the meds. That was all he had for evidence, and the New Age belle in the tacky ranch house hadn't bought it. No one would buy it. He wasn't sure *he* bought it. Except.

Strange, Ben Lieberman had said when he'd reported to Toby's room in Emergency. Not unheard of, but that Minipress dosage had a large margin of safety. You skip any of those yucko brown pills, champ? Toby had bit his lip; he'd cried a little. He'd admitted to one pill skipped the day before; he'd stuck it inside his cheek and spat it out later. Susannah had repeated, Yesterday? and Lieberman patted her arm, reassured her, reminded her how sly kids are, not her fault. Still, it's strange, he'd said. *One* skipped dose shouldn't bring on an SVT episode. You got today's okay? he asked Toby. The boy had nodded, swallowing twice, and Nick explained about the extra dose they'd shoved at him before the ambulance came.

Lieberman had written out a slip upping the milligrams. No one but Nick had noticed Susannah's knuckles, white on the steel rail of the bed. Her hand when Nick had reached for it had been cold as a medical instrument.

Air rushed through the window—cooler, in the hills. What a stupid idea, coming up here! Between him and Susannah the thing lay—Susannah who was smarter than he was, who knew her profession, who had earned, maybe, some right to risks. Linsey Hunter entered the scene only as Susannah's pet project, Susannah's thank-you note to the world. A gutsy woman surely. But these things were always trouble, the guy at Life Givers had warned them. Expectations, incriminations. All this spring, while Susannah had been painting Linsey's kitchen, reading Linsey's *Asana Mind*, figuring Linsey's taxes, weeping over Linsey's lost daughter, Nick had been sandbagging. He didn't need Linsey's help babysitting. He didn't have time to hear about her little girl, the accident. On spirituality he had nothing to share. Thanks anyway, thanks, thanks.

And now, on the excuse of Toby's school project, he hurtles out here. He implores her to spy on his wife; he begs her to put brakes on Toby, who thinks Brooke's mom hung the moon.

That neck of hers. Long and milky, her hair clipped over the pearly knots of her spine. The flinch of her freckled cheek this afternoon when he stung her: *Under other circumstances, that heart would not be beating at all*. When had he become a cruel man?

Just before the arterial, he pulled into the Shell minimart. Brightly lit, the loss-leader milk in its own case, young guy behind the counter watching ESPN on his six-inch screen. "They still rehashing that draft pick?" said Nick, putting down a five for the skim.

The guy nodded, made change almost without looking. "Making trades already. Johnson's gone to the Heat."

"Has he now. Sonofabitch."

Back on the road, planes passing low over the arterial, Nick remembered Toby at the hospital, his heart once again under control. From his gurney, waiting to check in overnight, the kid had kept tugging on Nick's sleeve. Finally Nick had turned and crouched, Yeah Tobe what's up, what's the problem, kiddo? The paperwork could wait. And Tobe had apologized: sorry he'd spat; had he got any in Nick's eye; he would never do it again; he was so so sorry.

And Nick had run the stubs of his right fingers through his son's hair, the silky warmth of it, grateful again.

There was that moment, his hand on his son's head, Toby fingering his yellow admittance bracelet. Then the next, when Toby's face had brightened, his eyebrows up, a world glistening before him. "So, Dad," he'd said, "I get to watch the NBA draft now, right?"

And Nick had seen how it would be—*Toronto, yes! I knew it! Turn that defense around*—a sea-change from last year. He could put them together like a diptych: Toby languid on the bed in Durham, the spirit punched out of him; then Toby slapping his dad five when they both got the pick right, swigging his ginger ale and guessing how the Kings would trade Webber now, laying odds on New York.

He could have made Toby a bet, say fifty cents on the first pick—a bet Toby would have won, would be around and healthy to win, much later when the snow fell in the Blue Ridge and the games began.

Cars passed him, shortcutting through Roanoke out to Richmond, down to Research Triangle. A place to pass through. He steered with his right hand, a habit that hadn't changed when he lost the fingers. The thumb held the wheel, the primary knuckles gripped. Linsey had gazed at the hand with revulsion, a fairly usual reaction. Most people, seeing the pink stumps, took him for a machinist, the victim of an industrial accident. That he had *chosen* the risk, that risk had been part of his *amusement*, sucked away all the sympathy. As it should! he told himself. As it should. A dozen years ago, just before they moved here, a guy in New York had offered to build him prosthetic fingers, and he'd turned the guy down. I do most things I need to do, he'd said. What he hadn't said was he wanted the stumps, to remind him.

And then Toby had blossomed into his life, and each time Nick dreamed of flying away again, he woke with love inside him like a heavy stone, like the stone that had blessed him with half a hand.

I get to watch the NBA draft now, right? Toby had asked in the hospital, and Nick had hesitated. Surely the kid had been through enough punishment. Surely each moment of joy was already purchased and paid for. But then, just as surely, he found himself shaking his head. "I don't think so, Tobe," he said. "You were supposed to stop playing, to watch that draft. You didn't stop playing. If I went back on this one, I'd be a bad dad." Wheeling his son up to the hospital room, he'd glanced from the side to see the wet glimmer in Toby's eyes, the tremble of his lip, the narrow bridge of his nose white where he'd inherited the bump from Susannah.

Nick would tell him about Obatu Johnson, if he was still awake, about the luck of the Heat.

But the bedroom lights were out, the downstairs silent. Nick tiptoed into the kitchen, where Coal met him madly wagging. "And no one," Nick said, cupping the dog's muzzle, "has walked you, you poor S.O.B."

Light on upstairs, in Toby's bathroom. The children's bathroom, the realtor had advertised it, when they first looked at the house. Already Toby was sick by then. Nick remembered rubbing Susannah's back, as they'd followed the realtor past the second, smaller child's room. They didn't use it for much, now—a sewing machine passed on from Susannah's mom, an exercise bike gathering dust. Coal panting behind him, Nick picked up the clothes Toby had strewn around after his bath. In the pocket of his son's shorts he found a cut straw, the metal ring from a soda can, and a ragged, half-eroded brown pill.

Nick shut his eyes, saw Toby shooting hoops on the asphalt, then running away from him over the grass. Yes, he had been wearing these same shorts, the other day. Susannah had brought them home in a plastic bag from the hospital and tossed them in the wash. Only the Minipress was a tough pill, tougher than Tide.

"Yup," Nick said aloud. He flipped the pill up, like a coin, with his one hand and caught it. Then he dropped it into the toilet and flushed. "C'mon, boy," he said to Coal.

Warm night and cicadas whining already, the heavy scent of lilac. Coal tugged at the leash. The dog had been a gift from Nick's father when Toby was two. "Get him used to having a younger brother," the old guy had said, with a wink at Nick.

They hadn't been trying, then. It was two years later, the diagnosis just in on Toby, that Nick had been desperate to get Susannah pregnant again. Every night that winter they'd made love, and he'd made sure she didn't have her diaphragm in, though they didn't talk about that. Maybe, he'd considered down the years, she'd had the same idea in mind: they could replace Toby while Toby was still with them, could replace him without it seeming like a replacement.

Coal stopped by the stream, sniffed for small creatures among the boulders and bunchgrass. How young they'd all been, back before a single surgery was scheduled! Taking off her shirt, he'd given Susannah back-rubs with fingers and stumps, kneading one shoulder blade then the next, kissing the mole on her neck until the neck softened and, swanlike, curved. Tired as she'd been, she came suddenly, those nights, a sharp cry and convulsion and then she begged him to be inside her, quick, now. He really thought his seed had taken, in her. And maybe, if they'd kept going like that, it would have.

He pulled the dog back to the sidewalk. The neighbors' houses were spottily lit, closed up for the air-conditioning. A far, far cry from Brooklyn, everybody's music spilling onto the street, a backyard a place to grill on, a rail to hang laundry. It was these big, quiet, houses, he thought, that made the South so profoundly lonely for a transplant like him.

"C'mon, Coal," he said. It was a humid night, a good time to sweat. Wash it off in the shower later. "C'mon, boy," he said and began to jog. Over the bridge, along the moonlit path by the Roanoke River, a few cars in the parking lot, lovers and smokers. Coal loped alongside, red nylon stringing them together. Perspiration gathered in the small of Nick's back. He had a nice gait; it felt good, to stretch his long legs over the hardened ground. To dismiss Linsey, her tchotchkes and weavings, to dismiss his own foolishness, to dismiss even the pill in Toby's pocket. The river was still high, from the spring rains and the snow melt in the Blue Ridge. Brown and sinewy it flowed beside him. As he picked up the pace, he felt his heart pumping oxygen-rich blood, the arteries opening.

His son would never know these sensations. No matter what Susannah said; no matter what Lieberman promised. Brooke's heart, he remembered as he passed the bandshell, had been a few centimeters too big for Toby's chest, at first. They'd had to extract fluid and wait for the inflammation to recede before they closed back the ribcage. Fact was the thing didn't quite fit. It was like a pewter soldier he'd seen once, painted to look like the rest of the lead collection into which it was dropped—he'd laughed and told the dealer it would never pass.

Rounding the bend of the river, Nick felt his own impetuous heart, the heart he held in check by force of will. He always wished he'd gotten his dad's heart, the solid, steady, unassuming heart of a midsized man who built houses, who took his greatest pride in a neatly fitted joist. Long ago in Brooklyn, he used to work next to his father, used to match his breath to his dad's as they struggled with a panel of sheetrock. Together they'd exhale when it was in place, and shake their muscles out. They had everything in common except biology.

Which was, in the end, the thing that mattered.

It didn't come from me, it didn't come from me, Nick's steps thudded on the dirt path. At the second bridge he slowed. He let Coal trot down the shallow bank and drink. He pictured Lieberman's pared fingernail, stopping like the cup on an Ouija board at the square Nick had checked on the family-history form. "*Adopted,*" Lieberman had read out. "Is that a fact?"

"The form asks for facts," Nick had said.

"You made any attempt to contact your birth parents?" Lieberman had a thick brush of a mustache and tended to chew his words. Like Nick, Lieberman had come down from New York, only it was Susannah he'd known in that other life, the geography of medical work.

"I never went for that approach," Nick had said. "Why dig up pain?"

Lieberman had run his finger down the page, past all the hereditary conditions that Nick couldn't answer to. "Because," he'd said, "we're talking 75 percent genetic on this condition. And if Susannah's family has no prior history—"

"Then it's me, probably. All right. Let's say it's me. What difference does it make? He's still the same sick kid; you still treat him the same."

"It might help you and Suzy"—Lieberman glanced at Susannah; he was the only one who seemed to call her that—"make plans."

It was Susannah who'd protested. Up to bat she'd stepped, against her old med-school pal. Okay, she'd argued, let's say there's a history. They were still talking about 25 percent non-genetic. Toby could be in the 25 percent, couldn't he? Even if they knew about Nicholas's biological family, they might decide to gamble on another child. Mightn't they?

In that case, Lieberman had argued, with quick little accusatory glances at Nick, they would at least know the odds.

"C'mon, boy," Nick said.

He pulled on the leash. Coal started to trot again, but Nick held him back. Tired; he was tired. It had been a long day. "Got to check our goldfish," he told the dog who flashed his inane pink grin.

The odds. Nick didn't play them. Ever since that day—three years now? no, more—he'd kept track of Susannah's periods. He started keeping

Trojans in the bedside table. And when she wouldn't let him put them on, and no, she wouldn't put the diaphragm in either, he'd started withdrawing before he came. Once last year, as his semen spilled gelatinous onto her belly, she'd hauled off and smacked his face with the back of her hand.

Since then, their times were rare and mute and filled with absence.

The cool water of the goldfish pond was gurgling in from the pipe; under the spotlight from the deck, the white bricks glinted. Beneath the dark surface of the water, Nick could make out four slow orange torpedoes, brought to life by the sudden light. But in the corner, nested in a scrim of dead grass blown onto the surface, a flat side of floating copper, a dead eye. "Aw, Jesus," he said. Reaching through the loop of the leash, he picked the fish up by its sharp-scaled tail and lifted it quickly away from Coal's nose. Tomorrow, he and Toby had been going to give them names. "Fish," he said aloud, with a sour gleam of satisfaction at not knowing the dumb creature better.

Setting the thing down, he pulled the cover off the trash can; dropped it in. His fingers smelled of fish. When he let Coal off the leash, the dog bounded onto the deck as if home, too, were an adventure. Nick followed. There, by the plastic lounge chair, rested Toby's Kobe Bryant ball. He picked it up one-handed and shot. The ball clanged noisily off the backboard, off the rim, and missed, landing soft on the grass.

He would not mention the pill. He would not ask them anything. He would despise no one. He would buy a new goldfish. He would not ask for help again but would keep them all as safe as a man knew how.

It didn't come from me, it didn't come from me.

He would go in, now, check ESPN, find some news to greet Toby with in the morning. Maybe Susannah would wake with the sound of the TV, or the shift of weight as he lifted the sheet from the bed and slipped in next to her. Maybe he would touch her face, and she would wake. Already, the door sucking behind him, holding in the cooled air, he could taste her skin, salt and the almond soap she used; he could feel the curve between waist and hip.

Chapter 6

*B*en Lieberman had an hour between patients. With a view to the clock on the wall, he had taken the seat by the cafeteria window. He could focus on Susannah without stopping to check his watch. She was telling him now—finally—about the Minipress. All week, she was saying, she had been meaning to explain to Nick.

"About letting Toby skip the pill, you mean," said Ben.

"Not just that. Nick already suspects that I knew Toby skipped. He's heard me arguing with *you* over that med."

"You were trying to do my job, as I recall," Ben said. He studied her eyes, the way the lids hollowed below the brow, the almost languid crease and hood, the reddish lashes.

"Look," said Susannah, brushing at her hair, "blame the database. No longitudinal studies on liver tolerance in children. The medical establishment gone pill happy again."

"That's what you've been meaning to tell Nick?"

Susannah leaned toward her coffee, then drew her mouth back. "Hot," she observed.

He blew on the surface of his own brew. He'd taken it black, forgoing the leathery-tasting creamer that Susannah stirred in. This cafeteria, in Marcus Griffiths's research building, was even dingier than the one in the hospital.

"Toby gets nauseated in the morning," Susannah said. "He kneels by the toilet and dry heaves. Then he won't eat anyhow, because he's watching his weight. He stands on the scale and squeezes his tummy and turns away dinner. The fuzz growing on his arms? He picks at it like a monkey! Last week, he took my razor and tried to shave it off."

Ben nodded, his mustache damp from coffee. "That's the Minipress, doctor."

"Right. All right. But it affects me. *That*'s what I wanted to tell Nick. How knowing the pharmacology doesn't keep you from dreaming of your kid's body clean of this crap."

"Crap?"

"You know what I mean."

"Just saving lives, ma'am."

"Oh please, Ben." The muscles around her eyes tensed with shame. "I am *whipping* myself. Does that make you happy?"

"Not exactly."

"I don't have the right to change the dosages. I don't have the right to ignore the dosages. My opinion is just that, an opinion, I—"

"Okay, Suzy. Okay." Ben pinched Susannah's scarred chin. She'd told him about it one night long ago, when they had both been working late and her skin was so pale the scar stood out like a cut. A Rottweiler had kissed her there, she said, and the nurse at the clinic had stitched the wound into a half-inch frown and then made Susannah promise to keep smiles planted on the rest of her face. "Toby is fine," Ben said. "I've got a safer margin on the dosage, and you've learned your lesson. Now let's get this tissue sorted out. Patients are waiting."

"And cells," said Susannah, wiping a stray tear.

"Do cells wait?"

"They wait," she said, setting down the Styrofoam cup and picking glass jars from the box Ben had brought over, "very patiently."

Ben was donating cell-wall samples from biopsies drawn last month, for Susannah and her lab group to grow into malignant tumors. In return he would get a line of acknowledgment in whatever article Susannah managed to pull out of this line of research. Enough for Ben, who had known back at Columbia not only that he wanted clinical practice but that he wanted cardiology, the care and healing of the human heart.

From the minute he met Susannah Hubert, he'd seen it was not the work she was cut out for. "I have got to be a doctor, love it or hate it," she'd confessed to him, another one of those endless-loop day-nights in New York. These were the stories residents told one another—how they first knew, or which teacher first told them they could make it. Suzy Hubert's was a backing-in, heading-out story. There had been her third brother, the original Toby, who died, stupidly, of a burst appendix. There had been a schoolteacher father who wanted one of his nine children to fly out of their West Virginia coal town, the mother who said rosaries for three years until breast cancer silenced her. There had been one of those goodhearted, misplaced priests who told Susannah over and over how bad their town was going to need a doctor in ten years, and who finally helped her get the scholarship that launched her into Ben's territory.

She dated no one back then, as far as Ben could see. She was this deep red rose from West Virginia, her bloom and her thorns both intact.

"I never thought I could work miracles," she said to him on that long-ago night. "I had a friend who was always after setting some cat's paw or bringing some broken-winged starling back to flight. I was never hands-on like that."

"I think," Ben had said, daring to part her veil, "you like what you see in the microscope better than what you meet on the street."

"I understand it better."

"So do your work in the lab. More compatible materials. No bedside manner required."

How many times, since then, had he told himself that he was glad to have given her good advice? Even though it meant she was gone from the program by that summer; even though the nights at the hospital had quickly acquired a gray, caffeinated taste. How many times had he told himself he was too busy to look her up, that he felt no need of her sharp tongue?

He was a smart Jewish kid from Brooklyn who'd grown up wanting to heal the paraplegic Orthodox girl down the block. He wasn't going to change his course. He put off calling her apartment, once she'd changed her degree. And then one day he did make the call, only to learn she'd moved—down to Greenwich Village, to live with an adventurer named Nicholas Ames who played bar piano and didn't mind how sharp a tongue she had.

They left the cafeteria, took the stairs up to the second floor. "Got to go put balloons in hearts," Ben said when they had the tissue stored in Susannah's incubator.

"I'll walk you out. Maybe we'll bump into Marcus."

"I'll prepare myself."

Susannah gave a little grunt. "The great Marcus Griffiths is too intense for you?"

"Not at all. I expect madness from my scientists. Why? Is he too intense for you?"

Walking, he slid an arm across her shoulders and was rewarded with hers around his waist.

"You know," Susannah said, squeezing him a bit at the ribcage, "I am the only woman he's ever given a lab to."

"So the man knows brilliance."

"Nick and I were just thinking about having kids when we got here. I came home after a week in this place, and I told Nick, 'No can do.' Not that I'd ever known a mother *anywhere* who did research oncology. But I'd thought, you know—"

"Superwoman," said Ben. He let go the shoulder. *Nick*, he thought. How easy it was to forget.

"I thought times were changing. Only Marcus ran me on all cylinders—the way he runs himself. You direct committees, you deliver lectures, you publish articles, you complete experiments, you don't have babies."

"Well, you did."

"That was Nick, screwing up my courage."

Ben bit his tongue. *That wasn't the only thing he screwed.* He'd have said it, once. They were that frank with one another, and that barbed.

They'd reached the heavy oak door; Susannah pushed it, and they emerged to bright sunshine. "Nick went with me when I gave Marcus the news. He told Marcus about the shop. Pointed out how he could take up where I left off. He could lock up the shop and leave. He could stay up all night minding colic and catch sleep later. And Marcus—there he is now, on the hill—he nodded like an old bull that's been worn out by the picadors."

"And he didn't fire you."

"Not yet."

"Happy ending."

"I don't know."

"If you mean the cardiomyopathy—"

"No! I feel blessed, given Toby's chances."

"So do I."

"Sure you do," said Susannah. "But you don't have this—attachment. You don't know how a kid lays *claim* to you."

Ben looked away. His voice came thick. "You're complaining?"

"No, silly. I am in love with my kid. And it scares me to the soles of my shoes." She and Ben both looked at her shoes, white pumps worn gray at the toes, her small plump high-arched feet. "One day," she went on, shading her eyes and waving at Marcus Griffiths, "I went to this birthday party—you know, out by Bluegrass Lake?—and the birthday boy's mother had Toby sitting in the shade, drinking a glass of water. He got flushed, the mother says. He fell down in the middle of balloon races. His heart's going like mad, this mother says. And then you know what she says?"

"She says, 'He has hypertrophic cardiomyopathy.'"

Susannah worked on a smile. "She tells me Toby's *lucky*, because he's got a *doctor* for a mom."

"Hey. Hey. Take a tissue. He *is* lucky."

Susannah blew her nose. "You *do* this to me, Ben. You make me so fucking *emotional*." Quickly, she tucked the tissue into a pocket and looked up. "Hello, Marcus. You know Ben Lieberman."

They shook hands, exchanged compliments of Susannah's work. If he'd gone into the army, Marcus Griffiths would have been a war-room general, stabbing his pointer at the map. The spring wind blew his unruly fringe of hair; when he sneezed, his face went purple for a fraction of a second.

Then he goose-stepped into the building. Ben checked his watch. "We were saying," he said to Susannah.

"What?"

"Do me a favor."

"Keep a med schedule. You got it."

"Not that. You remember Harvey?"

"The invisible rabbit. James Stewart."

"Not the movies. *William* Harvey."

"You mean like the seventeenth-century guy? The one we studied in history of medicine?"

"Time for you to go back and read him. *De Motu Cordis*. The Circulation of the Blood. Read it, okay? Promise me."

"Jesus, Ben. That was a lifetime ago!"

"Look, when you start believing your kid has got a small thinking creature in his chest, I don't want to go into a boring lecture on valve mechanics. So promise me, okay? Gotta run."

Which was true, he did. As he neared the top of the hill to the parking lot, though, he turned, just in time to watch her disappear through the heavy double doors, the glass refracting her red dress.

It was enough. He told himself often how it was enough, to be ministering to the child of an old friend, to see her successful and happy, weathering this storm. It wasn't as if he had spent the last ten years pining for Susannah Hubert. He had been married, hadn't he? Briefly, to a religion professor in New York, and they had entertained thoughts of beautiful dark-haired children in excellent health, of family visits and the sort of luxury vacations his older colleagues talked about almost to the exclusion of everything else save platelets. Then he had finished his residency. Had cast about for private practice and turned up Roanoke, Virginia. Not West Virginia, but still the Blue Ridge, and that awful lit-up city star, and bluegrass music, and it was where he wanted to be. And when the religion professor had said no, no, she couldn't see it, giving up tenure, no. . . . The visions of dark-haired children had vanished like so much smoke, and he had made his way south alone.

There had been other women since then—several, in fact—but none now. Tonight, he would finish his rounds and go for a late workout at the gym. Privately, he divided his history in Roanoke into two eras—the four years before he knew Susannah was in town, and the time since, that second era subdivided by Toby's illness. That's me, he'd said when his eyes lit on her at a Cancer Awareness dinner six years ago, good ol' boy cardiologist, at your service ma'am. And she'd run her eyes over his curly hair, Semitic nose, eyes of coal, and laughed that full-bellied laugh he hadn't heard since the cafeteria at Sloan-Kettering. And said, "Come meet Nick."

Who was a helluva nice guy, you had to admit. *He* had to admit. A little testy when Ben had first diagnosed his son, but who could blame the guy?

In fact, Ben was thinking as he scrubbed at the hospital, he liked Susannah's husband well enough that it ought to feel a little odd, keeping this business of the Minipress from him. But Suzy would tell Nick Ames, in her own good time. Meanwhile, it gave Ben a little rush to have a bit of Suzy's sauciness in his palm. Call him pathetic, but when he dwelt on her and her boy, his heart strained against his bonds and he thought, not of the enlightened William Harvey, but of the old Greek physician, Galen. He pictured his heart's action as Galen had described it, like the movement of tides, swelling and receding. And just as with romance, knowing the idea was wrongheaded did nothing whatever to drive it from his thoughts.

Chapter 7

*T*hat night the first mealworm turned into a beetle, its small black back shining in the oatmeal. "I'm the first," Toby said when he'd made a handful of phone calls. "The first beetle in the class."

"Way to go, Tiger," Nick said as the beetle crawled onto his finger.

"When school's out, Max and I are going to start a beetle farm. We'll feed them leaves and apples. He's got a terrarium in his basement, from the turtle he had last year. They'll lay eggs."

This time last year, Susannah thought. This time last year, Toby had missed two months of school already, and summer meant the hospital, the transplant center, the long wait, and terror. Now he was just overexcited.

"When I'm retired from basketball," Toby said later, as he slipped into his nightshirt, "I might raise bugs. Can you make a job from that?"

"I don't know, honey. Probably. You can do mail-order ant farms, so I guess so."

"I'm good at taking care of stuff. Dad's not so good. Another goldfish died, did he tell you? He thinks we're overfeeding them. He's going to pay me to monitor the water temperature."

"Okay, honey. Okay. Ssh, now." Susannah flicked off the light. Through Toby's French windows, the full moon shone. "Look, Tobe," she said. "There's the Man."

"Cool," he said. His fingers rested on her wrist, stroked the smooth face of her watch. She couldn't remember when they'd started sitting like this, with the light off, sharing the minute before sleep laid its claim on Toby. Last year at the hospital, maybe, or just before hospitals became part of their lives.

"You know it's not really a face, right?"

"Duh, Mom."

"Okay, smartie. So you know what makes it look like one?"

He shrugged. "Shadows. Some kind of trick."

"Craters, actually. And you know what makes it full?"

"Sure. The light from the sun. Though I forget how come it waxes and wanes. And I don't want you to explain."

She smiled. She touched his forearm, where the hair had grown in stubbly. Patted his chest where she'd rubbed cream after his bath. The worst of it, she would have told anyone who asked, was how the scars had itched. For weeks. Same way that a toothache is worse than childbirth because you don't know when it will go away. He no longer scratched, but she rubbed lotion every night on his old-man skin. "Little kids think," she said, "that there's a real man in the moon who decides to visit and then go away."

"There isn't."

"No. The moon doesn't have any say in it at all. Kind of like your heart."

"*Brooke's* heart," he corrected her. This was one code she hadn't been able to crack, the way he called the heart Brooke's, as if it were on loan and might be reassigned.

"You are the sun," Susannah went on. "You put the light in Brooke's heart. Do you know what I mean?" He shook his head, a dark wavering on the pillow. "By taking your meds," she said. "Every time you take them, you're deciding, 'Okay, I want to be alive today. I want this ticker to tick today.' The rest of us don't make that same decision."

"I hate the meds," Toby said. He yawned; time for her to get up. She touched the bridge of his nose, the narrow bone that had grown out, the last couple of years, to a shape sharp and distinctive as a beak. Until men began admiring her own profile, she'd thought it ugly. On a small boy—she traced Toby's bone to the cartilage tip—it was startlingly elegant.

"I'm just reminding you, Tobe," she said as he turned on the pillow. "You know the schedule. Just like you know how long it's safe to exercise. For a while, Daddy and I can help, we can remind you. But in the end, you have to decide it's worth it. The heart won't decide for you."

"Yes, it will," said Toby.

His eyes shone, little moons reflected in the dark pupils. He wasn't going to talk about the lie he had told Ben Lieberman. "You are such a stubborn kid," Susannah said.

"Aren't I though." This was a new phrase, heard somewhere—TV, the teachers at school. Pleased with himself, Toby risked a quick smirk toward his mother with his moon-studded eyes, round like hers, then turned his attention back to the window. "Wonder where I got it from," he said.

Susannah kissed him lightly and stood. In the upper hall, above the wide stairway that had sold her, from the start, on this house, she paused. Tonight, she would tell Nick about the Minipress. Tonight or tomorrow. Five days it had been, since the SVTs episode. Two days since she and Nick had made love, the night he fetched the mealworms back from Linsey's. Made love with that strange sexiness, the way he'd surprised her in the hallway, his hands cool from tending his goldfish. As if he'd expected making love to bring a confession to her lips, *I saw him slip the horse pill into his pocket; I saw him, and I didn't know about the day before, and I said nothing*. Well, she would confess then. All right. Worth it, to feel his hands mold her skin again, to taste the clean salt of his sex.

The stairway was polished oak, the handrail resting lightly on the spindles; wainscoting ran waist-high around the curve of the risers. From the landing, Susannah regarded her husband, at work in his studio below. Where he worked had once been the parlor, an arched doorway leading to a narrow room designed for an overstuffed loveseat and a bridge table. A trio of Tensor lamps shone onto his materials. She could almost make out the canister labels: "cinders," "polyester grass," "roots," "white sand," "brown sand." Bags of dried lichen, herbs, and kitty litter tucked under the table. The roots would transform into miniature trees, the lichen to clumps of leaves, the litter to small boulders, all of it to simulate scenes of war.

As she watched, Nicholas was painting the uniform onto a Civil War cavalryman. A breeze blew in the open window; outside, moonlight whitened the blossoms that brushed against the screen. The scent of lilac, amalgamated with turpentine, floated up to Susannah. Nick had flicked off the radio, and she could hear peepers, their clicks and scales coming from the woods, frog fertility songs. From a tall jelly jar, he picked a new brush and dipped it in black.

It was a kind of play, a cleverness so lightly worn it approached art, though Susannah and Nick both laughed at the dour miniaturists who handed out business cards with "Artist" engraved in the corner. A good trade for a one-handed bandit, Nick called it. Of course there were lots of those. But ever since the rafting accident, he'd been content with this tiny, simulated world.

She could just barely remember his right hand as it had been. There were photographs, of course, but none of the two of them together. They had known each other six months; had slept together a dozen times, maybe fewer. If she shut her eyes, now when they made love, she could sometimes imagine his right fingers traveling down her spine to her buttocks, sliding on her sweat. He had been a part-time pianist, then, in a Soho bar. Summers he spent rafting, gliding, ballooning. He was going to get certified, he told her the second or third time they went out, as a guide. She loved how his eyes lit when he described the air, the wind, the water. Sure, she would have told him if he had asked, she could live in a wild place. She could do her research anywhere.

Now they lived where she did her research, and Nick played brilliant five-fingered piano and made little worlds out of stone and lichen, and they had Toby. How could she tell him what she yearned for? It wasn't just another child. It was the roar of his rapids and the silence of his thin air; it was the smell she remembered from his skin, before, when he'd been off somewhere pushing the envelope, and then had come back to her.

Nonsense, she told herself. He had lost four fingers, nothing more, and like the monkey's paw she would not wish them back for the world. And she would tell him about the Minipress; she would tell him now. It would be no big deal.

He was facing Susannah, bent over the latest scavenged set. Through a long window over the staircase, the moon cast shadows, white oblongs descending. Good *feng-shui* this house had, Linsey had assured Susannah. She had also offered to spend a day sometime, whenever Susannah wanted, to adjust the *ba-gua* in certain rooms. A science, Linsey had called it. Susannah tried to picture the people from her lab—her assistants Cutter and Tomiko, or even Marcus Griffiths—calibrating *ba-gua*. Sure, come on ahead, she'd said to Linsey. I like science.

Nick stood back from his new Rebel. It was almost done. The gray looked too shiny, but Nick knew it would dull, and the black buttons were perfectly spaced pinpricks. All he had to do now were the honors.

He'd got this batch from an estate sale up in Charlottesville. The Northerners had all but rusted away, but the Rebels were intact, only their paint chipped off from the alternating moisture and cold in the old woman's attic. *She'd be pleased to see it,* the woman's portly son had observed. *She always said the good side would last the long battle.*

Upstairs, Susannah was settling Toby down. Nick didn't mind. Nothing but relief, really, when she swooped in at the end of the day and took his son off his hands. If he got this dozen painted and dried by the weekend, he could sell them to one of the tourists who starting flocking through the Blue Ridge this time of year.

A relief, even though she was so tired that half the time he went up after twenty minutes and found her asleep on Toby's bed—her feet still in shoes on the floor, her generous body twisted awkwardly to let her head rest on the pillow next to Tobe's. Gently he'd shake her shoulder. She'd open her eyes, confused about where she was, then she'd let him lead her across the hall, past the empty child's room.

Another child. The question, or the possibility or the chance, it wouldn't go away. The other night, Susannah had dutifully worn her diaphragm. How close he'd come to arresting her polite hiatus in the bathroom, to saying *who cares? who cares?* and making love the old, unguarded way, his fingers and mouth eager explorers in and around her labia, his cock reaching deep enough to make her gasp, no fear of the rubber rim. But then she was gone and the bed cooling. By the time she came back, he felt caution like a sleeve over them both, love like a gift they owed each other. He reached for her breasts, the pink stars of her aureoles, and said nothing.

Adjusting the magnifying glass, he pushed up his glasses and worked his red-sable brush to a point. We both work with tiny things, Susannah had observed once. Linsey Hunter too, he thought, and felt again the weight of the jade piece—what had it been? A turtle, a lizard, a pregnant lady? Well, he wouldn't go back to find out. The next day, two days ago now, Linsey had come around the house, but he had managed to be at his shop downtown. It would pass, somehow, this strange relationship. They would all move on.

No, not all of them. He painted an epaulet, thread-thin gold over burnt red, and put the figure down. Not Toby. Toby had this alien heart, and that was that. In a year or two his fierce, feisty, focused little kid would see that pro basketball was even more out of the question for him than for any of the thousands of other dreamers out there. He'd realize that his endorphin highs would come slow, if at all, and at the expense of lengthy negotiations between his physiology and the drugs he poured through his bloodstream. Finally he'd see the shortness and difficulty of the life ahead of him. The courage he would have to summon came from a place where Nick had never even set emotional foot.

That was the real issue. Not another child, but who Toby was, what Toby could become. Susannah thinking grit and determination can take you to the moon even if you're a little short on oxygen. For this folly he raged at her, for this folly he loved her.

He dipped the brush, swirled the tip, executed the last flourish. Then he lined the figure up next to his comrades, a half-dozen doomed fighters.

"They look new," said Susannah, holding her hands together behind her neck and stretching her elbows upward as she came downstairs.

"I hope not. They'll sell because they're old."

"You know what I mean. Good as new." She bent over his work table. "What a steady hand you've got. You could be a surgeon."

"Sure thing. The one-handed appendectomist."

"Brooke had her appendix out. Linsey told me."

"Well, that's, uh, that's . . . Jesus, I don't know. It's not exactly *too bad*, is it? I mean, what do you want me to say?"

"Nothing, Nick. Nothing. Just, she sounds like a little girl who didn't have the easiest short life."

"She is a bone that you and that Linsey are chewing together. The one with the tricky *life* is Toby."

Susannah picked up one of the unrestored soldiers, a rusty corporal with a broken nose, and twirled it between her fingers. "Ben's got me reading William Harvey," she said.

"Does he now. And what has Mr. Harvey got to say?"

"Nothing very useful. It's all very male. The heart's a prince in his kingdom, he gets erect and pumps."

Nick grinned as he dotted buttons. "Sounds like soft porn"

"Harvey also studied oysters, clams, mussels, that variety of zoophyte. He looks at them and he writes, 'The whole animal is a heart.'"

Nick replaced the brush, sat back on his stool, adjusted his glasses. "So?"

"So, I don't know. Sometimes I wish we had let that little girl rest in peace."

"And our boy die?"

"I didn't say that."

"I told you, Susannah, you should never have written back to her. This goes nowhere."

"Hold me," said Susannah, coming around the table.

He wrapped his arm over her back, smelled her almond hair. He put his lips to the bump on her nose.

"I've got to get up to the lab," she said.

"What, this late?"

"Two weeks till data is due in to Cantrex. Cutter's been pulling all-nighters."

Nick sighed. "Maybe you can take a break next week."

"Why next week?"

"You know my customer, McGowan, the one who collects miniature Corsairs? He gave me a poster for the window. Seems he's bringing his hot-air balloon for some carnival by your lab."

"Oh, great. I'll just forget the cell-death assays then."

"Trade 'em for the ring toss."

"Hm." Susannah nestled into his chest, and he considered persuading her to stay home. "I just barely remember," she said to his shoulder, "*your* windy days."

"Over and gone." He laced his hand into her hair.

"I loved that one time you took me up," she said.

"Susquehanna Valley. Pretty country."

"Like being up in a kite." Pulling away, she took the stool on the other side of the table. He let his glasses slip down his nose, to get a good look at her. When she was tired like this, her eyes paled to opal. "You're really salvaging those guys."

"They're worth it."

"Are they?" Susannah touched a tiny pewter head. "They seem so—I don't know—*reduced*."

"Well, that's the point, isn't it? Miniatures?"

Susannah tucked her lower lip into her teeth—though it was hardly worth the pinch, since he could read the thoughts held back. He was, indeed, the man who'd taken her white-water rafting two weeks after they met; who'd sold his car once to spend a summer rock-climbing in Vancouver. And now he painted dolls.

"Toby and I had a little talk," she said. "About his meds. I'm trying to get him to take more responsibility."

"He's not going to do that, Susannah." Nicholas picked up a weathered drummer boy, his sticks broken off. "He's nine years old. He hates the meds."

"He does. And he can't believe—it *is* hard to believe—that all those pills are really necessary, every single day. You have to treat the routine as an insurance policy. It's like wearing his bike helmet or fastening his seat belt—"

"Which is why you let him skip the Minipress?"

He hadn't meant to say it, right out. Setting the drummer boy down, he knocked over the freshly painted Rebel. Carefully he righted the piece. Drawing a Q-Tip from the jar on the work table, he swabbed the back of the soldier's coat, where the paint had smeared. He turned the Tensor lamp back on and dipped his brush.

"Go on," said Susannah. "Like the Minipress."

"Nothing. Go do your lab work. The sooner you go, the sooner you're home."

"You think I ignored his blood pressure med."

He filled in the place he'd swabbed, three quick strokes of gray. His voice urged gently, like his hand. "I didn't say that."

"You might as well. It's been your attitude for a week, you've been watching me like a hawk."

"You heard Lieberman. One missed dose wouldn't do it."

"Look, everyone makes mistakes, Nick. I tried—"

"Don't tell me what you tried. Tell me what you did. If there's one thing I know"—he held up his crippled hand—"it's that life doesn't grade us on effort."

Susannah slid off the stool and took a step back, as if the floor near the table were filling with mud and she needed to keep her feet dry. "You think you can control this thing," she said tightly. "You think if something goes wrong, it wasn't controlled. But it's total risk, Nick. Total risk all the time. If you can't deal with that, then—" From where her arms were crossed over her chest, she lifted one hand and waved it in a circular motion, as if swatting smoke from her face. "Then I'm going to the lab," she finished, "while you downsize your life."

He stayed like that for several minutes after she'd gone, brush in hand. She had been going to tell him. She had opened the door to telling him and had waited for him to invite her in. Only he hadn't, and so she had slammed it shut. He bent the little soldier he had been painting toward the light. What a stricken look the guy wore on his face—his drooping blond mustache, his knit brow—as if he, too, were guilty, though no one knew of what.

Chapter 8

No matter how his parents argued about her, Toby thought Linsey was awesome. For one, she never went out to work. For two, you couldn't even imagine her raising her voice in an argument, the way his mom and dad did when they were talking about meds or b-ball or old issues from the past that he couldn't remember, like his dad quitting his job to go on that rafting trip. For three, she had all these great things to eat and do at her house, like sweet-potato chips and African mancala, that you would never think you'd like but you did. And for four, she gave him pictures of Brooke to keep under his sport cards in his room, so he could check out Brooke's happy face whenever he got to feeling too gross to live.

That was how he'd been feeling, ever since Dr. Lieberman upped the meds. Gross. Fat. Greaseball. Hairier than Coal. Stinkier than Coal. Stupid in school, he'd missed so much and they were giving out the math awards and he got nothing, only he had to stand up while Mr. Loving the principal said some garbage about being brave and having a big heart and the whole third grade laughed and clapped like he was their pet gerbil come back to his cage.

His parents weren't any help. His dad acted like, get a grip, just a few extra rules to follow, don't regress to a four-year-old. Look at my hand, his dad would say, you're lucky they even know how to *replace* a heart. His mom made it like all her fault, as if she ought to have birthed him different so the whole thing wouldn't have happened and he'd be on the basketball team already.

Linsey was always glad to see him and share her cool stuff with him. If she was only interested because of Brooke, that was okay. He figured Brooke's heart needed her mom. Plus she said Brooke's brother Charlie would come visit sometime. Charlie. And they'd shoot hoops together, and Toby would give him the '89 Rodman card.

Still he felt like crap most of the time, and his mom said it was the extra meds, the Minipress and Ecotrin and cyclosporine, the prednisone that he was supposed to have quit by now, but it was all messed up because he'd ditched the Minipress those couple days. Which, thank God he'd just told them about one of the days or it would be worse. Plus Max was gone. Poof like that, the second school let out.

Max lived right across the street, but his dad lived in Atlanta. For three years now Toby and Max had been shooting on Toby's driveway, playing h-o-r-s-e or p-i-g or Max's favorite, e-l-e-p-h-a-n-t. Max was twelve but he was small. His mom Cindy worked for an insurance company out by the mall. Usually she came home with takeout and Max's baby sister right when it got dark and called Max across the street. The whole time Toby was in the hospital, all last summer and fall, right through Christmas, Max had brought by basketball cards. A card every single day. Then the first couple weeks home, with all the germs Toby could supposedly catch (he never believed that; they wanted to keep him to themselves was all, they wouldn't even let Coal into his room), anyhow Max couldn't come in the house but he dropped the card off anyhow. I got an allowance, Toby heard him telling Toby's dad downstairs, and a collection I can pull from.

That was in January. By March, Toby was giving Max Mortal Kombat competition. In April, when Toby went back to school, Max stuffed a hundred sixty cards in his bookbag on the bus. And now Max was in Georgia for a month.

"So call some other kids," Toby's mom said. "Call your school chums."

"Nobody from school likes to play basketball."

"Don't be silly. I've seen them. On the playground."

"That's just goofing around."

"So let Daddy take you to Bluegrass Lake. There's a hoop there, and the beach. And kids you know from before."

"They'll see my scar."

"What, they don't know you had surgery? Scars make your body more interesting, Tobe."

"Scars are *gross*. You don't know. You don't have them."

"I do *too*," his mom said, pointing to her chin. It was like showing him a wash-off tattoo; he rolled his eyes.

Anyhow Max was gone, till July sometime. Toby shot hoops as long as his mom or dad would let him, one set after another, his arms just working the ball like a machine, pitching it up and over the rim in the hot sun. Then he holed up in his room. He tuned the radio to WHYY and read the old Batmans his dad had dug up at an auction of lead grenadiers. He weighed himself, and the weight kept coming on. One night he stole his mom's razor and shaved his arms, and the next day they itched and had red pricks all up and down where the hair had been, and he didn't even bother going out to shoot hoops. That was when Linsey came by and showed him how to make a bead belt on this crazy loom she said the Indians used, and they spent all that afternoon threading tiny plastic circles onto string and squeezing them down into the pattern, and she sang him these crazy bootlegger songs from South Carolina that he could teach Max when Max got home. She was awesome.

Still, the next day he went back to feeling gross, and the day after that. There wasn't anything going to "snap him out of it," the way his dad insisted to his mom—until his mom and Linsey both came up with the balloon.

It happened the night Linsey stayed for supper. His dad didn't want her to stay, but she'd brought a bag of Brooke's old games over for Toby, and before his dad had a chance to say anything, his mom was pulling out artichoke fettuccini, which she'd never cooked before Linsey came to town. Toby finished eating—no offense to Linsey, but it tasted like clay—and went to play Megaman in the living room. Keeping the sound low, he could still hear the grownups. His mom was telling Linsey he'd been depressed, and Linsey said Brooke used to get like that. *Hear that, Brooke?* he whispered to his heart while he executed a triple jump stomp.

He'd been glad to get a name for his heart, four months ago when Linsey first came to visit. Sure, it was a girl heart, but still better to have a name than nothing. He'd already started talking to it, little things like *Toby to heart, come in heart*, or *Fifty-yard dash, let's get the rate up!* Like his heart was a shy pet that needed encouraging. He knew other people didn't talk to their hearts, but theirs weren't new arrivals. And he'd heard his mom once say, "Come on, legs, get moving," when she didn't want to get up from the patio chair, so he figured he wasn't crazy. Still, he didn't tell anyone about talking to his heart; he didn't tell anyone he called the heart by Brooke's name.

Brooke's slew of despond, Linsey was calling her moods. "She used to climb this oak tree in the back meadow. She'd sit there for hours. 'Leave her in her slew,' my mama used to say."

"Toby doesn't get depressed," said Toby's dad. "He just gets pissed off. This is reaction to drugs."

It is not, Toby said to his heart.

"John would jolly Brooke right out of it," Linsey went on. "He'd say of a sudden, 'Come on, girl, we are going to the circus!'"

"She's always sounded like a happy child, to me," said Toby's mom. Toby's mom was always looking for the thing to say that wouldn't bother anyone. Toby turned up the sound. Now they were going to say nice things about Brooke, which he didn't need to hear. From the open window he could smell the moon vine, which bloomed when the morning glory had closed up for the day. He'd helped his mom plant it, back in March, and shown Linsey the little shoots when they started peeking up from the ground.

Now he was on Level 10, but with only two lives. He always died here. The voices in the kitchen were getting louder. Linsey was saying something about Brooke being a genius, that was why she got her slew of despond, and Toby's dad did not—thank God, did *not*—laugh. "Of *course*, it's hard," Toby's mom said, and then a little louder, "It *is* hard, Nick, and you know it, because a slew of despond is what we've got here. Yesterday he wouldn't even play pig with me. He sits in front of that TV screen zapping creatures. If we can't lower the dosages—"

"Which we cannot," said Toby's dad, pretty loud.

"—then I'm open to suggestions."

Toby turned the sound down, but just a fraction, so they couldn't tell. His hands were sweating. His dad had wanted to turn the air-conditioning on, but his mom said Toby got cold too easy, with the meds. When they ate out on the porch, they always heard the highway, like a huge mosquito. In fact, Toby hardly ever wanted to be outside, any more. That was part of the grossness. He heard the clink of plates—Linsey, stacking and carrying up to the counter. "My boy Charlie is coming to town in a few days," she was saying.

Charlie, he repeated to Brooke's heart.

"He's a musician. And the absolute best at cheering Brooke up. Next to John, I mean. I could bring him around."

Yes. Charlie.

"Next week Toby's got his nine-month biopsy." This was Toby's dad. "In Durham."

Toby turned up the sound. He was at the Megaman. Now he'd die for sure.

"Toby, turn that thing down!" his dad called.

"In a second."

"*Not* in a second." His dad was in the living room now, a beer in his good hand. With the stubs of his right fingers he punched the TV off.

"Dad! I was at the last level!"

"Yeah, well my patience is at the last level. Get up to bed. Go on." His dad turned the Nintendo off with his shoe. Toby thought all the bad words but didn't say them, this time. He started up the stairs; his dad went back to the kitchen. From the stair landing he could see his dad lean over his mom where she still sat at the table, and from the way she looked when he straightened up, Toby figured they'd kissed. He tiptoed back to the indoor ficus tree, by the doorway to the kitchen. He could smell the bitter artichoke noodles, his mom's coffee.

"So how about I take him to the lab on Friday?" his mom was saying.

"Now there's a terrific idea," said his dad, moving over to the fridge. Toby backed off. "Show him what a malignant cell will do to healthy tissue, and we can't stop it. Should cheer the kid immensely. Make him glad he doesn't have cancer."

"I was *thinking*," Toby's mom said, "what Linsey said about John cheering Brooke up. And about that poster you taped up."

"What poster."

"You know. The one for the carnival. With the balloon."

"Toby oughtn't to get dizzy, ought he?" said Linsey. She was over by the sink, where he couldn't see her. He liked hearing her use his name.

"Balloon won't make you dizzy," his mom said. "A little vertigo maybe, if you look down. But it's calm as a lake mostly."

"Mightn't it blow up?"

"They fill it with hot *air*, Linsey," said his mom.

"Oh well, all right."

"You could meet us there, see for yourself. It's not far from your house. Will your son be here?"

"He wouldn't say just when. He's got a gig somewhere."

"It's not like when I took you up, Susannah," said Toby's dad. He didn't sound so grumpy, now; more serious, like there was a big explanation coming. Toby heard the sound of his sucking on the beer. "They'll tether the basket," he said. "You won't travel."

"I just mean to cheer up our son," Toby's mom said, pushing back her chair.

His dad set the beer down with a loud *tink*. They were all standing, there, in the kitchen, plotting to ambush his slew of despond. Toby felt goose bumps on his prickly arms. "He's all yours," said his dad.

Tiptoeing back up the stairs, Toby whispered to Brooke's heart: *balloon*. He'd seen the old photos of his dad, a young guy with heavy sideburns standing by a bright blue hang-glider, a silver glider plane, a fire-orange vinyl raft, a brightly striped hot-air balloon with an aluminum basket.

He wondered if his dad felt gross sometimes, like him, only from looking at the snouty dead ends of his fingers. It had to feel extra gross, knowing the thing was your own fault. Still he used to want his dad to take him on one of those rides, somehow, before his old fat heart gave out and he blobbed into death. Now, with Brooke's heart, he'd get to go. With Linsey. With Brooke's mom, who wanted to cheer him up.

He leaned over the railing, feeling the good news pump through his veins like a med, the buzz in his fingers and toes.

Chapter 9

*C*lusters of new brick buildings dotted the landscape that housed Susannah's lab. To the north, where the land rose, sat the branch of the med school that sent research-minded students in the direction of Marcus Griffiths. Other buildings boasted computer technologies, beauty products research, and a lab for industrial chemicals. All of them looked over a broad flat flood-plain that local environmentalists lobbied to turn into wetlands and local developers lobbied to drain and develop. For now it lay fallow, closely mown, in a dry spring, and the carnival had moved in.

"I wish Dad was flying it," Toby said when they finally got within sight of the balloon.

"Oh, honey. Dad hasn't gone up in years."

"That is so unfair. I get born, and he quits doing all the fun things. That stinks."

"It's not that you got *born*, Tobe. It's that he injured his *hand*."

"Same thing."

Far off on the field, the colorful nylon was slowly filling, its stripes rippling in the breeze. Susannah pictured the carnival organizers sifting through glossy, bulk-mailed brochures: a Native American healer, a juggler, a mime troupe, a belly-dance work-shop. Ah! Balloon rides! Apolitical, colorful, and apt to show up as promised. Someone, somewhere, paid to organize such things, had picked up the phone and dialed Blue Ridge Balloons, and the deed was done.

Susannah took the dirt path down the hill ahead of her son. It hadn't been easy, Toby at the lab. Three years ago, she'd brought him all the time. Cutter, then a mere lab tech, would set him up with an experiment in the corner, adding phosphates to proteins or something, and two hours later he'd show off the mess he'd made, and they'd all have a chuckle and a Coke from the machine. That was when Toby was six, healthy and cute. Susannah was a postdoc fellow. And Marcus Griffiths was nowhere near a groundbreaking article in *Cell*.

How things change, she thought, gazing down the hill. The Cantrex people were calling every day, badgering Marcus for data from three research groups. Today, for the twentieth time, Marcus had barged through the narrow door to Susannah's lab, his notes highlighted in optic yellow, his eyes popping. He wanted calibrations checked, the transference fine-tuned, figures broken down. In the middle of a heated argument over radiated nuclei, Toby had left his Game Gear on the couch in the lobby and come to tug at Susannah's sleeve. Come on, *Mom*, come *on*, he'd whispered, and when Marcus was done making his point, he had snapped at her not to bring members of her family to work again. "It's my lab, Marcus," she'd pointed out.

"It's my *building*," he'd replied darkly, and passed a sheaf of lacerated notes to Tomiko.

As they reached the plain, the balloon was still filling. The oblong colors wrinkled and wafted between breeze and hot air. Drawing closer, they could hear the whooshes of the flame, just like the last scene in *The Wizard of Oz*. Already people were lining up, as patient as grade-school kids at a pony ride. Puffy clouds raced overhead, a stiff breeze. "Where's the balloon going to fly to?" Toby asked.

"I don't know, honey. Dad said not far."

He took her hand, a gesture he'd started making again. His skin was moister in the warm days. Before the transplant, he'd considered himself too big a boy for hand-holding. She loved the feel of his hand in hers, the way his fingers fit neatly around her palm. It more than made up, she thought, for a lecture from Marcus.

"Rides cost a dollar," he said when they got to the line.

"I know; I've got it."

"We shouldn't go without Linsey, right?"

"Oh, sure. We can go without her."

"I don't want to."

Funny, Susannah thought, this loyalty to Linsey. As if he'd known her a long time, or had been given charge of her. Not once had he been bothered by the idea that his new heart had a name attached to it; never had it seemed that the grieving mother was coming to Roanoke like the uninvited fairy to Aurora's christening. *Just keep it quiet that it's a girl heart, okay?* he'd asked way back in winter, and Susannah had pinkie-sworn, *Okay*. When the curious ones, the unstoppable ones, asked her how they'd cracked Toby's ribcage, opened his heart and taken it out and nestled a strange organ in its place (*how could they do that? and that? and that?*), Susannah said, "They opened us all up, really. They cracked us all. There's something strange beating in all of us."

Which was true, but nowhere so true as for Toby since he'd come to love Linsey. These days, more than Susannah herself—was she *jealous?* could she be so mean-spirited?—Linsey held, as it were, the key to Toby's heart.

Just as Nick had described, the basket was held by three inch-thick ropes tied to two trees and a car. Along one edge ran a brass plaque with *Mustang Sally* in black script. When the operator opened the heat jets, the balloon rose about fifty feet, where it hung for a few moments and then floated down. You got a view of the carnival and the branch campus of the med school, and maybe a peek at the next ridge of mountains, out toward Lexington. "I guess we can go up without her," Toby said when they'd reached the front of the line. "Then when she gets here we can go again, right?"

"We'll see, honey. Now listen to the man about climbing in."

It was a wicker basket like the one Judy Garland had missed in Oz, more old-fashioned than the aluminum number Susannah had tried with Nick in Pennsylvania. As people climbed out of the back side of it, one at a time, new people climbed in. The guy in charge, McGowan, had his hand on the spigot for the flame, which he'd turned down low; his assistant, an acned kid of maybe sixteen, was helping people out with one hand and keeping the basket steady with the other. At the front of the line, Marcus Griffiths's son Danny, in his second year of med school, was collecting dollar bills and liability release forms. "Ah," said Susannah. "Fundraiser for the med school."

"Scholarships," said Danny.

Toby squeezed her hand. "We still going up?" he asked.

"You want to?"

"Maybe."

"Okay, then. We'll still go up. Though it doesn't look like much."

"Why don't they go somewhere?"

"You've heard Daddy, honey. It's hard to land one of these things. This is just to give everyone an idea."

Toby shielded his eyes and watched the balloon rise. It was impressive, up close. The basket held six people including the operator. Not more than a dozen waited their turn; this wasn't going to be much of a fundraiser. Up went the balloon to where the ropes held it like giant kite strings. The people in the basket waved and shouted; behind Susannah, a pair of pony tailed girls giggled. "Great day for it," Susannah said to Danny as she signed two release forms.

"Yeah. We worried about the wind, but this guy says he's seen much worse."

"You don't even feel the wind when you're traveling." Susannah squinted into the sun, watching McGowan tighten ropes. She hadn't ever seen him, stopping by the shop. Nick's customers were oddballs, men mostly, wistful sorts with bits of knowledge packed into their brains like grain in a silo. "My husband's a balloonist," she explained to Danny. "Or was."

"Yeah? He make it around the world?"

"Not yet."

"He stopped doing that stuff when he lost his fingers," Toby piped up.

"In a balloon?" Danny crouched a bit.

"No. In a river. He used to do *lots* of stuff."

"Did he now."

Toby nodded. "When I get bigger, I'm going to make him teach me."

"Well, you be sure to hang onto *your* fingers." Danny tapped Toby's hand. "How's that new ticker doing?"

"Okay," said Toby.

"You're not—uh—worried about him here, are you?" Danny asked Susannah as the balloon floated to ground. "Getting too excited or what not."

"It's not *exercise*, Danny. It's just standing in a basket."

"That's what I want to do," he said. "Cardiac." He tousled Toby's hair. "You're our big experiment, buddy," he said.

"He's not—" Susannah began, but then the acned kid gestured, and Toby tugged at her hand.

It was a high basket to scale. As a teenaged girl stepped out, Susannah hiked her skirt and stepped in. Danny Griffiths gave Toby a boost; then she hauled him in beside her.

"Excited?"

"Yeah. I guess."

But he was, by his voice. The breeze lifted his hair. Linsey had been right: newness and a thrill, the best therapy.

"All set?" asked McGowan. He was a gravel-voiced, stumpy man with a face like a clown's without the makeup. The small crew of passengers nodded in unison. Susannah looked down at Toby. It was as if a sponge had gone over his face, wiping off the sour film left by the meds. His eyes half-closed in the breeze, he gripped the side of the basket. Light bounced off his high forehead, his nose, off his soft bare shoulders under the Hornets jersey that reached past his shorts. Parted, his lips tasted the air as if it had already gotten thinner.

"Set," Susannah said, and the guy fired up the jet. Up they went, a fresh-air elevator, to the top of the ropes, where the basket jerked in the wind. Looking up, they saw the colorful stripes from the inside, a skyful of rainbow. Looking out, their view went over the tops of the hill buildings, to the thunder-like rise of Tinker Mountain on one side and the gray network of highways on the other. Toby waved and called down to a couple of older kids who'd joined the line. On the green hill, a figure approached. Linsey, dressed all in blue, Bo-Peep on the hillside.

Behind her, jacket slung over shoulder, sauntered a tall young man.

Susannah waved, though Linsey didn't see them up in the basket. She would tell Linsey what a great idea this had been. She'd tell her, too, what rotten tension there had been at the lab. She would meet this young man, who had to be Linsey's Charlie—a lone son, like Toby. They would welcome and appreciate each other. And at the same time, unable to help herself, Susannah spotted Linsey and thought, Fuck.

Linsey's pretty caramel hair caught the afternoon light. She turned back to her son, was pointing them out to him. McGowan reduced the gas flame. Gentle as a feather, the balloon came down.

"That's all?" said Toby as Susannah lifted him out.

"For now, kiddo."

"Can we go again?"

"Maybe. We'll see. It costs a dollar."

"Linsey!"

He'd spotted her. Susannah found a hangnail to pick at while he ran over.

"Did you see me up in the balloon? They keep it tied down but it's neat. Are you going to go up? Did you see me?"

"I saw you! I saw you!" She caught his hands and squeezed them together. The blue was a long, loose-woven peasanty dress that took the breeze nicely, as did her curtain of hair. "And guess who this is?"

"Charlie!"

Toby shouted it as if he'd known Charlie all his life. It was only as Charlie came forward, his right hand extended, that Toby seemed suddenly to contract into himself, and he put his own hand forward reluctantly.

"I've heard a lot about you," said Charlie. "You're one brave guy."

"I'm sorry," said Toby. "About Brooke."

"Yeah," said Charlie.

He looked like Linsey—more so than the photos of Brooke, more than his own photos would suggest. Same turned-up nose, same wide temples. In his left ear, a trio of small gold loops. He smiled crookedly.

"Are you going to come up?" said Toby, glancing from Linsey to her son. "In the balloon?"

"I'll watch a round," said Charlie. "Then maybe."

"Linsey?"

"Oh, no, honey! I'm scared of heights!"

Linsey took Charlie's arm, as if the balloon were about to carry her off. Charlie turned to Susannah.

"It's an odd way to meet," he said. His voice didn't have Linsey's pure drawl; it was raspy, as if he'd missed a night's sleep.

"Yes," said Susannah.

"My mom's been glad to have . . . all this. In her life." He made a feeble gesture in the direction of Toby, who was dancing back toward the line.

"Come on, Linsey!" Toby said. "Go up! Tickets are just a dollar!"

Linsey was looking doubtfully at the balloon rising, as if it were a horse not used to being saddled. Her blue dress had a low, square neck that showed off her collarbone and a trio of small moles, like a tattoo, just underneath the hollow spot at the base of her neck.

"Did you tell the guy"—Linsey waved toward the balloon—"that Toby was a transplantee?"

"For heaven's sake, Linsey," said Susannah. "They don't ask for that kind of info."

"There might be something we don't know."

"About what?"

Linsey shrugged. "Altitude?"

"Tell her to relax, would you?" Susannah said to Charlie. Toby had begun pulling on her arm. The balloon was coming down, with its last batch of passengers.

She wanted to shoo Linsey away, along with her tan, earringed son. But why? *She doesn't get her hands on you,* she thought to herself as she joined the thin crowd with Toby. She didn't know what was possessing her. The lab, surely; tension at the lab. She had *invited* Linsey.

"Don't get out yet, folks," McGowan said in his gravel voice.

Leaning over the side of the basket, McGowan had some discussion with Danny Griffiths. From the other side of the field floated the tinny melodies of the merry-go-round, the odor of fried dough. A couple of new people had drifted across the beat-down grass, but mostly the balloon wasn't drawing.

Charlie hung back, lanky and uninterested. Linsey meanwhile came up behind Susannah. She put her long-fingered hand on Toby's warm head. Anyone looking would have thought she and Susannah were a pair of sisters, one willowy and the other full-figured, held together by long acquaintance and easy affection. Under the bright sky with its racing clouds they waited, like the others, for a patch of excitement.

"Okay," said Danny Griffiths. He turned to them. He was a weedy-looking young man, trying to grow a beard. He'd been to the lab a couple of times, but he could not, Susannah surmised, be prodded into research. "This guy is here for an hour one way or the other, and if he hasn't got people in the basket he's got to turn the jets off, and then if people come he's got to start the whole thing again. So we're offering free rides for awhile. Till another crowd gathers, anyhow. Anyone want another chance?"

"Yeah!" Toby cried, and now he looked as if the first time up had been the thrill of his short life. "Okay, Mom? It's free. I can, can't I, Mom?"

Susannah glanced at Linsey. With her eyes fixed on the gay colors of the balloon, she shook her head slowly, as if she'd already spotted a puncture in the fabric. Susannah bent down. "I don't know, honey," she said.

A couple of the new arrivals pressed to the rope, where the insurance releases sat under a rock. Startled, Susannah recognized Marcus Griffiths, out of character in a T-shirt and jeans. His hands fisted into tight pockets, he squinted through pale sunglasses at the rope set-up, as if deriving a new experiment from the evidence.

"Marcus," Susannah said tentatively.

"Doctor," he greeted her. "You—ah—reminded me this afternoon. I've got a son, too." He smiled nervously at Danny, who was talking to the pimply helper. In the T-shirt Marcus's neck looked fleshier, older, like a man nearing retirement. "This worth a try?"

"Worth it for nothing."

"So my boy's not exactly raking in funds for new respirators."

"We're thinking more people might come," Danny called over, "once they see the balloon up a few times."

"So you need demonstrators. Okay, then! I'll volunteer."

"Gotta sign a release form, Dad."

Susannah couldn't help laughing. "Sorry, Marcus," she said when he turned. "I've just never pictured you in Oz."

"Pay no attention," Marcus said to his son, "to the woman behind the curtain." And to Toby, "You coming, champ?"

An apology, Susannah thought, and warmth filled her chest. Sympathetic nerves, connecting the heart.

"Mom, *please*," Toby said. He was tugging.

"Wait," said Susannah. "Some people haven't gone yet, Tobe."

A young woman stepped out of the basket as Marcus, ungainly even in casual clothes, amber wire-rims yellowing his eyes, his wispy top patch of hair blowing in the wind, climbed in. "It's full now," said Linsey. "Thank goodness."

"I'm ready to get off," called a burly fellow from the basket.

"*Mom*," said Toby. He was pulling on her hand, pumping it the way he had her sleeve at the lab.

"If he steps down, I'll take one more," called McGowan, counting his five passengers.

Ahead of Susannah stood a pair of teenagers. The boy looked at the girl. "Let's wait," the girl said. "We can go the next round. They said free till more people come."

"*Mo-om.*"

"You'd have to go by yourself." Susannah felt Linsey's eyes on her, but she bent down and addressed only Toby. "It might be scary. They can't take us both. You really want to go up alone?"

"I'll watch him," called Marcus.

"Yes," said Toby impatiently. "I *do.*"

"This is bad," said Linsey in a stage whisper.

Toby ran toward the basket. "A little guy, huh?" said McGowan. "Well, in that case I should take your mom, too. For ballast."

"Great," Susannah said. She trotted toward the basket. "Let me get in first, honey," she said. "Then Danny can boost you up."

"Don't!" cried Linsey. At her shrill tone, Susannah couldn't help glancing back. She grinned, her boss behind her, happy to face down Linsey's disapproval. In that moment, as she turned, Toby scrambled into the basket, while the burly fellow stepped out.

Instantly as the balloon lifted, Susannah knew what was wrong. The big guy stepped out and Toby stepped in. Two hundred pounds stepped out and seventy pounds stepped in. The balloon lifted. Not the way it had lifted before, with a push of hot air and a slow ascent, but sudden and jerkily, like a huge butterfly escaping. "What the—" said the assistant, his hand thrown from the rim. McGowan was messing with the controls. The burly man looked up, amazed at what he'd released.

Susannah took hold of Danny's arm. "It's okay, right?" she said. Danny was scratching his soft chin, where the beard grew in spurts. "It was just a little sudden because of weight. I mean, it's tethered, right?"

Danny shook his head. "I'd ask your husband, if he was here," he said. "Ballooning's not my thing."

Nick, Susannah breathed, shutting her eyes. As if the Nick of the past were some kind of spirit. Who could appear. *Nick.*

When she opened her eyes, Toby's head just cleared the top of the basket, a bird in a nest. He wasn't looking up this time, at the clouds and the great balloon, but down at his mother and Charlie and Linsey, and Nick was miles away. "It's okay, honey!" Susannah shouted. "Don't be scared, you're going to come down!"

But he didn't, not right away. The wind buffeted the basket; McGowan worked the controls. Charlie, who had donned dark glasses, came and stood at Susannah's side, looking up. The balloon jerked at its stays. Like a boxer returning the punch, another gust came back toward the small crowd on the ground.

Too fast, the balloon descended. It hit with a thump on the basket's corner. The thick rim clocked Toby in the chin. Crying out, he fell back into the basket.

"Toby!" Susannah cried.

Then they were all shouting something.

Charlie called, "Hold the thing! Catch hold of the basket!"

Linsey rushed behind Susannah to hold the rim and the anchoring ropes, but the wind came up again, and the thing jerked from all their hands.

"Mom!" Toby cried. "Mommy!"

Out of the corner of her eye, Susannah saw Linsey running, jumping into the air.

"Jesus!" said a guy from the ground, as the balloon rose.

"Linsey, what are you thinking?" Susannah cried.

"Mom, hold on!" said Charlie. "Christ. Hold *on*."

Linsey didn't answer. She hung from the rope that ran between the basket and a maple tree. Between rope and ground, gravity stretched the tendons of her arms. Her hands gripped like monkey claws. She looked down at the ground, then over at the unballasted balloon. The wind blew her blue dress around her thighs. Then it blew her sideways, and when Susannah looked for the cause, she saw the third rope, the one from the oak tree, waving in the wind like a snake—snapped, or loosened, no longer tethering the balloon.

McGowan turned his faucets and made nothing happen. Next to him, Marcus Griffiths looked frail, his hand on his heart. The basket headed toward ground again. Just before it hit, as she let go the rope, Linsey's voice rang out, "Charlie! Grab him!"

"Right," said Charlie, at Susannah's elbow, and suddenly he grew in size. Clearing the others away, he reached into the shadow of the crashing basket. "Alley oop," he said to Toby. With one great jerk, biceps bulging, he had him out of the basket and on the ground, and then Toby was enfolded—his precious head, his heaving torso—in Susannah's arms.

"Darling, darling," she said. "You're all right, darling."

The basket had lifted away with its scarce four-passenger crew. Earthbound, the rest of the crowd yearned upward. Over their heads, the rope that had come loose from the oak tree whipped angrily.

"Mom," Susannah heard Linsey's son say. "Mom, your ankle."

But Susannah didn't look up, not right away. She had her boy to hold.

Later they said the operator had finally doused the flame, knowing they would crash-land but afraid of the other options. The rope around the car handle had started to work free; if the basket flipped, the whole thing could spill its passengers and ignite, all at once. Danny Griffiths had scrambled to the roof of the car, trying to head the basket off. From there, perhaps, he had already seen his father clutch his heart.

By the time Susannah did look up, they'd all heard the tinkle of glass and the groans of the passengers left in the basket. The Volvo's passenger side was smashed in. The two college girls who'd been in the basket were standing on the wide spread of deflated sailcloth, holding each other. McGowan was standing tragically by the balloon, as if it were a favorite broken-legged horse he was going to have to shoot. The acne-faced kid and Danny were together lifting Marcus out, laying him flat on the windswept grass. The ambulance stationed at the entrance to the carnival was charging across the field, siren wailing. "My god," said Susannah. She touched the back of Toby's neck. Then she left him with Linsey, who had sunk to the grass. She went to where Danny and Charlie were bending down.

"I'm a doctor," she said. "Or almost."

"I'm an EMT," said Charlie. Already Danny was bending to his father's mouth, giving him breath. Marcus's glasses were off, his eyes half-lidded. "One. Two. Three. Four. Five," Charlie said, pumping Marcus's chest. "You want to take over?"

"You're doing fine." Susannah licked her dry lips. "Has he got a pulse?"

"Feel," said Danny, between breaths.

Susannah took Marcus's arm, pale and meaty. "Maybe something faint," she said. She put a finger to the carotid artery under his jaw. "Very faint." Kneeling, she tipped her watch out of the glare of the sun. "Faint and fluttery. Over a hundred, but I can't really be sure, it's so faint."

"Turn him," said Danny.

Expertly, the two young men tipped the older one. Marcus's eyes were half-lidded. As his backside lifted from the ground, Susannah saw the stain at his crotch. With a sputter and gag, Marcus vomited onto the fresh grass. "Good," said Danny. "Now back."

"Here," Susannah said to Danny. From her pocket she handed him a clean tissue. He wiped his father's gray, spewed mouth and began again.

"One, two, three, four, five," said Charlie. Danny breathed into his father, then straightened. "Okay. One. Two. Three. Four. Five." Breathe, straighten, count; breathe, straighten, count. Susannah pressed harder on the unresponding artery. She kept her watch tilted.

And then the medics were there, with their tanks of oxygen, their electrical stimulators. Susannah backed away. As the team went to work, she saw only the stain, the meaty wrist. "Oh, Marcus," she said. "Marcus, please."

Only after they'd put Marcus Griffiths's body through its humiliating paces, only after they had finally removed the equipment and hung their heads, only after the sheet had gone over Marcus's determined, doughy face, and Danny Griffiths had sunk against the crashed Volvo, his own face buried in his hands, only after the police had arrived and taken the balloon operator aside to question him about the accident—had Dr. Griffiths hit his head at any point? Had the rope whipped his face? Had he exerted himself to bring the thing under control?—only after the curious crowd had begun to disperse like oil in water, did Susannah look around. Only then did she realize that Linsey had done the wise thing.

"She said to tell you," said Charlie.

Susannah nodded. Of course. Linsey had known, even before Susannah had noticed the verdict of Marcus's stained trousers. She had seen death, and she had taken Toby's hand and led him away from it. It had been the right thing to do, the absolute right thing.

Chapter 10

*T*he noisy car outside Nick's shop had to be Linsey's. Dread snaked through him. Casually he stood from where he'd been sliding armor kits onto the hanging display. From the window he saw his son step from the car—his bruised chin, his scraped cheek. And more, a trembling at the corner of Toby's mouth, a darkness in his eyes, round like his mother's but like dark stones when Nick tipped his chin to gaze into them.

"I don't want to talk about it," Toby said. He went to the castle set-up in the back of the shop. He started moving knights around.

Putting up the Closed sign, Nick locked the door. Linsey wore a sturdy blue dress, but standing between the Napoleonic display and the Bunker Hill diorama, she trembled as if the hot breeze had chilled her. "The whole thing was my idea," she said, looking straight ahead. When he put his arms around her, it was to hold her steady, like a figurine half-loose from its base with the solder still drying. "I thought," she went on, "you know, cheer him up. With Brooke, I—" She broke off. "Anyhow, I did *try* to stop them." She drew away, leaving a damp spot on his shoulder. As she fished for a tissue, she knocked against a table of Victorian-era Viking figures. "Omigod. Oh, I *am* sorry."

"No harm done," he said quickly, ducking down. "What about Susannah?"

"Oh, she's fine. Charlie's with her."

"Charlie?"

"My son."

"Oh yes. Your son. Of course, he's here, I—"

"They're helping. Her boss—something went wrong. With the weight, and the wind. And the ropes. I'd got this bad feeling. I said 'Don't' to Susannah, 'Don't.' But I guess she was determined by then, and her boss was on board, and Toby so excited—" Linsey found a tissue and honked, noisily. "She just didn't want to turn back, I guess. Do you—do you mind if I sit down?"

"Oh. Please. Here. Sit." Nick scooped a pile of catalogs off a small red bench by the Civil War display. He didn't keep the shop as neat as he should. When he first rented the space, he'd had visions of historical murals with spare, well-lit displays in front of them, a set of tables in the back for modeling classes, a reading area. He had underestimated the public's passion for pure collecting, the accumulation of things. "Can I get you, I don't know, iced tea or something?"

"No, thanks."

"So Susannah's all right?"

"She's just fine."

This information somehow annoyed him—that Susannah, unhurt, had dispatched Linsey to bring him his son. Worse, he saw when Linsey lifted the hem of her dress, she herself was hurt. She'd fallen, she said. Twisted the ankle.

"Sprained, more like," said Nick, rotating it while she winced. Obediently she sat while he fished an Ace bandage from the shop bathroom and taped where the joint was already swollen, twice normal size.

"I always forget," she said as he wound the bandage, "about your fingers."

"Do you? I don't."

"They look as though they hurt."

"I wish they did," said Nick.

"Why?"

He shrugged and reached for the metal clips for the Ace. "So women would kiss the pain away, I guess."

He folded back the edge of the pink elastic. Suddenly she took his right hand in hers and put the pinkie stub to her mouth. Her lips were cushiony and warm, but he pulled back as if they'd pricked him. "There," she said.

"I meant metaphorically."

"Course you did." She didn't smile, but kept her eye on the ruined hand, as if by her kiss the digit would begin to regrow.

"Well, you're done," he said, gesturing at the Ace. He sat back on a folding chair. The pinkie stub still felt the imprint of Linsey's mouth. He had said that, about women, to offend her, and now he'd embarrassed himself. Over at the table, Toby was lining up Cathars against Tuscan knights. "*He* doesn't want to talk about it," he said with a jerk of his head. "Do you?"

She stroked her bandaged ankle. Her hair was tangled, the part uneven on top. Her eyes flickered around the crowded shop before they landed on him. "Sure," she said in a husky voice, "I'll talk."

Part of what she told him, with her wide vowels and fallings-off at the ends of sentences, sounded like pure accident. A bad trick of ballast, the sudden wind. She'd been worried about that wind, she said. Only Susannah hadn't waited for her, they'd gone up one time already, and then of course Toby was so excited. They could only take one in the end—or maybe two, but Susannah was all set for Toby to go alone. Maybe that was why Toby had gotten into the basket first, Linsey couldn't say. She'd had a creepy feeling. And had tried to cry out to them, but Susannah just smiled at her. Like she said, Susannah's boss was there, he was the one who died.

"Died!" He jumped up suddenly as if they had to go somewhere.

"I *think* he's dead. He sure looked dead. Charlie was pumping his chest. Not a mark on him. If I had to, I'd say he died of pure fright."

"Christ." Nick ran his hand through his hair. "Can you keep that foot elevated, a minute? Just—give us a minute." He made a gesture at her that he recognized as a sign he might use with Coal, the stay command.

"I'll just run along home," said Linsey. "Charlie might have got there by now."

"With that foot? You're not driving."

"I've got automatic transmission!" Taking her right sandal in her hand, Linsey stood up. She leaned on the counter and took a step, and her breath came in a sharp gasp of pain.

"That," said Nick, strangely pleased, "is your right foot, Miss Independent."

"I don't understand. I drove here fine. I walked fine."

"Initial shock, and then the pain and swelling. Has your son got a cell phone?"

"In his van, yeah. He followed me down there in his van. He thought he might have to pick up some equipment. For his gig, you know."

"Well, here." He pulled the cordless phone from its cradle. "Try calling him. I'll check back with you in a sec."

In the back, Toby had knocked out two of the knights and tangled the last pair up. Normally he took no interest in these little figures at all, and Nick was just as glad—the kids who came here were high-strung, myopic, and generally mean-spirited, full of their own arcane knowledge. If it hadn't been for a major in history, a steady left hand, and a right hand that couldn't play Gershwin, he wouldn't be here himself.

He crouched by the table. "So," he said.

"I *told* you," said Toby.

"You don't want to talk about it. Fine. Do we need to check in with the doctor?"

"No."

"Where'd you hit? Your head?"

"Here, and here," said Toby. "You can see. Nothing came near my heart."

"You can get hurt in other ways besides your heart. Mom probably should have had the ambulance guys look at you."

"They were *busy*. Dr. Griffiths is *dead*."

"I know. It's sad. But I think I'll call Dr. Lieberman, okay? Maybe when we get home."

"I don't *want* to go home. I want to stay with *Linsey*."

"Well, we may need to drop her off. She's got a sprained ankle, I think."

"That's why I should stay with her. To *help* her."

"She's got her son here now, champ. He'll help her."

Toby bit his lower lip. He paired up the knights, Cathar against Cathar. The whine went out of his voice as he said, "He pulled me out."

"Who, Charlie?"

Toby nodded. "I fell, in the basket. And then it hit the ground again. He reached in and got me." He picked up a knight, weighed it in his palm. He whispered, "Or else I'd be dead too."

"Don't say that, Tobe."

Tipping his son's head, Nick looked more closely at Toby's cheek—a bruise starting there too, moving up to the delicate skin below the eye.

"I'm calling Mommy," he said. "We'll do what she says, all right?"

Toby looked darkly at him, as if he'd asked a trick question. He pursed his small, soft mouth, and for a moment Nick thought he would cry. Then he knocked the knights down and started a new arrangement.

Linsey handed him the phone. She couldn't get through, she said. Her son was out of range. Nick stepped to the window as he keyed in Susannah's cell number. Outside, a brisk, sunny day, the outdoor market setting up. It took five rings for Susannah to pick up. He pictured her rummaging through her mesh bag, cursing in whispers, apologizing to the others.

"Nick," she said when she finally picked up, and she expelled a long-held breath. In the background, murmurs and machines. She was at the hospital, she said. There was still a lot to deal with. Marcus's family. Danny. *Bleep, bleep, bleep* in the background. She was glad Linsey had taken Tobe. It wasn't the balloon guy's fault, she kept saying. A freak accident, no one could have predicted it.

"I wasn't blaming McGowan," he said.

"It wasn't your fault either."

He looked around the shop, as if something there might make sense. Linsey had her ankle elevated; Toby had given up on the knights and was touching his bruised chin.

"You there?" said Susannah.

"Yeah. Yeah. I was just—how could it be *my* fault? I was here in the shop, talking early resin figures with two old guys from Lexington."

"I don't know. I just thought you'd think. Since you got Toby all fired up about ballooning."

"Well, I did *not* think. And I haven't been off the ground in anything but a passenger *airplane* in ten *years*."

"But Toby always thinks of you as—as—"

"As ten-fingered. Okay. And adventurous. Neither of which I in fact *am*."

"Right. And I am *not* blaming you; that's the point. And I'm not blaming myself either."

"Good. Don't. A freak accident," he repeated. He tucked the portable phone under his ear and pretended to rearrange the bay window display, the other side of the shop from Linsey. Between the slats of the blinds, he saw a pair of clients, traveling salesmen who liked to stop in and tell him about their sex lives and buy Napoleonics. "But Susannah, our son has a freak condition. He went up once, he came down. Why wasn't that enough?"

"I don't know. I think I told him it was enough."

"But you didn't tell him *no*, did you? *Did* you?"

"Maybe I did, in fact. I don't remember. It happened very fast, Nick. This big fellow got out, and my back was turned, and suddenly Toby was in the basket."

"I'd like to believe you, Susannah."

"Then believe me! Christ, Nick. Toby is *fine*. It's *Marcus* who's dead!"

"Of a heart attack."

"I know very well," Susannah replied—he could picture those round eyes, cool as nickels—"what Marcus died of."

"Look, I'm sorry your boss died. I'm sorry. I liked the guy."

"No, you didn't."

"All right, I found him a little officious. But I'm sorry he died, and I'm goddamn sorry it had to be in such a stupid accident." He took the phone in hand and started to pace. Toby was sitting on the castle table, glowering. "Where is Linsey's son?" he asked.

"I don't know. He performed miracles and left. Probably at her house."

"Right. Of course. Look, Susannah, there is a point here."

Bleep bleep bleep came from Susannah's end. Then a series of background blips and static. "What point, exactly?" her voice finally broke through. "Since Toby is suffering from all of a bruised chin?"

"Well, you do have *some* experience with a hot-air balloon. Enough to know about *ballast*. Other people didn't know what to watch for. *You* knew what to watch for. My God, Susannah, you let him get in the basket first!"

"Who says I let him in first?"

"Your best friend Linsey, that's who." He thought Linsey would look up at this, but she only flipped a page and rocked the elevated leg. He pressed his own mouth to the stub of his index finger, felt the bone under the flesh.

"That's *not* what happened. And more important, what *did* happen is that your loyal customer McGowan forgot to teach his measly assistant how to tie a *knot*."

"I thought we'd agreed it wasn't Mac's fault," he said, wheeling around with the phone.

"I think we need to agree that *fault* is not the *point*."

Toby had come up from the back of the store. He tugged on Nick's sleeve, then stopped his pacing by putting his forehead against Nick's belly. Nick tucked the phone again. "The point," he went on, stroking Toby's wayward hair, "is that I trusted you. Now I've got to take care of my son," he said to Susannah, and hung up.

Up Tinker Mountain, Toby brooding. Nick had not suggested calling Charlie again. Solicitously Linsey asked after Susannah—*how just like her to stay for her boss, I know she was frantic, she'll be tired when she gets home, you tell her I'm fine I want to help*—until at her house Toby sprang from the back seat to help her out of the car. Parked in the driveway, a blue van with black stripes on the side and a bumper sticker reading *Musicians do it in harmony*.

"Would you like to meet—?" Linsey began, but Nick shook his head.

"Not now," he said.

"Will Charlie be here tomorrow?" Toby asked.

"All week," said Linsey.

"I'm going to Durham."

"I know, honey."

The *honey* was a sock in the gut.

Linsey's front door opened, and a young blond fellow stepped out, and Nick gave what felt like a lame wave while Toby walked the hobbling Linsey up the walk and turned her over.

Then home, Toby wiping tears, in the sharp light of a solstice evening, where Coal sniffed and whined over Toby and the sprinkler system started up like suburban vespers, whispering comfort to the dry grass.

As he slid pills over to Toby at the kitchen table, Nick put in a call to McGowan's answering machine ("Blue Ridge Balloons, the hottest air west of the Beltway. Leave your message at the beep"), then another to Susannah's cell phone, which indicated out of range. Toby wanted to read comics, he said. He felt fine; he didn't need ice on the chin; he just wanted to read.

Nick watched him mount the stairs, then called Ben Lieberman, something Susannah hadn't thought to do. After the story, the shock— he hadn't heard about Marcus Griffiths, what a loss, how tough on Susannah—Ben said to take the boy's blood pressure through the night.

They had the biopsy scheduled in a couple of days, he said; Toby would get his once-over then.

Nick stepped outside. The sprinklers had stopped, the green blades shone. Above, the sky was deepening, its blue solid as glazed clay. No view from this back yard, but Nick held in his head the panorama they'd enjoyed from the first place they'd rented here, above the city to the southwest, the contours of the rich land sculpted and fissured as if by a great carving paddle. One day, they'd told themselves when Toby was little and healthy, they would buy land out near the Blue Ridge Parkway. Every night, they promised each other, they would watch the sun set in flames over the Alleghenies. Roanoke's was one of the hardest airports for bad-weather landings—that steep descent over either mountain range, and the unpredictable winds rushing up the valley. Still they'd loved it, looking down over the bowl.

He checked on the fish—a hardier breed, the pet-shop guy had told him, mottled orange and yellow, not as sleek as the others but more gregarious; already they came for food flakes when he tapped on the rocks by the tiny fountain. Yanking the motor into life, he gave the lawn mower a couple of turns near the deck. He shouldn't have argued with Susannah, he told himself as damp grass flew from the side of the machine. She was grieving, exhausted. Under pressure at her job. He should have taken Toby to the carnival himself; he'd have noticed the bad knots, have observed whether McGowan was really competent. Only himself to blame, when you got down to it.

In the kitchen he washed his hands, coated with motor oil and grass; he gripped the tiny brush in his right palm to scrub the grime from under the left-hand fingernails. Then he tiptoed, pressure sleeve in hand, past an old Coltrane score gathering dust on the piano, up the broad oak staircase. It was the staircase that had sold Susannah on this house, a house he couldn't have afforded alone. They'd moved down from the hills to be nearer the hospital, Toby's lifeline.

Now he pictured Susannah, letting Toby step first into the basket, opening the door to risk, for a kid who had already risked so much. A sharp pain concentrated behind his eyes; his hand clenched.

Freak accidents, he would tell anyone who asked, they happen. We all know they happen. McGowan landed the thing safely, Linsey's son rescued Toby. Marcus Griffiths's time had come. No place for blame.

He slipped into Toby's room, where the June sun still cut through the west window. Silently he pulled the chair over to the bed. There was the dark smudge on his son's chin, the same spot as Susannah's scar. In a moment he'd push up Toby's nightshirt sleeve to check diastole and systole. In a moment, when he was done touching his hair, listening to his breath, eyeing the translucent flesh lidding his son's round eyes, the rapid movement underneath which spoke of dreams.

Chapter 11

*I*n the warm June evening, Ben Lieberman made his way far from the rounds he was due to perform at the hospital, out Peters Creek Road to the research park and Susannah's lab. There they shone, the lights of a carnival on the broad flood plain below the square buildings, the bright bracelet of the Ferris wheel still turning. Vaguely he wondered who'd been called in, to pronounce on Marcus Griffiths. He'd been up to his neck in angioplasty, putting balloons into people's hearts at the other end of town.

Inside the lab building, his steps echoed on the cheap linoleum. Sixth floor, south end. Excepting days like that one last month, when he managed to drop off tissue samples, this was a foreign planet to him, shaped and peopled differently from the buzzing, efficient hospital. But to Susannah it was home. Sure enough, as he stepped out of the elevator, he saw the lights on in her lab.

Inside, Susannah paced. Ben used to watch her pace the back of the cafeteria at Sloan-Kettering, after she'd gone a round in the ICU. Through the bubbled squares of glass in the door, now, he watched again. Every three steps she clenched her fingers; every three steps she let them loose again. Deliberately she blew her breath out. Her gauzy hair caught the harsh light, as the fingers of one hand unknotted to skim the gray edges of the tables.

Twenty years, he'd known this woman. How high she set her standards, how hard she took each blow. Her A-type brain processing: *What would Marcus have us do? He would have us go to the lab and work work work.* As if. During her near turn, he twisted the knob and pushed the door open.

"It's the vision thing, isn't it?" he said softly. Her back was to him. "The king is dead, long live the dream of the king."

"Ben." She stopped, but didn't look over. "You heard."

Moving into the light of the lab, Ben felt his own fatigue, like a rubber band pulling at his shoulder blades. Nick hadn't said where Susannah was, but it hadn't been hard to guess. "Your hubby called," he said, advancing close enough to stroke a hand lightly down her arm, shoulder to elbow.

"About Toby."

He nodded. "He'll be fine."

"I know."

"Marcus, on the other hand—"

"I'm still trying to believe it." Slowly she turned, faced him. Her eyes were swollen and bloodshot, her lips puffy. He pushed her hair back from her temples.

"God, Suzy. Must have been grim."

She shrugged, moved her head away. "You've seen a fatal heart attack."

"More than once, pal. Doesn't get any easier."

"I don't know," she said, her voice a little high and thin, "that it was so bad for *Marcus*. He was frightened up in that basket, and then he felt a pain. The worst was what we put his poor body through. Trying to bring it back from the dead."

"I don't think he minded, Suzy Q."

She drew up her eyebrows. "Not for us to say."

"No." Ben leaned against the table, breathed in the chemical air of the lab. When she didn't answer, he began to stack stir sticks, their glass flashing blue in the fluorescent light. "I reached Danny Griffiths on his beeper," he said. "Apparently there was a pulse, when you started CPR."

"I thought there was, something faint. I wanted there to be. For Danny's sake, maybe. He was trying so hard."

"Yeah, he's a good kid. He knew about his dad's heart."

"And you?"

Ben shook his head, embarrassed. "Marcus was seeing some guy in Blacksburg. He was on digoxin; he knew his chances."

He felt the brush of Susannah's sleeve against his arm as she moved to the doorway, her hands hugging her elbows. For a while she stood staring down the long corridor lined with boxes of notes, old incubators. The building smelled of alcohol and formaldehyde, things taken apart and recombined and preserved. The windows were small and dusty. Other medical doctors called the research people *squirrelly*, meaning crazy, but

Ben pictured them more as hoarders of nuts, as tree-hollow dwellers. He joined Susannah; absently he chipped dark green paint from the wooden doorframe. Pale tubes lit the way to the far end of the hallway, where the glass door faced them with its black letters, *Chief of Section.*

"This place seems too big," Susannah said finally, "without him."

"I hear he took up a lot of space."

"I was glad for him to take it up."

"You never wanted to go off on your own?"

"Are you kidding? When I could work with Marcus Griffiths?"

"The Great Griffiths."

He shouldn't have said that. She turned back into the lab, pinching the prominent bridge of her nose. When she finally spoke, her voice wobbled. "He *was* great. And good. Good to me, to my work. And what do I do to thank him? I bring my whining kid in *right* when we're at the final end-run for data. He says a little word about it, and I shoot him a dirty look; I shoot the one guy who's ever been proud of my research a nasty *look*. So he changes, you know? He changes from his blue button-down shirt and his paisley tie and his white coat to this T-shirt with a Santa Cruz logo—"

"That must've been from his daughter. Danny told me, she's flying in from California." At Ben's tapping, a handful of sleepy white mice, half-blind, lifted their noses out of the wood shavings.

"So he wears his daughter's silly shirt and follows me out to apologize. To be with his son, like I'm with mine. And so because of me—because of *me*, Ben—he goes up in that shitty balloon and he *dies*."

"He died of coronary thrombosis, Susannah. Could have happened here in the lab."

"But it didn't!"

"No, it didn't. And you held a gun to his head and told him to get into that balloon."

She came back into the light. Through her tears, the faint hint of a smile—that upper lip of hers so naked, he'd always thought, the lip an artist would paint to give away his subject's emotion. "It's selfish, isn't it?" she said, leaning on the table near him and the mice. "To feel so responsible."

"I don't know. Hey fella." He held his finger near the glass, and an unsuspecting week-old mouse came sniffing after it. "It's a way to make sense of death. What'll happen here?"

"Here? You mean, in my lab?"

"I mean the whole section. It's Griffiths's biggest legacy, isn't it? They'll probably name you chief."

"God, I don't want that."

"You refuse the throne? Come on, babe, I *know* you."

She fished in her pocket for a tissue, blew her nose. She shook her head quickly. "I'm not ready," she said, her voice under control. It was her skin, Ben thought as she tucked the tissue away, that made Susannah lovely. Not white-pale, but barely honeyed, her neck mottled now with crying, the little chin-frown red. "I know people say that, and then they rise to the occasion. I can make the leaps, sure, like from manipulating cell lines to planting tumors. That's what I'm brilliant at. I have the energy, I'm smart enough. God knows I'm old enough. But I am not *ready*."

"Because of Toby?" Ben adjusted the mouse's glucose bottle.

"If Marcus had had a son like Toby," Susannah said, picking up a ream of papers from the opposite table and bringing it over, as if something could be gained from rearrangement, "he'd have understood the whole thing—the illness, the cure—in terms of the broad history of organ transplants."

"And you?"

"I can understand it in terms of Toby. That's all."

Ben took Susannah's hand from off the stack of reports. He adjusted her wedding ring, plain gold with a tiny inset diamond, which sat a little crooked on her finger. "You ever get around to reading William Harvey?" he asked.

"Well, I found *De Motu*. Fell asleep at the part about zoophytes, I think."

"I've got a little anecdote about Harvey."

"Oh, please, Ben, not now."

"Ssh." Letting go her hand, he put his finger to his lips. His mustache needed trimming. "It's about Marcus, really. And you."

She sighed. "Okay. Distract me."

Leaning over Susannah's gray lab table, Ben tapped on the glass of a cage labeled *Injected Adenovirus, 3 June*. Inside, fat white mice lifted their heads and sniffed. "Picture William Harvey," he said, "in 1647 or something. Stuck out in the countryside for some reason, nothing to do. Someone tells him there's a witch living in the woods nearby. Okay?"

"Okay." Susannah pulled a tissue from her pocket and dabbed at her leaky eyes. "Marcus would go extract juice from berries, looking for monoterpene."

"Harvey's not an oncologist. He doesn't know from cancer. He goes to the woods and asks the old woman why it is she thinks she's a witch, and she produces this toad. And she says"—making one hand into a witch's claw, Ben rose to falsetto—"'This is my *familiar.*'"

"Cute." Susannah slid onto the other lab stool. Next to her was an incubator, growing mutations from human platelets that Ben had supplied. The light glowed lavender.

"So Harvey tells the woman he's tired and thirsty, can he have a cup of tea. She goes into the next room to fix it, and while she's gone he vivisects the toad."

"No!" Susan gripped the sides of the stool. A dawdling tear dropped from her eye, and she brushed it away.

"I'm not kidding! He vivisected the damn toad! And of course it's an ordinary toad, no black blood or horns on its heart or anything. So the woman comes back into the room, and he holds the animal out and he says, 'This is not your *familiar.* This is a toad.'"

"So what did the poor woman do?"

Ben shrugged. The mice had curled up in a white ball, already back to sleep. He could stay all night in this musty place. "She wept and wailed," he said, "and chased him out of the house with a broom. He went home and wrote it all down as an instance of the scientific method."

"And a proof against the existence of witches. Are you saying I'm a witch, Ben?"

"Not you, Suzy. No way."

Abruptly she slid off her stool and went around the lab table, to the window. Ben followed. Below ranged the lights of the arterial, Roanoke Mountain beyond, its tacky star lit like a phony Bethlehem. He felt the pull of his hospital rounds, patients with heart murmurs, hardened arteries, thinned blood. "She was lonely," Susannah said. "She wanted a pet frog."

"Toad," he corrected.

"Toad, frog, lover, who cares? Along comes this stranger and kills it." Susannah put a hand to the back of her neck, but Ben lifted it away and replaced his own, his thumb and index muscle working the upper deltoid. She flushed. "You're saying Marcus was like that?"

"I'm saying Marcus would have wanted to further the Enlightenment. Whereas you, Dr. Ames, would have wanted the old woman to keep her self-respect. Marcus was the better researcher. If I were in oncology, I'd have worshipped him, too. But you." Lifting his hand from her neck, Ben stroked Susannah's flyaway hair. "You've got the bigger heart."

"It's a muscle, remember?"

"Not the one I'm talking about."

Moving out of the circle of his arms, Susannah stacked a stray set of papers. "Marcus had a whole new theory, you know," she said. "About cancer as an aberrant process. An unstable system. That's what we've been working on here. You remember when I took that leave, last summer?"

"Before Toby's open-heart surgery, with me."

She nodded. "*Cancer Journal* was expecting an update from my lab. It was supposed to coordinate with what Marcus had submitted. You were giving me platelet cells, I was working late nights, the whole bit. Then one day he comes in here and tells me to take six months off. Just like that. I told him we needed the money. We were hitting the ceiling on insurance, for Tobe. So he says, 'Paid.' He says he'll take my salary out of the next set of grants. So I object, right? I tell him Cutter and Tomiko don't have the background to finish the follow-ups. And he reminds me that they also haven't been needing to repeat the protocols to get the details straight, like me. He tells me I'm no damn good to the section, the way I am."

She put a fist to her mouth. Her eyes glistened.

"He hurt your feelings," said Ben.

"No. It's not that. I hadn't been needing to repeat protocols, and we both knew it. He finished up my work, and put my name to the piece in the *Journal*. The day Toby came out of recovery, Marcus was there, at the hospital. He said he was just happening by. He had bags under his eyes. Two months later, when we were in Durham, he happened by there."

He took both her hands. "Thus nature, ever perfect and divine," he said.

"Oh, you and your Harvey, again."

"Say it. I know you know it."

"'Thus nature ever perfect and divine,'" recited Susannah, "'has not given a heart where it wasn't required.'"

"'Nor produced it before its office became necessary.' I'd say its office was necessary, by then."

Turning, Susannah leaned back into him. He crossed his arms over her torso, the deep tuck of her waist in his hands. He put his lips on her hair. "Do you know," she said as if to herself, "why I turned from the clinic to the lab?"

"Because I told you to."

"Yeah, you told me."

"Because you didn't much like patients."

He felt her smile. "Oh, I liked patients all right. Just not when they died. That's what you see, isn't it, Ben? I don't mean because of your mistakes."

"Well, sometimes."

"But even if you're a family doctor. Even if you're a plastic surgeon, or an allergist. I mean, people die in all *kinds* of ways. But mostly they die like my brother, like Marcus. They die with a doctor around."

"Okay," said Ben, microscopically tightening his grip. "So you got a degree in molecular biology. So, fine."

"And then I bear a son whose heart develops hypertrophic cardiomyopathy. So much for running away from death."

"You are not running away," said Ben. He kissed the top of her hair. He beat down desire. "Right now," he said, "you are going home."

ven though Toby said he really, really wanted to go to the funeral for Dr. Griffiths, even though he told Linsey and his dad the same thing about how nice Dr. Griffiths had been to him when the balloon started to crash around, he wished someone had said he was not allowed to go. The whole idea of doctors dying was a spook-out. He knew his mom was, technically, a doctor, even though she'd never healed anyone, and that she would die. But this wouldn't happen until she was very old and he had made his career, so it seemed natural, in the course of motherhood, and nothing to do with his special circumstances. Other doctors, the ones that had been poking and prodding at his heart since first grade, the ones who looked him not in the eyes but in the chest, were supposed to have the cures. And no matter how many times he tried to skip his morning doses, he knew the cures worked. The cures kept you alive.

Sitting next to his mom in the sixth row, he tried to remember Dr. Griffiths from the balloon ride. What he could bring to mind were mostly legs, bumping and kicking inside the basket after he'd fallen. He remembered the sudden quiet and dark at the bottom of the basket, like the time he'd been in the hold of Max's dad's boat, years ago on Otter Lake. He remembered feeling sick, grabbing an older boy's jeans leg, pulling himself up. His chin was stinging by then, and when he got to his feet the basket shifted and threw him against the rough side, scraping his cheek. He'd cried out for his mom, but he couldn't see her. The operator had been muttering fuck this, fuck that, pushing them all away from him like it was their fault.

And Dr. Griffiths. Dr. Griffiths was moaning. Holding his chest.

Then the rope had come flying. The tall girl, the one who'd been singing Up, Up and Away before they took off, yelled like she'd been shot. Bright dots of blood had coiled up her face, her hand cupped over her eye. *Fucking rope*, had cried the boy whose jeans Toby had grabbed, *what's with the goddamn rope?* Then they'd hit ground, and he'd lost his balance again, a hard toe punching his side as he went down. He'd felt his heart, taking adrenaline from the bloodstream. He'd prayed to it to beat. *Beat, Brooke*, he'd said. And then Charlie's arms had reached into the basket.

Now he heard all the words Dr. Griffiths's friends said as if they were words supposed to bring Dr. Griffiths back. Stuff about how important he was, how he was in the middle of his life's work, how he helped all the other doctors who were trying to cure cancer. Stuff that made Dr. Griffiths sound like he was worth about a million of any other person in the church, and like this heart attack he'd had was an enemy who'd been lying in wait for him, just licking his chops at the thought of getting to kill Dr. Griffiths up in that crazy balloon.

And then he had this stupid thought. What if the heart attack had been supposed to get him, Toby, and got Dr. Griffiths by mistake? It was that thought that started him crying. He never cried when he was sad, or even like the other kids when he was hurt. He cried when he was scared. Max teased him about it all the time. Now, at the funeral, he was scared that someone else would realize what a mistake it had been, that the heart attack had gotten the totally wrong person. They would crowbar open the casket and lift Dr. Griffiths out, weak and hungry, and then they would come after Toby.

He cried, big gulping sobs. His mom put her arm around his shoulders. "Ssh," she said. "It's okay, honey. I love you, honey." She was crying too, but differently from him. She didn't get what was happening.

The choir sang. A violin played a sad piece that he'd heard his dad play one-handed on the piano. His dad wasn't there; neither were Linsey and Charlie. The older kid, Danny, who was Dr. Griffiths's son, who'd helped Toby into the basket the first time, read some things from the Bible, but he was hard to understand because he was crying too—which Toby figured he would, since he'd been right there, and he hadn't been able to stop the heart attack.

Toby stopped crying to hold his breath. If anyone would figure out about the attack getting the wrong person, it would be Danny Griffiths.

So no one would notice, he put his hand carefully between the buttons of his button-down shirt. He hiked up the T-shirt his mom had made him wear underneath. In there, against his sweaty skin, his hand found the scar and the ribs, the cavity where they'd nestled Brooke's heart. On Monday, his dad would drive him to Durham so they could do a biopsy. They'd stick him with something that would make him numb from his neck to his knees, and then they'd open up a vein in his thigh and run a little tube up with a set of little teeth on the end of it, to take a bite out of Brooke's heart. They'd tell him he wasn't going to feel anything, but he would feel it, the tube snaking its way under his ribs, pushing down the vein. To keep himself from scream-ing, he'd think about Latrell Sprewell. He'd shut his eyes and picture Sprewell on a breakaway, his big feet covering the court and then his legs springing him up, up and over everybody else to where he could dunk the ball. That usually worked. And then it would be over and they'd be telling him how great he did, and his dad would be promising him ice cream which he didn't really care about, but it made his dad feel good to fetch it.

The violin played. Toby put his hand over Brooke's heart. It was beat-ing fine, steady and strong. He wasn't being fair, to talk about Dr. Griffiths's heart attack being meant for him. He'd been forgetting he had Brooke in his corner, too. Brooke wasn't the type to die of some stupid heart attack. If you tried to make her think she might, she'd have laughed; heart attacks were for old people. She was young—well, Toby admitted, older than he was, technically, but really a lot younger in the way she saw things. Like Max. Jesus, what was he so scared of? Brooke's heart wasn't going to turn on him.

He handed his mom one of her clean tissues, out of her purse. From across the aisle, Dr. Lieberman winked at him, and Toby gave him what felt like a stupid wave, pulling his hand out from under his shirt and sort of waggling the fingers like they'd gone to sleep. Times like this, when the scare had passed on, Toby felt like he had something his mom and Dr. Lieberman could never have. He had a twin. Sort of. Like those con-joined twins Max had shown him pictures of, in *People* magazine, two girls who shared most of a body but had their own heads and shoulders. He and Max had agreed, you'd have to get along with your twin if you were like that. If you fought you'd just hurt yourself. It could be kind of neat, they'd agreed.

He slipped his hand back under, to where Brooke's heart was working. He hoped the doctors wouldn't take much of a bite out of it. He didn't think Brooke's heart could build itself back, the way a heart could if it was attached to the body it was born in. What he was working on was getting Brooke's heart to feel so totally at home in his body that they would stop doing these biopsies. They would realize he was hardly even a trans-plantee any more. Brooke and he understood each other so well, it could just as easily be her body as his own. He had about five years to pull that off, he figured. Between now and tryouts for the high school varsity.

They closed the service with "Amazing Grace," which Toby heard his mother singing among the others with a clear, vibrant soprano. Toby didn't sing, but he listened hard to the words, especially the part about being lost and then found, like Brooke's heart. When it was over, the mourners stood and greeted each other, glad to be surrounded by the liv-ing. A young heavyset woman who had to be Marcus Griffiths's daughter hugged Danny; Ben Lieberman hugged Susannah; people Toby didn't recognize fussed over him. Outside, the sun had gone behind a scrim of clouds. The wind had stopped, and the June air hung heavy and damp in the valley. If only it had been like this, they all thought as they stepped out from the church, the day of the balloon.

Chapter 13

*T*he way she'd brought up her son Charlie, Linsey would have been the first to admit to anyone, hadn't been right. From the start. She'd gotten the guy who was responsible to drive her to the abortion clinic in downtown Myrtle Beach, she'd made it past that wall of red-faced protesters, she'd filled out the forms, and she'd gotten changed into one of those flimsy blue gowns that opened at the back. Then the nurse had come in with a Dixie cup and said Swallow this dearie, and she'd asked what was it, and the nurse had said it was a Valium, and she'd said she wouldn't. She had to be to work at the Nice 'n Easy two hours later, she said when the head nurse came in to argue with her; she couldn't be dopey. If you're going to have the procedure, these nurses said—two of them now, standing at the door of the little white changing room—you've got to take the Valium. Next thing she knew she was back out at the van in the parking lot where what's-his-name was swigging a beer, all the protesters cheering and whooping behind her.

It's not in the cards, she told the guy. He drove her back to the room she was renting, and they never spoke another word to each other, then or ever. That was how Charlie made it, because she was over-sensitive to Valium.

Not that Charlie was a bad boy. No. God or somebody had smiled because Charlie had been a ton of fun when they were just the two of them, the first ten years of his life. They'd played music together, her on a tin can and Charlie on her dad's old recorder. They'd caught crawdaddies under the rocks in the stream near the trailer. They'd made fun of the old boogers who bought brand-name cigarettes at the Nice 'n Easy just so they could lean over and blow their breath in her face. Charlie was a good little mime. He'd push his belly out , curl his lip, and try to look down her blouse with one eye.

When John joined the picture, Charlie pulled into himself. That was normal, people told Linsey, a boy with a new father. Brooke came along, with more moxie than he'd had when little, taking up more air. And then when Charlie came back out of himself, he was gay.

Which was the one thing, the only thing John had a problem with. You know me, John used to say to her. I am an old-fashioned nineteen sixties hippie. I smoke grass, I don't mind what other people smoke or snort, I like blacks and Jews and all them, I don't make my money off capitalism, and I believe you can live eternally in the present. But those are all natural beliefs. This thing is not natural, and I do not believe it is something a man is born with like a hump on his back. He chooses it and lets you know he's chosen it because he wants to offend you. I don't like being around those kind of people. I'm sorry. They make me violent. A fellow just wants to slap the shit out of them for strutting it around like that.

Charlie was gone already to Nashville by then, but he stopped pretty quickly coming back for holidays or summer. She called him on the weekends when John was out with his buddies. She put Brooke on the line with him a few times, and he made Brooke laugh, though neither of them would ever tell her what the jokes had been about. I have a big brother, Brooke would tell people sometimes when they asked if she was the only kid, and John would frown and correct her: No, you don't. Half.

At the funeral for Brooke and John, Charlie had played his clarinet, a slow piece like water falling. When he'd finished and come to sit next to her, she'd realized how tall and good-looking he was, a young man making it on his own. His father had been a looker, she remembered— that and not much else, an Agway salesman who'd had a wife somewhere.

When they put Brooke into the ground Charlie had burst into sobs, the only man crying, he went right onto his knees on the ground. Afterwards they'd both gotten pretty blotto on white wine in the kitchen, and he'd kept thumbing the glass over a photo of Brooke that he'd taken six weeks before, the one time he'd visited in years, when Brooke had got her new bike and the new helmet for her birthday.

Weird, he'd said, to think that her heart's still beating somewhere.

And she'd tried to ask him, a week later when he was catching the bus back to Nashville. Did he think—? Would she be too crazy to—?

Fuck, Mama, Charlie had said. That's like a birth mother changing her mind ten years after she gives the kid up. Nobody'll want to see you on their doorstep.

But he'd grinned at her the old way, like when he was a kid, and she was his only family, and they could do what they wanted. It hasn't been ten years, she pointed out to him, and I never gave up my little girl.

That is exactly, he'd said, what I am worried about.

Now here he was in Roanoke, where no one but her nagging conscience had wanted her to come, and already in four days he had dipped into the same lives she was coating her own sorrow with.

"It's our first tour, Mama," he'd said when he called, "so I can't stay long." But he had come out early anyhow, ahead of the rest of them, so she could steal some of his time.

Come out, that is, in time to meet and save Toby all in one afternoon.

Since then, there had been the funeral for Susannah's boss, which Charlie had talked her out of attending ("You do not need another coffin in your life right now, Mama"). There had been Toby's departure with his Dad for Durham, where they would cut a little piece of Brooke's heart and have a look at it. There had been a lot of talk, she and Charlie remembering the Nice 'n Easy, the Sisters of Mercy nursery school, the road trips for craft fairs.

Tonight, the other members of Charlie's band would get here, for the performance. They'd stay downtown, mostly, he'd said, at the hotel. All except Jermaine, he'd said.

She'd woken late, and cotton mouthed. Charlie had taken her up to Lexington last night, to hear bluegrass, and then they'd stayed up drinking Wild Turkey and now her head hurt. Lying in bed, she tried turning the bad ankle, and the pain shot up her leg and landed in a dull ache at her stomach. "Aa-aah," she said, and laid the ankle back where it had been.

Thank Heaven she had made things ready before Charlie showed up, the day of the accident. That very morning she had swept the house, then got on her hands and knees with the Wood Preen and scrubbed all the way to the corners, the way Eustacie had taught her when she was a girl. She had stocked the pantry—After the Fall juices, carob bars, beer, and a couple bags of onion rings. You never knew what Charlie and his friends would want. She'd mowed the front lawn with the push mower she'd brought up from Granite Falls, though it was rusty and caught on the turns. She had showered with oatmeal soap and stepped out of the stall just as the phone was ringing, and it was Charlie calling from the road, saying he was pulling into town, hadn't she said something about a carnival?

She couldn't even do her yoga now, much less housecleaning. Even Toby, who'd been by with Nick yesterday on their way to Durham, called her a cripple. Give it ten days, Nick had said, and retaped the Ace before they left.

She pushed up on her elbow. Ten-fifteen. Her ankle felt like it had an iron weighing it down, inside the skin. It had started, she thought, with Toby's eyes, the way he'd looked at her when she got to that carnival with Charlie. Toby's eyes had shone just the way Brooke's used to, when John talked about little rides on the motorcycle, little safe rides where he'd be with her all the time. Your mama's a mouse, John had said, holding Brooke on his lap and laughing at Linsey. Your mama goes squeak, squeak, squeak and hides in her hidey-hole.

Brooke had giggled as her daddy tickled her ribs; she'd tucked her head into her daddy's chest.

There were times you knew. You smelled the karma, like motor oil on the skin of a pond.

Next thing she knew there had been the wind buffeting the basket with Toby in it, the basket without enough ballast, and there she had stood praying to the god she'd known back in Wardleysville, the one you had to make all kinds of promises to. *God, if You bring him back I will patch things up with Charlie. I will visit my mama and finish that rug for her. I will repent all the harsh words I ever said to John. If You bring him back unhurt. I will be humble. I will go to church. I will stop making designs on Susannah's husband.*

Now, that had been stupid, Linsey thought, carefully swinging both her legs around to the edge of the bed. You didn't promise what didn't make sense: to do things you couldn't do or stop doing things you weren't doing.

Then there had been Toby, crying out. He sounded like Brooke too—just like the Brooke Linsey heard in her dreams when Brooke hit the tree, just before she lost brain function. "Ma!" she cried. "Mama!" In the dreams, Brooke flew slowly, like a feather, from the truck chassis to the tree, and Linsey was always running, running with lead feet. And so she had run, the other day, toward the ropes that held the thing, to jump up and grab one, to pull it down.

Pouring the Wild Turkey last night, Charlie had finally laughed at her. "Just how strong d'you think you *are*, Mama?" he'd asked. "You just said to yourself, 'I'll pull this old balloon down to earth'? Hercules, watch out!"

"I was like a tail on a kite," she'd said.

"You're lucky you didn't *break* your damn tail."

Using the bed stand for support, she pushed herself up. Still no *asana* today. One or two positions she could manage, but not without feeling always the distraction of pain. Sequence, Priya Roy used to counsel, *vinyasa*. The sequence holds as much importance as the *asanas* themselves. And this time last year Brooke had done the *vinyasa* with her, that little rubber band of a body holding the poses like she was born to it, giggling when she had to hold too long.

Linsey shut her eyes. *Hey Brooke honey. Your big brother Charlie's here. That rascal!*

That was what Brooke would say, because Charlie called *her* a rascal, and he was the only one who did.

By noon he was up, her long-limbed boy. Awaiting his comrades, a little jumpy. They sat in her back yard, by the stream that ran to Carvin's Cove, and drank iced coffee. She liked this back yard. It was more orderly than what they'd known in Granite Falls, but across the creek there was a rising tangle of vines and small trees, and most evenings if you were quiet, you'd find deer down a ways, where the slope gentled. And even if the grass was non-native and chemically fertilized before she got here, it was thick and smelled sweet. There were three dogwood, two pink and a white, past bloom now but like dressed-up ladies all spring, and now the magnolia at the side of the house was in bloom, its perfume saturating the yard. It seemed like a yard where no harm could come to a person—and indeed, while she was still working on the house, adjusting its *ba-gua*, she'd spent a couple nights rolled in a sleeping bag out here, and she'd felt safer than she had those months alone in the house in Granite Falls, haunted by ghosts.

Charlie was telling her about the gig, tonight.

They were booked at the Blue Wall, he said, which did bluegrass mostly but was starting to venture into jazz, or that's what their agent told them. After this they went on to Richmond, then back by way of Greensboro and Asheville. "I can revisit the stomping grounds," he said.

"Better you than me," she said. "I can't bear the thought."

"But Ma, you got friends there. People who know what you went through."

He was sitting backwards at the old picnic table that had been left here. His hair was longer than she remembered, pretty enough to be a girl's. But for that and the earrings, she thought, you could never have told, with Charlie.

"It hurts too much, honey," she said. "Every time I would turn around, I'd hear your sister's voice. I couldn't go to sleep at night, thinking I ought to be tucking her in. And there were all John's things around, reminding me how he walked. How he smelled." She sipped at her lemonade. "Here, I remember with my mind, is all."

"You ought to come to Nashville, Ma."

She waved him away. "Not on my map," she said. "Anyhow, you probably live in some kind of communal house."

"I do not! I have an apartment. I pay rent."

"I don't know how you keep body and soul together."

He grinned, his dimple cutting his cheek. "Same way you did, Ma."

"Don't you go be getting any kids in your life, then."

When the tears spilled over, he touched her arm.

"I miss her too, Ma," he said. "She was going to come visit me. I keep expecting her great little face."

"Her skin," said Linsey. "You recall how warm her skin always was?"

"Sure I do."

"And that little line of freckles across her nose. And the way her shoulder blades kind of rounded into her shoulders."

"She had a lot of upper body strength, for a girl."

"You miss her, really?"

"I took a couple shirts of hers, Ma. I put my face in them, sometimes."

They had been doing this, off and on, for three days. It wasn't depressing, Linsey thought. It was just what they did, she and Charlie.

Charlie went on down to the hotel. When he got back, he had another young man with him, a skinny black fellow with a goatee.

"My beautiful mama," Charlie said, nodding at Linsey as he got out of the van. And then he nodded at the black fellow and said, "Jermaine."

"This cannot be your mother," said Jermaine. "This has got to be your big sister."

"Not what she tells me."

Jermaine stepped forward, took her hand. His was dry and cool. "Overjoyed," he said.

"You do look young for your years, Mama," Charlie said. He kissed Linsey's forehead, his butterfly kiss. "Like a weight lifted off you."

"Why, Charles Andrew. I never had any weights on me."

"Didn't I tell you?" Charlie said to Jermaine.

"You want tea," Linsey said to this stranger, her boy's friend, "or something a bit stronger?"

"Now tea would be just the ticket," said Jermaine. He looked like he'd never gone near a teabag in his life.

Jermaine, Charlie explained when they were settled in the tasteless kitchen—get a load of these eggplants in the wallpaper, Charlie said, they make you want to move your bowels, or what?—had come down to Nashville from New York, where he'd graduated top honors from Julliard. "It's a music school," Jermaine said politely, and Linsey said she knew, though she hadn't. One of his front teeth was capped with gold, which gleamed when he smiled. Jermaine had been headed to Memphis, Charlie said, for a teaching gig, but he'd stopped to visit an old boyfriend in Nashville and decided it was too early to lock himself up in some tower where jazz came at the end of the course list.

"Your son's skewing the story," Jermaine said. His walnut-colored hand came onto the table and covered Charlie's pale one. Linsey tried, but she couldn't take her eyes off those hands. Jermaine's voice was nasal, not from the South. "I jammed with Charlie and his ensemble, and it was like magic. And I made him promise I wouldn't starve."

"And you promised?" Linsey asked her son.

"I took my measure of his sax playing," said Charlie. "Nobody plays like that and starves."

"Well, said Linsey, passing Jermaine a basket of rice cookies at which he winced—she should have gone for the onion rings—"I can't wait to hear you all. My friend Susannah might come too."

"She's the one with the boy, right?" said Jermaine. "The boy got caught in the balloon?"

"That's the one."

She saw the look pass between Charlie and Jermaine. Three years ago, when Charlie told her, she'd been nothing but glad. Here was her son who she'd worried didn't know how to love except as a son, and now the problem was just that he loved boys. Only when you loved you shared secrets, and she wasn't sure she was ready for this Jermaine to be giving his opinion on her life. "Susannah's boy," she went on as if Jermaine didn't already know the facts, "had heart failure, so he got Brooke's heart. He and his daddy are down at the Duke Center this week."

"Something wrong?" asked Jermaine. He sipped his tea as if it was medicine.

"No, no. Routine." She didn't want to say what they were doing to Brooke's heart, or why. "Anyhow, Susannah's nice. You like her, don't you?" she said to Charlie.

Charlie took a hit of the Scotch he'd brought and elected over tea. He pursed his lips. Such a rangy, uncollected sort of young man he was. "Any friend of yours," he said.

She had no complaint to make of him. That she had come so close to losing him, back there with the Valium, was the one piece of her personal history that stopped her breath, each time she let herself dwell on it.

hen his mama first moved with him to Greensboro, Charlie told his friend Jermaine, they lived in the Crystal Estates Trailer Park, on a flat ashy road outside town. Fully half the trailer was filled up by his ma's loom, which they stepped around to get from the two bedrooms in the back to the narrow kitchen up front. They ate canned goods at the bar stools that came with the trailer, tucked into the counter behind the stove. During the day, while he was at the Sisters of Mercy Nursery School, his mama worked the checkout at the Nice 'n Easy, where she was three times held up at gunpoint. After school and deep into the night she worked the loom. In his sleep he could hear the clack of the shuttle, the low thump of the beater. She drank black coffee to keep awake. On weekends she'd load her wares into the trunk of the neighbor's Chevy Cavalier and they'd drive through the mountains to the craft shows. There, he'd fill his belly on fried dough and cotton candy and fall stickily asleep under the folding table while she opened up the rugs and shawls and hangings for suspicious people to paw over. When they returned the Chevy late at night, she'd carry him into his bed and wipe his mouth with a rough cold washcloth. Then she'd have to go over to the neighbor's for a couple of hours. To pay for the car, she said.

When the Sisters of Mercy caught him peeing underneath the cross they'd tacked onto the playground fence, they locked him into a basement closet for the rest of the day and told him to think what God was going to do with him. When his mama came to pick him up and found him in the closet, his lips blue with cold and the feces loading his pants, she marched out into that yard and tore the cross off and broke it in two with her foot. "That ain't my god," she said. Next day she quit the job at the Nice 'n Easy. For four years they got along on her weaving and what she picked up from magazine phone sales. Then one night she left Charlie alone to go crawl through John Hunter's window, and their lives took a turn.

How many years had it taken him to forgive her? For loving that ignorant arrogant bully, for acting like you could sit in so-called meditation and let the world crash around you? *But she is your mama, man,* Jermaine would remind him, *and she bought you your first horn.*

Which he remembered. And he remembered the solid gold cross her own mama had given her, which disappeared from around her thin neck when her world fell apart last summer. Now she was chasing the shards of that world, and he didn't see what role he had to play. Even though he, too, had loved that little girl, loved her shine and her softness; even though he'd been missing a piece of his own heart since last summer.

It was still light when they pulled up to the Blue Wall, east of town. It was not a bad-looking place; the owner had said they would draw a good crowd. Behind them lay the mall and the arterial, trucks whining by; before them lay the misty blue-green wall of the mountains. Jermaine and the rest set to unpacking and setting up the equipment. Charlie went over to where a red Saturn had just wheeled into the gravel lot, and his mother waved her hand excitedly.

"Susannah!" his ma was crying. "You made it!"

Charlie stood back a moment, before going over. Under other circumstances, he would have found Susannah Ames to be a decently interesting person. But under other circumstances, his contact with her would have been limited to an article in a newspaper read idly while waiting for the bus. She had surprised him, he would give her that. From what his ma had said, he had expected a tough-looking science type. Susannah looked like she had been painted in watercolors; she was always patting down her blowzy hair. Yet she regarded him much the way he regarded her, with the wariness of seconds in a duel, as if between them they could ward off whatever bloodiness might ensue, or else go at it themselves.

Really, his judgment had nothing to go on. One afternoon was all, the day before her boss's funeral. He'd gone with his ma to pick the kid up from school and take him and a friend to a skateboarding park. He'd gotten a little high before they left, and so done a few tricks on the board that the boys had cheered. Toby had made a big deal of giving him a basketball card, a pre–cross-dressing Dennis Rodman. When Susannah showed up, she thanked him effusively for lifting her boy out of that basket.

You like her, don't you? his ma had asked.

You had to step back from it. You had to remember how quickly time went by, and how, soon enough, they all—even his ma—would be leading different lives. This whole thing, with the boy and Brooke's heart, was only a bump on the way.

Patting down her hair, Susannah stepped over. "I bring Toby's regrets," she said. "He was dying to come, but he's in Durham."

In her ivory blouse, with her matching cheeks and thin nose, she resembled one of those Italian Madonnas. He took her outstretched hand and squeezed it without any intentional rancor. "I'm sure he won't miss much," he said.

She made the usual protestations, from which he was distracted by Jermaine, looking for speaker wires. He glanced back as he dug them out of the van. He saw the way his mother touched Susannah's shoulder to point out all the players; he saw the way she tried not to lean on her crutch. She was still young, his ma, but sometimes, like now, he saw her the way she would look as an old woman, still bending and smiling, trying to please.

"Nervous?" said Jermaine, placing the flat of his palm against Charlie's chest as he straightened up.

"Not about the music."

"Aw, your ma's going to love you, man."

"I told you. It's not that. I just see her in this *place*. I don't know—"

"And I see her standing tall. She has got backbone."

"She did once. Steel backbone."

"Have a little faith, then. If she wants your help, she'll ask."

They kissed quickly, then Charlie brought the wires inside.

Charlie's group did two sets. Susannah left after the first one. She had to get back to her lab, she said. Marcus Griffiths, the scientist who had died, had been pushing a deadline to submit lymphoma data, and now she and her team were finding holes in it.

"I thought we had saved him there, for a minute," Charlie said, remembering the stocky chest, the gray face.

"Me, too," said Susannah.

"Charlie learned CPR back in Greensboro," Charlie's ma put in. "It think it was a Boy Scout thing, wasn't it, Charlie? He was trying to please his stepdaddy."

"Mama, please," said Charlie. He glanced around. They were sitting in a quiet corner of the club, drinking beer. The rest of the band was at the next table.

"It's a great skill," said Susannah.

"Can't your—ah—deadline be pushed back?" Charlie said. "Under the circumstances?"

She rolled her round eyes. "There are people out there," she said, "who would love to see this research group taken down a notch. Who would love to say that without Marcus, we can't contribute anything."

"Well, cancer," said Charlie. "It's not like anyone's got a cure to it or anything."

"No," said Susannah, but she bit on her lower lip, like a child guarding a secret. "What we're trying to do, basically," she said, "is to make cancer cells sick. We've been growing a sort of virus that, if it infects a malignant cell, could possibly make it behave like a normal cell. Meaning the cell would die in a normal cycle."

"Can you do that?" said Charlie.

"If we can get more time, maybe."

She's real ambitious, his ma had said admiringly of Susannah, and he supposed that was a good thing.

When Susannah rose to leave, his ma sat up.

"Toby'll be back tomorrow?" she asked.

"Or the next day," said Susannah. "Depends."

"Depends on what?"

Susannah paused. Charlie could see the sigh pass through her body. Truly, under other circumstances, he might have liked her. "Nah, he'll be back tomorrow," she said at last. "Late, though. And he'll be tired."

That was when Charlie's ma started to push, to say she'd see them on the weekend, right? Or Sunday anyhow? As Charlie shifted in his seat, the manager came over, asked if they were ready to go back on. With relief he fetched his clarinet, headed for the safety of the stage.

Back at his mother's house up on the hill, the night felt wrung out like a thin towel. It had been a good gig, not great; a bigger crowd at the first set than the second. Afterward, they had traded the beers for bourbon, and the manager had sat with them till closing, taking an inordinate interest in the long-haired lady with the sprained ankle. Which his ma, Charlie noticed, had not seemed to mind.

"So, Mama," Charlie said, opening the living room window to the air, cooler here where the breeze rose, "you ever going to start dating again?"

She was putting away mugs from earlier. Jermaine, who had come along, was sacked out on the couch. The blow-up doll she called Safe-T-Man sat in the corner of the square kitchen, a little deflated. Looks more like Don Knotts, Jermaine had observed, than like Clark Kent.

"What?" she said, leaning on the counter. "You mean like a man?"

"No," said Charlie from the living room. He winked at Jermaine. "I thought maybe you'd changed your voltage. Of course a man, Mama."

"They don't exactly line up," she said, "at my age."

Jermaine snorted lightly and hauled himself off the couch. Scratching the back of his head, he took to examining the wall hangings, wild scraps of weaving that Charlie had seen his ma pull off the loom in a weekend. Now she limped out from the kitchen.

"Give me a break," Charlie said. "Your age. You're never going to stop being a looker, Mama."

"Damn straight," said Jermaine, still studying the hanging. "You see that guy at the Blue Wall?"

"She doesn't even color her hair. Get a load of that hair, Jerm."

"Pollutes the water, hair color does."

Charlie's ma raked her fingers through the finer hair, above her ears. In fact, Charlie thought, he'd like to give his mom a trip to the beauty parlor. Let them brighten her blond locks, fuss over her face. John had liked her plain, but John was dead. And in Charlie's opinion, one reason he had liked her plain was so no one would come carry her off.

He sat on the warm couch that Jermaine had vacated. He pulled a book of rolling papers from his pocket. He felt Jermaine watching him, but Jermaine didn't know his ma.

"I don't like to think," she said, coming closer, "that everything comes down to looks."

"Then your age shouldn't matter either, Mama," he said. "You shouldn't be saying 'at my age.'" Spreading a paper on the glass coffee table, he produced a clear Baggie and started sprinkling the contents. "You just got your confidence shook up," he said.

"And just when would that have happened?"

He didn't quite look at her. He picked out the seeds.

"When?" she said again. She'd hobbled to the couch, perched on the arm.

"You cannot tell me," he said, arranging the grass to make a substantial but elegant joint, "you were a hundred percent sorry to have him out of your life."

"Are you talking about John?"

"Well, I'm not talking about my daddy."

"John was a sight better than your daddy, if your gene pool will excuse me," she said.

She was watching him roll. Jermaine had moved farther away, toward the front hallway. *Don't be taking it out on her,* Jerm had told him before he left Nashville. But Jerm did not completely understand what Charlie meant to do.

"John brought up his child," his ma said.

"He sure did," said Charlie.

He kept his eye on the table, the paper, the weed.

"He took her motorcycle riding," he said.

"Hush your mouth!" she said. It was as if he had stung her. Standing by the couch, she raised her arm as if to strike him. Charlie just held, his tongue on the edge of the rolling paper.

"Hey now," said Jermaine, stepping over. "Let's be cool now, Char."

"*He* never scared me, Mama," said Charlie, sealing the joint. "I don't think you're going to."

"You have no right to talk about him!" she said. She let the arm drop. "Now he's dead, he can't defend himself."

"Oh, I don't think he wants defending."

Pulling his lighter from his back jeans pocket, Charlie lit the joint and sucked it in. He started to pass it to Jermaine, but Jermaine, standing, nodded toward Charlie's ma. Charlie had never smoked with her. He thought maybe she smoked alone. The other day, he'd come out of his weed-smelling room to go to the skateboard park, and she hadn't given him more than a knowing look. That she used to smoke with John he knew, because those nights had been the easiest.

In any case it was time; the weed was good; and they were maybe going to have a conversation at last. Slowly his ma sat back down, right on the couch this time. Reaching out her thumb and index, she toked lightly. "There wasn't many men," she said when she'd passed the stick on to Jermaine and let the smoke out, "were going to take on a boy almost ten. John never raised his hand to you."

"No, he did not. Just offered to slice my dick if I ever brought a fairy home with me."

His ma glanced from him to Jerm and back. "Maybe he didn't approve of your—of your lifestyle."

"Maybe he tempered his world love with a good lick of hate."

"Maybe he didn't understand everyone. But he had a good heart. I chased *him*, Charlie. He didn't come looking for the kind of trouble a girl like me could give him."

"Kind of trouble? You hear her?" Charlie said to Jermaine. Jermaine had gone into a crouch by the coffee table where he'd found the turtle-shaped brass ashtray Charlie sent his ma long ago from Texas. He didn't say anything, but passed the joint to Charlie. "Trouble," Charlie repeated when he'd toked. The stuff burned his throat, where he'd been blowing Coltrane two hours ago. "That's exactly what I mean, Mama. You held the job, you bought the groceries, you did the man's laundry, you brought a beautiful brilliant girl into the world for him, and he's got you thinking you are *trouble*."

"He didn't have to hang on to anybody," his ma said. "Why, he could have lived—well, on air you might say. But he chose to stay in my bed. Now maybe that doesn't matter to you in your—" She took a quick peek at Jermaine. "In your lifestyle. But you know how it was for Brooke. The sun rose and set on her daddy's behalf."

"He charmed, all right. He made his daughter into his creature."

"So what if he did? She loved him. When he was gone, she watched out that window, and when she caught sight of his truck, it was like she'd entered heaven." She turned to Jermaine. "I can't tell you. Hours they'd sit there, her on his lap and this notebook of numbers. It was like they had some other language together, like they—"

"Like he owned her," said Charlie.

"No!"

"He owned you both. You danced to his bidding."

"Why, *everybody* danced, then. You get a man like that, with a strong personality—"

"And he exploits you?"

"He never exploited anybody. He didn't believe in that. He believed in personal freedom."

Charlie held a toke in, and snickered. "His own," he said.

"You're just jealous."

"I just don't want you carrying a torch for him!"

Charlie passed the roach to Jermaine, who pulled a clip out of his pocket. Yes, he could have left it alone, this business of his ma and John. But you didn't see someone you loved tied hand and foot and not do anything about it. It wasn't his ma's desire to chase after Brooke's heart, he was sure of that. She was being, still, the dutiful wife.

Oh Brooke, he thought, the weed making him maudlin. Brooke little honey.

His ma had gotten up from the couch again. "You put him up to this, didn't you?" she was saying to Jermaine.

"No ma'am. I am just hearing it, myself. I'll take a little drive, Char."

Charlie tossed him the keys to the van. On his way out, Jermaine put a hand on Charlie's hand, let it rest there an instant.

"Char," his ma repeated when Jermaine had gone.

"It's a nickname."

"So you two going steady now? Or what d'you call it?"

"Jermaine's my partner. I guess that's what we call it."

"Well, John was *my* partner."

"I know, Mama."

"He built me a hot tub. Finished it just before the accident."

"I remember. I saw it."

"He could have made millions of dollars, if he'd cared about dollars. He could have run a company. He was smarter than Bill Gates. First in his class at Duke. He showed me the yearbook."

"Forty-two years old, and showing you his college annual. Well, Mama, that is a great accomplishment. Yes Ma'am."

He fired up another joint, just for the two of them.

"Just because he didn't treat you right—"

"Tell me this, Mama. He ever notice those incredible rugs you wove?"

"Those were just old patterns. Something to sell."

"He ever notice the garden you planted?"

"Why should he notice a thing like that?"

"Because you made a beautiful form of it. Because every flower was tended, every color had a place in the scheme, every vegetable made its way to our table. I mean, look what you've done with this ordinary house, Mama." Charlie swept an arc with his hand, taking in the colors of the walls, the hangings, the arrangements of small carvings on the shelves, the cloth of the chairs. "I know you call it that Chinese thing. But you made our home like this, and he moved through it like you'd done nothing more than sweep cobwebs from the cave."

"John didn't care"—she was starting to cry—"about material things."

"Didn't he? Then tell me why, when his money was running out, he was going to put his daughter out there. Why he was getting those publicity shots done. Not for the Buddha, he wasn't doing that."

"Oh, stop." She had taken the joint from him, but toked too fast and coughed. She coughed and the tears came, and she took the glass of water from Charlie and her hands trembled. "Stop. Just stop," she said when she had breath. "You don't know—him. You don't know. Brooke—with him—"

"All right, Mama, all right. I'll stop."

Neither of them said anything for a long while. Through the open window came the whine of the interstate. This time last year, Charlie thought in a kind of waking, stoned dream, he had taken his sister Brooke outside with a flashlight. They found possums, coons, bats. They smelled a skunk. From the top of the rise, they spotted a trio of deer at the stream.

"Why did you wait till now," his ma said at last, "to talk this way to me?"

For the first time since he'd started to spread the rolling paper, Charlie looked at his mother. The skin around her eyes was as finely lined as crushed silk. This time he saw her, not as old, but the way she must have looked years ago, before he was born, when her name had been Lynette, and she was just leaving Wardleysville, South Carolina, and everything about her was pure and unbroken as water. Like Brooke.

"That time you stood in the meadow and wept," he said after a while. "You remember that visit, Mama?"

"I remember something, yeah. Crying for no reason. I was getting my period maybe."

Charlie chuckled, a rasp in his throat. "I talked to Brooke that visit, too. She wasn't eating right. She wasn't moving her bowels right. She was like you, scared to death she'd let him down somehow. Only she was ten years old. And I didn't do anything. I didn't confront him. I didn't lift the pressure off her."

"I thought he didn't scare you."

"Yeah, well." Charlie tried to grin, a twist of his mouth. "That's a later revision."

His ma rose and went to her loom. She ran her fingers across the interrupted weave, the warp waiting to be filled. He got up, stubbed out the joint, followed her. When he was standing next to the loom, she said, "You know how they were going down the hill, that afternoon."

"Too fast, the coroner said."

"Hell for leather." Her fingers brushed the weave, back and forth. "And no one could figure, even the guy who ran the woodworking shop, he couldn't say why they would have been going so fast or decided to take that turn right then. But I know. It was what he was going to do. No one was going to tell him what he could do and what he could not do. That was what we fought about, that morning. He said—"

Charlie put his hand over hers. He squeezed the fingers.

"He said," she went on, "I was always telling him what to do. That was what he hated about marriage. It was all—all bourgeois bullshit and people telling you what to do. He said I was always telling him to lay off Brooke. Well, we both knew, he said, which one of us Brooke would choose."

"Oh, Mama," Charlie said, and then he held her, her thin face against his chest. "Forgive me, Mama," he said. She didn't answer. "Forgive me," he said again, and then he could feel her nodding, against the cotton of his T-shirt, short sharp nods.

Chapter 15

Waking in the darkness of the motel room, Toby thought for a second that he was in the hospital, and they had finally shut the lights off. That was one of the things he'd hated about living in the hospital—they never let it go all dark in your room, as if without some bluish light shining on your face, you might suddenly die off. So now, for just a split second, he thought it was the hospital, but all the nurses had gone home, and some older kid had found the switch and flicked it off. Then he heard his Dad's light snore, from the other side of the king bed, and he knew they were in a regular place. Not home, but Comfort Inn, where they tucked the sheets tight and had free breakfast in the morning, cherry Danish and Fruit Loops and cranberry juice.

For a while he lay still, hearing the whoosh of the air system and adjusting his eyes to the dark blue of the room. Yesterday he'd seen his old team, the guys who'd taken out his sick heart and stitched Brooke's heart into place. He didn't like the way they treated him. They were always so cheerful, in a fake way that made him feel like a little kid. The called him Tiger and Big Guy; they pulled nickels from behind his ear and high-fived him and showed him where they were double-jointed or could talk like Homer Simpson. But they weren't his friends. If he and Brooke's heart died, it would mean they had messed up, was all. They didn't want to mess up.

And so yesterday they'd done the thing where they ran a tiny little pincer called a bioptome up his artery from the inside of his thigh. They always liked to show him the bioptome first, as if it would make him feel better to know the thing was so small. But his veins were small too, and it hurt, still, the place where they'd run the catheter in. He touched his fingers to the gauze bandage there, and then he touched them to the scar on his chest.

Where Brooke lived.

Well, he knew she didn't live there. He had known, way back, when he could barely climb stairs, when his arms and legs felt like water balloons, that his one big hope was for some other kid to die. That was when he slept in the double room at the hospital with that kid Shawn on the other side of the curtain. Shawn needed both heart and lungs, and he was younger than Toby—he had his seventh birthday their second week at the Transplant Center—and funny the way little kids could be funny, because they don't have the whole picture. Shawn had had this idea they were making him up a heart and lungs, like out of spare parts somewhere. Shawn's family prayed a lot, and every night Shawn prayed to the baby Jesus that his heart would be ready soon. One day, in a bad mood, Toby had said, "What you've got to pray for, Shawn, is a lot of really lousy weather. Like, hurricanes. Snow up north."

"How come?" Shawn had asked in his peepy voice.

"Cause then there'll be car accidents, and kids'll break their necks, and you'll get your heart and lungs."

He'd peeked around the curtain. Shawn had thin, white-blond hair and a face like soap. "I don't want that!" he said.

"Sure you do. *I* do."

But it was like telling an even littler kid that you can't get a McDonald's burger without killing a moo-cow. As soon as the truth was out, you had to soften it a little. "Hey, it won't be any *good* kids. It'll be kids who didn't listen to their moms and dads and didn't wear their seatbelts. It'll be kids who're ready to die."

"Why?"

"Because," said Toby, getting into the story now, "because God said it was time for them. Because he'd rather keep you alive than them. Cause you're better."

"No, I'm not," said Shawn, but you could tell the idea was already not bothering him so much.

Even back then—even when it was hard to remember what a kid might do with a day that didn't include IV checks and EKGs, that meant fifteen hours of awake time and nine hours of sleep time instead of the other way round, that got its excitement from things like basketball games and water slides instead of left ventricular assists and a visit from Hoho the Hospital clown—even then, Toby thought all the time about the heart he might get. What kind of personality it would have; whether he would get along with it. He called his own, swollen heart The Blob. He saw himself as being enslaved to it, the way the androids were enslaved to that sort of bald, brainlike thing in "Next Dimension." The pills he took were supposed to be his weapons, but they just went into the maw of The Blob, and he still felt run over by a train.

And then one morning his mom was at his hospital bedside, shaking his shoulder, saying, "They've got one, Tobe. They've found you a heart. It's coming up from North Carolina. Oh, honey. This is your time."

Shawn was already gone, by then. They'd moved him into intensive care, and then he'd died. The nurse said he'd gone along home, but Toby knew better. You didn't get to go home without a dead kid's organ stitched up inside you.

Sitting up in the motel bed, he fished around for the remote and flicked the TV on without sound. His dad stirred but didn't wake. Sports Center was on, with replays of the Braves in Houston and the New York Liberty in Seattle. He'd learned, in the hospital, not to get too excited while he was watching sports on TV. If you got excited with something, the nurses came in and flicked it off. Now he just studied the moves, the quick footwork, the no-look passes. If you got good enough with this stuff, eventually the coaches wouldn't care about a little handicap like a transplanted heart. You'd have made yourself too valuable to the team.

The real team, that was, not this sort of phony team like the doctors.

Funny how he couldn't remember September. Not at all. He'd said this to his dad once, and his dad started singing "Try to remember that time in September," which just made Toby mad. It was awful, to lose a month out of your life! They'd told him everything he did, how it was like being a baby again, taking baby steps. They told him he'd been hard at work, the whole time. To Toby, it all seemed like sleepwalking except for the baseball cards that came from Max. Until one day he woke up and there was his new heart, beating away in his chest like it had found a home there. Almost from that moment, he went looking for a name to put to it, a name totally different from The Blob. He had little conversations with it, even when they'd let him go back to school, and there were other kids to talk to. "How'm I doing, heart?" he'd ask, and he'd put his hand there, to feel it beat. When they took the biopsies he felt bad, like he'd hurt his best friend.

He was glad, though, that he hadn't known right away it was Brooke's heart. By the time he found out, Brooke was six months gone, and her dying wasn't anymore his fault, no matter how many time he'd stood at the hospital window and wished the rain would come down harder and faster and make the cars skid.

He surfed the channels—cartoons, shopping, weather, cartoons, golf, John Wayne. He swung his legs out of bed and rose to pull the heavy drapes open. Below the closed window, a parking lot, then the highway. Above it, nesting below the eave, a family of birds. He felt okay; Brooke's heart felt okay. He wanted to get out of here. Max thought it was cool, how Toby got to stay in a motel every couple of months, but Toby would take Max's house and the meadow any day. He climbed back into the king bed and touched his dad's shoulder.

"Dad? Can we get breakfast?"

His dad stirred; threw up an arm. Underneath, in his pits, dark nests. On his chest too, hair in a T shape—if he'd had a scar like Toby's, his dad's chest hair would cover half of it. "Your turn will come," his dad had said, but Toby had his doubts. The hair he got, with the medicine, was more all over, like fur. He'd shown Brooke's brother Charlie where he'd shaved it off, on the arms. Charlie had said he should definitely let it grow, and then bleach it, like a blond shimmer all over his body. Next time he came through Roanoke, Charlie said, he'd bring peroxide.

"Dad?"

"Yeah, sure Tobe. Sure."

His dad opened his eyes; smiled. For once, maybe because it was early morning and they were at the Comfort Inn, he didn't even look worried.

"Are the fish okay, you think?" said Toby, worrying in his place.

"I think Mom can handle fish."

"You sure? Because up to now—"

"That's why you've got two parents, Tobe. We pick up where the other one leaves off."

His dad pushed Toby's hair from his eyes. Last night, when Toby was released, his dad took him for spaghetti and meatballs and a round of duckpin bowling. They'd done ten frames with bumpers and then Toby wanted to try without bumpers but his dad said no, that Toby looked too pale. If his mom had been there, Toby might have worked her into the argument and gotten five frames, anyhow. But she wasn't there, so he'd shrugged his shoulders and asked if they could watch a movie at the motel. And his dad had hugged him, a big bony long-armed hug with his stubby right hand against Toby's ribs, which was something he did practically never.

"Next time," Toby said, as if his dad had been hearing his thoughts, "I want to just go without the bumpers from the start."

"Sure, Tobe."

His dad stood and stretched. He didn't sleep in anything, and you could see the marks of the sheets on his butt. A little hair there too, Toby noticed. Toby slept in a Knicks T-shirt. His mom slept in a nightie. He wondered what Linsey slept in. Charlie was like his dad, probably. Brooke would have known. You knew stuff like that about your family.

"Let's get breakfast," he said.

"Meds first," said his dad.

"No, breakfast."

"Meds."

"Breakfast!"

"Toby. It's meds first at home; it's meds first here."

"I get two bowls of Fruit Loops then."

His dad pulled on his boxers, stupid-looking plaid things. "Okay, buster. Sold."

"And a Pop Tart."

"Jeez, Toby. I thought you wanted to keep the weight down."

"It's Comfort Inn, Dad."

His dad grinned, and waved at the air like there was a cloud of gnats in front of his face. He wasn't all that tough, Toby thought as he scrambled for his knapsack with the change of clothes. You just had to get him alone. You just had to work him right.

Chapter 16

Susannah woke to the telephone. For a few cotton-mouthed seconds she couldn't understand why Nick wasn't picking up the receiver on his side of the bed. Nick wasn't there, that was why. Nick was spending the night at the Comfort Inn in Durham, with Toby. She lunged across gathered sheets. It could be him, Nick, with something wrong, something they'd never thought of, Toby's heart.

But the voice belonged to Danny Griffiths, who began by scolding her for not being at work. "Faye didn't know *why* you hadn't come in," he said. "There's nobody in your lab at *all*, she said."

"What time's it?" mumbled Susannah. Shutting her eyes, she lay back on the pillow. She didn't want to see the red read-out on the digital clock by Nick's side of the bed. Closed, her eyelids looked purple, plush, comforting.

"Almost noon!"

"Then I left my microscope station almost eight *hours* ago. How right you are, Dr. Griffiths."

"I just—sorry. I just wondered. There's someone with me that I thought you could talk to."

"I'll be in before you can say stem cell factor backwards."

She walked the dog—unleashed, the little luxury of Nick's absence—all the way to the river and back, showered, and choked down black coffee. One day with them gone, and already she was falling into dissolute habits—no milk in the fridge, no regularity to her hours, no vitamins. *Bad girl*, she said to herself on the way out the door. *You'll have to change your evil ways.*

Danny was waiting in the lounge, with a damp-looking, gray-faced man he introduced as Leonard Tuck, his lawyer. "Oh my god,"

Susannah said, pouring herself more coffee, "I know where I've seen you. On local TV."

"You might have."

"You're a—" She felt giddy, from curtailed sleep and Tomiko's new theories, spread over the tables back in her lab like cut pieces of a new pattern. Once she returned from the Blue Wall, they had labored through the night, she and Cutter and Tomiko, logging quantities of virus and bcl-2 patterns, chasing the combinations. "You're an ambulance chaser."

Leonard Tuck cleared his throat. His hair was steely and straight at the sides, smoky and kinked on the top. "I have never chased an ambulance in my life, ma'am," he said, lacing together his large hands. "I run a law practice out of Blacksburg. This young man has *engaged* me."

"Well," said Susannah. "Sit."

Though the administration had made an effort—wallpaper, enlargements of electron-microscope photos of nerve cells and aberrant chromosomes, flavored coffees—the lounge exuded an inescapable tinge of hospital, with humming soft-drink machines in the corner and stale pastries under a plastic dome next to the steaming coffee machines. This late in the morning, only a few lab techs were apt to wander in, and they tended to fill their Starbucks mugs, grab a stale doughnut, and head back to the rodent room to gossip. In the blinking overhead light, her linen blouse indifferently ironed, Susannah looked as exhausted as she felt.

But she heard Danny out, and she did her best to rise to McGowan's defense. "Nick says it could have happened to any balloonist," she said, addressing herself to Danny. "And Ben Lieberman said your dad's attack could have come anytime."

"Who is Nick?" said Leonard Tuck, scribbling in a wire notebook. "Who is Ben Lieberman?"

"My dad never had a heart attack before," said Danny.

"Oh, come on, Danny. You want to be a heart surgeon. Your dad had an arrhythmia. He was at risk."

Danny pulled nervously at his half-grown beard. "That's not the point. He didn't sign a liability release. Before he went up in the balloon."

Sick as she was of blaming and being blamed, Susannah couldn't help herself from saying, "And whose fault is that?"

Danny hung his head.

"The company was responsible," Leonard Tuck picked up. "Mr. Griffiths was a volunteer and in no way liable. The company should have overseen the signature process itself."

"*Himself*, you mean," said Susannah. "Mr. McGowan."

Danny stood up suddenly, and poured himself coffee. "Not to mention the ropes and everything," he said from the doughnut table. "My dad could've lived another ten years. You don't know."

"No," Susannah said. She drained the Styrofoam mug dry. "I only know I'm tired of looking for someone to tar and feather."

How many times had she gone over it with Nick? *Linsey called my name. I turned around. The big guy was getting out, and Toby in. I never wanted him to go the second time. I told him to wait. But Linsey called my name.*

"Are you saying," said Leonard Tuck, looking down at his thin file of papers as if he had his lines there, "that you won't cooperate with our inquiry?"

"I'm saying I don't care. Look, Danny." She turned away from the sad, wet-paper attorney to Marcus's son. *You reminded me. I have a son, too.* Those had been his last words to her. "Go ahead and sue the poor bastard if it makes you feel better. This guy probably won't charge you. I'll bet Mr. McGowan has a lousy insurance policy, and it won't bring your dad back. But if anyone wants me to say what happened, I'll say."

Danny Griffiths and Leonard Tuck had tracked her down, too, Linsey admitted. "Nasty little man, that lawyer," she said, weeding the little patch of vegetables she set out behind her ranch house. "Droopy-eyed. I think he wears a rug."

"It won't make Danny Griffiths feel better, to do this," said Susannah.

Linsey adjusted her wide-brimmed hat. Her hair was gathered into a loose braid and swung over her shoulder like a pet. She didn't seem to mind the heat—her freckles multiplied but she looked cool as a picture. The gig, she had reported, had gone past midnight, and this morning Charlie had taken off with his band for Richmond. Meanwhile her ankle, five days past the accident, was markedly better—wrapped still, but she could walk on it, and garden.

"I told that lawyer," she said, "we were *all* liable. He might just as well sue us all."

Lah-bel, Susannah repeated to herself. She yanked on a hunk of crab-grass threatening the peppers, and the stem broke off in her hand. "I don't see how that's true," she said. "Marcus had a heart condition. The operator had a new assistant. The wind gusted. You and I had nothing to do with those things."

"One thing I learned from John," Linsey said, pulling a string of clover from around the ferny carrots, "is we are each of us responsible for everything that happens in our lives. We just have to open up to that responsibility, the way you got to open up to pain when you're hurt, or joy when it comes." She stood up and flexed her back. There were patches of dried mud on her knees, and Susannah realized how rarely she'd seen Linsey's knees—she wore long cotton skirts, usually, or torn jeans—and how they had the same crêpey skin above them as Susannah's, and tiny patches like fossil marks from old scars. They were not young knees. "I could of bought Brooke a real motorcycle helmet," she said. "I didn't because I didn't want her riding. But she rode anyhow." The tears had started again, brown streaks on Linsey's dusty face. "I accept what I did and what I didn't do."

"Oh, Linsey."

Susannah pushed herself up and tried to put her arm around her. The gesture was awkward with Linsey so tall and bony; she found herself pressing her cheek against Linsey's warm shoulder. She wanted to exonerate her. They were friends. But it hadn't been Linsey who took Brooke on the motorcycle; it hadn't been Linsey who turned too fast into a gravel driveway. Didn't you have to be guilty of something first before you received pardon for it?

"I didn't make anyone get in that basket," she said, echoing Ben Lieberman, "and neither did you."

"You let Toby get in."

"Toby got in while my back was turned. Anyhow, that's different. Danny's suit—*if* Danny sues—is about *Marcus*. We *signed* the release for Toby and me. And Marcus was responsible for himself. This is all about a piece of paper."

"Well." Linsey dabbed at her tears with the back of her lavender gardening gloves, and managed a smile. "I guess I would say the same thing as that Griffiths boy if the balloon *had* hurt Brooke."

"You mean Toby."

"Didn't I say Toby? I meant Toby. I'd say, we were all liable."

Lah-bel.

"But we *weren't. You* weren't."

"I should of got there quicker. And stopped you." Linsey had turned her back to Susannah; she was picking up her gardening tools, the cardboard box with her organic plant food, her seed packets.

"Stopped me from what? Linsey, if we're talking about ballast here, everyone would have been better off—Marcus Griffith might even still be alive—if you hadn't called *out.* I was going to get into the basket before Toby. My weight would have held the basket down. But you called, and I turned."

"You asked him if he wanted to go without you."

"Yes, I did." Susannah felt her head bobbing, like a toy. "Earlier. But then the operator said we should both get on. And *then* you stopped me."

Her face felt flushed, the sun hot on the back of her head. Linsey had turned, with the box, the tools, but the brim of her hat shaded her. Susannah felt as if she were sliding down a gravel slope. All night she had worked, and all day, and then she had stopped by here trivially, as it were. To talk about a silly lawyer. "You told Nick I let Toby go," she went on. "You told him I practically caused that accident. Didn't you?"

Linsey almost passed her without looking. Then she stopped. She drew a deep breath. She looked down at Susannah as if she'd just noticed her, standing there; as if she felt, was surprised by feeling, a great pity for Susannah. "I can't answer for what *you* did, Susannah," she said patiently. "*I* tried to stop you. To stop the whole thing. That's all I know. That's all I told Nicholas."

"Why, you. That's a lie."

"Excuse me," said Linsey. Her voice choked the way it did when she was going to cry. Hobbling slightly, she pushed past Susannah into the newly painted kitchen. It seemed to Susannah that she was expected to follow, but her own words had taken her aback, and she rested a minute in the shade of the veranda, trembling in the heat.

In the middle of the sloping yard, Linsey's garden bloomed brilliantly—corn rising silkily toward the back, peppers blossoming midway, runners of beans grasping their eager path along the trellis at the side. Last winter this had been a denuded mud-patch, a shit-strewn dog run. Wildflowers from seeds Toby had helped plant in April crowded now against the fence at the far end. In her shoulders Susannah felt the memory of muscle fatigue from the hoeing she had done at the end of March.

Yet last December, she had never heard of this woman, never thought of the family connected to Toby's new heart except with a melting sensation of bittersweet gratitude. It had all happened too fast, like the balloon. It had all seemed safe, an act of healing. In fact the whole process was more like tumor growth, invading the good tissue, establishing its deadly place.

Reluctantly she went inside, the house dark after the fierce sun. "This isn't about Toby," she said.

Linsey stood at the sink, scrubbing her nails with a brush. "For some of us, it is."

"It's about you and me. What we have a right to."

Linsey turned. Without the sun hat, her hair hung flat against her head, and the bones of her face looked raw. "I want to see your boy safe. I told your husband that. I don't know why you can't keep him that way, but you can't seem to. Now if some lawyer or other asks me, I'll tell him just the way I'm telling you."

"You're jealous, and bereaved, and guilty, and you want your pound of flesh."

"I want to do some good!"

"Bullshit," said Susannah. At the table, slightly deflated, sat the permanent resident of the kitchen, a blow-up bit of tomfoolery called Safe-T-Man, intended to fool cops cruising carpool lanes. Unaccountably she touched its plastic hair. She drew a long breath. "I want you to stay away from my family for a while, Linsey. It may astonish you, but we were managing okay before. It was a really hard, hard time, but we were managing. We didn't make all that many mistakes. Now we're at risk, and Nick was right; it's because of you. I will never *ever* stop being grateful and sorry. But I want you gone."

"You can't make me go," said Linsey. She'd turned away again; she spoke toward the sink. Her voice was stubborn, the voice of an adolescent girl.

"I can't make you leave Roanoke, no. But I don't want you"—Susannah backed toward the door; she held her hands palm-out in front of her, doing a sort of abbreviated breast-stroke, pushing away the air—"I don't want you in our *lives*, any more."

Chapter 17

*B*y midday, Nicholas and Toby were home. Nick was at the point where he made the three-hour drive from Durham in a hypnotic state, and found himself on the arterial skirting Roanoke Mountain without quite knowing when or how he'd made the switches that had brought him north and west. He and Toby had spent the time playing Sports Twenty, which was Toby's version of Twenty Questions, only restricted to sports personalities. Toby's last choice had been Rebecca Lobos, who played basketball for the New York Liberty. He couldn't believe his dad hadn't guessed that one. Is she a figure skater? Nick had asked. Does she play tennis? Do gymnastics? When he gave up, he asked Toby if his mom had coached him on girl athletes. Geez, no, Dad, Toby had said, everyone knows who Lobos is. She *rocks*.

Funny, Nick thought, how the first real lie they'd ever told Toby had been about the sex of his new heart. A boy, they'd said. A boy who died in an accident. And they'd have stuck with that lie, defended that lie, if Linsey hadn't gotten in touch. A girl heart is different, Toby had repeated, weeping angrily on his bed. He'd rather have died than sew a girl heart into his chest.

Next he'd said that Max must never know. Max wouldn't play with a girl heart. That's the stupidest thing I ever heard, Nick had said. Max plays with *you*, not with your heart. But Susannah said Never mind, never mind, and promised that Max would never find out. The girl's mother lived three hundred miles away; it wasn't exactly a difficult secret to keep. Then Linsey had come to Roanoke, and Brooke had come out of the closet.

Susannah was at the lab, of course. Coal needed water. Nick filled the dog's bowl, then boiled water for himself in the microwave and spooned Folger's Instant. He waited until the granules dissolved on the surface, their rock-candy sheen gone oily and flat, before he stirred and added sugar. Susannah would wrinkle her nose at such brew, but Nick sipped and remembered cold mornings in the Sierra, water boiling in a tin saucepan over an open fire, a knife-opened can of Pet milk.

Another life.

He opened the piano, set his mug on a coaster, ran a few left-handed scales. From here he could see Toby, on the blacktop. The kid had slimmed down from a month before, despite the occasional Pop Tart. Every morning he weighed himself. You really going out for the team in the fall? Nick had asked on the way home, and Toby had answered, Duh, Dad. But then the kid had changed the subject, wanted to know if Brooke's heart would replace the cells they'd just nipped off in Durham. He'd grown up a little, their boy, grown more aware. Natural, Nick thought, reaching for his coffee with his right thumb and palm while his left fingers ran a Coltrane bass. Natural for any kid to change. Though if you looked at Toby the way that space-head Linsey Hunter did, part of the change was Brooke.

It wasn't hard to believe, now that he'd seen pictures of her. You could spot the sturdy, brainy, sad-eyed kid in Toby's quick fluid movements on the blacktop. Her heart helped push the basketball off Toby's shoulder and loft it to the net. It was like—what was that called, when a painter painted over an old canvas? Pentimento. Or like the echo of Bach polyphony in a Miles Davis riff. Yeats had said it—he was pretty sure it had been Yeats—in that poem about his daughter. *Hearts are not had as a gift but hearts are earned*—he could hear the prof recite it still, her bony chin and trembling voice. His kid was earning, had earned plenty.

The phone rang: Susannah. Yes, the drive was fine. Yes, Toby was shooting hoops. He had fifteen minutes left. Yes, Lieberman had said they could stretch it to forty now, and Nick would be gentle, but Dennis Rodman was coming in when Nick called time. No, they hadn't stopped at McDonald's. Yes, he knew she had to be at the lab till eight. No, Linsey had not called.

She was so tight. Tired and tight. She'd called, surely, to ask about the biopsy results, and then fired off too many questions and lost the main one. Nick sighed, his hand resting on the phone. Even with all the tension around these trips to Durham, he was glad when his turn came, and he got away with Toby for a night. Susannah accused him of down-sizing his life. Well, maybe. Sipping his oily coffee, Nick sniffed the latent odor of caution that hung around all his little projects. But if so, then she upsized hers. Used up all the air and complained she couldn't breathe. Even those six months she'd taken off from the lab—she'd spent it with Toby, yes, they both had, spent the time fanatically. But then late at night, she'd glued herself to med sites on the Web, digging out the lat-est on cardiomyopathy to challenge Ben Lieberman's diagnosis; she'd signed on for another committee at the med school; she'd helped that lab assistant, Tomiko, with her dissertation. And do you notice, he'd asked, how you've been leaving the coffee machine on? How you let Coal go thirsty? How you left the groceries in the rain, the lights on in the car, your grant proposals in the hospital waiting room?

Thank goodness, she said when her mood was light and sweet, I have such a man to watch over me. Her full upper lip, the white teeth below as she grinned, stretching the scar on her chin to a curved dimple. Think-ing of her even now—the tense voice on the phone, raspy with espresso, burdened with agendas that didn't include him—Nick started to feel aroused. He let his hand graze past his crotch, anticipating.

The fact was that even in overdrive, Susannah ran through his mind like a tune he couldn't shake. Always it had been this way. The remark-able density of her breasts, the slope of her hip, the way goose bumps rose to his hand there. In bed, night before last, in the middle of quar-reling, something to do with the balloon, the accident, he'd pulled her toward him by the hips. Carefully he had undone each of the covered buttons of her silk blouse. Naked, he'd laced his good hand through her fine spun hair. When she'd come, her cry had set him off, and he'd cli-maxed inside her, no time to withdraw. Oh love, love, she'd said, and they hadn't argued, any more.

She had no way to comprehend how deep she lay in him. By Susannah's grace, he sometimes thought, he existed.

Closing the piano lid, he went to check the fish pond. Outside was all rich light and sharp shadows, the high sun of June. The lush plant life exhaled oxygen, and he sucked it in. Later he'd drive to the shop down-town, open it for after-school hours. Meanwhile, deep in the yard, where a pocket of cool remained, the tiny water outlet was burbling away. Tanger-ine fish roamed the gray depths of the pond. It gave him disproportionate pleasure to tap the block of cement at the side and make them gather, as if hooked, and then suck down the confetti of their food. He'd even starting risking names: Althea, Guinevere, Marguerite. Already they had their favorite crevices; they anticipated the slant of light and the falling of papery seeds from the tall maple. They knew no other world and missed none.

The rhythm of the bouncing ball halted. Nick heard Toby, trotting over the long grass. "You feeding 'em?" Toby said breathily.

"A little. I forgot to ask Mom if she did."

"That one's Marguerite, right?" Toby pointed with a dirty finger at a slender, green-speckled carp.

"No, that's Althea."

"Does that one have a name?"

"Which?"

"The kind of pale one, by the pipe."

"Not yet. That guy's still new."

"I want to give it a boy name."

Nick tossed a few crumbs in the direction of the fish Toby had pointed out, but one of the others got there first. "Okay," he said.

"Charlie," said Toby.

"Charlie," Nick repeated. "Here, Charlie!"

Briefly the pale fish darted toward the surface, grabbed a sprinkle.

"But I'm not sure yet." Toby crouched. "Another one might be Charlie. Can I think about it?"

"He looks like a good Charlie to me," said Nick, straightening.

"Maybe. I just want to be sure," Toby said. He stuck his dirty finger in the pond, and one of the more aggressive carp tried to kiss it. "I might name a couple of them," he said.

From the open door of the back deck, the shrill of the phone. Nick jogged toward the house. Behind him, Toby headed back across the yard, dribbling. "Five minute warning, kiddo!" Nick called on his way up the stairs.

"C'mon, Dad!"

"Half-hour rest and we'll play horse."

"No! One on one!"

"If you'll say half-hour rest."

"In five minutes."

"In five. Right."

"Okay," said Toby, and he executed a flawless reverse lay up. If the kid had had a strong heart, Nick sometimes thought, there'd have been no telling.

"We don't know yet, Susannah," he said as he picked up in the kitchen.

"Hi, Nick. It's Ben Lieberman."

"Sorry. The wife's been badgering me. Hi."

"Badgering you for the biopsy report."

"More like afternoon sex."

Ben laughed. He sounded as if he was in training for a laugh track. "I hope she gets it," he said.

"It's those lab tables. Too high up. And she refuses to come home."

"Women." Ben put on the laugh track again, a shorter version. "Listen. Speaking of labs."

"Mine's a black mix. I thought you were a people doctor."

"Skated past me, Nick."

"Dog joke." Nick lowered himself to a kitchen chair, and Coal crawled out from under the table, tail wagging. "Give me the good news."

"We're at 3 percent tissue degeneration."

"This is not the good news I'm used to, Ben."

"Well, 3 percent is just over the edge. It's not, you know, disastrous."

"More like alarming."

"A little alarming, yeah. The guys in Durham detect rejection at 2 percent degeneration. Toby's been well under 1 percent, up to now."

Nick scratched Coal behind his ears. The dog was getting old, white around the jowls. It had arrived in their lives as an omen. One day, while he and Susannah were hoping to have a kid, one of his customers had walked in with a Lab pup that he refused to take away. Nick had owned the shop less than a year, then; the rafting trip had taken place only the summer before; his expedition equipment still filled the barn behind the house he and Susannah rented in the hills. He'd brought the black puppy home, and a month later Toby was conceived. "So," he said to Lieberman, "what do we do?"

"I've faxed Susannah the report. The team out in Durham usually recommends notching up the cyclosporine, moderating exercise, and taking another biopsy in four weeks. And calling them, of course, if we notice anything in between."

Ben Lieberman, according to the degrees on his office wall, was board certified. Patients came to him from Blacksburg, from Charlottesville. Yet his best asset seemed the ability to remind people to call in situations where only a fool would *not* call. "We haven't noticed anything," said Nick, running his fingerless hand over his face.

"You wouldn't necessarily. That's why the biop is so crucial. But not to worry. This is all routine. Thirty percent have some sort of rejection crisis in the first year. Right now is Toby's turn, is all. Sort of like marriage, you know. The honeymoon's over, and he and his heart are having their first tiff."

Hanging up, Nick finished his coffee in small, controlled sips. Then he went to the screen door. Listening carefully, blocking out the noise of the interstate, he could hear Toby muttering under his breath, like a sports announcer: "*And then Iverson takes the ball, and it's a breakaway, dishes it off to McKee, nope, there's a magnificent steal by Latrell Sprewell folks, and he's at the three-point line and shoots, there's the whistle, foul by Matumbo, he'll go to the line now with three minutes and fifteen seconds left in the quarter.*"

In a minute he'd call him in. Toby would say he couldn't have been playing more than a half-hour, and Nick would say yeah, but Dr. Lieberman called and we have to cut back, and they'd fight it out, and he'd end up swearing silently at his only son the sickly spoiled brat.

For now, though, he watched him pivot and soar, his graceful offspring. Ten months ago he'd been near death. Nine months ago they'd said good-bye to him, pasty and bloated and drugged past personality, and watched the gurney wheel him away to a room where a dead girl's heart sat in a Styrofoam cooler.

Nick shut his eyes. He saw Toby's chest laid open like that video the team at Duke had shown them, the ribs lifted like a big chicken breast. He saw Toby's sick heart lifted out, the girl's healthy heart stitched in. When the clamps were removed, the pink muscle had quivered and then beat hard, bang once and then bang again and again. Nick squeezed his eyes and saw it. Like a blind animal bound and flayed, it beat; like a newly harnessed slave.

Chapter 18

*T*here's news, was the way Toby's dad had put it. News from the team in Durham, the ones who ran the line up Toby's vein and nipped at Brooke's heart. News, and now they'd increased the cyclosporine, because Brooke's heart was dying.

Rejection, they said. But that was just another word, like when you talked about putting a dog to sleep. He wasn't rejecting Brooke's heart. At first, maybe. Because it was a girl heart. Now, she was his conjoined twin, like those sisters in *People*. He felt what she felt. Like when Charlie had arrived, walking down the green hill at the carnival, when Toby was up in the balloon, and the heart had kicked. A transplanted heart wasn't supposed to do that, have those sudden reactions. Or when they were skateboarding, the day before Dr. Griffiths's funeral, and he felt his heart tug and float away while Charlie was doing those awesome spirals, even though he'd never cared much about skateboarding before.

You didn't reject your conjoined twin's heart. It was your heart, too.

And still he had to take more cyclosporine, and it was making things worse on the rest of him. Before, it was just the extra hair he had to worry about. Now the medicine was fattening him up, inside and out. He'd found a pimple, like Max got, even though Max was three years older. He did forty sit-ups and twenty push-ups a day so he wouldn't get flabby. When he was in the NBA, he didn't want people saying stuff about him the way they did about Shaquille O'Neal, calling him a tank. You couldn't use excuses like having someone else's heart when you were in the NBA.

At least he could tell Max about the medicine. Max was back from Atlanta, the same old Max. Yesterday Toby had shown him his upper arms, where the dark hair was growing even on his shoulders. "Monkey man!" Max had called him. He'd shown Toby how to pop the pimple. They played like always. Only Toby didn't talk about Brooke being his twin. Especially not now, not when her heart was dying.

Lying down for the cyclosporine drip, Toby pressed his hand over the spot where Brooke's heart labored. In circles he massaged the muscles, the way he'd seen Max's mom do on Max's baby sister's back when she fussed. Don't die, he whispered. And felt sure, the way a twin would feel it, that the dying hadn't started with him. Hadn't even started when her brain died. But had started before then, her heart begging off. Heading for the showers, the sportscasters would say, and he had just this one job, to get her back in the game.

From the couch in the TV room he could hear his mom on the phone with Linsey. He'd picked up, when Linsey called. "Hey, Linsey!" he'd said in this fake cheery voice. He didn't want her to know, about Brooke's heart dying. "How was Charlie's show? Were there lots of people? Is he coming back?"

"It was *awesome*, Toby," she said. "You have got to hear Charlie play. I felt so proud I could bust. You doing okay?"

"Sure! I'm great!"

"Those doctors didn't give you too much of a work over, huh?"

"Piece of cake, Linsey," he'd said, and then she'd asked to talk to his mom. And his mom had made her wait while she got the drip going and set Toby up to lie here in the den. Now she was talking out in the kitchen where he couldn't make out the words. He hadn't liked how Linsey sounded; she'd been just as fake as he was, though she didn't know anything about the biopsy. And now he heard his Mom's voice sharp and bitter, like she was talking to one of those telemarketing morons. Finally she got off and came to check his drip, and he asked if he could go up to Linsey's.

"No, honey," she said. Not *Later*, or *Not today*, but *No*.

"Aw, c'mon," he said. "Max is at his aunt's house till five. There's nothing to do around here."

"Read a book. Walk in the meadow."

"Linsey's got better books. I haven't seen her for a *week*. She needs help weeding her garden."

"I said no, Toby."

"But you didn't say why."

"I am learning," his mom said, rolling away the IV pole, "to be more like your dad. No means no. You know the reasons. I don't have to repeat them to you."

He didn't know the reasons. She sounded angry, he knew that, and he couldn't remember the last time his mom sounded angry. Slowly he stood from the couch where he'd been lying for the drip. When she came close to him, he reached out, like a blind person feeling for the wall. She turned and hugged him close. His head came up to her chest now, and when she held him he felt her breasts on either side of him. Now that felt great. And then she held on even longer than he did, as if she'd lost something. "My Toby," she said. "We are going to lick this thing. You bet we are."

He thought she meant the dying of Brooke's heart, the *rejection*, but he couldn't be sure. She could just as well mean the heart attack, the one that got Dr. Griffiths and was waiting to get Toby. With Brooke dying, what protection did he have against the heart attack?

But his mom didn't mean those things. She just meant he wouldn't always have the drip. He nodded, his nose bumping her soft skin.

"Come walk the dog with me," she said, letting him go.

"Nah."

"Sure. We'll look for blackberries by the river. Come on."

"You can walk him yourself. You don't need me."

"Not to walk Coal, I don't. For company, I do."

They crossed the street and cut around Max's house to the meadow, thigh-high now with grass and wildflowers. The bluebonnets were bright eyes following them. Coal lunged and waded through the growth, his black back like a dolphin's. Toby's mom held the leash coiled in her hands. She didn't like to leash the dog. His dad always did, and his dad took the sidewalks; he said there were ticks in the meadow. Once or twice Toby chased after Coal, and when they got back, his mom said she couldn't believe how fast he could run. The sun pricked the back of his neck, where he was already burnt.

"It's hot," he said, panting as they left the meadow for the dirt path that led past the tin-sided warehouse—*Auto Parts* fading on the shingle, a lopsided basketball hoop in the gravel lot—down to the river.

"We should have signed you up for something, Tobe. Camp, or something. We didn't realize you'd be doing so well."

"Camp's stupid."

"How do you know? You've never gone."

"Well, I would have. After second grade. If I hadn't got sick."

"But you did get sick, so you haven't had the chance yet."

"Give it up, Mom," said Toby, stopped at the stone fountain in the park. "Too late for that stuff."

When he straightened up, she put her hand on his head. She didn't want to think it was too late for anything, that was his mom; she wanted to go back in time to that baby basketball camp and start everything over only with Brooke's heart in place and not dying.

They picked the ripest berries, at the river, while Coal plunged neck-deep in the water. Toby wandered ahead to check what the thin line-up of fisherman had brought in. "Brooke used to go fishing," he said when his mom caught up.

"With her dad, yeah. I know."

"She must have been real patient."

His mom shrugged. "Maybe. I guess. Sometimes they stock the ponds, and the fish bite fast."

"Not where Brooke and her dad went. They went to wild places. She baited her own hook, with grasshoppers."

He didn't like the way his mom chuckled. "Linsey tell you this?"

"No. I just know it. From the pictures. From what I know."

"Well." She picked through the berries in the palm of her hand. Running beside them, the river gurgled exactly the way it was supposed to— as if a bunch of people underwater were tuning up instruments. "It was a tragedy. Like Dr. Griffiths in the balloon, that was a tragedy. But we go on, Toby. It doesn't help to look back."

"Is that what you were mad at Linsey about on the phone? Because she's looking back?"

"Toby, Toby. Here." His mom plucked the fattest, blackest berry yet, like a jammed-up cluster of grapes, and gave it to him. Her own lips were stained purple, like a kid's. "I wasn't *mad* at Linsey. I have no reason to be mad at Linsey."

"How come I can't go up to her house then?"

"You—" His mom held her breath and then blew it out. "These are grown-up things, Tobe. They don't make a lot of sense to start with, and if I tried explaining them to a kid they'd make even less. Let's just say Linsey needs to stay away from us for a little bit."

"Is that what she says?"

He could tell his mom didn't want to lie. Lying was one of those things grown-ups almost never did straight out because they'd made such a big deal of it that they couldn't just go and do the thing, the way he'd lied about taking the Minipress that time. Instead they slipped and slid, and you weren't supposed to notice that the truth was over *here* while they'd traveled all the way over *there*. This time, sliding, his mom lifted her chin and said, "Yes, actually. She might even go away. She doesn't even want us calling her, honey. Not for a while."

"What's a while?"

"A while is a while." She offered him another fat one, but he shook his head. "Okay, then," she said, as if they had made their way together through a narrow gate. "Let's call that pooch and get home."

She uncoiled the leash. "Co-oal!" Toby cried. The fishermen looked annoyed at them for scaring the fish. "Co-oal!"

His mom turned and shaded her eyes against the sun. The river was flat. No splashing got in the way of the current by the bank. "C'mon, Coal!" she said as if Coal was a kid. "Stop fooling!"

Toby started back, looking left toward the park with its gazebos and trash cans, right toward the fringe of high grass and the water. His dad would have had Coal on a leash. Even when Coal wanted to wade in the water, he kept the leash hooked; it was extra long, he said, and nylon, so there wasn't any reason to let the dog off it. But his mom liked Coal to be free. Toby walked and called. Then ran. He tried to whistle, but it came out like wind through a window crack. "Co-oal!" came his mom's voice behind him, the voice that tried so hard not to lie. They called and searched, ran and stood still. With the useless blue leash, Toby's mom beat at the tall growth as if she was looking for a small cat or an escaped turtle. Toby lifted his head and shouted Coal's name to the trees as if he was calling Brooke, calling Brooke's heart back from whatever heaven hearts float off to.

Finally he thought he was going to have to tell his mom one of those grown-up half-truths. He was going to trudge back to where she stood straining her eyes over the river and tell her not to worry, Coal would find his way home, Dad wouldn't be all that mad. He was just putting the words together in his head when the black streak went by on his left and Brooke's heart thunked right back into his chest.

"Coal, you bad dog," his mom said when she'd got her face licked. But Toby noticed she used the leash, all the way home.

Chapter 19

*I*t was not Linsey's first nighttime visit to the Tudor house. Way back in March she had come, just once, to peek, in a funny panic, thinking Brooke's heart could have stopped, and she wouldn't know till morning. The second month she'd come each Saturday night. By Wednesdays she was already feeling tight in the chest, thinking what she would do. Thursday, Friday, Saturday until midnight she waited; then she coasted to the bottom of Tinker Mountain and took the arterial through the city. Parking a few houses down, she would make her way down a neighbor's drive, then through the forsythia bushes to the Ameses' back yard. Toby's room gave onto a little balcony against which leaned an oak limb that she'd heard Nicholas say he meant to lop off. From the balcony she could make out how cluttered Toby's room always was, how the night light in the corner cast shadows from sports equipment, piles of clothes, the IV pole standing guard—like Safe-T-Man—from the corner. Slowly she would turn the knob on the French doors of the second-floor balcony. Like a breath of wind she stepped into the room.

Stretched on his side, arm flung out from under the pillow, Toby inhaled sleep. His breath shuddered; a kind of mist came off his cheek, like from a garden. Once she'd touched her hand there, back when the steroid dose was low and you could make out his cheekbones. Another time she terrified herself when she slipped into the dark room, stepped gingerly over the clothes strewn on the floor, and made out a form half-curled over Toby's, on the narrow bed. Dark jacket, white skirt, fine cropped hair on the pillow: Susannah. Backwards Linsey had stepped, not daring to turn. In silence out to the balcony, then madly down the oak, scraping her wrist, stumbling down the sidewalk as if she'd been mugged. Then she was back in her car again, out of their neighborhood, following the lights toward the arterial and back up the mountain.

"Get a cat," Charlie had told her before he drove on to Richmond. "Get a canary. Get a two-toed sloth; they're calm and very affectionate."

Now it was July, hot even at night, the fireflies swarming. Six times Linsey had called since Toby came back from Durham. The first time, she had exchanged maybe ten words with Toby before Susannah picked up. Yes, Toby was fine, Susannah had said, and the biopsy was normal; everything was as normal as it could be; would Linsey please leave them in peace? When Linsey called again, the machine had clicked on with Nick's Yankee voice. So she had called again the next day. And again, and again.

Just the other day she had dared to drive into their neighborhood in the afternoon, and had spotted Susannah and Toby taking their big black dog for a walk. Parking, she'd followed to the bridge over the Roanoke River and then stood there, watching them pick and eat blackberries. They almost lost their dog, which Susannah let run off by itself. It swam a ways out in the river and then came back and shook off. Losing their scent, it trotted up the bridge to where Linsey was standing. "Hey guy," she'd said, leaning to scratch its wet head. She could have stolen that dog and no one the wiser. But she shooed it on back and got, instead, the pleasure of watching Toby clap his hands and cry out "Mom! Coal! Coal's here!"

John wouldn't hear talk of a dog. Got to be a pretty sorry human, he said, goes looking for his best friend in some other predator species. Ninety-nine percent of domestic dog breeds, he said, wouldn't survive two weeks in the wild. Every fit thing bred right out of them. He preferred to sit rock-still three hours in the woods that rose behind their house, a bowl of apples and corn cobs at his feet, waiting on the deer that normally wreaked havoc on Linsey's garden, to see if his stillness and smell would convince them he hadn't touched meat for twenty-five years. The days they came—Linsey remembered a half-dozen, maybe, in the ten years—you'd have thought he was a big game hunter who'd bagged an elephant and pulled the tusks. He was that happy, that high. He made love to every inch of her body those nights. Then she'd go out the next morning and find the deer in her spinach. Right then she'd have given anything for an old hound dog to keep them at bay. She'd even thought, once, of her dad's shotgun. She didn't mention either of these ideas to John. She planted more spinach, set the garlic out, fixed the wire fence.

She would have liked to take Susannah's dog, but she hadn't. She hadn't taken anything. Only now she crept around Nick's goldfish pond, its four plump orange carp gliding invisible under the dark surface. She could just barely make out the gurgle of circulating water. On one of the flat rocks by the pond someone had left a mug of beer, and a moth was struggling in the amber. Dipping two fingers in, she lifted the creature out. It panted on the table a few seconds, drying its wings, then lifted limply off. Overhead a bat swooped; probably scooped it up.

Coming around the house, she steered clear of the deck. "It comes on with movement," Susannah had said of the spotlight that looked over the back yard. In May, when the dark still fell early, they would sit out here and move their arms or heads each time the light blinked out, and it would flick back on.

Linsey started up the oak tree. From inside the house she could hear a light, quick jazz piece on the piano; Nicholas, playing one-handed. A professional—that's what Susannah said he was—before the accident that took his hand. Brooke could have been a professional, one day. She could have played with Charlie, little duets. Ramrod-straight, Brooke used to sit on the black bench, her hands spidering the keys.

Inside, Susannah paced in her study. Portable phone to her ear, she trooped in front of a big mural she'd told Linsey she'd bought at an auction in London, one of those abstracts people are always saying they could have painted with their fingers when they were five. Books were stacked everywhere, and little throw rugs that didn't match each other. Mail loitered on a side table, and someone had left shoes on the floor with socks lolling out of them like dogs' thick tongues. A messy house, Linsey thought. The antique clock on the mantel read a permanent five-thirteen; broken clocks and clutter, bad *feng shui*.

Up the tree, out onto the thick limb. Four days ago she'd taken the wrap off her ankle. It held as she climbed, but like a joint of glass. Above her head shone Toby's light, the amber square with the top of his Charles Barkley poster barely visible. As she reached the balcony, the window went dark. He'd taken his meds, finished reading his *Sports Illustrated for Kids*; he was settling under the covers, one hand under his left nipple to bid goodnight to Brooke. His French doors were open. She scratched at the dark screen.

"Linsey?" he said from the bed.

"Ssh." She unlatched the screen and stepped in. "How'd you know it was me?"

"Looked like you," he whispered in his high boy's voice. "You going on a sneak?"

"I couldn't sleep. Came to see how you're doing."

"Not too good." He hung his head. "They put me on more meds. How come you don't want us to call you?"

"Who told you that?"

He shrugged.

"Well, I do want you to call me. Why else you think I went to all this trouble to visit you?"

"You sneaked up here," said Toby. "Don't you have a sprained ankle?"

"It's better now."

"You shouldn't of hung on that rope."

"I thought I could reel you in."

"Like reeling in a whale!" Toby shook his head. "Stupid."

"Scooch over in the bed. I'll sit on the side." She straightened the coverlet; snapped on the light from where she sat, and taking a clean tissue from her pocket ran it around the lamp and over the base. She scooped a dozen baseball cards from the floor and tapped them together, like a deck.

"I'm not supposed to be reading," said Toby, thumbing his book. "I'm supposed to be asleep. Don't tell my mom."

"I won't if you won't."

"I think the meds keep me awake. They make me jumpy."

"Why d'you have to take more meds? What'd the biopsy say?"

"I don't know." He glanced quickly at her, but the bedside light was behind him.

"I think you do."

"They never tell me anything. Just 'Take your meds.' They never tell me why, or what'll happen if I don't."

"One of those meds makes you hairy." Linsey ran a finger down Toby's arm.

"Yeah. Another makes you fat."

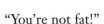

"You're not fat!"

"*And* it gives me pimples. Look."

"I think pimples are very grown-up."

"Fine, then *you* have 'em."

"What'd the biopsy say?"

"I *told* you."

"Are these different meds?"

"Had to do a drip. Today was the last day."

"Toby, did they say"—she was tracing his cotton coverlet with her hand, she wasn't any more able to look at him than he was at her—"Did they use the word *rejection*?"

"I dunno."

He shifted in the bed. It was like a knife slicing her, breast to gut. "Let's just—let's just say they did. What d'you think about that?"

"I dunno."

"I don't believe you."

"Okay. Don't." Toby pulled the light coverlet up to his chin, as if he were cold in the steamy night, and slid his body downward. He turned his face away from her. "Maybe they did," he said in a whisper.

"Say they did. How you feeling about that?"

"I don't like it."

"Cause you'd have to have a new transplant?"

"No." He squirmed a little, under the sheet. From downstairs Linsey could hear stray notes, on the piano. No talking, though. No scratching from the dog. "Because," Toby said, "I would die."

Carefully Linsey lifted a lock of his hair from his forehead and brushed it over to the side. "You like having Brooke's heart, don't you?"

"It's not that way."

"Course not. It's hard to explain. But you think . . . if Brooke lived here . . . don't you think you'd be friends?"

Toby turned his face. He looked at her for a long while. His face—pudgy, but she'd seen pictures, she could make out the lines of his cheekbones and jaw, a heart-shaped face they called it, the chin slightly pointed—was so still it reminded her of Brooke's face as she'd seen it in dreams, staring dead but floating toward her through water or mist. "Brooke was a girl," he said.

"So?"

"She didn't like sports. All my friends like sports."

"But except for that."

"Except for what?"

"Except for being a girl, you'd like her?"

"I told you. It's not like that."

"What's it like, then?"

Under the covers, Toby was rubbing his chest. "Every morning I wake up," he said, "and it's like there's somebody else in bed with me. And not just in bed. In everything. It's like the whole world is this other person. It's not about liking her. It's about"—he licked his lips—"learning to be in her. So she won't just click off, the way you can click off the TV."

"You've got it backwards, Tobe. *She's* in *you*."

More sounds from downstairs—Susannah, saying something sharp. Any second and she'd come check on Toby. As Linsey started to stand, Toby caught her by the wrist. "If you ever talk to her?" he said, whispering again. "I mean, I know that's a weird thing to say, but I saw a movie, in the hospital, where this lady could talk to her boyfriend once, after— you know. Will you tell her, I did my best? Okay?"

"Okay, Tobe." Linsey leaned down; brushed her cheek against his moist forehead. "You know, this is the second time I've climbed into a boy's bedroom."

"You did it to Charlie?"

"No, not Charlie. Another boy."

"Was he asleep?"

"If he was"—she tiptoed backwards, toward the French doors—"I woke him up. Sweet dreams now."

"Don't let the bed bugs bite," said Toby.

Silently she stepped onto the balcony and swung down the tree. That night—the night she'd first bedded John, better than the nights that followed—had been a lot like this one. Dry, windy, moonless, clouds scudding across the twinkly stars. The feeling inside her was the same too—as if she might see a black cat or a shooting star, might draw the Queen of Spades from her pocket or the Jack of Diamonds. She looked to see if Toby would watch for her from the window, but he didn't. In less than a minute there came voices, and his light went out.

Chapter 20

For all that the plastic knights and lead Rebels bored Toby, he was a diligent helper, those days when Susannah spent each waking hour at the lab and Nick had to keep the shop open. He was especially good at razoring open the new boxes and setting up the displays. He faced the plastic packages out, in logical sequence, on the long hooks, moving the slow sellers down and bulleting the new prices. And he had a talent for posing the new figures, half-hiding them behind resined trees or balancing them down mountaintops so that the kids who did love this stuff came in and wanted to buy the whole scene.

On the older, valuable collections, Toby was less helpful. Trying to clean them with the tiny metal brushes Nick hung over the sink in the back of the shop, he missed most of the residue and over scrubbed the rest. "Their faces aren't as good," he said of the lead soldiers.

"You're wrong, champ. They're better. Only they're made of soft metal, so they've rubbed off a little."

"That's why they're not as good."

The boys who came into the shop acknowledged Toby, but not as one of them. They were dropped off by their mothers, with their allowances fisted and destined partly for Soldiers on a Shelf and partly for On Deck, the shop across the square that sold baseball and Magic cards. They gabbled fiercely and looked on Toby as a source of information rather than opinion. They knew who Toby was at school, too, Toby told Nick. He'd hear one say to another, "Hey, there goes the kid whose dad runs the soldier shop," and they'd ask him if any new Imperial kits were in.

"You like it, that they know you?" Nick asked. They were midway through the trial period, between the news of rejection and the next biopsy. They had yet to see whether the hit of cyclosporine was working. But already the drug tired Toby out; he was content to hang out at the shop and play Nintendo at home.

"It's better than when they say, 'Hey, there goes the kid with the monkey heart.'"

"Do they say that?"

"Sometimes. Not since I beat Kevin Ryder up."

"You didn't beat Kevin Ryder up!"

"Well, I punched him. On the playground. I had to go to the principal's office."

"Toby! You didn't tell us this!"

Toby shrugged. He'd just finished setting up a jousting display, one knight half-toppled from his horse. "I don't tell you a lot of things," he said.

"Such as?"

"I saw Linsey."

"Okay. That's okay. What's the big secret there?"

"Mom's mad at Linsey. And you always hated her."

"I have never hated her, Toby. I don't even know her all that well."

"Well, you could if you wanted to."

"Thanks for the advice," said Nick. He finished tallying the delivery, then came over to inspect the display. "Great job you've done here, buddy."

"Mm."

Nick paused. He adjusted his glasses. Toby was looking away from him, affecting keen interest in the line of trees edging the display. "You want me to try harder," he said gently, "with Linsey?"

"Well, it's not like she did anything to hurt you."

"You have a point, there."

"She could even come in and help you here. When I go back to school, I mean. She could use a job."

"You think she'd like selling miniature war-mongers?"

"What?"

"Never mind. If I need to hire, I'll keep her in mind."

The door tinkled; a pair of boys, browsing the new kits. Toby lingered near them; he knew part of his job was to make sure nothing slipped into a boy's pocket. They each bought Star Wars figures—solemnly, setting the boxes on the counter as if they were conducting weapons sales. When they'd left, Toby perched on the stool by the counter and flipped through the catalog. "Where'd you get the name, Dad?" he asked.

"What name?"

"Soldiers on a Shelf."

"Oh. Well. It was a little joke your mom and I came up with. I mean, first off, that's where the little guys sit mostly, right?"

"Well, not if you're playing with them. And not here." Toby waved his arm over the tables and window displays, the racks and counters.

"For collectors, though."

"Okay."

"Plus there's this other meaning. When you stop doing something— when you get too old or not good enough at it anymore—people say you're on the shelf. So for these guys"—Nick held up a Russian grenadier—"the shelf is their retirement. They don't have to fight for the Tsar, any more."

Toby took the grenadier. He looked pale with the increased meds, his skin waxy as cheese. And yet, Nick thought with surprise, a painter would love him this way. The eyes wide and glassy, the tiny, noble hook of the nose, the downy hair at the back of his neck. He looked like a beautiful Victorian child. "Did you really want to do this," he said, "when you grew up?"

Nick chuckled. "Hardly, kiddo. But I'm not complaining."

"What *did* you want to do?"

Nick took the other stool. From the back room, where the sink was, came the tinny chatter of the radio. "I wasn't going to spend my whole life running rapids and flying balloons, if that's what you mean."

"So you're on the shelf. Like the soldiers."

"Well." Nick snorted. "Look. A body has to quit on that stuff one time or another, Tobe. Even if you don't hurt your hand. Even if you don't have a heart problem. Bodies slow down. If I'd been a little luckier"—he held up his right hand and wiggled the knuckles—"I'd have tried to do something with the piano. Maybe taught lessons, or played with the orchestra, or something."

"That doesn't sound like much fun."

"It would have been fun enough. But the shop is fun too."

"When you retire from the NBA," said Toby, settling his head onto his arm, "you usually run a camp, or become a sports announcer. I think I'll do the sports announcer."

"When you retire from the NBA, you mean."

"Yeah."

Nick looked at his son's waxen face and felt a sharp pain in his chest. They hurt, dreams did. It was out of that pain that he said, "You aren't really serious, are you, kiddo?"

"Course I am." Toby lifted his head; a spot of color came into his cheeks. "You never think I am. Just because it's Brooke's heart. If I'd got a boy heart you'd believe me."

"Toby—kiddo—it's got nothing to do with the sex of your heart. There are just some things that a transplant person can't do."

"There's nothing I can't do. Dr. Lieberman said so."

"He wasn't talking about the NBA."

"He was talking about the basketball team. I'm going to make the basketball team in the fall."

"I don't even know about that one, Tobe."

"Well, I do."

"You can't. Okay? You cannot now. We're in a new crisis here. That's why you've got to lie down for the drip every day, that's why—"

"Fuck you, okay?"

The words came with a gentleness that was even more shocking than the fact that Toby was saying them at all. He slid down from the stool and walked away, stiff as a mannequin, to the back of the shop. Nick took his glasses off and ran his palm over his face. All he wanted—all he needed, like a hunger—was to fold his son in his arms.

"Toby," he whispered, not calling him; wishing him back.

The door tinkled, opened, the afternoon light flooding in. Looking older and beat down came McGowan, the balloon operator, the Corsair collector.

"Come for a little free advice," McGowan said. "You busy?"

"Never too busy," said Nick. He glanced back at his son, bent studiously over the castle. "Coffee?"

McGowan had discovered ballooning when he retired at fifty-one after thirty years with the postal service. Collecting he'd taken up years before.

"I used to find little things along the route," he explained to Nick. "I'd ring the closest bell and ask if they'd dropped this or that, and they never wanted to be bothered. Pretty soon I had five thou worth of old coins, a couple thou worth of precious stones, and a few boxes of these little guys." He'd bought the balloon from the fellow who first took him up in it, a second cousin up in Lexington who died of liver cancer. "He followed all those hot-shots, you know, the English or Australians or whatnot, with their high-tech balloons and their fancy expeditions, looking to make it around the world. But me, I said the balloon wasn't for going nowhere in particular. Said it was meant to get a view of things, was all, and travel with the wind. The wind don't go nowhere in particular."

McGowan could understand why the Griffiths boy wanted to sue him, but he didn't see what satisfaction could come of it; he was divorced, lived on his pension, had sunk his savings into the balloon. As carnival entertainment, he'd managed to get a policy that offered $10,000 in liability per passenger. "They can have that," he said. "I'm all paid up, premium-wise. Soon's this blows over, I'm selling my rig. Going down to Florida—that's where my daughter is—and do some deep-sea fishing. You ever fished?"

"Not like that, no," Nick said. But he did know a guy, if McGowan was interested. A guy up in Pennsylvania who was always looking for a good balloon, and had the cash.

"That'd be real kind of you," said McGowan. "I guess I ought to sell my Corsairs, too. But they're a little more portable. Otherwise there's just my personal stuff, you know, you could fit it all in a Volkswagen. Me and the wife split years ago. You got a family, Mr. Ames?"

"My son's in the back."

"Hey, look at that. Likes his dad's hobby, does he?"

"Not much, actually. He, ah. . . . Do you recognize Toby, Mr. McGowan?"

"Well, now, I might could."

"He was in your balloon, the other day. The day of the accident."

"Oh," said McGowan. "Oh, my." He took off his glasses and shined them with a gray handkerchief. Nick pictured him in his blue postal uniform, his slight shoulders bent a little from the weight of his bag, trudging his route and dreaming of thin air. "He wasn't hurt, was he?"

"Couple bruises."

"I sure am glad. You'd probably be suing me, too, wouldn't you? If something happened to him."

"Hey, not all of us are litigious. An accident's an accident. Toby," Nick called, "come say hello to Mr. McGowan."

"I need to go home," said Toby darkly. He wouldn't look up from the castle. "I need to get the drip."

"Well," said McGowan, putting his glasses back on his thin nose, watery eyes, "I've taken up enough of your time, Mr. Ames. You sure are a kind man."

"Would you say"—Nick hesitated; he had just been called kind, and yet he did not feel kind—"as best you recollect, that Toby had anything to do with *causing* the accident?"

"Well, now, that." McGowan looked over at Toby, then down at his hands. "That's the part clearest in my mind. After that, it gets all mixed up, and mostly I got the damn gauges to blame for not adjusting the way they ought. But that part. It was all the big fellow, how he got out. I was going to put your wife in, see, for the ballast, and then the boy. Only something distracted her at the last minute—perfectly normal—and the fellow just had ants in his pants. Lets the boy in and he jumps out."

"So she was planning to get in. My wife."

"Oh, I insisted on it. Yessir. I never put a child in harm's way in my life. Got three of my own."

"*Dad*," Toby said. He'd moved to the front door, which he opened and shut to make it tinkle.

"Say hello to Mr. McGowan, Tobe."

"We gotta go."

"That's all right. I probably scare the little guy." McGowan set his coffee mug down and approached Toby. "I'm sorry about what happened that day," he said.

"'S all right," said Toby, keeping his eyes averted.

"I sure am glad you didn't come in harm's way."

"Yeah. Thanks."

"No one's fault," said Nick, and he meant it, or tried to mean it. Though when he finally caught Toby's eye—crouching down, taking Toby's chin between thumb and forefinger, turning Toby's face towards him—he couldn't read the answer he wanted there. He couldn't read anything at all.

Chapter 21

*T*here were times—over the Fourth of July, for instance, while they watched the local cheerleaders perform with flaming batons at Bluegrass Lake—when Susannah wondered about Linsey. Worried about her. Could imagine, even, how she sat in her balanced, light-filled kitchen awash in loneliness and grief. Susannah had seen her mother sit that way, the weeks after Toby died, her brother Toby, and behind the grief there had smoldered this unquenchable fury at a world that had so badly botched things.

He had been on a camping trip, Boy Scouts. Had complained of a tummy ache the night before, but Toby was always getting butterflies in his stomach, and anyhow when the Scoutmaster's station wagon drew up at their house just after dawn, Toby jumped out of bed and said he felt fine. The troop drove a hundred fifty miles, to Lake Moomaw in the Alleghenies, and there they hiked two hours, to a spot where they had a fine view of the dam. How long Toby held the pain in, who knew? No one, the doctors would say, can disguise the symptoms of acute appendicitis—but then no one knew Toby the way his family did. The campers made a litter for him, true Scouts, but on the way back, in the dark, one of the boys carrying fell and broke his leg. Toby reached the hospital in a coma.

You wanted someone to blame. Susannah, when she was little, had blamed the doctors, and then set out to become one. Her mother had driven the blame straight inside, where it nestled in malignant cells and did its business.

So Susannah sat with the other families, the display of local talent tossing feverish batons in the dark, and yearned after Linsey. Until she leaned back against Nick, and watched her own Toby's eyes shine in the dancing torchlight—and knew that the deeper emotion was relief.

Most of July, in any case, her waking minutes were consumed. New results from Tomiko's protocols had to be charted before the National Institutes of Health conference in August. She had to hold off weekly demands from Cantrex. A new shipment of mice arrived to be injected, monitored, their tick-sized tumors recorded. And there was the request, still sitting on her desk, for her résumé. From the dean's office. From the committee cobbled together to find a replacement for Marcus Griffiths.

When she paused long enough to feel anything—watching the robins in the morning from her study behind the kitchen, or sitting with Toby while he endured the IV—she spiraled around Nick. She felt him watching her. Even when he mentioned, lightly, that McGowan had been in the shop. McGowan, the balloon operator, looking pathetic, he said. Had Susannah known that Griffiths's son was suing the poor bastard?

"Yeah," she said. "They came to talk to me."

"You didn't tell me."

"I didn't want anything to do with it."

McGowan was wiped out, Nick said—accusingly? Or was that the twist Susannah added to his tone of voice? McGowan's business was done for, whether the lawsuit went through or not. "He says it was that big guy, getting out of the basket, that did it," Nick said. "If you had been in the basket rather than Toby, of course—"

"But I wasn't." There she went, spiraling, spinning downward into the trap. "I wanted to be, but I wasn't. Linsey—" She stopped herself. She was done with Linsey, not about to trade accusations. Had Nick simply believed Linsey, whom he disliked so much? They were sitting on the back deck, the night air studded with fireflies. "Linsey distracted me," she said.

"And so the whole thing's not your responsibility." He picked wax off the citronella candle. Toby had gone over to Max's. Nick was drinking a beer, his glass coppery in the light. He was tanned in midsummer, his muscles tight from six miles every morning, only his receding hairline giving proof to years. If she'd had to put a name to it, Susannah would have called Nick's condition bilious. Ben Lieberman's favorite Greek, Galen, would have prescribed cold sponges and a Spartan diet, rigor for the impetuous heart. "Is it?" he said.

"What's that got to do with McGowan?" she said, punting.

"It has to do with responsibility," he said, rolling the warm wax. "That's what a lawsuit is all about."

"I see." Even as she spiraled, she felt, strangely, calm. If she was losing Nick's trust—if that was the disaster looming here, as failure was the threat in the lab—then she had no choice but to plow ahead and lose it. "I am the sole person responsible then. Are we seeing maybe a little transference here, Nick? I mean, who really knows about hot-air balloons in this house? Who saw his son getting more and more depressed and did nothing but watch the meds and the clock?" Susannah sipped ice water, the glass sweating in the warm evening. "Let me think back. 'He's all yours,' wasn't it? I believe those were your words."

The air was heavy, a storm brewing by morning. "He is all yours," echoed Nick. Standing, he leaned against the deck railing and talked to the back yard. "That means he is *yours* to take responsibility for. If you decline that responsibility, you should say so. 'He's all yours' does not mean 'Whatever you do will be my fault as well.'"

"Oh, I see," said Susannah. "I am glad to understand the rules."

Nick started down the back steps, on his way to his goldfish pond, a dark stain at the back of the yard, still barely lapped by the setting sun. "Fine," Susannah called after him. "Fine. It was all my fault, and my boss is dead. I get it, now."

That night she lay awake as the thunder rolled down from the Blue Ridge and through the valley. Coal came and put his nose over the edge of the mattress, and she stroked his flank. The windows went white with lightning, then black as if someone had punched a switch. All the while, Nick was downstairs, fussing over his Rebel soldiers. She saw the clock slip past two, then the storm quieted, and she slept.

When she woke to the green day, Nick lay asleep, fully clothed, on his side of the bed. Shifting onto her elbow, she studied the cross-hatching of wrinkles on his tanned neck, under the jaw. She watched the button-like pulse of the carotid artery. Then she slipped from the bed, checked on Toby, took her clothes to the bathroom to dress.

Later she reconstructed, if not the whole day, at least the afternoon hours up to the point where she found Toby. In the morning, after meds, Toby went with Nick to the shop. A handful of customers came and went; Nick spent time on the phone with his catalog printer; maybe the balloonist, McGowan, came in for commiseration. At two Nick closed the shop for three hours. At home he gave Toby another round of meds. Getting the IV drip, Toby lay on the couch, watching Simpson reruns. Nick walked Coal, then for an hour he let Toby play with Max across the street. Then the phone rang, or Nick got involved with an internet sale, and Toby said he was going to check on the goldfish, or weed the ivy, or who knew what. And while Nick finagled, Toby stole away down the road. He held his basketball but didn't dribble it. He scratched at the Band-Aid Nick had taped over the bruised spot where the loc had gone. It itched there. Everything always itched, for Toby.

The air was hot, but getting cooler. Rounding the corner by the path where they always walked Coal, Toby must have turned left instead of right. Down another block, then across the street. Behind the Baptist church was a cracked parking lot and a hoop missing its net. Not as nice as his hoop at home, but away from Nick and the clock. Slowly he started dribbling, passing the ball left to right to left, then a few turns around what had once been a painted three-point line. An easy lay up, rebound, dribble out. Surely he felt the cyclosporine in his veins like liquid lead. Still he was all focus. Reverse lay up, rebound, pass to Camby. Seventh game of the playoff series, Heat up by six. Three-pointer by Sprewell, it misses. Sprewell gets the rebound but Hardaway steals it, breakaway down the court, pass to Mourning for a swish, Heat up by eight. Foul on Houston, another chance for the Knicks to get the ball.

Or something to that effect.

Susannah, on the other hand, had not been focusing all day. Tomiko and Cutter, her two young and extraordinary lab assistants, had been at the scopes when she arrived, tracking the mutated bcl-2 protein on the outer membranes of lymph cell mitochondria. Their brilliant brains were filled with virus vectors, mutant genes, bcl-2; there was no room for doubts about one's spouse. Tomiko was spare, vinegary, precise; Cutter, gangly and contemplative. Susannah drifted through their eager calculations like a lost moth.

It was easy enough to say what Nick wanted of her. She should admit she let Toby skip his Minipress. She should take the blame for putting him at risk in the carnival balloon. Nothing was so hard about these confessions. She had done worse things; Nick had done worse. He would forgive her long before she forgave herself.

When she finally left the lab, the sun just beginning to angle west-
ward in the late afternoon, she didn't even concentrate on her route home,
but circled around by the movie theatre and down the back streets into
her neighborhood. And there she saw him, her boy. Stumbling like a
drunkard on the uneven asphalt behind the church, lobbing the ball. He
failed to see her as she pulled the sharp left and parked her red Saturn by
the broken glass. His breath came in quick stutters. His brown hair flopped
into his eyes. The backboard clanked, the pole shook.

"Toby!" she called. "Toby!"

He looked at her as if she was upside down, and then he stumbled
into her arms.

"Heart attack," he said as she caught his damp and trembling body.

When she got him home, Nick was in the back, tending his lovely, lazy
fish. Susannah lifted Toby from the car and carried him through the front
door, up the wide staircase to his room. She had already taken his pulse,
but she got the blood-pressure sleeve on: ninety over sixty. She fetched
him orange juice. After five minutes she checked his pulse, which was
coming back down toward ninety. From below she heard Nick bang back
into the house. "Susannah?" he called.

"Here!"

"Tobe with you?"

"Uh-huh!"

"Great, I'll go on back to the shop, then."

She put a cool cloth to her son's head, and waited. She reconstructed
the day. She was all focus, now.

She waited until she and Nick were walking Coal. Ever since Toby had
been out of the deep water, walking the dog together late in the evening
had become the equivalent of a nightly date. If Toby woke and found
them not there, he was to understand they'd be back in ten minutes to
share a glass of brandy in the living room. If something couldn't wait, he
was to call over to Max's house. Susannah could not remember who—
after the months of vigils, of spelling one another by the hospital bed—
had hit on this brief, low-risk escape. Once, a long time back, they had
even walked Coal to the park by the river and found a bed of moss behind
a thick cluster of trees, where with deft hands and swift nibbles on his

neck and earlobes Susannah had persuaded Nick to a sharp, erotic coitus that delayed their flushed return by perhaps three minutes.

Now on their dusky tour of the neighborhood, Nick holding the leash while Coal alternately pulled forward and stopped short at a dog's whim, Susannah made the argument blossom like bacteria in tissue culture.

The air was still steamy from the recent rain, mosquitoes out after the last light faded. Susannah had changed to a sleeveless white dress that shone in the streetlight almost like a nightgown. Loose on her moist skin, it dipped in the back and showed off her shoulders. "So," she began, "I found Tobe at the Baptist church this afternoon."

"What do you mean?"

"While you were—well, who knows? Chatting it up with a collector, or maybe Linsey, or—"

"Linsey! What are you on about?"

"Toby almost fainted on that basketball court behind the church, that's what I'm on about. He thought he was having a heart attack. He thought it was Marcus Griffiths's heart attack, out to—I don't know— *haunt* him, or something. He had a pulse of a hundred twenty five, and blood pressure in the basement."

"Well, you never told me—"

"I'm telling you now. What else should I do, Nick? Should I sue you? Or would a good whipping do?"

"So that's why you swept in the front door. You'd scooped him up."

"Literally. And I wasn't going to mention it because he was fine in a few minutes. But who let him go there? Hm? Who, Nick?"

They had reached the far corner of the block, where Coal was nosing around in a clump of bushes. "C'mon, Coal," said Nick.

"I'll take him."

"No. You let him off the leash, I don't trust it."

"I keep him leashed on the *sidewalk*."

"Well, I've got him."

Nick kept his gaze on the dog. The argument had to continue, it had a momentum of its own, but his voice when he hit on his next move was hesitant. "You're saying Toby disobeyed me?"

"I'm not saying anything except I found him close to fainting on a glass-strewn basketball court. I found him saying 'heart attack' and muttering about Marcus. 'The one that got Dr. Griffiths,' he said."

This was true, as was Toby's referring to the heart as "Brooke's heart," but Susannah didn't mention that part. "He's not supposed to be playing basketball till the next biop," she went on. "You were the adult in charge."

"Yes. Yes. I was." Now it was rolling again, the argument. They stood on the corner, Nick taller than Susannah. Above his head moths crowded the lamplight. He spoke more quickly. "And it sounds like the kid deliberately sneaked away where I couldn't see him. Which is a little different from your putting him into a balloon basket—"

"My back was turned. I did not put him in. Linsey—"

"—different from that, and then you enable his disobedience by not reporting it to me."

"He was fine! And I am reporting it to you now, oh Psychobabble Master!"

"No need for sarcasm, Susannah."

"No need for sarcasm, Susannah," she echoed.

"You know, I don't get you at all. You control experiments all the time at work. What is it—change one variable at a time, right? And yet you are incapable of controlling—"

"Our child is not an experiment! He is not a toy soldier that you fix and put on a shelf, Nicholas Ames! He is a human being! And I am terrified as can be that he will have a short life! But I am even more terrified—even *more*, Nick—that he will have no life *at all*."

"And that's why you let him ride in the balloon."

"In part, yes. Not by him*self*."

"That's also why you let him skip his blood pressure med."

"I let him skip nothing!"

"You know, your idea of a life, Susannah. Your idea of a life is hanging by your fingernails off the edge of a cliff."

"Sometimes it is. Whenever you're unlucky enough to have a swollen heart courtesy of your father's genes."

"Ah! *There* we go." He slapped the lamppost with his right hand, a flat percussion. Coal's ears perked up; anxiously, he wagged his tail. "Below the belt, Susannah."

"Was it? You've had pretty good control below the belt. I'd think you could fend anything off."

"That was uncalled for."

"Well, your presence is uncalled for at the moment, okay, Nick? You want company, go play soldiers with your friend McGowan."

"Fine," Nick said. "And you talk to your little Buddhist pal whose kid's heart is working so great for Toby."

Linsey lied, she had meant to tell him. *She lied.*

Instead, Susannah strode up the sidewalk ahead of her husband and the dog. Across the dark road, a blue Celica hid in the shadow of a wide beech. Linsey. Perfect.

Susannah stormed into the house and took the stairs by twos. But the upstairs lay undisturbed, Toby sleeping on his back, his right arm flung wide. She descended to her study and slammed the door behind her. Within seconds she heard Nick in the kitchen. He gave Coal two biscuits, then three. He tried to whistle as he put away the brandy and the glasses.

Chapter 22

*B*en Lieberman thought Toby looked good. "With severe rejection," he said when he'd checked vitals, "we'd be seeing cardiac impairment, by now." Turning to Toby, he said, "Do you know your mom's getting to be famous? Look here."

From the shelf above the metal cart Ben pulled down the fat conference program for the NIH, now barely a week away. Susannah and one of her students were presenting their findings on the bcl-2 virus. For a week or more, Ben had toyed with the idea of going to D.C. for the conference. But he had no research to present and too many terminal patients.

Ben passed a manicured hand across the shiny surface of the program before flipping it open and handing it to Toby.

"It's just her name," said Toby. He sat in his white briefs, his skin the same fine ivory as his mother's, his growing legs swinging against the side of the examining table.

"It's her name next to Peter Simon from the UCLA labs. Pete Simon is like Michael Jordan in your mom's world."

"Okay. Hooray." But Toby was proud. He ran his index finger over the listing.

"You get on dressed now, buddy," said Ben. "I'm going to talk to your mom a sec."

While Susannah, looking tired, settled into the one armchair in his office, Ben ran the test results off his printer. "This'll be a good break for you," he said, passing them across the desk. "Getting out of town."

"You mean now, to Durham?"

"And the NIH conference, too. I get this funny feeling you've been on duty for twelve months."

Susannah riffled through the dense pages of Toby's report. Reoentgenograph, echocardiogram, ECG, EEG, sonograms all held in place, the foreign heart still loyally beating. "Guess who I've been reading," she said.

"William Harvey."

"Wrong."

"Marcus Griffiths."

"Wrong again. Galen."

"Galen? You mean Galen the Greek?"

"No, Ben. Wilbur Galen the rap poet. Of course Galen the Greek."

Ben rolled his eyes. "Suzy, we are losing you. You are talking humors if you're reading Galen."

"Yellow bile, black bile. Phlegm and choler."

"Dr. Ames, please. We have a mild case of organ rejection here, nothing more."

Susannah smiled. She was wearing a new lipstick, pinker than usual, but as usual, applied slapdash. The corners of her mouth looked hurt. "I found him on my shelf, Ben. Next to our friend William. Do you realize Galen's theories of the heart lasted fifteen hundred years? In spite of all evidence to the contrary?"

"Well, they're not in common usage now. Are we talking maybe about being up for chief of oncology? Not that the two problems have anything in common."

"That, and other things." She tugged at an earring. "The dean does want my résumé."

"You make it sound like he wants your pot of gold."

"Tomiko's got some interesting stuff going on. I want to encourage her. I don't want to play it safe, like an administrator."

"You don't want to be phlegmatic."

She curled her smudged lips. "Or bilious. Or melancholy."

"Is that how you see administering a section? As a case of humors?"

"No. No, of course not. I need more sleep," she said.

"You look great."

"Don't tell fibs. I'm worried about Toby. Not about the rejection. I just wonder. Maybe he should see a therapist."

Ben leaned forward. "Depression?"

"Not exactly. I caught him shooting hoops in the heat, the other day."

"Which he has always done."

"Yes, but he was a little farther gone than usual. And he talked a little crazy. As if he and his heart had been out there fighting a war. He thought he was having a heart attack."

"You didn't call me!"

"Because he was nowhere *near* a heart attack. He was flushed and winded. But to Tobe, it was like a heart attack was a giant bee, waiting to get you if you didn't fend it off. I got him cooled down, got his heart rate down. He took a nap. He didn't say anything more when he woke up. But he's been secretive. He won't stop calling the heart Brooke's. As if it doesn't belong to him."

"And so you started reading Galen."

"Well, calling it nonsense wasn't getting me anywhere."

A faint knock on the door, and Toby shuffled into Ben's office. His hair tousled with clothes-changing, he looked as if he had just awakened. "Hey, champ," said Ben. He liked Susannah's boy, liked his pluck and resolve. He wondered what it would be like to love him.

Susannah held out her left arm and roped her son in by the waist. "Dr. Lieberman says you look great," she said.

"Can we go now?" said Toby.

"Got a present for you first," said Ben.

Toby raised his eyebrows. Ben reached inside his desk drawer. He had picked the thing up on a lunchtime whim, meaning to give it to the boy on the anniversary of his transplant. Now, though, was better. He held out an envelope, and kept hold as Toby reached for it.

"First," he said, "you've got to promise me to hold off on shooting hoops until after the next biopsy."

"That's in three days," said Toby.

"Exactly. No time at all. But you have to promise me. Not your mom," Ben said as Toby turned to Susannah. "Me."

"Okay," said Toby, and Ben let go.

It was nothing—a 1984 Michael Jordan rookie card, encased in plastic from the sports trivia shop. But Toby said "Oh wow!" and "Thanks!" and Susannah gave Ben the bit of satisfaction that he told himself he should not be looking for.

"I wish," she said, "Nick had thought of something like this. Instead of just saying no."

They were Ben's last appointment of the day. After they had shaken hands and left, he stood by his window until they emerged below, a mother and son, Susannah's vivid hair and Toby's baseball cap stepping out from beneath the hospital canopy. Toby was looking at the rookie card, but Susannah took it from him as they crossed the parking lot. They held hands all the way to her car.

He turned away from the window. He shook her off. He had to shake her off.

At the hospital, there seemed to be a package deal the others had all bought: the bright unfulfilled wife, the three indulged children. Sometimes it even surprised Ben, coming home past midnight to his split-level below the Star, that the spouse and kids weren't there, waiting, concocted by his concerned colleagues in a family-brewing lab. He wouldn't have minded.

There had been no lack of women, he reminded himself, here in the south. Back in New York lived an ex-wife that he found himself, these days, hurrying to mention to new acquaintances, so they wouldn't start seeing him as a peculiar case, the supposedly heterosexual guy who never marries. There had been women transplanted from New York, Jewish women, black women, one Japanese lawyer who'd gone up against one of the tobacco companies and won a small victory. Only he couldn't seem to reach past the women's carefully done hair, their quick, uninvolved laughter.

It wasn't good, he told himself as he left the office, to compare these smart, attractive, gratingly eligible women to Susannah Hubert who was now Susannah Ames. Sometimes he had even resented her moving to this marginal city. Without her, he might even have bought the package, the wife with polished teeth and the children with their sticky hands in his. Without her, he might have gone back on the market at some reasonable point in his career, might have joined a practice in Philadelphia where his brother was, or gone west where Kaiser Permanente was king and doctors had stopped hustling.

Instead, he was supplying her with research tissue, like a good colleague. He was endowing her son with trinkets. He woke in the wee hours, sometimes, with thanks on his lips for having stumbled into a cardiac specialty, that he might have the excuse of helping this one boy survive childhood.

*T*he heart's primary function, Galen said, was to attract. To receive blood from the liver, loan it out to the parts of the body that needed its nutrients, then pull it back. To make a home for the blood; to warm and rekindle it.

The heart was essentially female, nurturing the depleted capacities of the veins. The heart had ears and arms. It made love to the body. If the body refused to make love, it hardened or broke or bled. When it sent forth its fecund spirits, the tissues of the body received them as fields do rain, and their fruitfulness was muscles and movement, energy and growth and the healing of limbs.

Thus it was that the receiving into itself of blood and air, and the driving out of blood, venous and arterial, coincided with the movements of the heart. The movements were like the tides. They complemented one another like Scylla and Charybdis.

Life was balances—moisture and dryness, heat and cool, phlegm and blood and the biles. The four rivers of Paradise had their twins in the heart's humors. The heart had a lot of thinking to do. It was dual, like the tablets of the Law, like heaven and hell. If it gave too urgently, the over-nourished body must be leeched.

Who wants to abandon such a nursemaid? Who would first declare her a figment of the Greek imagination? Who would replace her bounty with a heart that rules like a prince in his kingdom? That works like a machine inside a complex of machinery? Whose only purpose is the ceaseless and circular motion of the blood?

No wonder that puckish royal physician, Sir William Harvey, wrote: "It is no wonder that Spirits, whose nature is left so doubtful, do serve for a common escape to ignorance. And those who make corporeal Spirits say that the Spirits are contained in the blood as flame in smoke."

Because we wanted to believe—in fire, in heat, in nourishment. Even now, they believe—Ben as well as Susannah, Nick as well as Toby, Charlie as well as Linsey. They believe in the face of fact because their hearts leave them no choice. Like us, they miss the old days, the days when our hearts made a hearth within us, when we could listen to them as we might our absent, perfect mothers. When between heart and mind, the contest was already won.

Meanwhile midsummer, time of desire.

Max and Toby stood at the thick honeysuckle bush at the back of Max's yard, pulling the stamens and sucking the sweet droplets. Pluck, pull, and suck. Pluck again.

"Let's go inside," said Max. "It's hot."

"No," said Toby. "Let's get a few more."

Nick ran along the bank of the Roanoke River at a pace just faster than what felt comfortable. Passing the slower runners, the picnic pavilions, the children in their short overalls, the fishermen in their waders and khaki caps, he kept his eye on a red-winged blackbird that zipped from side to side above the thick gray water, scooping gnats in its beak. He remembered a woman's high-arched foot, the swollen ankle above.

Linsey stood at the window by her loom, watching the wasps enter and leave the hive hanging from the soffit. Out of the corner of her eye, she saw her again—Brooke, waving from the yard. Goodbye, Mama, goodbye. A hot breeze came through the screen. The four parts of the breath: inhale, hold, exhale, hold empty. From the fat weeds by the stream, cicadas whined. The sour, dry scent of summer pressed in upon her.

Susannah's laboratory in midsummer felt to her like the hot-air balloon, unballasted and impossible to steer, the ghost of Marcus Griffiths like the wind buffeting the basket. The road to Durham by contrast lay wide, straight, over easy rises and shallows of land. In Durham, she sat in a white room while Toby had his biopsy. She refused to think about the bite of heart tissue, refused to match its rate of cell death and genesis against the ideal and the unthinkable. As they drove back to Roanoke, the countryside had darkened a hue under the glaring sun. At the edge of the horizon, thunderclouds slowly massed. The white light was haunted by orange.

"It's all different," said Toby as they began the long descent from the Appomattox plateau toward the Roanoke Valley.

"Well," said Susannah. "It's August."

Chapter 23

*A*s soon as he'd waved good-bye to Toby and Susannah—a cool nod from Susannah, they were at that point—Nick descended the basement stairs and inspected the balloon that McGowan had so unceremoniously dropped off. The basket had taken a bad hit on one side, no question, but the frame was surprisingly unbent.

Once the lawsuit was settled, McGowan had said, he'd be leaving town. He would impose himself on his daughter in Florida as long as possible, then drift farther, to the Coast or Mexico, one of those postmarks he used to note as he slid other people's Christmas cards into cold iron boxes. Nick would pass his days with military-history buffs who complained of prostate troubles. What was it Yeats said about dreams? *This is no country for old men.*

McGowan had folded the balloon regulation style and tucked it into its huge nylon bag, cinched at the bottom. It was a good Ingelhoff balloon, though not nearly so stylish as the first one Nick had bought, direct from the factory in Pennsylvania, a dense swirl of blue and white that disappeared on a partly cloudy day into the mix of cirrus and nimbus above the low hills. A rich man's sport, ballooning. The aerial pleasures belonged to those who already held dominion over the earth. If ordinary people wanted to risk their lives, they drove fast cars or got into bar brawls. Nick himself had sold his car, a serviceable Datsun, to buy his balloon, and he'd got the basket used from a guy who'd invested badly in commodities futures. Maybe it was part of the allure, he thought as he ran his palm over the one undamaged edge of the basket. Ski bumming, balloon bumming, spying on the fancy folk. The first time he'd taken Susannah up, she'd gotten airsick. "Fix your eyes on the horizon," he'd told her.

"The horizon's too far off," Susannah had said, her knuckles white on the basket rail. Her teeth had chattered; he'd thrown his anorak over her hooded sweatshirt. But when he'd offered to bring them right down, she'd shaken her head. "All I'll remember later," she'd said, "is how gorgeous this landscape is. Feels like an acid trip, not real."

"You ever done acid?" he asked.

"Don't be ridiculous. I was pre-med."

"Just checking."

Mustang Sally, read a brass plate that hung loose along the side of the basket. The rig couldn't be sold, McGowan's insurance company had informed him, so long as a lawsuit threatened. McGowan couldn't afford to store the thing. Leave it with me, Nick had offered, and when the cloud lifts, we'll hawk it to Patterson in Pennsylvania. An easy favor, Nick told himself; a matter of storage room.

Down in the cool basement, he took a close look at the fuel pump. Amazing, really, how little it had been harmed in the accident. Henry Patterson in Pennsylvania would be getting a steal. Coal, following him down, pushed a wet muzzle into his curtailed hand. Five hours since Susannah had risen at dawn and walked the dog. From the bedroom window, he'd seen her unhook the leash, let Coal run ahead and vanish around the corner. She brought him back safely, of course; she always did. She'd grown up with dogs, she said, and knew how to control them with her voice.

Why, then, this fury he'd felt, watching her twirl the loose leash? Why this voice in his head that said *Stop her*? It was a puzzle he could almost make out the shape of, but he had to feel its edges first, its crooked pattern.

Mounting the stairs, he hooked the dog to the blue nylon cord; he took the plastic scooper from the closet. But he couldn't, just then, with the balloon in the basement and his wife and son gone, stand the idea of a dutiful stroll through the neighborhood. Instead he hustled Coal into the van and drove. West through the city, out onto Peters Creek Road and past the little college with its columns and rising lawns, onto the half-paved road where the slave cabins used to lie, under the near shadow of Tinker Mountain. Coal kept his nose to the inch of open window; the air smelled of dust and pine. The trees where Nick parked the car rustled in the strong breeze, and it was hard to erase from his mind's eye the idea of *Mustang Sally* floating somewhere high overhead, rounding the mountain and heading down the valley. He started along the path, Coal slathering as he pulled at the leash, snapping Nick's wrist.

How easy it would be, to let the dog run.

To fix the balloon.

To give Toby ten extra minutes; fifteen; twenty.

To get Susannah pregnant.

No, his steps thudded as the leash strained. *No. No. No.* And the fury was back, sticking in his throat, and he yanked on the leash to make the dog stop choking. How hot it was, and mosquitoes in the woods. He concentrated on the mosquitoes, and then on the pewter set he could start resoldering tonight, and then on the meds they'd have to move to, if Toby's heart still showed rejection. He concentrated until nothing was easy, and then he and Coal were at Carvin's Cove.

"I ought," Linsey was saying aloud to the stream that emptied into the cove, "to get out of this place."

The stream didn't answer, only gurgled along. Water bugs skated the surface. The trembling in her hands started to abate. She wouldn't think about the dream from which she'd woken, the dream in which a pair of old, wrinkled doctors were making a meal of Brooke's heart. Most of the night she had not slept, and then this morning she had come in from the garden and lain on the shag carpet and fallen into the dream.

Surely, when Susannah returned with Toby, she would thaw. If the news was good. You don't have to be a Christian to forgive, John used to say. Linsey would bring Susannah a basket of peas, and Toby would talk to his mom, and she would put past things by.

If the news was good.

And then Toby could come up here to collect crawdaddies, the way Brooke used to collect them from the stream that ran along the back of their property in Granite Falls. Now, Toby wouldn't like it the way Brooke had. He wouldn't make a family of the ones they caught; he wouldn't take the pure delight Brooke had, in cold toes squishing through stream mud. Instead he'd rope Linsey into a stone skipping contest. He'd pretend to teach the crawdaddies how to play basketball. That was all right. She would take pictures of him. *I need you like that,* she'd said a half-dozen times when the light twinkled over Brooke's cheeky face. But she'd never had the camera with her.

Oh, those doctors in the dream, their wrinkled necks. Their steak knives flashed over Brooke's purply heart.

Her throat was dry. She had walked the road down from her house, past the other development and along the steep side of the hill, the pines leaning over to give scant shade. Both trucks that had passed had offered her rides, then peeled away, jacking up the radio.

Bending, she scooped stream water into her mouth. Surely polluted, but who was she to care? Slipping off her sandals, she held them and the hem of her skirt high, then stepped into the cold stream. Pebbly at the bottom, no mud; her feet felt for sharp edges. At the mouth the water got suddenly warmer. An apron of pebbles quickly descended into the murky lake, and the sun bounced off the dark surface. You weren't allowed to swim here, Susannah had told her; you had to go to Bluegrass, which was private. Shielding her eyes, Linsey glanced toward the old dock. And there between the willow branches, resting his right foot on one boulder, the dog thumping its tail on the ground, was Susannah's husband. Her heart—unlike Brooke's heart, she thought at the very second it happened—jumped.

"Now, if *I* were to park my car and come spy on *you*, I'd choose this cove," he said. His voice was dangerously soft, a sandy beach on a warm afternoon.

"Why, Nicholas Ames. You scared me. Hey, dog," she said to Coal. He padded forward, sniffed her outstretched hand, and sat back on his haunches. "Come to walk him in the woods, huh?"

"Well, I don't have to scoop, here."

"I hear Toby and Susannah are out of town."

"Gone to Durham, yeah."

Linsey nodded as if she approved. "They get back when?"

"Tomorrow sometime. You could do it in one day, but we never do. Something about the trauma of the experience. Pretty routine by now, though." He forced a chuckle and rubbed the dog behind the ears. In the open air, the woods at her back and the water glistening below the shelf of rocks, Linsey felt trapped.

"And Brooke's heart?" she tried, not looking at him. "Have they got any more idea on it?"

"Well, they—they always, you know, collect a bunch of data."

He started walking in the direction Linsey had come from, and she followed. From the back she saw he'd just had his hair cut, and she noticed his ears—on the large side but nicely formed, thick on the outer curve, resting close to his head.

"What I mean," she said, stepping along the side of the path, "is will they know for sure whether Toby's rejecting her heart?"

"What makes you think he's undergoing rejection?"

"I—I don't know. I guess Susannah told me."

"Susannah did not tell you."

That was all he said for a few minutes. They walked around the small beach where the rowboats and canoes were tied to a rickety dock. Farther up, by the parking lot—she didn't see Nick's van there, he must have come through one of the paths—the old guy who rented the boats dozed on a bench outside the bait shop. Coal sniffed at a praying mantis in the sun, and they all paused for a second, then Nick tugged the leash.

As they entered the shady woods again, he spoke. "I noticed your car," he said, "on our street the other night. Were you visiting someone?"

"Why, no. Sure it was my car?"

"Toyota Celica."

"There're lots of those!"

"North Carolina plates. Bumper sticker about guns and day care."

"Not so many of those."

"Just happened to notice it."

"Which other night?"

"Two weeks ago, maybe?"

Linsey dropped back then caught up. She could feel herself reddening, that heat you can't stop, maybe it was the sun lowering. She shouldn't have asked about Brooke's heart. She could have kept guessing. They came out by one of the jetties where people fished, but it was empty. "I just wondered," Nick said, stopping, "because I didn't think you knew anybody but us in the neighborhood."

"I don't." The heat was in her eyes now, warming tears.

"Hey, look. Look. It's okay. I used to do that."

"Do what?"

"Hang out near people's houses. Just to see if they were going to come out, or hear what kind of music they were playing, if their windows were open." He rummaged in his pants pocket and brought out a ragged tissue. After she'd taken it he looked away, over the bright water. "I just thought—well, I don't know what I thought. I was a kid when I did that."

"I won't do it any more."

"Yeah, well," he said, his voice changing like a TV channel. "Maybe you shouldn't."

She blew her nose, folded the tissue. "You don't know anything about me," she said.

"No, I don't."

"All you know is my daughter saved your son's life."

"Well, that's the problem, don't you see?" He was leaning against a thick willow trunk. A tall drink of water, that's what her mama would have called Nick Ames. He had those crow's feet by his eyes that always looked better on men than women. "You eat organic foods. You believe war is bad for children and other living things. You lost your family. You've got a halo on your head, and petty people like me can't stand that." Reaching with his stubbed hand, he described a circle over her head. "We try to knock it off," he said.

She stepped onto the jetty. Fish line littered the rocks. You weren't allowed to use worms here because of some disease they could transmit to the fish and the water. She'd never seen anyone catch anything. If John were here, she had thought when she first came, he'd probably sneak in a worm and catch a fat bass. "I shouldn't of contacted you people," she said. "My boy Charlie told me not to. Life Givers told me not to. I was just pigheaded."

"You missed your little girl's heart. And you thought you could teach us a thing or two."

Retreating from the jetty, Linsey set down her shoes and peeled a strip of bark from the willow. Underneath, it was red-tinged and moist. "You don't take someone's heart," she said with a quaver, "and give nothing back. It's not in nature."

"And what are we supposed to give back?"

She looked sideways at him. His dark glasses reflected her shape and the sparkle of the water behind her. "You want me to go poof," she said.

"No."

"If I could've died on that motorcycle with them, you know, I'd have wished for that. Then no one would've been unhappy except my Charlie, and he's strong enough."

"Well, but you didn't."

"So much the worse for you."

"No." Crouching, Nick picked up a long dry twig. Snapping it into pieces, he pitched them with his good hand one by one into the cove. "You see us managing badly. Susannah and I."

"It is not my job to rescue you."

Nick brushed off his palms. He was about to stand up and start walking again. Coal rose, wagged his tail.

"People talk about being out of the woods," Nick said, patting the dog's back. "But it's a very thick woods."

Without thinking much about it, as Nick straightened, Linsey tipped her face. Sure enough, he kissed her. It was a bruise of a kiss; she could feel the shape of his teeth under his lips. She pulled away. "I think," she said, stepping backwards, "you are out of the woods."

And it was an old kind of knowledge she carried away with her as she walked fast, leaving Nick by the jetty. She half-strode, half-jogged across the parking lot to the path that led upwards, cutting through the switchbacks the road took, up Tinker Mountain and around to the other side. She didn't look back. She carried away knowledge like a dusty coin, like a cache of wine on the edge toward vinegar. Knowledge she'd been sneaking around trying to get, only here it was in plain daylight speaking to her. She carried her sandals as she walked; she heard the soughing of the willows.

Who owed her, mother to mother?

Who would pay?

Slowing her pace, she saw Susannah's round eyes, how they slid past her that day in the garden. Nick asking for her help, like he had a right. The sun flattened over the trees, on the far side of the cove. Hawks circled overhead. In some cold white room in Durham, the nerves of Brooke's heart were crying out. And Toby's nerves were listening but like phone lines picking up nothing, not even a dial tone, nothing since they'd gathered up his sick, swollen muscle and stuck it in a jar. Inside Toby's chest— she had put her hand on it in the dark, felt the steady pulse—floated the ragged ends of two souls, unjoinable.

The heart itself was nothing. It wasn't for the heart that they owed her. Later, when the flame she'd lit had spent its force, when the winds had abated and she and Nicholas Ames had both come back to ground, she would tell him this. She would tell him, she could have let the heart go.

luegrass Lake was private, but not very. It nestled in the hills a few miles from Susannah's lab, with its short stretch of imported sand, its trail around the lake, its peeling picnic tables and solitary tennis court. A few times, Susannah had seen Ben Lieberman there. More often there were families, and they were mostly white and double-incomed and boasted two children and a dog who stayed in the car or walked the children around the trail. They made Susannah nervous; and when she trained her eyes on the pairs of children, whispering or squabbling, towheads who had left the hospital at birth and stayed away from it since, she fought waves of jealousy like nausea. Nonetheless, every April, she and Nick threw four hundred dollars at Dennis, the club's owner, to keep up their membership. Benefits included fireworks on the Fourth, swim lessons for Tobe, and a termite-ridden clubhouse with ping-pong and shuffleboard for rainy days.

Even last year, when they never drove down the winding dirt road, never pulled into the banana-shaped gravel lot, never touched bare toes to sand, they had paid. Writing the check had been like planning Christmas, like tutoring Toby in math, an act of faith.

And now, in the ecstasy of good news from Durham, in the ripened warmth of August, Susannah had indeed forgiven Linsey for lying, and brought her to Bluegrass Lake.

It was a confusing time, she had said on the phone, and then she'd persuaded Linsey, who loved to swim, to come to Bluegrass. No—that wasn't quite true. Toby had been the one to key in Linsey's number when they got back from Durham. "You've been mad at her enough," he'd said matter-of-factly to Susannah, and then he'd just picked up the phone. Now he was catching salamanders in the shallow water with a handful of other boys, his T-shirt self-consciously on. Every half-hour, the lifeguard hopped down from his perch, stepped over to the boys, allowed them to count their salamanders, then tipped the buckets over in the water before the heat sucked the last oxygen from the slimy creatures. The shouts of the children lifted into the hot air like dragonflies, and like the flies' wings, their high-pitched voices seemed to cool the skin.

"*Out* of rejection," Linsey was saying, her sharp chin tilted toward the sun. "I like the sound of that."

"Do you?" Susannah pushed damp hair off her shoulders. "I think it makes rejection sound like a place. Like jail."

"Like a morgue," said Linsey.

"You don't get out—" Susannah began, then stopped.

A muscle pulled at the corner of Linsey's wide mouth. "I set myself up for that one," she said. She took a draught of iced tea, from a can stuck into the imported sand. A pine forest rose to the back of them; on the lake's far side, the sun washed a series of hills patched by grain fields.

Every now and then, from her beach chair, Susannah lifted her sunglasses to study her son. His very movements, his crouching and digging, his high-gaited prance into the gleaming water, might as well have been magic tricks. *This time last year*, she thought. *This time.*

"Any adults go swimming here?" Linsey asked.

"A few. You're not supposed to venture outside the ropes."

Susannah uncapped a tube of sun block and rubbed her pale legs. August already, and she hadn't been in the sun; she was as pale as last year, when she practically lived in the hospital. The bathing suit flattered her, the high cut of leg showing the thighs' shapeliness, the top scooping toward melony breasts. Linsey wore the cotton leotard Susannah had seen her gardening in, a nubby rose knit that clung half-heartedly to her long torso. She looked not slender but skinny, not mysterious but merely frail. "We had a lake in Granite Falls," she said. "Anybody could go there. You could swim one end to the other. I was stronger then." She rested her sharp chin on her fist. "I went one end to the other," she said.

"Sounds nice," said Susannah.

"It was nice. Not exclusive, like this club idea. John didn't like anything that kept people out."

Susannah rubbed cream onto her shoulders. She was not going to get annoyed, not on a day of such good news. "You see the guy over there?" she said, nodding toward the new dock on the lake. "Blond guy with the beard, getting out of the canoe? That's Dennis."

"Yeah, I see him."

"Dennis's parents left him all this land. He's kind of a latter-day hippie—maybe a little like your John—and he hadn't found anything to do with himself, so he moved home and opened the property up. Rebuilt the dock, cleared the weeds away from the tennis court, called it a club. You want to talk to someone about what's exclusive, he's your man."

"John wasn't," said Linsey, her eyes on Dennis.

"Wasn't what?"

"A latter-day hippie."

"All right. All right, I'm sorry." Wiping the last of the cream on her thigh, Susannah dipped her hand into the bag of whole-wheat pretzels that Linsey had brought. Even with the good news, she felt off-key, out of sync. Her hair hung heavy with sweat. Mysterious grains of sand dug under her swimsuit. Her period was due; her lower back had started to ache, and the beach chair curled her spine painfully.

Abruptly Linsey slipped her sunglasses back on, stood up and stretched. "I'm going in," she said. "You?"

"No. No, thanks." Susannah shifted in the chair and rubbed the back of her neck. Below, on the beach, Toby was lifting his T-shirt, allowing a select few to view his scar. "I pinched a nerve, I think. Moving all that stuff around my house." That had been yesterday, the rearranging of Susannah's downstairs to fit Linsey's geomantic chart onto the floor plan and enhance the Tudor house's karma.

"I got a yoga technique, fix you up in no time."

"I am not a yoga person, Linsey."

"My teacher, Priya Roy? She says we are all yoga people. Yoga means union with yourself, that's all."

"Then for sure I am not a yoga person." Susannah squinted up. In the white light of the beach, Linsey looked like one of those pre-Raphaelite water nymphs, all elongated bones and hair.

"I'll fix you up," Linsey said, lifting the hair off her neck, "when I get back from this water."

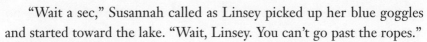

"Wait a sec," Susannah called as Linsey picked up her blue goggles and started toward the lake. "Wait, Linsey. You can't go past the ropes."

"I can't what?"

"Go past the *ropes*. Dennis has to have the rule, he says. Or he can't keep his license to operate as a club."

"Is that right."

Susannah followed Linsey's gaze as she turned it on Dennis. Dennis's was the wrecked beautiful body of a former surfer with more drug habits kicked than most people ever indulged. As far as Susannah knew, women drifted through his life, and he was kind to them. She had never thought, until now, of putting him together with anyone. "Besides," she pressed on, "he says there are snapping turtles, toward the other end."

"I'll just be a sec," Linsey said. She leaned down to tuck her sunglasses in her canvas bag. Then she sauntered, hips forward, over to the dock.

Susannah leaned her head down to her knees. Her neck did hurt. Maybe she and Linsey had spent too much time excavating the nourishing energy of the Tudor house. Linsey had judged the house craggy and heavy with yin, a notion that Susannah found herself surprisingly ready to accept. The entrance hall, fortunately, buffered the house from destructive energy, and opened to several rooms to let the benevolent energy flow. The broad oak stairwell had good *feng shui*. But Susannah and Nick's bed had to be moved out from under the exposed beam in order that its malevolence not crush their spirits, and in her study Susannah's desk had to be moved toward the other window, to synchronize the combinations on the geomantic chart.

It was at that point of moving the desk, Susannah thought as she watched Linsey importune Dennis, that pain had needled through her neck. She ought to have waited for Nick, she thought, to move such heavy things. Only Nick wouldn't have wanted to; would have laughed; would have called Linsey *your little Buddhist pal*. She ran her fingers under her fine hair and massaged the twin hollows at the base of her skull. Nick was gone for the weekend—to Annapolis, Maryland, ranging his John Hill hollow-cast Highlanders and Mignot French Colonials alongside the offerings of his fellow fanatics. Before he left, he had given Susannah the gold heart locket she wore now around her neck, a peace offering. They wouldn't talk about the balloon ever again, he had promised, and then he had shown her what he had stashed in the basement.

Susannah had even thought they might make love last night—no fireworks, just healing after a quarrel, and she'd showered and put in her diaphragm. But he'd been on his side already, the light off on his half of the bed. When Linsey had pronounced bad *ba-gua* in the bedroom, Susannah had been only too ready to agree. Get out from under the beam. Align with the elements. Whatever it took.

She lifted her head. Dennis, over by the dock, was laughing. Then he waved in the direction of the wider lake, beyond the sacred ropes. Linsey dipped to wet her blue goggles, then touched Dennis's tattooed arm, already a familiar, and dove cleanly into the water.

Even with all the block his mom had slathered onto his skin, Toby felt the sun crisping it. Like chicken, he thought, when his dad put it under the broiler. Rolling his shoulders, he could feel the flesh on his shoulder blades, crackling.

He wondered when Linsey was going to step through his window again. Her stepping through his window had done it, had turned Brooke's heart around. This was something he could never tell his mom. That he was taking Linsey on as his mom, too. Like the Mormons, the way the men took more than one wife. Or let's say a kid whose parents got divorced when he was maybe a year old, and his dad's new wife was like a mom to him. The kid might even call her "mom."

Mom, Toby thought as Linsey knifed off the dock beyond the ropes. *Go for it, Mom*. He remembered what it was like for his own heart to swell, and he tried to swell with pride, watching how fast and sure she swam through the tresses of the lake.

He wasn't at all sure this was what Brooke wanted. He hadn't ever had a chance to know Brooke. That was the unfair thing. Like getting a computer game, one of the hardest ones, with no instructions.

The kids he was with were okay. Jason and Ryan, the two in his grade, had been the ones clamoring to see the scar. Jason'd said it was like Frankenstein, but Ryan said he liked the way the marks of the stitches looked, like the tweed in his dad's jacket. "So what happened to him?" Ryan asked now. They were digging a tunnel toward each other.

"Who?" Toby'd given up on the stupid plastic shovel and gone for his hand. Under the surface the sand was wet and gluey as grits; it filled his fingernails.

"The kid who died. Who gave you his heart."

"You can't give a heart when you're dead," said Jason. He was still catching salamanders. He held one by the belly, and it swam in the air.

"Why not?" said Toby. He was hitting small pebbles now.

"Because, stupid. You can't do *anything* when you're dead."

"Hey, that's right!" This was Robbie Hargrave talking, a year older than the others and a bully. "How'd you get him to give it to you when he was *dead*, Ames?"

Toby sat back on his haunches. It was always a *he* they asked about, the kids who asked about his heart. "I don't know," he said.

"You don't *know*? You've got some other kid's heart, and you don't know how he *gave* it to you? What an idiot."

Jason dropped the salamander in the bucket and turned to Robbie. "What, you want to take it back, Hargrave? You want to reach in Toby's chest like that freakazoid in *Indiana Jones*?"

"Ooh!" said Ryan. "Gross!"

"I think," Toby said, "your parents decide to give it, actually. Or you can write something down. My mom wrote hers down. Like, when she dies, she wants them to take her organs to help other people. But if you're a kid, your parents can do it."

"Not my parents, man," said Jason. He looked like he was still thinking about *Indiana Jones*.

"Why not?" said Ryan. "Hey, gotcha, Toby."

It was true. Toby could feel the ends of Ryan's fingers, wiggling, where he was scraping away at the end of the tunnel. "Couple rocks to pull out," Toby said.

"I mean," Ryan went on, "you're dead, right? So your parents can do what they want with you."

"That is too gross," said Jason.

"Yeah, well nobody wants your shitty little organs anyhow, Jay-boy," shouted Robbie Hargrave. He'd gone down to the edge of the water and was holding a salamander upside-down by the end of its tail.

Toby could feel Ryan's whole hand now. The boys flattened onto their bellies, reached, and clasped wrists. He tipped his head toward Jason, which meant looking into the sun; his face felt on fire. "I got to talk to my dad," Jason said. With the sun behind him, he looked dark and small and scared. "He's not selling *my* guts, man."

Toby wasn't much for arguing. A ways off, he could just make out Linsey's arms lifting, one after the other, pulling her through the forbidden water. "We're touching here, you know," he said. And with that he and Ryan gripped tight and pulled up hard, gritting their teeth and grunting, not letting go, until at last they'd blasted through the top of the tunnel, into air.

By the time Linsey got back, Susannah had abandoned the chair and stretched onto the warm sand. She had entered that sea of half-dream that the sun engenders. She wasn't thinking about sex but about work. Ben Lieberman was with her, and Tomiko. They were all in the lab together, working on Tomiko's bcl-2 project. The assays were coming out, not within a micron or two of predictions but exactly on target. They watched, a breathless trio, as the amino acids rose. Across the lab table, the tensor light reflected onto Tomiko's sharp face. Ben stood behind Susannah. She felt Ben's mustache brush her hair, caught just a hint of bitter male scent. The acids rose. She reached out and gripped Tomiko's small hand. *Holy smoke,* Ben said, his mouth at her ear, *what a rush.*

"How's that neck?" Linsey asked. Cold water dripped onto Susannah's thigh.

"Mm," said Susannah. She wrestled out from the dream, a sucking sound in her mind as she pulled free of the golden ocean. She tried to lift her head. "Hurts," she said.

"Well, if there's snapping turtles in this lake," said Linsey, dropping to her knees on the sand, "they are fat and lazy."

"We feed them children," said Susannah. Her eyes still closed, light purpled the insides of her lids.

"Lots of water weeds though, on the far end. And there's sulfur in this water."

"Talk to Dennis."

"I did talk to your Dennis. He may be one brick short of a load."

"Told you."

"But he's real fond of you and"—Linsey hesitated—"and your husband."

"Nick."

"Uh-huh."

"Yeah, well, he and Nick used to run the trail around the lake, till Dennis blew out his knees."

"He says he does t'ai chi."

"That may be. But he's had laser surgery on both joints."

"Certain forms of t'ai chi," Linsey said, "can be healing. Turn over, now, onto your back. Let me work on that neck."

Susannah cranked up on one elbow and took a quick glance at Toby. He was straddling three long Styrofoam worms, watching two of the other boys churn through the water from one rope to another. Pale, T-shirted, he looked younger than the others. She shifted to her back. "Dennis got divorced last year," she mused as Linsey moved to a spot on the sand behind her head. "I guess his wife was in some Christian sect, and she started sleeping with the pastor. Anyhow"—through her dark glasses, she squinted up at Linsey—"he's been lonely."

"I'm going to move your head around," said Linsey. Neatly, she loosed the clasp of the new locket and laid it on the canvas lounger. "Now let go those muscles in your neck." She lifted Susannah's head from the towel. Through her tangled hair Susannah could feel Linsey's strong, slender fingers, gripping. Linsey bobbed the head, as if her hands were waves and Susannah's skull floating in them. "You're not letting go," she said.

"I'm trying."

"Don't try. Just trust me. Let me hold your weight."

Like loosening a taut rope, Susannah abdicated from her neck muscles, and warmth traveled from the back of her head as Linsey moved it in half-circles and figure eights. "Dennis lived in Vietnam for a little while in the eighties," she went on. "Learned some incredible vegetarian cooking. I should get him to invite us all over."

"I thought he was a hippie."

"Latter day, I said. He can be fascinating. You'd like him."

"You're tightening the neck again. Let go."

Susannah shut her eyes. "Only if you're interested," she said.

"In what, Vietnamese cooking?"

"No, silly." Susannah grinned as Linsey tipped her head to one side and pressed her hand in a long caress from just behind Susannah's ear down the side of her aching neck and around the knob of her shoulder. "In meeting men."

Linsey's hand jerked upward, her thumb slamming into the base of Susannah's skull. "Oh dear," she said. "I *am* sorry."

"Hey. *I'm* the one that's supposed to be tense."

"It was the suntan lotion. My hand slipped." *Mah hey-und*, she said. She shifted Susannah's head to the other side, and this time the caress came slower, the loop more delicate around the shoulder.

"Your *heart* slipped, more like. Look, if you're not ready, that's fine. I just thought, you know, Dennis could be a good time for you."

"Course you did."

"I could ask Nick to set it up. Whoah!"

Linsey had taken Susannah's head in both her hands again and been stroking upward on the neck vertebrae. Then suddenly one hand seemed to lose contact. Though her head probably dropped all of two inches before Linsey caught it, a firm hand in her curly hair, in the heat and sun, Susannah felt the vertigo of a long fall. "There," said Linsey. "It's okay. It's okay, I got you."

"Maybe. But I think that's enough." Susannah pushed up, shook out her hair.

"No! You're supposed to lie still afterward! Till the headache goes."

Susannah tilted her head back, then dropped it forward. "Headache's gone," she lied. She pulled off her sunglasses and wiped grains of salt from them with a clean folded towel. Only then did she look squarely at Linsey. "You're trembling," she said. "You've got goose bumps. That water must be really cold."

But when she leaned forward to touch Linsey's knee, the knobby cartilage and the old scars from childhood skinnings, she found the flesh dry already, and warm. "What's up?" she asked. Linsey had dropped her head like a Madonna and didn't look up, only mumbled about how Susannah should lie back down, the headache. The shouts of the boys came from behind Susannah, belonging already to a time before she suspected anything.

Chapter 25

*T*he balloon sat in the basement until the week Susannah left for the NIH conference in D.C. Every couple of days, Nick went down to tinker with it—to wire *Mustang Sally* back onto the basket, to oil the fuel gauge. The insurance assessors had been by, hemming and hawing and filling in their forms. They'd be pleased, in fact, if Mr. Ames could find a buyer for Mr. McGowan. Not that the suit had any merit. But to know if the deductible could be met, should they settle. Nick should be in touch with them; here were their cards, beige and orange, embossed.

He'd gotten one postcard from McGowan in Florida, breasts on a beach, reading "Empty skies here. Hot. Expect to see you and Sally floating over. Mac." The August air sucked moisture from the Roanoke Valley, hot breezes kicking up over the mountains, good ballooning weather. It had been an August like this one, with Henry Patterson, when Nick had first tried his hand. Over the low hills of Pennsylvania they'd floated, in a bright orange balloon filled with combustible hydrogen and operated by an eccentric entrepreneur named F. J. Wormley, who loved the sport but wore a huge tear-shaped scar down the left side of his face from a flame that had caught him as the gas caught fire out of the cylinder. Eight flights later, half with hydrogen and half with hot air, Nick had clinched his license, which he tucked into his wallet along with his River Guide License, his Orange County Hang Gliding Permit, his para-chuting certificate. Where were they now, all those scraps of paper with their gold scrolls and embossed seals? He pressed the palm of his left hand against the stumps of his right. He remembered the water thundering into his mouth, his helpless legs in the current of the Joachim River. *They got fake fingers now*, one of his customers had said, and Nick had said yeah, he knew. But it wasn't the fingers, it was the fear, and the shame of the fear.

And now Henry had called. He was ready for a look at that balloon, he said. He'd heard tell it was one of the great balloons that guy Maelbeek, in Belgium, had stitched by hand before he died. Nick told him it was true, and true also that the thing had a capacity of eighty thousand cubic feet, enough to carry three men and a pump over the Alleghenies. And so, the day Susannah took off for D.C., Henry drove out. Nick woke early, set about repairing the wicker work on the basket, cleaning the fuel pump, calling the guy at the air field for clearance. His license had expired, he explained, but Henry Patterson had a license. There would be two of them going up, maybe three. Say three. The basket held five, after all. Maybe they'd give someone a ride.

But it wouldn't be Linsey Hunter, Nick thought as he oiled the pump.

Well, why should it be Linsey Hunter?

The woman was unstable, to start with. She would hate everything about ballooning—she had refused to get into this basket even when it was tethered to two trees and a car. Apart from her personal tragedy, she was one of those vessels of received ideas you ran into in the South's deep pockets—people who mixed Baptist smugness with chow-mein mysticism, who could just as easily be talked into voting for Ollie North as campaigning for animal rights. Forget about that sudden, embarrassing kiss. The woman was needy; he'd given in for a second to the need. And what she needed wasn't him anyhow, but to be cured of all this—of her fantasy that her daughter still lived somehow in Toby, her self-absorbed notion that she could attach herself to their lives like a barnacle to a ship.

Hoisting the basket onto a dolly, Nick managed to load it into the shop van. The balloon itself was clumsier, and would take help. He went into his empty house and poured himself a glass of ice water. Toby was spending the day with Max up at Natural Bridge—another miracle, added to the stream of miracles beginning with the new heart: that he could swallow a series of pills in the morning and then spend the day at a tourist site, miles from medical assistance, with just his cell phone and a list of emergency numbers for a safety net. The house felt empty. Coming in from the balloon, from thinking about the old days, Nick almost felt he was in someone else's house: its teal-toned kitchen, its Persian rugs, and the great stairway that led up from the reordered front hall.

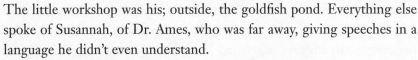

The little workshop was his; outside, the goldfish pond. Everything else spoke of Susannah, of Dr. Ames, who was far away, giving speeches in a language he didn't even understand.

On the table by the front door, neatly stacked, sat the bag Linsey had brought over. Toys, she'd said. They go to charity, Nick had warned Susannah before she'd even had a chance to unpack the bag—and yet it had sat there, lumpy and stubborn. He peeked in. Math flashcards; a tin of wooden peg games; a bead loom; a hand-carved chess set with *Brooke from Daddy* scratched into the side. And at the bottom, clothes. Unisex shorts, T-shirts, jeans, even sandals from a dead girl. Not many, but there you were. Well, they'd go back to her. Not to charity, but back to Linsey before Toby so much as opened the bag. You had to give a firm message, about these things.

He picked up the phone. Linsey would turn him down on the balloon ride. When she did, he'd tell her he'd be dropping off the clothes. If she didn't turn him down, the whole experience would cure her. She'd see him as a businessman, transacting with the very kind of country-club adventurer her husband had despised. She would back off after today, at least from him. She would be Susannah's problem again.

After two rings she picked up. "I am not the scaredy-cat you think I am, Nicholas Ames," she said. "Not for myself. It was Toby I was scared for. Now you give me twenty minutes to finish my yoga sequences," she said, "and I am your girl."

There were things that came back to Nick as if he had been living them daily. The need for symmetry in the filling balloon so that it would rise up as if plucked by invisible hairs on the crown of its head and not lurch left or right. The even, taut fastening of the four ropes from the basket toggles to the ring below the listless, tethered balloon. The satisfying whoosh of the flame lightening the air above it, pushing that suddenly lighter gas through the ring into the growing vault of splendid cloth. The first jerk upward, and then the doddering slow lift, the wind no longer ruffling your hair because you were moving with the wind, two feet then ten then thirty from the ground.

Then there were other things that Henry Patterson—blond hair streaked white like lemon ice, face tanned the color of doeskin—took care of with an efficiency that Nick barely remembered having in some other life. He foresaw the thermals over the hot cornfields, the cool spot over Carvin's Cove, the onrushing cumulus about to cover the sun because the air stream was moving faster at ten thousand feet. Deftly he adjusted the jet, read the altimeter, anticipated the second it would take for the balloon to react—and the jerking reluctance with which it might react, sending Linsey back against the rail of the basket, her face white.

"*Great* day for a flight," Henry Patterson said. Later he said, "You've got *gorgeous* country here, Nick. That ridge really is blue, you know it? I mean, look. *Blue*." And later he sang, as the country opened up toward Blacksburg and they had started descending at about a foot per second: "*Mustang Sally*, now baby. Think you better slow that Mustang down." He winked at Linsey then. "You scared, honey?"

"I think any reasonable person would be," she said. She'd worn a sheer Indian-print top and jeans shorts that looked unaccountably mannish. She turned and waved at a family standing outside a farmhouse, shading their eyes and watching the balloon. She had waved at everyone, as if she had a public relations job. "It's sure beautiful, though," she said, her voice clear over the hiss of the flame. "So quiet. I like quiet things." At this she looked directly at Nick. He felt filled with something, the old feeling, even here with this competent twit Patterson—the sense of owning the air he breathed. You couldn't feel that in a soldier shop or building a goldfish pond. He shut his eyes and then opened them. Everything dazzled—the colorless sun, the white edge of cloud, the green sward below.

"Well, I'll take old Sally," Henry Patterson said as they descended. "I'd take young Linsey too if she didn't look already bid for."

At this Nick said nothing. The balloon swooped down. He unfastened the trail rope and shouted at a dumbstruck farmer to catch hold of it. The woods at the end of the fallow field approached like a moving wall, and Henry cut the jets, and they came down fast and hit ground, and Linsey fell to the bottom of the basket with a high cry, and they bounced in a typical way across the dry, waist-high weeds, the wind suddenly loud in their ears, and Henry turned the fuel off completely and the basket dragged, then tipped. The balloon flapped wildly once, twice, then lay down like a dowager taking a nap, and the farmer came running, shouting were they all right, were they all all right? And Nick pulled Linsey out, regretting every second of it until she laughed, and Henry Patterson hugged her, at the sight of which Nick felt a strange stabbing somewhere below his ribs.

"Is it always like this?" Linsey asked when the ropes were untangled and the balloon safely tied.

"Always." He pulled Susannah's cell phone from his pocket, to call the guys at the air field to fetch them. "Only I won't be going up again, and neither will you."

"I wouldn't count on that," Linsey said, and Henry Patterson squeezed her shoulders.

"Good girl," he said. "Ride, Sally, ride."

The lawsuit would clear out, Henry said. He'd seen these things before; he was in the business, wasn't he? Nick gave him the insurance fellows' business cards, at which he smirked. A month minimum, he said, and he'd be sending for Mustang Sally. He would want repairs made to the basket; he'd ask for the fuel pump to be inspected. But the babe was a beaut, a real mustang colt. He peeled off four hundred-dollar bills to Nick, to make proper storage arrangements. As he handed the crisp bills over, Nick's hand wouldn't come out of his pocket to take them. He looked at the money and saw only the expense of blue, the race with the clouds, the land running beneath them. Finally he put forward his right hand, and volunteered the story of the stub fingers as if delivering a warning. When they shook hands on the deal, he tucked that hand away.

Nick and Linsey drove back down Peters Creek under the slanting sun. Linsey leaned against her door, her hair blown back by the wind, her eyes shut. "You must be sad," she said just when he thought she had dozed off.

"Letting Patterson take the balloon? Not at all." He cleared his throat. "It belonged to a customer of mine, was all, and it was defective to boot."

"You were all lit up, up there."

"Yeah." He drummed his good fingers on the wheel. "But you know— I never thought I'd go up in one of these contraptions again. And now I did."

"And lived to tell the tale."

"True enough. Unlike some others we know."

"You mean Susannah's boss."

"I guess that's who I mean. A few more bad gusts, and I might have meant my son."

When Linsey spoke, it was after a long silence, and as if she were answering a question. "I lied about that day," she said.

"What do you mean? You told me what had happened, and it had happened."

"Susannah wanted to get into the basket. I distracted her."

"Well, so what?" He turned onto the arterial. "Susannah's not exactly a model of caution."

"I wanted something to go wrong," Linsey said. Nick glanced over. Her eyes were still shut; she looked vaguely ill, the mud colors of her shirt unhealthy. "I wanted to scare her. It felt like she was getting away with something."

"Happiness," offered Nick.

Linsey shrugged. "I wanted to catch her at it, whatever it was."

"Well. Thank you for that little confession." They were underneath the Roanoke Star, now; he turned off and wound his way to the neighborhood, where Linsey's Toyota sat parked in his driveway. He pulled up and cut the ignition.

"Time had come," Linsey said, "to knock my halo off." Her eyes were open, now; she sat forward in the seat. She turned to him, her face like a painting, the full lips unnaturally red, the sharp little chin pulled up. As if she would do again what she had down on the trail by Carvin's Cove, Nick jumped from the car.

"I've got to get Toby from across the street," he said.

With the languor of the late afternoon, the hot day, she stepped out and stretched her arms upward. "I had a good time, anyway," she said. "Whatever you intended."

"Maybe the same as you." He wiped traces of oil from his hands onto his jeans. A tiny panic seized him; he could not figure why he had asked her, or what had possessed him ever to leave the solid ground. "Halo's off, I guess," he said, and turned, cruelly, away.

How to explain, then—after he'd given Toby his meds, checked blood pressure, heard about the awesome arch of Natural Bridge and the sad weird creatures at the Wildlife Park—that he let his surprised son go back to Max's for dinner and a sleepover?

How to explain how he drove—once Toby had tripped back across the street and the dog was walked and the goldfish happily fed—out Peters Creek to Carvin's Cove? How he sat cross-legged on the stony bank, rehearsing the glint of her white ankle, the one he'd wrapped, in the swift water of the stream?

It was an easy excuse. In the back of the van was the bag of Brooke's toys, forgotten in the balloon adventure. Aiming to return them, Nick drove from the cove through the cricket-chorused evening, up the road to Tinker Mountain. There wasn't, really, much of an explanation.

"We can't keep these," he said when Linsey opened the door.

"I gave those to Toby," she said. Country music played in the background.

"He doesn't need them."

"Come on in," she said. She was barefoot, in jeans, her straight hair wet and hanging down the back of a Save the Whales T-shirt. She looked about nineteen, a shade too thin. Her freckles, doubled by the sun that afternoon, blended across her nose. On the left side of her neck, a vein pulsed.

He laid his right hand on her hip, and with his left flicked shut the door.

Chapter 26

*I*n the lobby bar of the Washington Renaissance Hotel, Danny Griffiths was drunk. "Good lecture," he kept saying to Susannah and Tomiko. "Splendid. Splendiferous lecture. God. My daddy is dancing in his grave, ladies."

Susannah smiled through her fatigue. There had been a crowd in the room all right, but their exuberant applause had evaporated into the stale air of the hotel, and the anticipation of the previous days had already dried like a leaf and blown away. That Marcus Griffiths—such an odd little man, now she remembered him, with the personality of a grapefruit—would, as a host of oncologists had rushed to inform her, have been "proud" to call her his collaborator seemed a backwards kind of praise. When the fellow from Cantrex, waiting discreetly behind the other congratulators, finally stepped forward to give her a bear-claw handshake, he assured her that the funding sources would do all they could to extend her interim situation as section chief into something more permanent. She was grateful, she told him. And then had slipped away, with Tomiko and Danny, who had hit the bar even before slinking into his seat in the conference room.

"I don't drink normally," he said, staring down his Scotch. "In the daytime, I mean. But this is an occasion. Ladies, I am inspired."

"Thank you," said Tomiko. She was drinking tomato juice with a twist and looked like a million dollars.

"I sat there in the admiring crowd, and you know what I heard?"

"What did you hear?" asked Susannah. She ran a hand through her hair, sticky with spray and the heat. A bad hair day, whatever else good might be happening. Her period was overdue; she hadn't slept well. Her hair looked like a Troll doll's.

"I heard the voice of my father. No, seriously. That raspy little voice of his. And he said to me, 'Son, listen to those women. Now *that* is science.'"

"I'm not so sure—" started Susannah, but Danny held up a hand.

"'That is science,' he said. He wanted me to be a scientist, old daddy did. Scientists were competent people. I mean you ladies were"—he drained his Scotch, signaled—"*competent*, up there. Me, I can't even tighten the fucking ropes that hold down a balloon. That's how competent I am." He raised his empty glass. "To Dad."

Susannah lifted her glass—white wine, a bad idea, she'd have a headache—but didn't drink. "He would never have blamed you," she said.

"Well, I blame me. That's what I finally told that fuck Tuck. Cute, huh? That fucktuck. Tuck, I said, that old geezer in the Oz basket gave me the forms, and I didn't get my old man to sign one. The dweeb assistant asked me would I mind checking the knots and I said Nossir. And then I fucked up. There." A new Scotch arrived; he sipped and smiled. "I feel better."

"So you're not going to sue the guy?" Susannah said.

Raising and lowering his eyebrows, Danny looked momentarily like his father. "Tuck'll come after you next," he said. "He found out you have a kid with a heart problem, already. His pupils went to dollar signs. I swear, just like in a commercial or something."

"But Toby's fine. And we signed liability forms."

Danny waved a hand in the smoky air. Phlegmatic, Susannah thought. Melancholic. "Doesn't make a pisspot of difference," he said. "They'll sue anyone. He'll probably end up suing me."

Tomiko leaned over and took Danny's hand. She was younger than he was, by a couple of years, but right then she could have been his babysitter, settling him down.

"I'm not going into research," he said. He dug a twenty out of his pocket and rose. "Whatever mistakes I make, I'll make in private practice."

"C'mon, Dan," said Tomiko, rising too. "Let's get some food into you."

"There's more money in practice anyhow. Which I'll need now that old Tuck won't be garnering my million-dollar settlement."

"Come on."

They started off. "Hey," said Susannah.

"Hey." Tomiko turned. "Thanks, boss."

"Thank *you*. That last leg of the experiment was all yours."

"And it wouldn't have gone anywhere without you." Tomiko smiled, but only briefly. "I've got to help him," she said.

"Sure. Go."

The bar was quiet, the rest of the crowd gathered for a big stem-cell debate, up in the Renaissance Ballroom. Susannah's hand drifted into her bag, seeking her absent cell phone. It was the fourth time today she'd made the gesture. Just as well, she thought. If Nick wasn't at home or at the shop, she would have to think about where he was, in the middle of the day. Or if he answered, she'd listen for sounds of breathing in the background. If Toby picked up, if he said, "Dad's gone out. He wouldn't say where"—what then? Still her hand lingered, missing the phone.

"Dr. Ames, I presume."

Susannah started. "Peter Simon," she said. She looked at the fastidious, bearded man lowering himself into the opposite lounge chair. "You're not in on the stem-cell debate," she said.

He made a snickering sound. "We have all been around the track on that one, I think," he said. "Your little team, on the other hand, is bushwhacking a new trail."

Susannah blushed. She sipped the wine, felt the headache plant its seed. "I've got some energetic assistants," she said.

"That you do." Peter Simon signaled the waiter for sherry. "It is a terrible thing to say of the dead," he said, tapping a pipe against the ashtray on the little table between them, "but it was time for Marcus to leave the Roanoke section."

"You've got to be kidding. Our work was just getting started. People were actually starting to change their views about what cancer *is*."

"Cancer as process, you mean," Peter said. He lit the pipe; drew. He was about five years younger than Marcus, a Yale man, one of the few who tried to swim laps, during these events, in the hotel pool. "Not as product."

"You heard my presentation. You still think kill quotient is the standard of success?"

"No, I don't. I'm also not ready to call a four-year survival of brain cancer a success." His drink came; he tasted it and frowned. "Tumor malignancy is not AIDS," he went on, spreading his well-groomed fingers over the marble tabletop. "It's not a virus we should be content to 'manage.' It's a cellular invasion."

Susannah was tugging on a strand of hair just behind her ear, a nervous habit. She wondered how bad the hair looked. It felt like a mop glued to her head. "You mean a cellular *disorder*."

Peter Simon smiled. His eyes were a flannel gray, giving away nothing. The beard matched the stripe in his shirt. The pipe smelled like bourbon. He had a reputation for sleeping with his collaborators. "Funny," he said, "how much more reasonable that motto sounds, coming from you rather than Marcus. *Disorder*. Disorder," he repeated, "like a house needing cleaning."

"While *you're* preparing the infantry," said Susannah, "and considering a first strike."

"That's how you win a war," said Peter. He pointed to her glass. "You could use a refill," he said.

She hesitated. Her finger seemed stuck in her hair. Her lecture was over. She was enjoying herself. Enjoying the banter, the undercurrent of attraction. Such cachet she held, with Marcus's mantle wrapped around her. Pushing her unruly hair back, she hesitated just long enough to give hope to the famous Peter Simon. Then she looked up at the expectant waiter. "Rain check," she said. "I've got some errands to run."

It wasn't freedom, but it felt like it. Escaping out the side door of the hotel, Susannah executed a little skip over the sidewalk monogram, then headed away from the hotel shops, the restaurants, the valet parking. Nick at this moment, she felt sure, was doing as he pleased. Well, fine. So was she.

Miniscule bits of litter flew up and stung her eyes. Her hair whipped around to her face; she tasted the ends of the strands, metallic with volumizer. How did she know what Nicholas was doing? Ah, she knew. More than she had known anything, even the first sign of Toby's sick heart, she knew. She knew, as poets would say, in her heart. She slipped on sunglasses and fought the wind down the sidewalk, past a gray diner and a flower shop and a tired-looking computer accessories store. The headache had moved to her forehead. Her belly felt heavy, her period overdue.

When she finally stopped in front of a hairdresser, the pictures on the window made it clear the place specialized in black women, and when she stepped inside she smelled the ammonia of hair straightener. An obese African man looked up from his edition of the *Enquirer* and grinned at her as if he were ready to answer a question about directions. Otherwise, the place was empty. More photos of beautiful black women on the walls, their hair lacquered and braided, their faces resigned. *You know I have black blood*, Linsey had said once, but she possessed, Susannah noted with satisfaction, none of this smooth defiance. Susannah took the first chair. The hairdresser put his paper down and stood behind her.

"And what does the beautiful lady want?" he asked.

The hair, surprisingly, didn't look too bad—a coppery halo you could tame with your fingers. But she felt its weight as if the strands were made of lead.

"Cut it off," she said to him. "Cut it as short as you dare."

He lifted it from her neck; let it fall. He looked pleased, as if he had spent his morning hoping for her to come in and say exactly what she had said. "Come on, now, honey," he said, patting her shoulder. "Let's get you shampooed, first. Let's make you feel good."

hen he'd discovered Peanuts, last year, Toby had asked his dad whether Charlie Brown's name was just Charlie, or Charlie Brown. Charlie, his dad had answered, and his last name is Brown. But everyone calls him Charlie Brown.

Inside himself, now that Brooke's heart had come back from dying and was once again pink and healthy in his chest, Toby took the name Toby Brooke. He hadn't told anyone to call him that yet, but he was working up the courage to. His mom had said that if a person wanted to change his name legally, he could go to a judge and do it. That was what he'd do, as soon as he had the courage. For now, it was just his inside name.

Toby Brooke had figured a new basketball game, called Rebound, which he got Max to play with him. It wasn't one-on-one, which he wasn't allowed, but it wasn't so boring as p-i-g either. You had to shoot a sequence of three lay ups, three free throws, and two three-pointers. If you made the shot, you took a point, but the other guy got the ball. If you missed, you could both go for the rebound, and whoever got it took the next shot. But you had to keep track of your shots, too. If you'd sunk two free throws before the other guy got the ball, and then took it back from him three shots later on a rebound and went to shoot a three-pointer, he could call you on it and take both the ball and your free-throw points.

Rebound was a complicated game. Max, being faster, was better on the rebounds. Toby Brooke was better on the shots. They both lost track of the sequence. The day after his mom got back from D.C., he and Max got into a shouting match over Max's

three-pointers. "You already shot two of them!" said Toby Brooke.
"There was the one from the deck side, and the other that swished."

"There was not! There was just the swish! Before that I was on free
throws! I got two in a row, and then I got the ball back from you on your
second lay up, and I shot the swish!"

"That was when you shot the one from the deck. You just don't
remember right," said Toby Brooke, bouncing the ball on the asphalt as
he argued, "because it's so long between the shots you actually sink except
the lay ups! I'm at thirty-two now and you're at, like, fourteen!"

"You are not at thirty-two!"

"Am so! I shouted it out when I took my third lay up this round. You
have to shout it, that's a Rebound rule."

Max knocked the ball out of Toby Brooke's hand and took a shot,
which found air. "Stupid game," he said.

"Don't play it then! I don't care! I'll just keep track for myself."

"Oh, that's a lot of fun."

"What's fun, then? Since you won't play Rebound by the rules."

"What's fun, Ames," Max said, and he narrowed his eyes, "is one-on-
one. And I'm going to call someone who can play it. Since you can't. You
are such a wuss."

"You asshole!"

"You pervert!"

Max's mom, Cindy, was on them before they'd done more than shove
each other. She was a short, strong lady with Max's square shoulders.
They could take a break, she suggested, before the neighbors started
complaining. She suggested Popsicles, which the boys, mutually suspicious, agreed to.

Max's house was totally different from Toby Brooke's, and in many
ways better. It was a raised ranch, with a big industrial-carpeted room in
the basement that gave onto the back yard, which in turn sloped down to
a field of hay that remained incongruously intact this close to town. Right
now Cindy was having the back yard rototilled. They couldn't go out
there or over to the hayfield to leap the bales. She gave them each grape
and shooed them downstairs with a promise that they could come back
up for blue raspberry if they brought their sticky sticks with them.

You could tell right away, Toby Brooke thought, that Max's dad didn't
live in this house. The freezer had only Weight Watchers in it, and no

steak fries. The hall closet smelled of dry cleaning. There were little piles of messy paper around the L-shaped living room, but no half-finished projects, and no tools anywhere that Toby Brooke could see.

Downstairs, they could do whatever they wanted. Max had a little sister, but she was only two and more like a pet than a person. If they didn't want her to come downstairs, Max just had to shout to his mom, and she'd take her away. On schooldays, when their mom was working, his sister went to day care. Max let himself into the downstairs room by a hidden key, and took snacks from the little fridge down there, and watched the TV in the corner. It seemed like an okay life to Toby Brooke.

This time, they pounded down the stairs with their Popsicles, not speaking until they were both lounging on the bean bags in the corner. It was cool down here, the door to the rototilled yard open for the cross breeze, and Toby Brooke found it hard to stay mad about Rebound. "What's on?" he said as Max grabbed the remote.

"*Rug Rats* probably. Maybe *Saved by the Bell*. I hate Saturday afternoon TV."

"The Liberty are playing," Toby said.

"I hate girl basketball."

Max surfed. For a while he paused on the baseball game, but it was Cubs against Indians, and Max wasn't interested. He stopped on a Disney movie about a boy and girl lost on the African desert. "Your dad take you to see the Braves last month?" Toby Brooke asked. He wished Max would flip back to the Cubs, or ahead a couple of channels to the Liberty, but this was Max's house and Toby Brooke had been winning the Rebound game.

"Twice a week," said Max. He sucked his Popsicle. His lips were purple. "He's got season tickets."

"Cool."

"And his girlfriend is like this reporter for the Atlanta Constitution, so she can get us into the locker room."

"The locker room! Did you meet Greg Maddux?"

"Nope. He's got his own locker room, somewhere in the back. The big players get that. But I got Javy Lopez's autograph, and I saw Jones's naked butt."

"His butt!" Toby Brooke giggled and had to spit out the chunk of Popsicle he'd just bit off. "Was your dad's girlfriend with you?"

"Naw. She doesn't like baseball. She's got this cool boat, though. Where she lives, by a lake. She taught me how to work the throttle and everything. Next year I can take it out by myself."

"Sweet."

Toby Brooke finished his Popsicle. He licked the last cold layer off the stick until his tongue hit dry wood. "You seen my mom's hair?" he asked.

"Yeah. It's awesome."

"It is not. She looks like a boy."

"She does not. She's your mom, dweeb. And she's got the hooters."

"Hooters?" said Toby Brooke.

"You're too young." Max got the look Toby hated, lounging in his beanbag chair with his leg up and the ankle crossed over the knee, like some golf player just off the links. "Cheer up, buddy. It'll grow. Your hair grows, hers'll grow."

"My parents might get divorced," Toby said.

"No shit?" A commercial came on, and Max flipped to a superhero cartoon. "Because of the *hair*?"

"Don't be stupid."

"Hey, there's got to be a reason. And you guys have plenty of money."

"What's *money* got to do with it?"

Max shrugged. "That's what my parents fought about. I mean, they sure didn't fight over my mom's haircut."

"Your mom's got awesome hair."

"So?"

"So it's not money." Toby Brooke broke the Popsicle stick in half. The two ends were splintery, the way they always were, but when you pressed them back together you could hardly tell where the break lay. He was ready for the blue raspberry one. "It's Brooke's heart, I think."

Max laughed, the chortle of an older boy. "What's your *heart* got to do with it?"

Ever since Linsey had come to town and Toby'd had to confess that he had a girl heart beating in his chest, Max had smirked whenever he referred to the heart, the way you smirked when you talked about somebody's security blanket that they still couldn't give up.

"The old heart came from my dad, I think," Toby Brooke said. "Can you switch to the Cubs game for just a sec?"

"Okay," said Max, who was finally sucking the last of his Popsicle from the stick. He surfed back to ESPN. The Indians were up three one.

"I don't mean the heart came from him," said Toby Brooke. "I mean whatever was wrong with it came from him. *His* heart's okay, though."

"I don't get it," said Max.

"Get what?"

"Divorce. Your heart."

"My mom blames him. She's real soft on me to make him feel worse. He gets mad at her for being soft."

Max rolled his eyes. "Parents."

"And then there's Linsey," said Toby Brooke. "Will your mom give us the raspberry ones, now?"

Chapter 28

"Now I know what it means to weave a spell," said Nick, his hypnotized eye on Linsey's hands as they worked the big loom. "My grandma used to call me the spider girl. They say Grandma Spider wove the story of the world." Linsey's hands threw the shuttle, her feet pumped the treadles. The yarn she was weaving right now was the exact amber of her hair. She glanced quickly up at him. "You see a story here?"

"I don't see the end, yet," said Nick.

Linsey advanced the warp, gave an extra hit with the beater, shifted the treadles. She moved like an organist playing Bach. Yesterday it had been Linsey watching him, in the shop, while he put the finishing touches on a miniature Tsar's crown. We're both good with our hands, she'd observed. Funny how he'd taken so long to notice that. The care with which she arranged flowers in the glass pitcher on the sideboard, the flimsy cottons she'd draped into curtains. When he'd taken her up in the balloon, she'd coiled the ropes afterward so that they hung from their prongs on the basket like tightly curled ferns. "*Feng shui*," she'd said when he'd finally had the grace to praise her brightly painted living room.

"Gesundheit," Nick had said.

"Don't you start."

"I said it was a warm space. I said you'd done wonders I didn't think a ranch house was capable of."

"You think it's all hooey."

"Hooey feng shooey."

"This house had a little already, you know. When I rented it. None of the doors face south. The roof's red, the window shutters are green, it's perfect."

"Christmassy too," said Nick. He'd laced his hands through her hair. He loved the warm silk of it, the shape of the back of her head.

"You're never serious, are you?"

"I am always serious," he had said.

The assumption around Roanoke was that Nick felt inferior to his wife. He'd sensed it in the hearty greetings he'd gotten from her colleagues, in Ben Lieberman's efforts to dumb down his diagnosis of Toby's condition. Most of the customers in his shop were men; but the occasional woman, happening in, would change when she learned about Susannah. *You must be a godsend to her,* one might say; or, *Looks like you could do with a home-cooked meal.* When their praise of his shop went over the top—*This restoration is a work of pure genius! Is there a Nobel for miniatures?*—he knew they were wondering. If he fooled around. If he built up his injured ego by bedding available women.

They hadn't known him before. *Before what?* he asked himself as he watched Linsey's hands fly. Before he had lost four fingers to the Joachim River, yes, but that wasn't the *before* he thought of. Even leading up to that trip—a badly planned junket, too early in the season for safe rafting, not enough equipment, the sixth guy had bailed out at the last minute so there were only five of them and only him and one other guy with experience—something had started to slide. He'd seen it in Susannah's eyes when she came to stay over nights at his place in New York. She'd be pacing his loft, gesturing, explaining why she had to leave medicine, she just had to, and try for a life in the lab. *If only I could be like you,* she'd said then, and he'd asked, truly curious, *What do you mean, like me?* And she'd gestured again, a sort of setting-free of an invisible canary, and she'd said, *Just to do whatever comes to mind. To dare it.*

And he'd tried to laugh and explain that he didn't dare things; he prepared, he knew the risks. It wasn't, he said, like he couldn't keep a job. One time, she'd come to sit next to him on the piano bench. She'd played a high, two-fingered tune and rested her head on his shoulder so he felt her soft hair at his ear. *I like you to be daring,* she'd whispered, and already he sensed he would disappoint her.

"You weren't weaving this," he said now, touching the tight fiber on Linsey's loom, "when you came to Roanoke. It sat for months. Susannah said it was gathering dust."

"I told you. I sold hand-loomed rugs for profit. It was my old dad who thought to get the life insurance policies. I thought he was nuts. Spend your own money on our dying, I told him, I need my money for living. So when the accident happened and I collected the money, I thought, what on earth do I need to be weaving for?"

"And now?"

Linsey smiled at him, her broad lips. "I like it again."

"What about John?"

Linsey beat the weave a little harder. "What about him?"

For a minute Nick didn't answer. He went to the window on the opposite side of the living room and peered out, as if he expected someone to drive up, to handcuff him and take him back to his assigned place. What about John? John was a guy he didn't know who'd driven recklessly on his motorcycle and died. All those spring and summer days, sitting on the back deck of the Tudor house, Susannah had been the one to ask questions of Linsey. John's heart wasn't beating in Toby; why should he know the first thing about John?

"I don't know," he said, coming back to where the morning light washed across Linsey's back and onto the loom, "the first thing about John."

"Well, why should you?" Linsey's voice caught a little. For a half-second the hand holding the shuttle hesitated before throwing it through the warp.

"You loved him."

"Course I did."

"But I don't know what he did. In his life. For a living. Or hobbies. Nothing. Just that—"

"Just the motorcycle," she finished.

He leaned over and kissed her. He loved kissing her. Her mouth was ready for him, lips a little parted, breath tasting of cinnamon. "You sold rugs," he said, pulling away. He touched the weave again—pure wool, she'd said it was, tight and warm. "What did *he* do for money?"

"Little of this, little of that."

"Little of what, little of what?"

"All right." Linsey's shoulders dropped. She laid the shuttle across the top of the warp and pushed back in her wooden chair. Stretching her arms upward, she made her elbows crack. "John's daddy was a very big man at General Motors Corporation, and he died of colon cancer. Up to then John was in law school. Well, sort of in law school. He'd taken a little time off, before we met, to live on an ashram."

"Like, an ashram in India?"

"But he came back. He was in law school, and then his daddy died and left him a bundle. So he quit. He said he thought we should kill all the lawyers like Thoreau said. He'd only been on the way to being one so the old man wouldn't cut him out. So then after, he taught history at Spider Ridge Alternative. Where we sent Brooke."

"A little of this."

"Yeah."

"And that?"

Linsey fished a skein of cream-colored yarn from her basket. She kept her eyes from Nick. "He dealt a little."

"Dealt."

"Mostly just grass. He said he didn't need the money; he did it for the cause of individual liberty. What I've got, that's the life insurance money. There wasn't much of the other left."

With the yarn piled in her lap, she'd started to cry. Her tears weren't like Susannah's, which came in a rush and left her face puffed and mottled. These tears ran in a broad, thin stream down her cheeks. She wiped them with the back of her hand just at the jaw line. "Hey," said Nicholas, crouching, stroking her thin arm. "I don't give two cents what the guy did to be respectable. Look at me. I sell tin soldiers. He sounds like he had ideals. That counts. And he loved you, that counts more. And you loved him."

Fisting a tear, Linsey shook her head. "Brooke," she said.

"Brooke, too. He loved—"

"Ssh." She touched his mouth. Her cool fingers trembled a little. "It wasn't like he *hurt* her or anything."

"It was an accident, Linsey."

"I don't mean when she died. I mean when she *lived*. He just—" She thumped her fist like a hammer several times against her thigh. "He took her *away* from me."

"Death took her away, honey."

"No. No. In life. I loved her and he just—charmed her *away*. Like the pied piper or something. I mean, they'd go pick blueberries after school, and they wouldn't come back till after dark, and when they did, they were talking some other *language*. He'd have invented this language and taught it to Brooke, and they'd speak it together like that, and he'd look at me. Like, you know, 'I got her.' I wasn't—I wasn't *jealous*."

"No," said Nick. His hand grazed her hair.

"I was *worried*. When he wasn't home, she'd just sit and wait. Like all the life went out of her, and when he came back, the life came back, but it wasn't *right*. Even the piano. Even when she danced. I think he got her stoned sometimes, but I don't know. I don't know what all they did." She swallowed. "I lost every bit of my little girl, Nick. I lost her before she died."

With the palms of both hands, she wiped her cheeks dry. He tried to put his arms around her, to lift her from the rickety chair. Her slender body was dead weight. "No," she said finally, as if she were talking to someone else in the room. Straightening the yarn in her lap, she went back to working the loom. Her hands flew like hummingbirds.

Chapter 29

*A*s if by proving her reliability and competence she could prevent Nick and Linsey from sleeping together, Susannah bought a huge erasable chart and mounted it on the kitchen wall, above the table and by the phone. This will be so *handy*, the saleswoman at Office Suite had said as she fit the gleaming white board into an oversized plastic bag. You can just post your *life* up there. What Susannah posted were meds and notes on meds. Along the top, with her loopy cursive in blue felt marker, she inscribed the days of the week. In the squares for each pill, she noted time and milligrams; in the squares for special instructions, she noted pulse and temp. To reach the top of the chart, she stood on a chair and braced against the wall. Sunday nights, she wiped the vinyl surface with a yellow sponge that turned slowly green.

Nick declined to use the chart. When Susannah asked him at the end of the day, he reported on whatever he'd administered or injected, and she wrote it in erasable marker.

They made a partnership, Nick and Linsey. Not love or attraction. A joining of forces. Outweighing her, outweighing Toby. In the occasional bitter moment, rinsing blue water from the green sponge, she thought, They probably do it by the rules. Next, your second finger touches my labia. We continue this motion for twenty-three seconds. Time's up. Now I cup your balls in my hand.

Mostly, though, she was not bitter. Her cropped hair felt light. She kept putting her hand up, expecting to adjust the tortoise-shell comb that held her hair in place, but there was no comb; there was no hair to be held. The back of her head felt sleek as a cat. In D.C., once she was shorn, she had cruised back into the costume jewelry shop and bought a dozen pairs of chunky enamel earrings, which framed her newly revealed jaw. It was not a bad jaw, she thought. It was firm along the sides, the neck sloping down without double chin or wattle. On her chin, the old scar announced itself as a warrior mark. Her face was naked to the world.

At the conference, Peter Simon had been effectively shocked and had turned his attentions elsewhere. Back at the lab, Tomiko and Cutter voiced their youthful, short-haired enthusiasm. Nick, satisfyingly puzzled, said she never ceased to amaze him. Toby had stroked her head. "Are you going to grow it back?" he asked.

"I don't know. It's growing already, I figure."

"Grow it back."

"Maybe I will. I'll see."

"If you don't grow it back," he said, stepping back to survey her, "you'll have to buy new clothes. You know. More kind of . . . boy clothes."

In the swelter of late August, Toby lay on the floor in his air-conditioned bedroom and pushed up his new two-pound barbells. *Left, right,* he puffed, *hup, together*. He took his meds, and Susannah could see him fighting the munchies from the steroids. He'd wander into the kitchen after a session with the weights and open first the refrigerator, then the cupboard. He'd bite on his lower lip. Then he'd pour himself a huge glass of ice water and go out again. He kept a jar full of sugarless Bazooka in his room and chewed strenuously when the urge came on him. And he wasn't overweight; since the cyclosporine had been reduced, he even looked skinny again. He could go back to shooting hoops, Ben had said, so long as the temperature outside was below eighty-five and he didn't play one-on-one. But the heat blasted, interrupted by violent thunderstorms, and rather than argue, the kid stayed in, pushed weights, and went over to Max's to watch the Redskins slaughter Atlanta.

From her study by the kitchen, Susannah watched the robins in the scraggly evergreen where they nested each year. Their young had flown, but the male guarded the spot as if the credit union were threatening to repossess. At the start of the day, he flung himself from the branch below the nest at the neighbor's bay window, where the rising sun struck the glass into mirror. He came within an inch of crashing, then veered off and circled back to the branch. There he rested for a few seconds, his head turned away from the house so that one side-facing eye could keep his mirrored image in view. The other eye seemed to consider Susannah.

Stupid bird, she mouthed at him. Suddenly he turned and launched a surprise attack. He came around the other side of the bay, ready to peck his
rival from behind, only to find the mirror-bird vanished, the shaded glass
transparent. Just as his wingtip brushed the farther pane, he careened off
again. He settled on the branch, preened his feathers, performed an
eight-point check of his world, and began again. After twenty minutes, he
and the rising sun together persuaded his mirage foe to seek sanctuary
elsewhere. When the greenhouse window showed nothing but rubber
plants and hibiscus, he flew off—late for worms and disheveled, but calm
in his bird mind.

A couple of times, in the early mornings, Nick reached for her. Moving above and below him, Susannah catalogued all the little things he had
never done before. How he ran his index between her buttocks, like a
sculptor marking clay. The particular way he cupped her breasts, not like
when he used to marvel at their roundness and the secret fullness of their
sides, but as if weighing. He held the short strands of her hair between
thumb and forefinger, as if he could make them grow straight and honey
brown. Watching him, feeling him compare, she faked the moan of cli-
max, the spasm of her hips. "Stop now, Nicky, please," she begged, and if
he didn't believe in her orgasm, he didn't let on.

Twice a week, the first fortnight of her return, as Susannah descended
the broad stairs from sitting with Toby before sleep, Nick was just pushing back from the piano where he'd been exploring Gershwin, or stepping
in from the back yard where he'd been scooping algae from the goldfish
pond. "We live in a sweat box," he said the first time; the next, "We could
use some eggs for morning." And then he said he was driving to Kroger's,
even though the Kwik Shop two blocks off had cheap eggs. Another time
he announced he was going for a drive, get some cooler air into his lungs.
Coal thumped his tail at the jangle of house keys, then settled his muzzle
down on his forelegs after Nick had gone. Now and then the dog glanced
up, as if checking for the end of this strange trial of his patience.

The night before Toby started back to school, Susannah came home
after dark. She parked her Saturn next to Nick's van, then reached
through his open window. With the push of a prong, the van's trip
odometer tumbled back to a neat row of zeros. Next morning, after
Nick's late-night quest for cooler air, the odometer read twelve point two
miles, exactly the round trip to Linsey's house.

"Ah," Susannah said aloud, barefoot on the still-cool asphalt, her cotton robe loosely cinched and her short hair disheveled. A thin, sharp scoop seemed to empty her insides, the same sensation she'd felt once or twice when Marcus had persuaded her to perform a protocol that would prove the infeasibility of the experiment she wanted to perform, and the protocol had worked perfectly. Evidence, my dear, Marcus would say as kindly as he could, cannot be denied. Around the corner of the house she caught a glimpse of the little evergreen trembling, the robin up and at it. And just as in the lab, a strange fluttering began within her hollowed self, an excitement that the freedom of failure gave her, to step away from the problem and start clean.

Once she had turned to Nick like a plant to the sun. Back in New York, blasting bleary-eyed out of a twelve-hour shift at Sloan-Kettering, she'd skirt the subway entrances and keep walking south through Manhattan—past the Chrysler Building and Gramercy Park, past the tawdry storefronts of Fourteenth Street and through Washington Square to the Village. Her legs buzzing, she'd slip into a corner booth at the Macadam, where Nick played piano on alternate Tuesdays. She'd drink an icy martini while she watched him, shaggy head and narrow face following the music, his hands working the piano with ciliary motion. His loft had been filled with fascinating bits—two kayaks hanging from the ceiling, an old hand press he used for Christmas cards, a cache of wine he'd distilled himself. His friends dropped in from expeditions to K-2, from parachuting over gorges in Mexico; he was saving his money to raft the upper reaches of the Colorado. He made love to her as if she were his latest and most absorbing adventure. She feasted on him. The fermented oaky scent of his loft, the lazy smile with which he recognized her at the bar brought a rush of saliva to her mouth, a tingle to her nipples.

And still could, she thought, shivering in the warm air. Rarely did she admit to the depth of her love for Nick. At parties, especially when they first moved to Roanoke, she would come upon him charming a woman with an energetic explanation of beer brewing, and the woman would ask something that just missed being a compliment, like "Where'd you dig this guy up?" and Susannah would answer even more deprecatingly, "From under a mountain of beer bottles." Ben Lieberman, the first time she had lunch with him, before he became Toby's doctor, had listened conscientiously to the checkered quilt of Nick's past. Shaking his head,

Ben had said, "I can't figure what you guys are doing together," to which Susannah had said either, "Opposites attract" or "He makes me laugh," two standard responses. When she let down her guard—as she had, so inexplicably early on, with Linsey—Susannah remarked on the ease with which Nicholas exercised his talents. Before the heart disease, Toby had given off much the same ease. They could both, in the local phrase, turn their hands to just about anything.

At least she was calm about it, she thought when she'd checked the odometer. She knew and had known; the evidence was almost tiresome. Mounting the stone steps, she reentered the still-sleeping house—Toby at the top of the stairs with his school clothes laid out, Nick in the deep dreams of the unfaithful. She started coffee, got out the meds. The cool air of early morning brushed against her exposed neck. There seemed plenty of time for everything. Then, from her study, she saw the robin dart around the glass. She pushed her desk away from the wall and opened the window. "Stop that," she hissed. The robin landed on the branch, did his eight-point check. "You stupid bird!" she said, a little louder. He tipped his head her way. At the back of her knees she could feel Coal's nose, investigating. The robin flew at himself. "Stop," she said again. When he didn't, she pinched the locks on the screen and lifted it. She grabbed a pocket calculator from her desk. Ducking her head into the open window space, she hurled the thing. It shook the little evergreen tree, and the robin flew off.

"Well," she said, closing the screen, replacing the desk—she would retrieve the calculator later, or maybe not, maybe it would rot in the rain—"that's that."

Today, she thought, she would put in her formal application for section chief. She would color her cropped hair—black maybe, or blond, or streaked, hiding gray. She would write Peter Simon about lab possibilities in California—there were good doctors for Toby in California. She would outline new protocols. She would fill out the charts. There were things, surely there were things to be done.

Chapter 30

Ben Lieberman waited in a dark corner of the only decent restaurant in Roanoke, a Brazilian place that served spicy rice dishes at night and a variety of broiled sandwiches and bean plates during the day. People from the hospital didn't come here much. They liked brighter, louder places, like the New York Deli around the corner from the downtown market, the town's claim to quaintness.

He was meeting Susannah here to talk about epithelial tissue. The last time he'd sat in this same booth had been with a beautiful lawyer from Richmond that he'd met at a friend's Shabbat, who was both too young and too sure of herself for him to take seriously. She had ordered a ten-year-old Madeira, he remembered, that he didn't think could be found in the city of Roanoke much less in the Brazilian place.

His beer arrived, he sipped it, and Susannah came through the door. Dressed in what looked like an expensive suit, silk maybe, with a bright, nervous flush to her high cheeks and her hair—Christ, what had happened to Suzy's hair? For years she had complained, trying to tame her fine, tangled mane. Now it was gone, and she looked for the first time like a woman who could be hurt. She carried her pocketbook clumsily, as if someone else had asked her to tote it, and wove her way between the tables as if she were balancing on a beam. And she was missing all but maybe two inches of her lovely auburn hair.

"Late late late," she said, giving him a rapid hug scented with perfume. "God, will I ever manage not to make you wait?"

"It's part of your charm," he said as they sat down.

"Only if you define 'charm' as incompetence."

"Who made you cut your hair?"

"Nicholas."

"What, he likes the boy look now?"

"You hate it, don't you?"

He leaned back in his red vinyl seat. Clasping his hands to make the church with the steeple, he stroked his mustache with both index fingers. "I've never thought of you as a victim," he said.

"I'm not."

"But the wave's cut out. You look . . . pared down."

"Good. I feel pared down. I'll have what he's having," she told the thin waiter. "No, wait. I shouldn't drink. I'll have iced tea. And we should order, Ben. I've got my first interview in an hour, and I've got to be home for Toby."

"Right," he said, studying Susannah's small ears, the white skin just behind them. Once before, in medical school, she had cut her hair to a cap of fine frizz, like an exotic sort of seaweed clinging to a rock, and she had wept at her foolishness on Ben's shoulder and accepted his invitation to get very drunk. This time it was even shorter; he had to concentrate on her forehead, on the bump of her nose, the scarred chin, on her wide-spaced round eyes to find the Susannah he knew.

He took the rice and beans, she went for a blackened chicken sandwich. In the small space, his knee brushed hers without any extra effort. He brought out the list he'd had typed that morning. "These are the cells we've collected over the past six weeks," he said. "All benign, all showing normal molecular profiles."

"Lung epithelia."

"And a sheet of arterial cells, in case you want to compare genetic mutations. These are from the same patients, mostly."

"Wow. Thanks, Ben. You get a big mention in the next grant."

"Do I get to know why Nick made you cut your hair?"

"He didn't really. I just did it so I can throw him out when I'm ready."

"Is that like the Amazons lopping off a breast so they could shoot?"

"Sort of. A little easier to grow back."

"And what's Nick's sin?"

"Oh, it's too boring. These lung cells are more interesting."

Ben pushed his beans around his plate, a large white disk with an extravagantly raised rim. "Let's just run her out of town," he said.

"Ben, please."

"I mean it. Who is she? I know, some military history nut; she collects the little gray models and figured she'd collect the guy who carves their little noses. No? Okay." He finished his beer, set down the glass, rubbed his hands together. "The lady who runs that shop across from his, the one that sells recycled-plastic jewelry for just a little less than precious stones. I'm right, aren't I? That one with the piercings, a patient introduced me to her once, she said she had a shop just across."

Susannah washed chicken down with iced tea. "You remember Toby's heart?"

"Toby's heart, Toby's heart, let me see. Title of a popular song? No. Molasses in January? I think I'm getting closer. Gee, I must be getting old, I never used to forget a cardiac muscle."

"He's with the mother of the girl."

"The girl who gave the *heart*?"

"It's the only organ he's had replaced so far, I think."

"Jesus, Suzy. I told you it wasn't a good idea to be in touch, but—"

"But you didn't think Nick would be in such close touch?"

"I guess I thought your marriage was pretty problem-free."

She smiled, a little wanly. The makeup brightening her cheeks showed now, the mascara on the lashes, the powder camouflaging dark circles under her eyes. "The unmarried always think that."

"I am not 'the unmarried.'"

"I'm sorry."

"I'm not even 'the divorced.'"

"Neither am I, yet."

"But?"

"But I wasn't even going to do anything about it. Only Toby keeps asking where Linsey was, when he's going to see Linsey. He's friends with her."

"Hm. His heart's mother."

"You don't know." Susannah pushed her plate away. Her eyes looked damp, but she spoke brightly. "Nobody talks about it as Toby's heart any more. She *never* did. She believes her daughter is still sort of, well, *alive*, in Toby. Toby thinks he's part Brooke. Which he is, in a way."

"Oh, come on, Suzy. I thought I told you to read Harvey."

"I've *been* reading Harvey. 'A piece of machinery.'"

"There you go."

"Also, 'the prince in his kingdom.'"

"Well, that's a metaphor."

"Nick says everything's a metaphor. Nursery school, rocket science, you name it."

"Making you suffer? Is that a metaphor?"

Susannah drew a chocolate mint from her pocketbook. Slowly, willfully, her bright color came back, the skin of her bare neck blotchy. "Toby knows his dad's up to something. Next time he asks about Linsey—I'll tell him where his dad's spending spare time."

Ben drank beer, wiped his mustache. "That could break his heart," he said.

"No problem. He's got a fine team of surgeons."

"That's not what I meant."

"I thought we agreed it was a pump. I didn't think we talked in metaphors, Doctor."

"Oh, Suzy," he said. He reached over and took her hand, which was warm in the palm and cool at the fingertips. He leaned toward her across the table, but she pulled away and checked her watch.

"Interview," she said. She pulled out a tissue and blotted. "They've got three outside candidates for Marcus's job, plus me. Do I look okay?"

"Smart and competent."

"Not too butch?"

He raised his eyebrows. "To me you look all babe," he said. "And I would hire you over any national candidate they threw my way."

"For section chief?"

Ben managed to smile, feeling the laugh lines of middle age creasing his cheek. A bubble of hope—he hated to think he could be so cheered by Susannah's sorrow, but there it was—rose in his chest. "Call it," he said, sandwiching her hand between both of his, "whatever you want."

Chapter 31

*T*he first interview had gone well. Or at least, not badly. The three men on the other side of the table had praised Marcus; she had praised Marcus. Felix Hofgruder, who was head of the entire Med Research school but never appeared in the dim hallways of Oncology, had nodded and glimmered at Susannah over the tops of his rimless reading glasses. This was preliminary, they told her; this was an ice-breaker, not really necessary for Susannah since they all knew her fine work with Marcus, but the outside candidates were coming in, and they wanted a level playing field. She had impressed them, they said. They thought she should have a crack at the job. There were always politics, Felix Hofgruder said, and Susannah said she understood perfectly.

She refused to think any more about it. Other things puffed and swelled and filled her mind. Leaving the lab early in the lingering heat, she took Toby shopping for school clothes. Last fall, he'd sported mostly flannel pajamas and the cool teal of the hospital gown. Now, even with the meds suppressing his growth, he'd leaped to a new size; they carried home jeans, turtlenecks, a complete Knicks warm-up outfit. Meanwhile, the lab itself was ready for the next stage. Based on the *CR* article, the apoptosis-virus project had received enough funding from the National Cancer Institute to keep Cutter and Tomiko and bring in another grad student and technician for fall. And so she thought about clothes and cells, and she patted her short hair; she waited for it to grow, as she waited for the committee to make up its mind and for Nick and Linsey to give themselves up.

She might have waited longer. She might have waited weeks, even months, until another seismic shift did her marriage in, or until Nick came back with a magic paste-pot and glued things back together. "I am a tolerant person," she told Coal late one night, and the dog stretched his neck up and licked her nose. But then there came the Friday night when Nick kissed her before he went out for fresh air, his lips lingering as if to say he didn't plan on intercourse with Linsey tonight, and Susannah faced the prospect of faking another orgasm. Her heart constricted; she couldn't do it. Nick would drive his twelve point two miles and arrive home guiltily horny, and he would take off his wire-rimmed glasses and undress her, and she would fail to act the part, and their lovemaking would be like a dry plain.

Better to act, better no matter what.

It had been three weeks since the conference, almost a month since that afternoon at Bluegrass Lake. Her period was more than late. She waited until Nick had been gone for an hour, until she had walked the dog, given Toby his meds, folded the laundry. Unpacking her purchases from the hardware store, she found a Phillips's head screwdriver in the basement and set to work on the locks. The task went surprisingly quickly. Tiptoeing into Toby's room, she kissed his moist forehead and whispered, "I'll be right back, pumpkin," and he stirred and mumbled in the first stage of sleep. His skin gave off the odor of cod-liver oil, the cyclosporine at work. Susannah rolled her car silently out of the driveway, then turned on the ignition and headed for the arterial.

At the base of Linsey's drive—wider than theirs, flat and smoothly asphalted—she parked. The radio played Golden Oldies, "Light My Fire" and "Satisfaction" and "Ode to Billie Joe." Her hand on her still-flat belly, Susannah made mental lists of afternoon babysitters. Danny Griffiths, at least until he started his residency. Tomiko. That shy girl around the corner. There was Max staying by himself across the street—no, too dangerous. Toby could come to the lab sometimes, when they weren't up against a deadline. Now that Marcus Griffiths wasn't around to disapprove.

And Mama said to me, Child, what's happened to your appetite? Susannah slouched in the seat. Better reception, up here on Tinker Mountain. In Linsey's kitchen, the overhead light silhouetted Safe-T-Man, sitting motionless at the kitchen table. What a gas that had been, unpacking old Safe-T. She'd had fun, early on, with Linsey. Not something Susannah could say about a lot of other women. She'd liked stenciling Linsey's new kitchen, laying *feng shui* carpet in her bedroom, listening to her eulogize the middle-aged rebel who'd widowed her. They'd compared the trashiest sex they'd ever had, the stupidest idea they'd ever followed through on. When my college boyfriend broke up with me, Susannah had confessed to her, I stole his twenty-one-speed bike. I rode it to the edge of a cliff and then pushed it over. He knew you did it, Linsey'd said. He loved you for it. He was a rich boy, wasn't he? To think he could rouse you to that, he loved it. When I first got to Greensboro, Linsey said, I turned dry tricks. I'd get a rich lawyer to take me out for a nice dinner, I'd sort of promise him, you know, and then when we got to the dessert course, I'd excuse myself to the ladies' and slip out the window. They didn't mind. I saw one later. A girl has to eat, I told him, and he bought me a new dress.

Then did you sleep with him? Susannah asked.

A little, said Linsey. Not really.

They say that Billie Joe McAllister jumped off the Tallahachee Bridge, sang the radio. How many times, after spending a couple of hours with Linsey, had Susannah tried to bring Nick around? I know, she'd say, the girl's a walking cliché, okay, but can't you admire her guts?

She might have suspected the speed with which it had all gone. How it had been a matter of weeks before Linsey was dropping by with wine coolers late in the day, saying she happened to be in the neighborhood. How by May she was lobbying Susannah to bring Toby down to Wardleysville, South Carolina, so he could meet Brooke's grandmama.

"Good Vibrations," the radio played. Susannah snapped it off. She stepped out of the car and leaned against the door. Crickets whined, noisier than the interstate. Above, the sky curved starless and black; from the next range of hills, thunder rumbled low. Susannah and Nick had bought the house in town the year Toby fell ill. It was three blocks from the hospital. Someday, she'd said as they signed the deed, she would move back to the mountains. Not to a flimsy development like this, but to an old house set above a long curving driveway, tucked into the pines. As recently as last year, in the Transplant Center, she and Nick had talked about it. To see the next range, she'd said, and the valley below, to see where the clouds are moving from. I can live anywhere, he'd said, so long as my family's safe.

Linsey's front door opened, a long rectangle of light. Susannah stiffened. How tall the two figures were! To kiss Linsey, Nick scarcely had to bend down. In the yellow light, his high forehead looked vulnerable, a rangy boy cursed by oncoming baldness.

"Don't come home," Susannah said when he turned to jog down the shallow stone steps.

"Susannah?" he said. Shading his eyes from the porch light, he peered out into the darkness. Behind him, Linsey stood still as Safe-T-Man.

"Please. Don't even *try* to come home. I've changed the locks, Nick. I've never done things by halves in my life. I'm not about to start now."

"Susannah, whatever you got to take out, take it out on me." Linsey stepped out of the yellow light. She was wearing one of those deep-dyed Indian gowns that smelled of incense at the mall. Her voice had that hoarseness you get when you've been making out. "Not on him," she said.

"And make your day? Dream on, girl." Susannah narrowed her eyes, as if Linsey were hard to focus on. "I'm not even talking to you."

"What if I said"—Nick took several steps forward, stopping only at some invisible point about twelve paces from his wife—"that even if you've locked me out, I'm not going to spend the night here?"

"Then I'd say you were a fool to throw money at a hotel. Look, I'm not very good at this. I'm going to go now."

"No, you're not." Hair and dress fluttering, Linsey moved quickly to the other side of Susannah's car and opened the door. The latch clicked loudly, and Susannah wondered that she hadn't moved fast enough to lock it.

"Did you never watch *Lost in Space*?" she suddenly asked. Linsey looked over at Nick, as if he held the answer to this trick question. "Force fields," said Susannah. "They used to set them up around the spaceship, so aliens couldn't get at them."

"I am not an alien, Susannah."

Eye-liuhn, she pronounced it. Susannah shrugged. "Evidently not, or you'd have stayed out of the force field. Like my husband, there." She nodded toward Nick. A freakish, grim smile had crept onto her lips and wouldn't leave. Her period was going to start any second, surely, surely, she could just feel it. It wouldn't even be a miscarriage, just extremely late.

"Susannah," said Linsey, "we didn't make love."

"Course you didn't. He was going to go home and do that with me, pretending it was you all the time. Did you know he did that? Very common, I think, among middle-aged adulterers. The younger ones, of course, just get it up twice as often."

"If you want to play an insults game, Susannah, you won't find any takers here," said Nick. He wasn't even trying to crack the force field. He'd propped one foot up on the low stone wall that bordered Linsey's front yard, like a neighbor passing the time of day.

"I don't want to play any game. I want to get home to my son. Who is sleeping. Whom I will care for without any further lectures about responsibility. You can see him from time to time, naturally."

She got back into the car. She was trembling, and the smile wouldn't quit. Twice she dropped the keys before she finally got the right one into the ignition.

"Susannah," said Linsey, "you can't go off like this. It's not healthy."

"Susannah? Susannah? What is with my *name*, guys? Is there some other injured wife you're talking to as well, so you need to keep us *straight*? Susannah this, Susannah that! Do you think I'm not paying *attention*, or something?"

"We think," Nick started, and he stepped through the force field. His voice was too familiar; resisting it gave her a headache. "No, *I* think," he went on, "I don't know what Linsey thinks." Quickly he glanced across the hood of the car; sitting sideways in the driver's seat, Susannah rolled her eyes. "I think," he repeated, "that everything you say is right. Everything you *could* say is right. I should not be here. I should be home with you, working things out."

"There's nothing to work out," said Susannah. She blew out her breath, counting one two three, the way Linsey had showed her, long ago, demonstrating yoga postures. Sure enough, her nerves steadied. "I got the heart, you got the husband," she said, her head barely inclined toward Linsey. "Fair trade."

She reached to close the door. Linsey held it open at first, then at a signal from Nick let it go. Susannah turned the key. The Golden Oldies station was onto Aretha Franklin as she coasted down the mountain. The air smelled of rain.

Chapter 32

From Linsey's side porch, through the open window, came the hollow music of the wooden chimes Brooke had made for her at school that last spring. One two three, the chimes rang, the third note always a hair lower than you'd expected so it turned the happy sound into something a little mournful, like a dove's cry.

Brooke had wanted to fix the tone of those chimes, but there hadn't been time—she was such a busy little girl. When Linsey remembered that spring, it was a whirl of Brooke and John at the piano, Brooke making the chimes, the Afro-Haitian Dance Festival, Brooke up late doing the math problems John set for her, the ones for which he rewarded her with gifts to World Hunger Relief and rides on the motorcycle.

Somewhere in the stack of framed photos on the shelf was a picture of Brooke from the dance festival, posing in a squat, dressed in a brightly printed pair of knickers with a matching bandeau across her top and a long piece of cotton cloth knotted around her hair. The afternoon of the dress rehearsal, she'd given Linsey a full preview in the back yard. Linsey had sat on a bench, shelling early peas, while Brooke demonstrated. The music they danced to was just drums, so Brooke could sort of imitate it. "Boom shaka shaka boom diddy boom boom," she said while she danced. She rotated her hips, kept her center of gravity low; when she moved her legs, she led with her knees. The grass she danced on was new, bright green like the peas; her hair, peeking through the cotton band, was the color of the buttercups springing up that side of the woods. Linsey had been so proud she could have burst. When Brooke was all done, she did this sort of flirty bow, looking back over her shoulder, the bandeau knotted in the center of her sun-kissed back. Linsey had jumped up, spilling the peas, and clapped. "Bravo! Bravo!" she'd yelled.

"I didn't do the pivot quite right," Brooke said. She bent down to pick up a raw pea and popped it into her mouth. "I landed on my left foot."

"You looked perfect to me, baby," Linsey said. "Wait till Daddy sees you."

Brooke hadn't answered at first. She'd crouched on the ground to help gather the fallen peas. She was starting to show signs of spring allergies, and when she looked up her eyes were a little watery. Linsey started to ask if she needed some of that ephedrine tea. Then Brooke said, "I don't think dads are supposed to come."

"Don't be silly! All the parents are supposed to come."

"I'm pretty sure the teacher said no dads."

"Why would a teacher say a thing like that?"

"I don't know. Maybe I didn't understand her right." Brooke straightened up—so tall she was getting, still in her little-girl body—and slid her peas back into the bowl. "Dad says he's taking me fishing tomorrow," she said.

"Uh-huh. Trout season."

"I don't want to go."

"Why, you think you might miss the rehearsal? You're leaving early in the morning, Brooke honey. Daddy'll have you back here by noon."

"I don't like fishing no more," said Brooke.

"*Any* more. And you don't have to keep the fish if you don't want."

"Daddy says we do if they're big enough."

"Well, I'll talk to him. He loves to take you fishing; he'll just have to adjust a little."

"I got homework."

"It'll be Saturday!"

Brooke had unknotted the cloth around her head so her blond hair spilled over her shoulders. When she shook it over her face, Linsey couldn't quite make out if her eyes were still allergic. Grabbing a handful of unshelled peas, she had set to work, not looking at her mom. "I got a lot of homework," she'd said.

But she'd gone, in the end. Linsey had stood by while John pulled all the gear together and wrestled Brooke out of bed and kept saying Nonsense, nonsense, I need my fishing buddy to bring me luck.

At the dress rehearsal Brooke had missed a bunch of steps and had to stay after, and that night she cried and cried while John went over her mistakes with his barrels of patience, while he watched her do the steps again for him till she got them right.

What was it Charlie had said? He made her into his creature. Like he owned her. And here Linsey had always thought Brooke wanted to be owned, the way any girl would with a daddy who cared so much. I want my girl growing up *confident*, John told people. Linsey didn't know what that meant. Confidence was the main thing she'd grown up without. Maybe you needed to own a person to make them confident.

"I got homework," Brooke had said, but Linsey had pushed her to go.

When you don't want to think, you chant. Linsey couldn't chant *alone* because it made her see Brooke alone. She chanted *om* and pressed her lips together so the vibration of the *m* filled her head. Sure enough, the *om* turned into a small white ball and entered her body. It descended to her *dan tien*, just under her belly button, and circled nine times; then it spiraled up to the top of her head, around to her spine and down again. A series of colors it changed to, then it throbbed purple, indigo, green, yellow, orange, red. The red ball went out of her body, carrying her *gi*, and it entered the third eye of the Buddha. Nothing was left except her Buddha self. And inside her heart opened an eight-petal lotus, with the red ball and the white ball, radiating light.

"I got a *lot* of homework," Brooke still said, from the center of the lotus. "Hush," Linsey said. There was a word to meditate on. *Hush*.

After a while she heard Nicholas in the bathroom, and then in the kitchen mixing the instant coffee he'd brought in, his second night here. Out traveled her Buddha light, to the six realms of sentient beings.

Had she meant to have this particular man? Had she gone back on her promise to God to stop making designs?

Yes, yes, oh yes.

Had she wanted the scene with Susannah?

No.

Did she want him here, now, puttering in the kitchen with Safe-T-Man?

No. Yes.

He made her think about things. He was like Charlie that way. He made her think about Brooke, though he never spoke of Brooke, only now and then looked close at the picture on the fake mantel. That first night, after the balloon ride, he'd gone through her house like he was looking for something. Then he'd proceeded out the back door and down the hill to the creek, where he'd pulled off his shoes and socks. She'd watched while he stood there in the cold rushing water for a long while, his feet pale and splayed the way men's bare feet always were. Then he had asked, not with joy but like he was asking for a suicide weapon, if he could stay the night.

She padded into the kitchen. Last night, lying spoonlike against Nicholas's back, she had told him he still belonged to them, to Susannah and Toby. He'd taken her hand and pulled it over his waist. Then he'd said Susannah was like a prize he'd won, for knowing the right answer to the questions that didn't get asked. Like what? Linsey had wanted to know, and Nicholas had said like Toby.

Now, as if there wasn't a whole night's sleep in between, she poured herself a mug of herb tea and said, "So what is the answer?"

"To what?"

"To Toby."

"Nah, you don't get it."

Nicholas had pulled a rice cake from a brown plastic bag. He stared at it through his glasses. When he'd bit off a chunk and chewed, he crossed to Linsey's refrigerator and washed it down with guava juice straight from the bottle.

"That's terrible stuff," he said, running his tongue around his teeth.

"Scrapes your arteries clean."

He shut the refrigerator.

"Toby," he said, "*is* the answer. The question being what can slow Susannah down. You know that story, that Greek myth, about the girl who outruns her suitors?"

Linsey shook her head. The tang of rose hips filled the room. She used to cut the tea with honey for Brooke, add ginger for John, leave it alone for herself. "My mama used to read me myths," she said, "but they all run together in my head."

"Well, in this one the girl sort of wants to get married, but she doesn't want anyone inferior to herself, and she's the fastest runner in the land. The guy who finally catches her throws these golden apples onto the ground, and she can't resist them, and she slows down. Now, I don't know about her, but Susannah wanted all the way along to slow down. Only I didn't have the golden apples, to make her do it. Toby did."

Linsey nodded. She felt the heat coming off him; she felt the loose-ness of her own body. Outside somewhere, a lawn mower started up. Always there was a lawn mower, starting up. She pinched the placket of his shirt between her thumb and forefinger. "What about now?" she said.

"Now," said Nick, the breath of his voice running across the top of her hair, "Toby is the question. How much I could fight for him, I mean. How much I believe my way with him is the better way."

Linsey nodded, as if he'd said exactly the thing she had been think-ing, though for once the plight of Toby Ames was the farthest thing from her mind.

Chapter 33

A mother living with her only son. Susannah had been on her way to this one, it seemed, since the days her father had hauled them all to Mass in the dark church in Morgan-town. There by the outer aisle had hung the paintings, light against dark: the Mother and the Son, the fleshy baby on his mother's lap, the wise child leaning against his mother's knee, the gaunt son pulled down from the cross to splay across his mother's blue cloak. No one else in the pictures mattered. And so it was that she rose from her wide bed in the mornings and had only Toby to think of in the house.

Toby and Coal, whom she let out into the back yard, unleashed, to do his business and come scratch at the screen.

Often she touched herself, in the bed which still smelled faintly of Nick, before the dog whined and she rose to make coffee. She pressed fingers against her clitoris at first as a sort of containment. Hold on, the fingers seemed to say, right here. She thought back to lovers she'd had, long ago before Nick. The poet who'd lived in her building in New York, who paced like her only at night. His quick bird-like glance, the way he could crack her back when she came home late. Breathe in, he would say as she lay belly-down on the floor, then Breathe out, and he pressed perfectly so that the carti-lage in her spine released and the nerves tingled to the ends of her fingers. She spoke his name, and her fingers began to move in and out of the folds of labia. Then there had been the chief resident, married yes, and candid about it, conscious of his luck in her con-sent, finding places in the hospital where they could steal fifteen minutes, like a bad episode of *ER*, and she never came—but now, thrilling again to the illicit urgency of his cock in her mouth and vagina, she reached deep and sighed.

Nick too, the young Nick, entered her bed in this way. How he'd let her approach him, the only man she'd known who wore a smile all through the act of lovemaking, the only one who could make her come by caressing and kissing and sucking her breasts.

Oh, she whispered to herself. Oh oh oh.

Then the lovers vanished like the strings of clouds that hung over the mountains, and she heard Toby, stirring. She released herself, slid out of bed, snapped the shades up. The back yard sloped downward to Nick's goldfish pond and a tall hedge. Over the trees of the neighbor's yard, she could just make out the gray humps of the eastern mountains, but it wasn't what anyone would call a view. The goldfish circulated, anticipating breakfast. When she let Coal out, he would go sniff at the pond. The first morning of Nick's absence, Toby had automatically pulled the little shaker of goldfish food from the kitchen shelf and gone barefoot, full of responsibility, to take care of feeding. Not that she'd have let them die.

"School day, Tobe," she said, belting her robe as she passed his room.

"I have a headache."

"Let's check that after morning meds. C'mon."

In no time, it seemed, the kitchen had reverted. She'd separated out the foods only Nick cottoned to: prefab spaghetti sauces, Annie's Pasta Alfredo boxes, jars of macadamia nuts, Kellogg's Oats & Honey that he hid from Toby and consumed late at night, pretzel nuggets, sardine tins. These things she'd packed into a box and driven up Tinker Mountain one day before work, and left silently on Linsey's concrete front porch. In their place she'd stocked yogurts, dried fruits, chocolate-covered espresso beans, pesto sauces, frozen mozzarella sticks that she and Toby microwaved for a bedtime snack. Last Sunday, the first full weekend of Nick's absence, while Toby was across at Max's, she'd reorganized shelves and then put on the rock radio station that Toby liked. There in the kitchen she'd done a little dance, hands on well-shaped hips, bump and grind, *this kiss this kiss* wailing from the radio.

She laid out the pills, the psychedelic blue and the dull orange, the Minipress cut in two, the cod-liver-smelling cyclosporine, the hypodermic of gancyclovir at which Toby no longer even flinched. Since the moment Nick left, he'd stopped whining about meds. She should have been glad. But there was something a little creepy in the way Toby went through the line of tablets and capsules, raising and lowering his orange juice glass, forcibly swallowing then moving down the line. If she asked him a question while he was taking his meds, he wouldn't answer until they were all down, and he'd held out his arm for the swab and injection. While he was taking his pills he wasn't, in some spooky way, *there*.

"After school," she reminded him when the pills were all down, the chart checked, "I have that big meeting. It might go till supper."

"You told me already."

"And Tomiko said she'd come by here, get you settled, do meds and all that. If she has to leave before I get back, you can go to Max's."

"Isn't Tomiko part of the meeting?"

"No, this one's just for me. So you come straight home, okay?"

"I have a headache," he said again. "I don't want to go to school."

"I'll give you Tylenol. Not a good day to stay home, pumpkin."

"Can't I go to Dad's?"

"What?" Susannah stopped in the middle of scrambling eggs.

"To Dad's. You know."

"You mean to Linsey's."

It was the first time she'd said aloud what Toby knew, that Nick was staying up on Tinker Mountain. She had not, despite what she'd told Ben, given Toby the truth. On Saturday afternoon he had ridden his bike downtown to Nick's shop and passed the day there putting together an Austrian hussar from one of the kits Nick kept in the back, do-it-your-selfers in which Toby had never shown a jot of interest. Susannah had phoned the shop while Toby was on his way. "Don't break his heart," she'd commanded Nick. "Don't make any offers."

"I'll offer to come home," Nick had said.

"Don't you dare," she'd said.

She held, she'd thought, all the cards.

But now she had said it: Linsey's. "Max goes to his dad's six weeks in the summer," Toby answered, unruffled. "Plus school vacations. He says when his dad lived in Roanoke, he stayed there every weekend."

"Max's parents are divorced," said Susannah. Her son shrugged and attended to his cereal. "We're not at that point yet. We're a long way from that point. We're not even going to that point, necessarily."

"That's what parents always say."

"Oh, yeah? How many parents have you had, Toby?"

He looked at her from under his long bangs, but held back the retort. "I dunno," he said instead.

"Your dad and I have been under a lot of stress."

"Cause of me."

"Because of ourselves. It's better to have some time away from each other right now."

"So can I go there?"

"To where your dad's staying?"

"To Linsey's, yeah."

"Your dad has his shop to run. A headache isn't enough to make him close up."

"Linsey'll be home."

"*Linsey?*" Susannah examined her watch as if an answer lay there. For years Nick had been after her to hold her ground. All right, Nick, she said silently. Then to Toby, "No. You need your meds after school. Tomiko's expected. I don't have time to make new arrangements. Now finish up, you'll be late."

When she tried to hug him at the door, he pulled away. From the window she watched him walk to the corner, where the bus came. He had an athlete's rolling gait, Nick's sloping shoulders, her own lifted chin. If she could make another like him—stubbornness and sick heart and all— she would set right to it.

Chapter 34

*T*oby Brooke had been only the tiniest bit surprised to wake up and find his father gone. Not so much because of the fighting, though everybody knew that fights added up to divorce as surely as not brushing added up to cavities. Rather because his dad and Linsey seemed to belong together, like on a team, and his mom belonged on another team. You saw it all the time in sports. Team chemistry, the TV reporters called it, when one guy was shipped off to Detroit from Atlanta and another went from Seattle to New York.

He'd seen it that first Saturday afternoon, when he got sent to his dad's shop so his dad could have time with him. When his mom used to come in there, it was like a warm gusty wind in a forest. She talked fast. She exclaimed over the new things his dad had got in. He could feel his dad pulling away from whatever he'd been concentrating on, and then working to keep up with his mom. But when Linsey came in, on Saturdays, you hardly got a ripple. She had that accent, and she laughed a lot, picking up some of the funnier-looking models. But his dad was the same when she was there as when she wasn't, and both ways he paid better attention to Toby Brooke than usual. Of course, Toby Brooke figured, by Saturday his dad hadn't seen him in almost a week. His mom should be sending him there after school on days like this one, when she had a meeting and went to all the trouble of getting Tomiko to come over. She had to *pay* Tomiko, too. She wouldn't have to pay his dad.

School, Toby Brooke had discovered when he came back from all that time in the hospital, had become a question of reading. The teacher—Miss Cross last spring, Mrs. Saunders now—handed out worksheets every half-hour. All the kids sharpened their pencils or got out their crayons, and then Mrs. Saunders settled in at her desk with the batch of worksheets they'd done before lunch. If you finished the worksheet ahead of the others, she said, you could read until everyone was done. The worksheet usually took Toby Brooke about five minutes, and then he pulled a book out of his desk. Last spring he'd brought the worksheet up to Miss Cross and asked permission to start reading, but Miss Cross always said he had to check his work first. So now he didn't ask. His worksheets weren't perfect, but they were done okay, and he'd made it through the biographies of all the major living basketball players along with a handful of baseball guys.

The day his mom had the meeting, though, he only pretended to read. Mostly he was trying to listen to his heart. When Dr. Lieberman talked about listening to his heart, he meant with a stethoscope. When other people, in poems and so on, talked about listening to your heart, they meant deciding what you really thought about something. Toby Brooke didn't mean either of those. He meant something more like what happened when you listened to music. How it made you move a certain way, or want to be in a certain place. Now that he thought of himself as Toby Brooke, he heard the heart better than he used to. Listening to it today, he felt he had to run somewhere, only he couldn't tell if the urging of the heart was to run towards or away from something. And the towards or away, he was sure, had to do with his dad.

After awhile, Max had told him, your dad gets to be just this older guy you have fun with sometimes. Also he sends you money. When I remember my dad from before, Max said, it's like remembering this whole other person.

Trying to remember his dad, Toby Brooke got unaccountably scared. His face flushed. His hands started to shake. "Are you all right, Toby?" Mrs. Saunders asked. She was collecting the worksheets. At the exact same time, she and Toby Brooke looked at the one on his desk, a sheet about amphibians, which had nothing filled in on the lines. The girl next to Toby Brooke, curly haired and brown-skinned, started to giggle, but Mrs. Saunders shushed her.

"I think I should go to the nurse," Toby Brooke said. "My head hurts."

He had a fever, the nurse said with satisfaction. She wouldn't say how much. The office left a message on his mom's voicemail at work, but it was two o'clock already. So he stayed in the nurse's office, his head like a bowling ball, his heart singing a tune he couldn't hear. On his way out of the school, the curly haired girl ran behind him and said she was sorry, but Toby Brooke waved her away. As she went off to her bus, he felt suddenly very old, as if all his schoolmates around him were babies in diapers, and he was the only one who knew anything about the world. He was the only one in a hurry.

He ran past his bus to the number eighty-five. He knew it went up Tinker Mountain because he'd taken it once last spring, going home with a boy named Ewan whose three big sisters all made Toby Brooke pull up his shirt and show the scar. "Where's your pass?" the driver asked.

"I'm going to my dad's," said Toby Brooke, out of breath. "My mom forgot to write it. She always forgets."

"I don't usually take you."

"I'm going to my dad's. I said. In Tinker Estates."

His dad was at the shop, or somewhere. Not in Tinker Estates. Still, he was going.

"Better bring it next time," said the driver. Ewan was sitting in the third row. He punched Toby Brooke's arm as he went by, but he didn't ask anything.

As the bus wound its way out Hollins Road and onto Route Eleven, Toby Brooke leaned his hot forehead on the cool window. The landscape got more jumbled as they went along—seafood restaurants next to car dealers, a cluster of new townhouses sandwiched between Wendy's and Burger King, a vacant factory building rising behind a swimming-pool store. Finally they left all but four kids off at the bottom and started crawling up the back of the mountain. Toby Brooke's breathing got short and labored, as if he were hiking up the road rather than sitting in the bus. He gripped the metal bar along the seat back in front of him. His hand burned.

He knew he'd be in trouble—with his mom, with Tomiko who was waiting back at his house to give him meds. That wasn't what seemed to matter. The bus wound higher and higher. There seemed to Toby Brooke something complete about what he was doing. Linsey was Brooke's mom. His dad was his dad. And Brooke had been—Brooke had been—

Scared.

That was the feeling. His heart was scared as a rabbit and not of dying.

When you're scared, his mom had said, that's when you've got to get back on the horse.

"Tinker Estates," the driver said.

Toby Brooke grabbed his book bag and scrambled off, leaving two other kids on the bus. He started up the curving entrance road purposefully, as if he did this all the time. Then as he got closer to Linsey's house, he slowed. Tomiko was waiting at his house, but he hadn't gone there. He hadn't gone to his dad's shop. His dad wouldn't be here on the mountain. Linsey would be here. Linsey, his other mom.

A breeze moved the leaves on a pair of big magnolia trees overhanging the fresh black asphalt. His legs moved like a pair of pillars stuffed with sand. His heart was beating, beating. Not like the time he skipped the Minipress, but like that rolling drumbeat you heard before a big announcement. He was Toby Brooke, he reminded himself. He was Toby, she was Brooke. She was Brooke Toby, his conjoined twin. He was going to see his mom. She was going to see her—

John, came the name. Her head hurt. There was so much to do. She hadn't done anything right. Her feet felt hot enough to blister the road. John, who was John? She should have come sooner. She should have *gotten her act together*. It wasn't so hard as she was making it out to be, this ought to be easy for a *girl like her, a special girl my girl*. What did she have to be scared of? If she'd just *put her mind to it*. It was such a *bummer* when she *flaked*. Her heart banged in this too-tight chest. She would try everything again. From the beginning. Yes. And then his big arms would go around her, and the salty smell of his neck; she was his girl, his only girl, *and my heart belongs to daddy*.

Reaching the house, Brooke shook the bells her mom kept by the door, but no one came. No car in the drive. From somewhere down the curving street came the roar of a gas mower, pollution of air and sound. She had come the wrong way; she had *blown it again*. Where was her mind, how could she put her mind to it? When Brooke looked out on the valley below, the mountains and clouds seemed to spin. She was hot; her head hurt. She lay down in the cool grass.

Chapter 35

Nick and Linsey were on their way back from Lexington, taking the Parkway instead of the interstate because Linsey had never been on it this far north. Nick, driving, kept glancing toward the passenger seat. It was the first time they'd left town together, in a car, as if they shared an agenda, a man and a woman. Soon enough, guilt would bury him like a mudslide. For now he wanted only to capture snapshots of her face, tanned and bemused against the headrest, the rises and gorges flashing beyond her.

They had been to visit Mrs. Daphne Pinkerton O'Leary, widowed last week by former State Senator Archibald Jefferson O'Leary, who claimed descent in a zig-zag line from the prolific Thomas Jefferson. Twice while the Senator lived, Nick had driven up to examine his Revolutionary and Civil War collections, especially the primitive soldiers molded from melted bullets in the blacksmith shop at Andersonville. The Senator, unlike his ancestor, had died without issue; Mrs. Daphne O'Leary was finding herself with debts.

"I was such a very great admirer of your husband," Linsey had said while Nick inspected the collections, left to molder in cedar boxes in the dank back room of the O'Leary mansion. "That prison program he began? I tell you, I breathed easier at night."

"They fought him tooth and nail on that one!" Mrs. O'Leary said. She was a red-faced, blue-haired, high-pitched old belle, given to broad-shouldered dresses with flat lace collars. "Thought they should spend the money on remedial programs. You just can't remediate those people."

"You certainly cannot," said Linsey. Her South Carolina accent helped; she made two syllables out of "not," so that it sounded more sincere.

"You know who I mean," said Mrs. O'Leary.

"I know."

"The coloreds and them."

"It's a tricky world."

"All his life he was gentle to me," said Mrs. O'Leary. "I hope you'll be able to say the same."

"I thank my stars already," said Linsey, and Nick, bent over the Andersonville officers, felt her glance brush his back.

In the back of the station wagon sat four boxes. Two sets of Revolutionary figures, one lead, the other roughly carved black walnut that would need a great deal of sanding down and repainting but would bring a handsome price for the wood alone. The other two were Civil War. For the Andersonville collection Nick already had a buyer, a nervous professor at Virginia Tech who liked to bend unwilling victims' ears with pornographic disquisitions on the atrocities of the Andersonville prison camp. The other set was the sort Nick liked. It was a collection, not of soldiers, but of more common people, children and slaves and a preacher with the unlikely features of P. T. Beauregard, all of them dull but incredibly uncracked alabaster, china-painted by some rebel widow down on her luck. "So *dusty*," Mrs. O'Leary had said, turning her face away, ashamed, and she'd sold the box to him for seventy-eight dollars.

At Limestone Quarry Lookout, Nick pulled the car over. As they stepped out, the clouds overhead pulled apart, so that a cone of light spread over the valley and leaped up the mountain. Nick switched to sunglasses. His arm went easily around Linsey's smooth back. With Susannah, he'd have rested his stunted hand on her opposite shoulder, but Linsey's shoulder pressed into his chest at the armpit. "You were perfect, back there," he said.

"You got a steal of a deal, I hope."

"They're never a steal. Mrs. Daphne is no dummy. But I think she was kinder to a daughter of the South than she would've been to a Yankee boy."

"Sakes alive," said Linsey, and she wasn't even putting on the accent, "look at this view."

Below them, the old quarry yawned white. Across the valley ranged the greens and golds of ripened fields, interrupted by factories whose smoke, far off, blended with bluish mist. Toward the western horizon rose the Alleghenies, tentative and foreboding as an advancing army. Nick licked his forefinger, and held it up. "Ten knots," he said.

"You'd like to hitch your old balloon up to this, wouldn't you?"

"Or a hang glider. There aren't enough sheer drop-offs in these mountains, though. You need a younger range."

"Well, *I* don't."

He kissed her forehead—a stern brow, when you looked closely. The dark blond sprinkled with stray, unruly white hairs, refusing dye as she refused makeup, eye cream, exfoliant, all the mysterious magic of Susannah's bathroom vanity. "I liked being with you," he said, "in the air."

"That fellow come get his balloon yet?"

"Henry Patterson? He sent his minions. Mustang Sally is history."

"We are all history, one way or the other. I mean, look at that poor racist lady."

"So we are," he said softly. The wind puffed at his words. "But right now I want you to know—"

"Don't say it," said Linsey. She put her free arm to his chest, as if to stop him from going somewhere.

"Say what?"

"Don't say—you know. Love."

"I wasn't going to," said Nick, though he had been. "I want," he tried again, "to write our little history, right here." He swept his hand over the dark, plummeting slope. "So anybody traveling through time could look and say we had some right. Just a little right."

Linsey's arm looped his waist. "Look," she said. "Hawk."

They watched the bird circle upward on the draft, its wings held perfectly steady, tilting counterclockwise against the widening blue of the sky. When it finally crested and veered off, behind the next rise, Nick felt a startling absence, as if someone he knew had just jumped off the cliff.

He pulled off the sunglasses and squinted. "Let's get down the mountain," he said to Linsey. "It's getting late."

Susannah was fifteen minutes into the second interview with the committee when Tomiko called. She had already phoned the school, Tomiko said, when the bus went by and Toby didn't get off. Word was that he had left school on time.

"They said he'd had a fever," Tomiko said. "There's a message about it on your voicemail."

"They didn't call my cell."

"I guess they didn't think it was that serious. They didn't want to raise the alarm an hour before school let out."

Susannah leaned against the wall of the small vestibule outside the committee room, one hand against her free ear so she could hear Tomiko better. Inside, the committee awaited her return. "He had a headache this morning," she said. "I didn't think that was serious, either."

"He can get infections easily, right? With all the immune suppression they load on him?"

"I forgot to take his temp," said Susannah. Shame crept over her; she could feel her neck redden.

"The nurse said he had all his going-home stuff with him. He left straight from her office. Would he walk home, if he missed the bus?"

Susannah checked her watch. "He might," she said. She thought of the Baptist church, the basketball hoop. "He knows the way. He's never done it before, though."

"I'll trace the route if you'll tell me how he would go. I brought a math game for him. Last time he told me he was starting to like math. He said his—you know."

"His heart donor."

"He said she liked math."

Susannah gave her directions. She didn't mention the Baptist church. "Take the dog," she advised. "Maybe he'll sniff the kid out."

"Right, Chief."

"And call Cutter with whatever you find, okay? I'm switching this phone off, but I'll want to know."

Stowing the cell, Susannah reentered the committee room. Felix Hofgruder was penciling notes; Dr. Jamison, the chief of immunology, was pouring himself a fresh glass of ice water. There were six on the committee, all men. "Everything all right?" asked the youngest member, an AIDS researcher named Armel Singh.

"Missing kid," said Susannah lightly. "Now, you wanted more background on the bcl-2 project, is that right?"

But fifteen minutes later, a knock came, and Cutter put his head through the door. "Tomiko," he said, and handed her the cordless.

No sign of him, Tomiko reported, and in fact she had gone by the Baptist church, as well as the bridge over the river.

"I'll have to leave this meeting," said Susannah.

"It's an interview—isn't it?"

"A second interview. And they don't like candidates who pull the mommy excuse. Goddamn it."

"Wait." Tomiko was still short of breath. "Did I hear you—tell Faye—Toby's dad isn't living—at home?"

"Nick's moved out for the moment."

"He can be reached—?"

"Hold on."

Susannah had made her way down the hall to her office phone, where she keyed the shorthand for Nick's shop. "No luck," she said after it rang six times. "Though Toby could be hanging around down there, I suppose. In which case—"

"Susannah. He doesn't feel well. He wouldn't hang out downtown with a fever, would he?"

"Not normally."

"Is someone—at home?"

"What do you mean? You're *at* my house."

"I mean where your husband is staying." Tomiko waited; Susannah could hear her breathing, coming slower now. Down the hallway, the door to the committee room remained open. "Susannah," Tomiko said, "if you're not worried, I'm not. I can stay right here."

"I don't want to call her," Susannah said.

"So give me the number. Give me the address. I'll leave a note here in case he wanders home. Go back to the interview. I'm sure everything's fine."

Reluctantly, her neck splotched with worry, Susannah made her way back to the smooth maple table, the cushioned seat. The two representatives of Cantrex were ready to back up; they wanted to discover the origins of the virus project, what drug remedies Susannah might foresee. Meanwhile Tomiko was driving, driving. Out Peters Creek Road to Tinker Mountain, up the winding drive, into Tinker Estates.

"I'm sorry," said Cutter, when he stuck his head in again.

She had found him at the address Susannah had given. Curled, shrimp like, on the grass. Already she had phoned 911, but she thought Susannah should know.

"Yes," said Susannah. "Yes, of course."

The hiring committee, especially the members of the Cantrex board who had come all the way from New Jersey, frowned as the candidate made her excuses again. Felix Hofgruder shuffled through her papers looking for exculpatory evidence, but found only her six-month leave, the year before. Still, there was the initial apoptosis series, they noted; there was the loyalty and talent of her subordinates. Up to that point, they agreed after she left—taking the stairs over the elevator, racing out to the parking lot, jacket looped over her wrist, pocketbook hyperbolically flapping—it had been a promising interview.

Chapter 36

"Cryptococcus," said Ben Lieberman. "Not uncommon among patients with defects in T-cell function."

"Nobody told us Toby had a defect!" said Nick.

"*All* transplant recipients have poor T-cell function. They're immunocompromised, just like people with AIDS," said Ben. He leaned patiently over his desk. "You can get cryptococcus from pigeon droppings. Which is not to imply"—he held up a fore-stalling hand—"that you live in a house full of birdshit. It comes off the soil, especially soil that's getting dug up in dry weather so the droppings are aerosolized."

"They're digging behind the house across the street," said Susannah.

"Max's house?" said Nick.

"Yeah. Rototilling the yard. The kids go around it to the meadow."

"Jesus, Susannah, you never said—"

"That's just one scenario," Ben interrupted. "There are plenty of others, none of them anyone's fault." With a glare at his own fingernails, Nick was quiet. "We've done a spinal tap, which shows meningitis. You say he had fever and headache, right, Susannah?"

"Right. A headache. I didn't know about the fever."

"But the school reported it. And he was—what? Hallucinating, or something?"

"Tomiko said he was talking about Brooke. Just kind of . . . I don't know. Raving."

"Who is Brooke?" Ben ran a finger down Toby's chart, as if he could find the name there.

"Brooke is dead," said Nick.

"Ah," said Ben. "The girl with the heart." He looked briefly at Susannah, then at a spot on the wall, as if a tiny portrait of Brooke hung there. His eyebrows sloped upward toward the center like a pair of opposing accent marks.

"The boy," corrected Susannah, "with the girl's heart."

"I don't think it's a gender problem, Suzy."

"Ben, please."

Ben leaned back in his swivel chair. "Look," he said, "neurologic disturbances, which is what we have here, are a symptom of cryptococcal disease."

"How bad is that?" said Nick.

"Perfectly curable. We've got a drug that takes care of it. A day or two of intravenous in the hospital, then we'll send him home with a prescription. Give us a chance to check some other things, too." Ben riffled through the thick pile of paper on his desk. "I want to check a few things."

"I still don't get," said Nick, clearing his throat, pushing up his glasses, "what we did wrong."

"You did nothing wrong. You lived. Hey. Cheer up. There are dozens of these infections, folks. Suzy, you tell him." Susannah nodded, dumbly. "Dozens. And this is the first that Toby's caught. You might want to work out a better communication system with the school. But he'll be fine. He's a tough boy."

As he saw them out the door, Ben's broad hand lingered on Susannah's shoulder and traveled quickly over her neck. He shook Nick's hand with a doctor's reassurance, and told them to check with the nursing staff about seeing their son.

This time, Nick pondered some ten hours later, he had held his tongue. What *we* did wrong, he'd said. He had not accused his wife. He had not listed her previous screw-ups. She was better at argument than he. She was better, when it came to that, at apologies. It seemed clear to Nick— now that Toby had again been rushed to the hospital, again been put on a drip, again had the color sucked out of his face and the strength sucked from his limbs—that he had gone away from Susannah in the first place because of how she neglected Toby, and that his greatest sin was not adultery but leaving his son in her care.

He was washing the alabaster figures in a solution of white vinegar and sodium sulfate in the washbasin of his workshop in the Tudor house. Outside was not yet light. He'd left Toby's hospital room when Susannah arrived at four A.M.; he'd asked her simply for the keys to the house. The black pane above the basin gave back oily images of his face and white T-shirt, the benches and boxes behind him. Gently, with his good hand, he scrubbed the little people in the sink.

They looked like what they were: bits of stone refashioned. Toys. It was a way to make a living. You met interesting people, sort of wacky people. If you were halfway competent with your eye and your brush, you acquired a rep. No one told you what to do. Unlike jazz piano, there weren't a lot of other people out there trying to take the space. Unlike hot-air ballooning, you didn't have to become a carnival clown. Unlike beer brewing, it was commercially legal. Unlike—

He had led a trivial life.

He pushed such thoughts away. He had an important task. He had to get his son away from Susannah. Carefully he lifted the clean figures out of the solution and laid them in a tub of clear water. At first they floated, their hollow insides filled with air, then each one burped a bubble and settled to the bottom.

Coal, behind him, whined. "Okay, boy," said Nick. He reached for the hook by the back door, where they always hung the leash. Not there. "Fuck," he whispered. She wasn't even walking the dog properly. He went through the downstairs, flicking on lights. Coal trotted behind, tail bobbing. No leash on the kitchen counter or the mail table. Not hanging from any doorknobs—Susannah loved to hang things off doorknobs—or over the staircase railing. Fuck. He was not going to walk the dog without a leash; it was against the law and anyway Coal had run off twice last year. "Sorry boy, sorry boy," he kept saying, wheeling from room to room. This was it, this was the last straw. The rules are so *simple*, he heard himself saying to his wife, they are so *easy* to follow, you have to be *perverse* not to follow these rules. For Toby, for the dog, for anything.

He was striding through the living room when the doorbell rang. "Great. Just great," he said aloud. He yanked the door open to Linsey, who had a bag from Dunkin' Donuts. "I can't find the dog's leash," he said by way of greeting.

"Right over there," she said. She pointed to the hat rack in the corner of the front hall, where the leash dangled latch downward like a dead snake.

"Oh. Right. Jesus," he said. With the stubs of his fingers, he rubbed the back of his neck, then took the kiss she offered him. "I was worked up," he said.

"You're tired." The way she said it, *tie-yud*, made him feel the fatigue in his bones, in his lungs. "Brought you a pick-me-up," she said.

She held forth the bag. She looked tie-yud herself, her thin face drawn, her hair uncombed, as if she had tried to sleep but only tossed on the pillow. Coal was licking her hand. "Let's sit outside," said Nick.

Which was partly because he wanted air. Partly because he didn't want to be alone with Linsey in this house, his marriage house. Boundaries, he thought, the fatigue creeping through his limbs. He was a man of boundaries.

Coal was content to be tied to the bottom of the porch rail, to nose around the dark bushes, while Nick settled next to Linsey on the stoop and opened the bag. Hot coffee, three glazed doughnuts. "I thought you considered this stuff poison," he said.

"At five in the morning, a man needs a little poison," she said.

He drank and ate. They were comforting, the caffeine and the sugar. "Toby's going to be fine," he said when he'd washed down a doughnut.

"I know, I called the hospital."

"You talked to Susannah?"

"She was polite."

"Yeah. She would be."

"You can't say it's her *fault*, Nick."

"Yes, you can. Yes you can." He tipped back the cardboard cup; the coffee burned the back of his mouth. "Let's walk the dog," he said.

She slipped her hand into his as they walked. For a flicker he thought of the neighbors, but they were all asleep. "I'm going to separate," he said when they'd covered the first long block. "Susannah and I need to live apart. It's got nothing to do with you."

"Well, now, I *am* flattered."

He squeezed her thin hand, rubbed the back of it with his thumb. "I mean you don't have to take me in," he said.

"Oh, I see. In case I like to be intimate with you but I don't like to see your dirty socks lying around."

"Something like that. I have to do some planning. About Toby. About how I'm going to get custody."

"Is that what you think you're going to do?"

"Look, he had a headache yesterday morning," he said. They'd reached the stream; the pre-dawn light gave definition to the bushes, the slope, the water where Coal splashed. "Headaches are in the literature. You're supposed to watch for them. You or I, we would've taken his temp. He'd have stayed home, we'd have noticed other symptoms. By noon he'd have been at the doctor's. But Susannah had a big meeting. She didn't want to jeopardize her plans. She took a calculated risk with her only son. She won't *learn*."

"It couldn't of helped," Linsey said, "that you and I were off." She let go Nick's hand and hugged him. The length of her slight torso pressed up against his, her uncombed head on his shoulder. "*That* was a—what did you call it?"

"Calculated risk."

"When you think about it."

"I didn't change the locks on the house."

"She didn't sneak off to some man's house at night."

"Hey." Nick held Linsey off by the shoulders while Coal scrambled back up the bank. "Whose side are you on?"

"You got a boy. You got a wife who loves you."

"Do I?"

"Yes. And then you got me, too."

"Do I?"

"You don't know a damn thing, do you?"

He let go her shoulders and took a step back. "The man you're looking at," he said, his free, maimed hand against his chest, "used to know everything he needed to know."

"And how did that feel?"

"It felt good. It felt very good. And now, the one thing I know that way is how to be with Toby. How to keep my son safe."

"Good," said Linsey, very slow and deliberate. "I am glad you know that."

Her eyes filled and spilled over.

"Oh, God," he said. Like a proud vessel made of glass, he heard himself break and tinkle in cheap pieces on the pavement. "Oh God," he said again. He reached but she stepped away. Then he reached again with words; he was sorry, sorry, oh so sorry to be such a dumb ass, to say such a dumb-ass thing, and she let him hold her till his shirt soaked her tears, but that was all she would do. Her arms hung straight at her sides, her shoulders curled forward like a store mannequin. Through her sobs he could hear only the echo of his own voice in his head, explaining like an ignoramus to Ben Lieberman, *Brooke is dead.* Finally Coal pulled on the leash and whined, and they walked him back to the house together, and finished the donuts with milk until the sun rose September red over the dark hills, and it was time for Nick to drive back to the hospital.

"You tell him from me," Linsey said as she got into her own car. "You tell him."

"Tell him what?" Nick asked.

"Tell that Toby," she said, turning the ignition, "he ought to have known better."

"How?" he asked—tall and balding, a Yankee in the Virginia mist.

"Just tell him," she said with a twitch in her face, "from me. From Brooke's mom. Tell him."

Chapter 37

*S*he drove home then, in the bright dawn, and slept. All night she had only tossed. Now, mid-morning, she fell into the cheap bed she'd bought when she arrived in Roanoke—she'd left John's waterbed in Granite Falls, said she'd send for it but never had—and let sleep take her like a tidal wave. And somewhere at the bottom of the dark ocean she found a kind of pearl, which she seemed to hold in her teeth as she woke.

Except for the roar of the interstate, the house was silent. The hand-thrown pottery clock read eleven. While tea steeped, she showered. "A cat," she said to Safe-T-Man when she returned, steam-cleaned, to the kitchen. "Two cats. This house needs a pair of cats."

Then, sipping tea, she undressed Safe-T and pulled his three plugs. Gradually he deflated, his face caving slowly inward like someone aging in fast motion. When he was far enough gone, she took him off the chair and laid him on the floor, and with her knees and hands pressed the remaining air out, so she could roll him up like an air mattress and pack him back in his box.

She drove to the hospital. "You're lucky," the nurse on the ward said. "We just wheeled him back from X-ray."

For a full minute Linsey stood outside the hospital room. It was a double, but the near bed lay empty. Hazy light sliced through the vertical blinds. Half-drawn, the blue curtain hid the upper part of Toby's bed, but on the far side of it Susannah sat, reading aloud.

"So in his first year at Louisiana State University," Linsey heard Susannah reading, "Shaquille announced that he would be entering the NBA draft pick."

"That's not true," interrupted Toby. "He didn't go pro till he was twenty. I read it in *Rick Barry's Basketball Bible*."

"Maybe he was already twenty when he went to LSU. He wasn't much of a student."

"Huh-unh. His parents wanted him to finish college. He made it to his junior year."

"Okay, honey. Okay, so the book's got it wrong." Susannah leaned back in the plastic chair and rotated her neck. She looked fresher than Nick had, though she must have been here since the wee hours. Then she spotted Linsey. "Oh," she said.

"I meant to bring something," Linsey said. "A comic book or chocolate or something. But I forgot."

"Doesn't matter. Tobe's been asking about you. Here." Susannah stood. She motioned to the chair. She smiled with mouth closed, too tired to fake.

"You don't have to go," Linsey said, stepping gingerly into the room. "I'll just be a minute."

"Please. Be longer. I could use the break."

"Oh. Sure. Yeah, of course. Take as long as you like, Susannah. Get yourself some coffee. Sure."

Linsey took the blue plastic seat. Only as Susannah stepped out—not judging, not forgiving, just stepping out like a mother relieved on her shift—did she turn to Toby, in the bed.

He was pale, of course, a little glassy-eyed. The hand receiving the drip lay on the white coverlet, discreetly taped. The excess hair on his pale forearms looked freakish, a man's growth on a boy's limb. But none of these were what Linsey noticed.

It was the mouth. Still the flat upper lip he'd gotten from Susannah, but the bottom lip pressed upward in a tight, determined little gesture that Linsey recognized. Familiar too was the curl at the left edge of his mouth as if he hid a joke there. As if, whatever the deal was, this child wasn't taking it too seriously. Linsey leaned forward and touched her thumb to the lower lip. "Brooke," she said.

Toby had been regarding her, but his eyes suddenly lost their glassiness and flashed. The mouth jerked away, the lips parted. "Oh, I'm sorry," she said. She squeezed her eyes shut. Stupid stupid girl she could be. "It's just you looked, honey, for a sec—"

"It's okay," said Toby. His voice was hoarse, dehydrated from the night in the hospital.

"I've been trying to be your friend, honey. Only. . . ."

He waited for her to finish. "You can call me that," he said when she just waved her hands, like her words were things in the air. "But I've been thinking more, like, it's both."

"Both what?"

"Toby and Brooke. Toby Brooke."

"That'd be a cute name. If you grow up and have a son"—Linsey brushed at her jeans, as if she'd spilled something—"maybe you could name him that."

"It's what I call myself. In secret."

"That's nice, honey. But honey—" She took the free hand on the coverlet and stroked the back of the palm, the fingers with their pale, trimmed nails. "Brooke could never keep her nails clean," she said.

"Neither can I. It's just the hospital. They clean you up when you're not noticing."

She patted the hand and rose. Through the vertical blinds, you looked out over the ugly arterial, the squat buildings on the other side and then Roanoke Mountain, rising abruptly, the star decorating the top like a Christmas tree. "But you're not Brooke," she said.

"I am sort of, though. In my heart."

"That's a funny expression, isn't it?"

"It's not an expression," said Toby. "It's what I am."

Linsey shook her head. Below the window, traffic streamed down the interstate, everyone trading places fast. "My Brooke," she said, "was a girl with gold hair. She was chunky and sassy. She had a strong heart, and you've got that heart now."

"So I am a little bit Brooke."

"You are whatever you believe yourself to be, Toby. I used to believe I was a little bit black. But I don't nevermind it now."

Toby sat up and leaned forward. "Was Brooke scared of her dad?" he asked.

Linsey flinched. She'd known this was coming—maybe not right away, but sometime. He had the heart, after all. "Brooke wasn't scared of anything," she said. "She got nervous sometimes. She loved her daddy, like you love yours."

"I guess," said Toby.

She turned from the sunny window. He was scratching at his arm. "Honey," said Linsey, and she felt it like a lump in her throat, the pearl of understanding she'd woken up with, "you remember asking me once if I talked to Brooke?"

"Yeah." He scratched; he looked at the white coverlet.

"Well, I don't, though I've wanted to. But I think you do."

He shrugged.

"You wanted her to know you did your best. You remember?"

"Sort of."

"Well, you can just tell her yourself. You can tell her, and then just go on."

"Go on what?"

"I don't know. Live your life. Be a basketball player."

Toby smiled kind of crooked. "You're just like my mom," he said. "She says you can be anything you want. But that's not true. I mean, what if I wanted to be an astronaut? They make you take tests. You have to have perfect health. No way could I pass. Everyone just wants me to feel good about myself."

Brooke can be this country's top model, John had said, going through the studio pictures. She can be like Sharon Stone, only with more talent. And smarts. She can get a scholarship to MIT. Ought to, you mean, Linsey had finally answered him. She ought to do all those things. Well, why not? he'd said, and he'd waved the pictures at her.

"All I want," Toby was saying, sitting up a little higher, "is to bring Brooke back."

Through the gap in the yellow gown they'd dressed him in, the sun shone on the tracks of his incision, marching down his chest. If he grew to be like his dad, he would have ample hair one day, covering that old scar. If he grew. But Linsey made herself look away; she shooed off the image of Nicholas's chest.

"My daughter Brooke is dead," she said.

Toby's legs were crossed, Indian style, under the covers. Behind his back, he'd plumped the pillows. Light fell on his soft neck and delicate jaw line. With his bottom lip he made that gesture again, Brooke's little bit of stubborn. "Not all the way dead," he said.

"Maybe no one is ever all the way dead. For you she's alive. She is keeping you alive. But I can't wish her back."

"Don't you still love her?"

Linsey sat on the edge of the bed. She took his fingers in hers. "I want," she said, "to call you Toby. Just Toby, okay? So I can remember my little girl like she was, and not get us all more mixed up than we already are."

Toby Brooke didn't believe her. But then, he considered after Linsey had left, he didn't have to believe her. Linsey'd never had another person's heart in her body. No one around him had. They didn't know the first thing about it.

Chapter 38

S usannah had suspected, now, for more than a month. She had gone into the Cantrex interview suspecting, but it was too early to say, much less to decide what she might do about it. Only when the announcement had been made that Dr. Peter Simon from UCLA had accepted the directorship of the Roanoke oncology section, did she pick up a pregnancy kit from the pharmacy and watch the little strip of paper go from white to pink.

She was forty-one. Not all that old for a second child. Nick would not want her to have it, but Nick no longer lived with her.

She did the test the morning of Toby's tenth birthday. Already she had calculated the night it must have happened. Not the last time she and Nick had made love, but the last time before Linsey had been, somehow, in bed with them. The night after they'd rearranged the house and filled it with *feng shui*, and her neck had hurt. Two months ago plus a week—that must have been the time. She had felt him come inside her. They hadn't said anything about it, then or later. The time after that, he'd withdrawn, the way he always did, and she had faked an orgasm. The times after that were blurry, stupid.

She flushed the contents of the little plastic vial and disposed of the rest. No need to do anything right away. All week she had work at the lab, Peter the Great or no Peter the Great. In two days she would meet with Ben Lieberman to discuss Toby's meds.

She made espresso. While it steamed she checked for the foolish robin, but he'd deserted the nest, gone south where there were no ghostly attackers to torture him. She woke Toby, got meds into him including the new nut-brown tablet of flucanozole. Checked homework, took his blood pressure, watched him walk to the bus.

On the non-disastrous days, she would say to Ben if he were kind enough to ask, you might almost think we lead an easy life.

Ben came over that evening, along with Tomiko and Cutter and Danny Griffiths, for the grown-up celebration of Toby's birthday. Ten, the eternal age of Brooke. Toby had been home from the hospital for a week. Susannah served zucchini cake and champagne; she had weeded the garden and set pots of dark orange mums out on the deck. "Living well is the best revenge," she told Cutter after he'd complimented the garden, the goldfish, the crystal champagne glasses.

"Well, now, that's a great attitude," said Cutter, nodding his head approvingly.

"It's not original with her," said Ben, winking at Susannah.

"Really? Is that a quote? Did W. C. Fields say it, or something?"

"Cutter," said Susannah, "you are without price."

She was mildly drunk, not enough to harm the fetus. Toby tried the champagne and wrinkled his nose, the way kids were supposed to. The presents were Game Boy games and basketball paraphernalia. Tomiko brought the math game she'd had under her arm the day Toby fainted on Linsey's lawn. She opened it into a large foam mat, and everyone but Ben and Susannah played. "It's like Twister," said Tomiko, her fingers laced with Danny's, "only you have to think."

"I don't think at my own party," said Susannah.

"What do you have to think about?" said Toby.

"Numbers," said Danny.

"That's easy. That's not even thinking."

Susannah took snapshots. Ben drew the math questions from a deck of cards, and they had to put hands or feet on the answers. Tomiko and Toby got themselves tangled like a pair of crabs; Cutter bent straight from the waist, like the arch of a bridge. Danny, his goatee expanded to a neat Vandyke, always landed on equations toward the outside of the mat, so that he appeared perched, ready to spring onto the rest of them. At the end only Toby was left with his backside in the air, his hands triumphantly splayed onto *13* and 5^2. "That settles it," said Cutter, pouring more champagne. "The kid's a math genius."

"More like a human pretzel," said Susannah. "He only won because the rest of you fell down."

"It's called being ten years old," said Ben.

"I don't want to be ten," said Toby, sitting on the mat. "I want to be five. Or eighteen. Except not eighteen *yet*."

"I didn't know kids ever wanted to be younger," said Tomiko.

"Being younger rocks," said Toby.

"Prove that to me," said Ben. "Give me a game of pig."

"What, basketball?"

"No, chess. Of course basketball."

"You're not as tall as my dad."

"And you're not as tall as me."

"Elephant, then."

"Elephant?"

"Same thing, just longer."

While they shot—Toby graceful and businesslike, Ben like a misplaced squash player—Tomiko opened a thick composition book, the pages crowded with her tiny handwriting. "It's not at all the direction Pete Simon's going in," she said while Susannah glanced it over.

"No," said Susannah, "but he ought to be mighty impressed. We've already renewed your fellowship. And I bet he could get you a grant for a lab tech, to help with the next stage of this." She tipped her face up, into the equinoctial light. Her hair was growing out, but still short—shaggy, like Elizabeth Taylor's in some old movie where she crops it herself. Her skin felt burnished, like a brass vase. The test that morning had told her nothing she didn't know. Having a secret pregnancy made her efficient, made her invulnerable.

"That won't be necessary," Tomiko said. She reached across the picnic table and closed the lab notebook.

"But why not? You could use the help, you're going into that place at night—"

"I'm going to leave the lab, Susannah. I got an offer from Berkeley. Teaching and research. No commercial affiliation."

"Oh. Well." Susannah looked over at Ben and Toby. She liked the set of Ben's hips, low and slim. Toby was up, E-L to E-L-E-P. Farther back on the lawn, Danny and Cutter were crouching by Nick's goldfish, amazingly still alive. "It's not like you wouldn't have the freedom to do this line of research here," she said to Tomiko.

"I know. And if you'd been named section chief, I'd be staying."

"Because you'd have gotten my lab."

"Not so much that." Tomiko adjusted her thick glasses. "I think I want to work under a woman. Not just in the lab, but in a larger way. The chair at Berkeley's a woman."

"So am I."

"Yeah, but they didn't name you and they should have. Pete Simon's going to get on the latest bandwagon, and you know it." When Susannah didn't answer, Tomiko went on, "Or maybe it's just time for me to change. My family's in California."

"What about Danny?"

Tomiko blushed. "Ever since he dropped that lawsuit, he's wanted to leave. His sister's in San Francisco. He can finish his residency and follow me."

"Well," said Susannah, forcing her chin up a notch, "you'll have to stay in touch when you're settled. Maybe we can collaborate"—she waved her hand at Tomiko's notes—"on this."

"It would be an honor," Tomiko said.

If she were to decide not to have the baby, Susannah thought when they'd all left, she wouldn't have to tell anyone, not even Nick. She'd take a day off from work and then have what amounted to a really wretched period. Women did it all the time. Girls did it, and their mothers didn't even know.

But if that was her vote—to terminate and not tell Nick—she would be voting to end her marriage. Really and truly.

She had not thought about actually ending the marriage until Nick started his campaign to get Toby. About a week ago, now, as soon as Toby was out of the hospital. He'd started by sending her a list of all the ways she'd neglected Toby, all the mistakes she'd made. Times she'd administered the meds late, times she'd let Toby play too long, the inappropriate foods she'd let him have, the temperature she'd forgotten to take, the scuttled Minipress.

Late that night, the house quiet again, she sat with Nick's list on her desk. She minded it as one might mind a poisonous snake whose venom transmitted even through skin. Finally she took a sheet of lined paper. *Dear Nick*, she wrote. *Take Toby. Keep him safe from harm.*

Then she balled it up and lobbed it into the waste bin.

All the next week, she kept the scrupulous white meds chart with the blue marker. She posted, erased, re-posted. After twenty minutes, every day, she brought Toby in from basketball and no, he could not play Mortal Kombat; he could finish homework first. When Toby fought her, she hugged him tight, and said, again and firmly, No. He could have a snack, orange juice and raisins. She junked the old mozzarella sticks, bought new ones in low-fat, no salt added. *I do not need you*, she e-mailed Nick after another note arrived, this time by certified mail, *to play the heavy*.

Terminate the pregnancy. Divorce the husband. Rear the son. Follow Pete Simon to the land of the Nobel. Now there, Susannah thought as she drove from her lab in the still-cool morning to her appointment with Ben Lieberman, is a plan.

*B*en had, as he promised, been checking a couple of things while Toby was in the hospital. They'd done oxygenation tests, pulse, pressure, blood volume. He knew what he was seeing in Susannah's boy; he had seen it many times. With heart transplantees, you always saw it eventually. It wasn't rejection, or a virus, or a racing heart, or a fungal infection; it could be slowed but never reversed, and it had only one outcome. What Ben Lieberman saw on Toby Ames's chart was atherosclerosis, hardening of the arteries.

It was the last of the Days of Awe, the one ritual of his faith that Ben still held in high regard. Tomorrow the gates of heaven would close. He would stay home from the office, pin on his yarmulke, fast, spend hours on the phone with his family, maybe even make a pilgrimage to the synagogue to atone for his offenses.

From his office window he watched Susannah step briskly from her car. He admired her supple posture, her stride a little longer than her legs would seem to allow. In med school she'd tamed her hair into a short braid that ended in a tight knot at the top of her spine. One night she'd let him loosen it and spread the fine waves over her shoulders. Now that she'd had it chopped— though it grew each week, softening, the curl sneaking back—she seemed to stand defiant against gravity. A woman over forty, he thought, and shook his head. They always cut their hair eventually, like cutting the rope that held them to girlhood.

"I heard the news," he said when she sat down. "About the lab."

"Oh, yeah. Pete Simon. Pretty good catch, huh?"

"I suspect you were the bait."

Susannah shrugged, her shoulders erect under blue silk. "Marcus's reputation would be bait for anyone."

"Are you disappointed?"

"That I didn't get the post? No way. I excel in lab work, Ben. Not in schmoozing. Not in paper."

"Then you'll stay with the section."

"Jesus, Ben." She pulled a goofy face, rolled her round eyes, bigger with the hair short. "I'm *honored* to work with Pete. Plus the whole set-up for Toby's here."

"And your husband's business."

"Well. . . ."

Ben pretended to check his calendar for a few seconds. She didn't go on. "Nick is going to have to stay involved," he said finally, his eyes meeting Susannah's then dropping away, "for this next stage. With Toby's treatment, I mean."

"Of course. He's involved. There's no problem between us that way. Well . . . no. Not that way."

Ben raised an eyebrow, then hooked his glasses back on. "I've got good news and bad news."

"Good first. Bad can always wait."

"Toby's lung tests show no infiltrate from the cryptococcus. Once he finishes the oral sequence, he should be clear of it."

Susannah nodded rapidly. "And the bad?"

He slid the intravascular ultrasound across the desk. "You see the stenosis," he said.

She spread the print out; stared. "You mean the lesions here," she said slowly, touching her little finger to the image. "And here."

"Here, too." He tapped three dark areas. "All the epicardial arteries are affected. Sometime within the next year, he will have to undergo a re-transplant."

It wasn't as if he had delivered bad news. It was as if he had struck Susannah a blow on the head. Tears started out. A cry broke, between surprise and pain, that she seemed not even to hear. Before Ben's eyes, the graceful lovely doctor in the blue silk blouse crumbled like clay.

He came around his small gray desk. He pulled close the other visitor's chair—garnet-red upholstery with wooden arms meant to handle distraught patients—and sat holding her awkwardly. He patted her back. Still she seemed alternately to crack and to dissolve. He grabbed the box of Kleenex off the desk. "Here," he said, and she took three tissues.

"It's not . . . it's not the news I was expecting," she said when she'd used up all three and pulled two more from the box.

"It never is. The good part is that we have time, and that Toby's likely to get Status One."

"But it's—" She broke off. The scar on her chin trembled. "The end of Brooke."

"I'd think you'd *want* that whole fairy tale to end."

"Toby will think it's his fault. Nick will think it's mine."

"Send them to me. I'm the doctor. I'll tell them they are wrong. Look, Suzy." He sat forward in the chair and took both her hands. Except for the tiny frown on her chin, stitched to whiteness, her face had gone red, her nose swollen at the nostrils like a clown. He wanted equally to laugh and to kiss this puffy sorrow away. "You can't tell me *you're* subscribing to all this cellular memory crap. You're a *scientist.* You know the heart has certain physical functions. You know it's not a central part of a person's identity."

"Course not," said Susannah. "That would be the left front lobe of the brain, maybe, where the memory lies. Or the anterior lobe, where you see the regulation of emotions? Or how about the pituitary, since it secretes the hormones? Or how about a pianist's hands? Doesn't his identity lie—"

"You're getting philosophical on me, Suzy. I'm talking about keeping Toby alive."

Susannah rose from the chair. Slowly she walked around Ben's office. She ran her finger over the brown spines of the medical books, *tuptuptuptup.* "Toby is a guinea pig," she said, her voice hoarse. "He is a statistic."

"Yes, he is. He is also your son."

She'd reached the anatomy books, which she seemed to caress. "How much time do we have?"

"The atherosclerosis is at an early stage. Depending on diet, depending on what you want in terms of quality of life, depending on a donor heart. . . . I'd say six to twelve months."

"Six to twelve."

"It's a broad range, I know. But there aren't enough statistics to narrow it."

"In seven months—" He waited. She put a book back onto the shelf, nestling it carefully with the others.

"You've got something planned?"

"Sort of. I can adjust it, though." Her smile was strained. "Will he start feeling sick soon?"

"Not for another month or two."

"Then give me a little time. I'll talk to him when I have to."

"Sure, Suzy." Ben had come up behind her. He put his hands on her shoulders. When she didn't resist, he wrapped them across her torso. He felt her breath shudder in and out. Outside his office, patients waited. Once, he had longed for Susannah Hubert. Now she contained ordinary flesh and blood, and a door opened as onto a small garden, for him to walk through. "I think," he said close to her ear, "you are a remarkable woman."

Susannah shut her eyes and leaned back against him. He smelled of the starch in his white coat, of strong clinical soap. "There's even more," she said, "you don't know."

"I would like"—he released her to touch her saucy hair, fine as ever, shot with white strands dyed reddish brown, like cinnamon—"to hear the rest over dinner. Only the sun is setting." She followed his glance out the window, where the mountains glowed. "Yom Kippur," Ben explained. "Time to fast, until the gates of heaven close."

"Sin, right?" she said. "And atonement?"

"If I have offended you in any way, now's the time to let me know."

Susannah turned around and kissed him, first on the corner of the mouth, then fully. The kiss neither of a friend nor of a lover, as they both later thought, but of a promise keeper, a gambler, a maker of truces, a seal on the heart.

ix weeks—and neither Nick nor Susannah had moved beyond the changed locks, the key that he had scrupulously returned to her once Toby was out of the hospital. Wednesdays and Saturdays, Toby came to the shop or the house in Tinker Estates. Sure, he told Nick, Mom gave him all his meds. Dr. Lieberman had said he could still try out for the basketball team. Here was the note, Dr. Lieberman's note, Mom had wanted Dad to see it.

When Toby came up the mountain, Linsey took him on long walks down to Carvin's Cove. Once, she'd taken along an old fishing rod and shown him how to cast, like Brooke. "He's better than she was," she said when they came back to the house with a small-mouth bass. "He's got a stronger arm and a lot more patience."

She didn't seem to care whether Nick got custody. "You honestly think that's what I wanted?" she'd asked once, late at night, sitting up in her futon with the man's undershirt she wore to bed draped over her thin shoulders. "To be with you so I could be with Toby?"

"You talk about Brooke's heart. You're *here* for Brooke's heart."

"I am here," she said stubbornly, "for my own good reasons."

They made love silently, eyes open, as if to confirm that they knew one another. When Linsey announced that her son Charlie was coming back to Roanoke, Nick did his best to act unsurprised. "He's got another gig?" he asked.

"Nope. I think he wants to talk sense into his foolish mama."

"You didn't tell him—"

"About a certain Nicholas Ames? No. He just wants to meddle in my plans."

He did not ask what those plans were. Plans were the sort of thing that broke a spell. Neither did Linsey ask, when he told her this afternoon that Susannah had invited him for dinner. She only regarded him shyly, and he thought—for the first time, really—that she was beautiful. The spray of freckles, the high smooth plane of her forehead. He touched his thumb to her lips, right at the center where they blossomed, and her cool finger grazed the inside of his wrist.

He wouldn't be late, he promised, but she urged him. "Take your chance, Nicholas," she had said, his full name like an invention of hers, conferred on him like a gift.

It was a warm evening, for October. At the Tudor house, they ate on the deck, with blue votive candles that Susannah lit when the light leeched out of the sky. "I told Dad about basketball tryouts," Toby said when they'd made their way awkwardly through bowls of chili.

"Ben says it's all right," Susannah added. She sprinkled Tabasco on her beans. She liked them spicy, and the spice gave her face a rosy flush.

"I saw the note, thank you." Nick sipped his beer. He hadn't met with Ben Lieberman since the meningitis scare. Four days ago Toby had let slip that Ben had come by and watched a movie with Mom. "How often are practices?"

"Twice a week if I make the travel. We play games as far out as Richmond!"

"The coach says," added Susannah, with a glance at Toby that told Nick this subject was not supposed to have been raised, "he can modify practice for Toby. He's promised to make him rest after twenty minutes. And he'll put him in as a guard. They don't run so much."

"I'm a better forward," said Toby.

"Guard," repeated Susannah.

"Okay, Dad?"

"Sounds like a sealed deal," said Nick, finishing the beer.

"I think he wants to know," said Susannah carefully, "that you approve."

He set his glass down and regarded his wife. She was looking great. A few pounds heavier since summer, but it became her, and the hair she'd shorn was growing rapidly, curls trailing down her neck. He almost regretted the stern tone of the notes he'd been sending her. It seemed as though another husband had sent them, one living far away and out of touch.

"When's the first game, sport?" he asked Toby.

"The week before Thanksgiving."

From his back pocket he drew his small daybook and ostentatiously marked it. "I'll be there," he said.

Later, Toby glued to the World Series, Susannah brought two glasses of cognac out to the deck. While she'd been gone, Nick had been rehearsing the phrases he was ready to hear from her, *I want you to move back in*, *Toby needs his dad back*, *Let's talk about where we're going*. He blotted the word *custody* from his vocabulary.

"I got some medical news," was what Susannah said when she'd taken a sip of cognac, "a couple weeks back."

"News from—Dr. Lieberman?"

"Some of it from Ben, yeah. Toby's arteries are hardening. It happens to everyone eventually. Toby's case is on the early side. But Ben said it's never a surprise."

"Well, shit." Nick glanced inside, to where his son sat on the edge of the couch, cheering the Braves. "Can't we lower his salt intake, or his cholesterol, or something?"

"We can, yeah. I have. But it's not quite the same as when it happens to old people. With allografts it's quicker and less reversible."

Allograft, Nick repeated to himself, allograft. He wouldn't ask. He'd known once; he had explained it to Linsey. "Toby shouldn't be playing on the team then."

"Makes no difference." Susannah had a spit curl of her hair in her fingers and was twirling it. "So long as he doesn't overdo, he should stay in shape."

"So he can die healthy?"

"So he can handle the next transplant as well as possible."

"No," said Nick. He gripped the edge of the round picnic table, as if to steady it. Linsey's face swam before him, the way her eyes would shut at the news, her nostrils inhale fiercely. "No, Susannah. This heart was—was bad enough."

"It's been a good heart. We're talking about his arteries."

"That's not what I mean. We can't put him through the torture. He's just a kid, he shouldn't have to."

"This heart," said Susannah, letting go her hair, "was special. I felt the same way you do, at first. Then I realized we sort of—adopted this heart.

Apart from you and Linsey and—and Brooke. We'll get away from that feeling next time, Nick. It'll feel like a part. And we'll miss something, feeling about it that way. But it'll be easier, too. For Toby."

Nick stood up. He went to the porch railing, looked out over the back yard. Susannah was keeping it trimmed; she'd probably hired a teenager. The cognac burned his esophagus. "You told him yet?"

"He won't want it. He'll think he's killing Brooke. And that's why we have to do it. So if he ever decides it's not worth it, to go through the operation again—"

"Like how many times? Four? Five?" Nick turned suddenly. "How many transplants does the great Dr. Lieberman foresee?"

"I don't know! He doesn't know. But we now, and Toby later, should decide based on his own life, his own quality of life. Not on somebody else's life that's already over."

He came back to the table. When they'd sipped their way through the cognac in their glasses, Susannah rose and refilled them. Nick picked a splinter from the table, touched the lighter wood underneath. He saw the thing again, the way you see anything that you think you've put behind you. The biopsies, the preoperative drugs, the endless nights on Status One, the ward full of labored breathing and oblivious nurses, the terror of the false start, the equal terror of the real moment. The moment when they saw open your child's chest and run his body off a machine while they rip and suction. The stitches like Frankenstein's monster. Toby weeping with pain, hour upon hour of pure pain.

From inside they heard Toby whoop. He was standing on the couch, pumping his arms. "How 'bout them Braves?" said Susannah as she passed through the door.

"I'll take him to a game," said Nick. "Next season. Third-row seats." He smiled at his wife. But she'd sat and was looking down, as if at something in her lap. "You said *some* of it," he remembered. "Only some of the news was from Ben."

"I'm taking a medical leave," she said, "in the spring. Pete Simon says it's not a bad time. He wants to go slow getting started on his own projects, anyway. We'll replace Tomiko and then I'll be off. I'm going to have a baby."

Sympathetic nerves zapped Nick's heart before he completely understood the words. It swelled and hammered; it lifted him from his seat. "Oh darling," he said, going down awkwardly on one knee before Susannah, "that's—" He laughed, not from anything funny but because a gasp didn't make enough noise. "Fabulous," he said. "No matter what. I mean—you know. Genetically. It's still the best."

"I know," she said. He could feel her nod. She ran her fingers through what was left of his hair. "I waited to tell you till I decided. But it is. Good news."

"When?" he asked.

"Mid-April it's due."

"So you've known—"

"A month or so. No, two months. I'm sorry. I had to think about— about all of us."

Behind Nick the door swung open, and Toby stuck his head out. "Braves five, Indians two!" he shouted. "Top of the eighth!"

"Cheer 'em on, sport," said Nick.

"To bed right after the game," said Susannah.

Slamming shut the screen door, Toby melted back into the house. Nick took the blunt tips of his wife's fingers in his own. "Does this mean—" he began.

"That you should move back in? I don't know," Susannah said, and a vise took hold of Nick's heart. "I have—a little exploring to do, on that end."

"Ben Lieberman?"

"Maybe." Her fingers were warm. "I'll let you know," she said. "Promise."

Before he left, he offered to walk the dog. As he rounded the corner back toward the house, he saw her. Linsey. Her car was nowhere on the street, but still he thought he saw her slight figure on the balcony of his house, where he didn't live anymore. She was standing outside Toby's room, under the long arm of the oak tree that brushed the house. Through the panes you could see the faint yellow glow of Toby's night light. He saw Linsey's hand on the crossbar of the locked French doors, like a girl shut out of a party. Her name on his lips, he pulled Coal along the sidewalk, past the streetlamp. And then Linsey disappeared. Or not disappeared, but turned back into the whitened tree branch and elongated shadows that criss-crossed the balcony.

How he had wanted to catch her there. To wait at the base of the tree and lift her slight body down as she descended. To feel her hair fall across his face.

It had been a trick of light, nothing more. And still, later, Nick drove slowly back up the mountain, as if giving Linsey the chance to get there before he did and be spared any explanations.

hen his ma's postcard had come, Charlie had tried to pack a bag that night. "I cannot let her move back to Wardleysville," he said to Jermaine. "Those bigoted crackers will make grits out of her."

"Maybe they're her kind of people."

"She thought that John character was her kind of people."

"She is a grown lady, man."

"Hey, I'm a grown man. But if I was about to do something stupid, I'd want someone on my ass."

Jermaine had persuaded him to wait a few days. See if she didn't change her mind. Maybe she was just homesick. She was going into the second year of this, wasn't she? This could be second-stage grief.

After a week, Charlie phoned. When he heard his ma was listing the ranch house, he called his friend Dylan and got him to fill in for the next four gigs. He told the temp service to put him on the shelf. In his beat-up Honda Civic, tapes of Miles Davis playing through the night, he drove over the mountains to Roanoke.

When he arrived in the morning, he and his ma smoked a joint and didn't say much. He noticed there was a guy's stuff around. He borrowed his ma's bed for a four-hour nap. When he woke, the afternoon sun was blazing. He shook his head clear, stepped out, and said he thought they ought to go down to that cove nearby. "We could rent a boat," he said. "Float on the water and talk a bit."

The cove was like a pewter plate, yellow leaves littering the surface near the shore. With the rare gust of wind came a flurry of pine needles, their tips glinting in the sun. Charlie's ma stood by the dock, her hands on her hips. At her feet was a picnic basket to which Charlie had added a couple of Heinekens and his depleted bag of grass.

"You used to take me out on that lake in Granite Falls," he said, dragging the boat into the shallow water. "Now it's my turn."

He helped her in and they pushed off.

"So," he said. "I don't see you packing, yet."

"Oh, yes, I am. Jeepers, it's great to see you, Charlie."

"I didn't see boxes."

"Not yet, no. Just suitcases. They're all full, in the garage. And I've collected a few empty boxes for my kitchen things. And the photo albums, of course."

"I thought you were selling the house."

"Listing it. They say houses look better, furnished. I can always come back for the other stuff. You look great, honey. You've put on muscle."

Charlie leaned back against the pull of the oars. His hands felt good gripping the wood. Temp jobs in Nashville were mostly data entry, carpal tunnel work. He liked the stretch of his arms. "So had the time come?" he said when they were free of the dock area. "To go?"

"I saw it in Toby's eyes," his ma said matter-of-factly. "At the hospital."

"Saw what? Your marching orders?"

"You ever considered that we die," she said, "and dissolve into something greater?"

"I have heard that theory. Never comforted me much."

"Well." His ma trailed a hand in the water. She wore an old straw hat that he remembered seeing once on Brooke, bent at the brim and casting a checkered pattern on her face. "If there is any truth to the idea, you'll find it here. In what's happened to your sister's heart, I mean. Whatever's left of her has been transformed. I believe she is free of us at last."

"That is good news," said Charlie. "And are you free of her, Mama?"

"I should hope not ever." Her face was hidden by the hat. "She was my sweet girl."

Charlie pulled on the oars. He'd been working out at the gym in East Nashville. He wasn't a dandy, and he didn't care for beefcake, but it was good to have biceps that worked. He could hold his own in a fight, if it came to that.

"Do I want to know," he said after a time, setting the oars in the locks, "who the guy is?"

"You saw him?" She leaned back on her arms, her face to the sun aslant.

"Saw his gear."

"Is it okay if I say he doesn't matter?"

"Doesn't he?"

"He does, actually. But not to why I'm leaving."

They drifted. Charlie remembered the lake in Granite Falls, his ma rowing. He remembered Brooke as a baby, sitting on the floor of the boat, her fat feet with the toes curled. A knot came in his chest, and to relieve it he said, "You been on this lake before?"

"It's the town reservoir, not just any lake. And no, I haven't."

"Your boyfriend doesn't take you here?"

Blushing, she tucked a strand of pale hair behind her ear. "I'm not saying I've got a boyfriend, Charlie."

"Sorry. Your lover."

"It gets complicated, you know. When you get older."

"Hey, I was happy to see it. At least you're not going to Wardleysville to catch yourself a hillbilly husband."

"Well." His ma leaned back on her arms, her face to the sun aslant. "Maybe I am at that."

"Naw, Mama. You're not running toward. You're running away."

Charlie rowed. Glancing back, he saw they were advancing toward an island. "You ever swim here?" he asked.

"I said. It's the reservoir. You're not allowed."

"I didn't ask if you were allowed."

His ma giggled. "The places I used to take you." She shook her head. "I set a bad example."

"There's a lake near me in Nashville. You're allowed to swim there. Spring fed."

"Cold."

"Sure, but clear. They don't allow powerboats." He glanced behind him and pulled farther right, toward the island. "Gay people go there," he said.

"Good. Then I wouldn't be annoyed."

"I'd like to take you swimming there, Mama."

He paused; let the oars drift awhile. His ma looked over the flat surface. "That would be nice," she finally said. And then, "You always been gay, Charlie?"

He took up the oars again. "I thought you'd never ask."

"Well, have you?"

"Sure. I don't know. I've never been anything else." He pulled. His biceps bulged. His face felt itchy with sweat; he hadn't shaved before driving out. "Why, Mama? Do you think you're gay?"

"No, as a matter of fact, I don't."

"Did you really love him?"

"John?"

He didn't answer. He didn't want to say the guy's name.

"I did, yes," his ma said as they drew into the weeds by the island. "He had—you never saw this, Charlie, but he had a shyness about him. That I liked. And then, I think he wanted the best."

"For Brooke, you mean."

"I'm not saying he was a saint. But yeah. For Brooke."

Charlie shook his head. "Mama," he said.

"All right. Maybe his own life was a little empty. Or getting that way, day by day. And he couldn't help borrowing a little from hers, to sort of fill it up. Parents do that, you know. They think they can always pay it back."

"You must have loved him," said Charlie, resting his elbows on his knees, "to go to a length like that to forgive him."

"I didn't say," said his ma, "I forgave him."

Which, thought Charlie, was news.

The rowboat bumped into a tree fallen into the water. Leaning forward, his ma grabbed a branch and pulled the boat farther in. "I'll tie the rope," she said. "We can get out and sit a spell."

There wasn't much place to sit, only a thickly grown patch of damp grass and one ungainly boulder. The rest was cattails and brush. "They say a whole family got hit by lightning here once," said his ma. Though the warm air hardly moved, she was hugging herself—as if, Charlie thought, telling the truth had pulled the warmth right out of her. "They got caught in a storm on the water, and they canoed over here. But they stood on the edge to watch the storm, and a bolt came down and zapped them all at once. Parents and two kids."

"I doubt that," said Charlie, opening the picnic basket.

"You never know. It seems so sad, all of them at once. Sadder than if someone were left. Though that person might wish they'd got zapped too."

"Nobody really wishes that," said Charlie. He twisted open a beer and handed it to his ma.

"No," she said thoughtfully.

They drank. Charlie smoked a menthol cigarette, the last of an old pack. His ma ate a little, but he wasn't hungry, though he was sweating from the rowing. The sun began to dip.

"I came here," he said at last, "because I aim to stop you from going to Wardleysville,"

"Why? I told you. I'm all done with being here."

"What about the boy?"

"Who, Toby?"

"Well, he was the point, wasn't he? Whatever you think's happened to Brooke's spirit. He got her heart. You wanted to follow that out."

"I did." Gingerly, his ma lifted out a tin of tabouli, and unwrapped a bag of pita. "He's a good boy," she said. "He reminds me of her sometimes. And you know, the funny thing"—she tore a hunk of pita, but didn't scoop—"the funny thing is that *he* thinks she is part of him. It makes him better, to think that."

"So now you leave. Rather than disabuse him of the notion."

Charlie's ma didn't answer. She set the pita down in the basket and rose. Stepping partway out onto the tree trunk that jutted over the water, she surveyed the cove. "You know," she said, "I still got Brooke's ashes. I sprinkled John's over the hill in Granite Falls, the way I figured he'd of wanted. But I kept hers. Would you come out here with me again, tomorrow? And we can scatter them here. Before I go."

"Sure, Mama," said Charlie. "I can do that."

Satisfied, she settled onto the thick grass next to him, and ate hungrily. The sun traveled over the cove. They took off their sneakers, rolled their jeans, and dipped their calves in the cold autumn water. Charlie told his ma he was thinking of moving in with Jermaine.

"But before I do that," he said as he popped open a second beer, "I want to propose something to you. You want to leave here, fine. But don't go to Wardleysville. Not right yet. You got the whole world before you, Mama. You go back to that place, and they'll never let you out. I want to propose that you come stay with me awhile."

"Oh, Charlie. I couldn't do that."

"There's lots of good craft outlets around Nashville. There're places that see weaving as an art, you know, not just something old-fashioned."

"I'd just get in your way, honey."

"No, you wouldn't. You've seen my place. I've got that whole other bedroom, and that big empty room in the back where you could put your loom."

His ma had unrolled her damp jeans and settled her straw hat back over her hair. "You are the sweetest son in the world," she said, closing up the picnic basket. "But I didn't accept charity when I was twenty-two and making do with you on my own, and I am not about to start accepting it now that I'm a rich lady with a life insurance payout."

"You don't understand, Mama." Charlie stood. He felt a little wobbly, like the island was floating. Bracing himself, he helped his ma to her feet. "I am not offering this to you. I am asking this for me. You know, when you met John, I think I needed just a little tiny bit more of you in my life." With his thumb and forefinger, slightly drunk, he showed her just how much. "Now I would like to take that, please. Just that little bit. If you can spare it. And I warn you right now, I am not asking a loan. I won't pay it back."

The sun kissed her lips, and her row of white teeth, as she beamed at him. Beamed so hard she made crow's feet start up either side of her eyes. He'd never seen those before on his mother, Charlie would tell Jermaine later, and they were the most beautiful accent he had ever witnessed on a mortal woman.

Chapter 42

*T*hat Susannah knew Ben Lieberman's address and had never gone there once in six years hinted, perhaps, at what would happen once she crossed that threshold. When she finally did, it was after dropping Max and Toby at *Flubber 3* and picking up a bottle of Jack Daniels, which she knew Ben liked. He opened the door still in his scrubs. They both laughed. Susannah moved past him to the kitchen, to pour them each a glass. When she turned around, she could barely breathe.

She had thought they would go slow. But their kisses sang with sex. Their mouths gripped and tugged. Tongues flickered, teeth bit, lips would not stop tasting. They kissed even as they made their way to Ben's dark bed, even as they fumbled to nakedness and locked their furious bodies and finally let their nether regions fall away from each other, everything sated except their mouths, which touched again and again until the movie was probably over and Susannah had to go.

The second time, slower and sexier, was the night Ben came over to watch the video with Toby and Susannah. He stayed until just before dawn. In the early gray light he guessed Susannah's condition and seemed to make love to her belly, first his tongue in her navel and later his hands describing the faint plumpness from hip to hip. Then he let his index finger trail upward, through the passage between her breasts, over the collarbone and the dark mole on her neck. "Tell me again," he said, stopping at the scar, "where you got this."

"Dog next door," Susannah said, exhaling with relief. "It was digging baby rabbits out of a nest between our two yards. I remember how the rabbits looked like they weren't even ready to have been born yet, all pink and blind and naked. I thought I'd be their noble rescuer."

"So you weren't going to dissect them."

"No way. I was a nature girl, then."

"And so you are marked." He kissed the little frown, its pucker of skin.

"They put the dog to sleep. That was the worst part. From that day on, every time I passed the neighbor's house, he made a point of coming out. He'd wag his finger at me, like this." Susannah put up her index and rocked it back and forth like a metronome.

"So you felt sorry for the dog."

"I didn't have anything against the dog. It was doing something perfectly natural."

"Like biting you?" Ben fixed his teeth on her chin. She lay immobile. "You always forgive the things that bite you?" he asked. He moved his teeth to her shoulder, and she gave a little cry.

"Most always," she said, and bit him back.

The third time they made love, Susannah came as soon as he put his mouth on her clitoris. She said she couldn't help herself, apologizing like a man with premature ejaculation, and he said he loved her for it, and she said she loved him, and she rubbed her lips against the bristle of his mustache and then she wept. This was at his apartment again, while Tomiko babysat Toby. They mated fiercely and even heartlessly. Ben cried out as he came and then rocked Susannah's body as if in the grip of a dream.

Then they lay under the damp sheet, in the strange warm night of Indian summer, and Ben asked when she was due.

"April," she said, a little hoarsely but without surprise.

"So that's why you're taking leave in the spring."

"You have a spy," said Susannah. She blew gently on Ben's chest, the springy dark hair there.

"Danny Griffiths," said Ben, and Susannah nodded against his shoulder. Of course. Danny was doing a tour under Ben, part of his residency. "He thinks you're looking at offers, from other labs."

"Danny doesn't know much about being a mom. I'd take the time off for Toby anyhow, if your timetable's right."

"It's not an exact science."

"Yeah." They both laughed, a soft sound in the dark. "I think we missed the exact-science boat," said Susannah.

"I missed a lot of boats."

Susannah propped herself on her elbow. Streetlight cast a blue glow over Ben's strong-boned face. "We could've decided not to touch each other at all in this life," she said. "That would've been missing the boat."

Ben laced his fingers into her free hand, then kissed her knuckles one by one. His lips were velvet; Susannah shut her eyes. "Quid pro quo," he whispered.

"Hmm?"

"Tit for tat. That's how this started."

"That is not true."

"Is too."

"How can you say that?"

"A woman's revenge," said Ben, "can be a man's only opportunity."

Susannah didn't answer. She opened her eyes, tried to read his.

"All I want to know"—Ben laid her hand on his chest, where she could feel the lub-dub of his heart—"is whether we traveled any distance from that."

"Oh, Ben." Shifting her weight, she kissed his shoulder, his ear, his forehead; her breast grazed his nipple. "Revenge," she said, "is like a little creature waving at us from a distant shore."

"You sure?"

"Sure." Her hand lingered, then reached further. He let his legs draw apart. "You married once," she said. "Someone told me. One of the old gang from Columbia. You never talk about it."

"No." Growing aroused, he thought, This is the last time, and a taste like bitter oranges came into his mouth. "It was after you left the program," he said. "She was a religion professor at Columbia. We met at a seminar on ethics. Her father was a Jew, her mother was a Quaker. She'd thought she could get a doctorate in religion and figure herself out. After I left, she took up with the chief resident."

"And what was he?"

"Good Catholic boy."

He turned her onto her side and entered her from behind. "Oh, sweet," she said.

"Mmn," said Ben.

"Nicholas," she said, "has been spending his time with a Buddhist."

"Well, now." He moved in her, the depth of her. "We've covered, what? a third of the world's religions."

"Confucius say," she said, reaching her hand back to cup his buttocks, "oh Ben, oh Ben, he say you a good man, he say you a sweet fuck. Oh Ben," and he reached around, deep in her now; he would make her come a last time, "I believe in this, Ben, in this. This. Oh."

When they kissed at the door, Susannah showered and fresh, her fluffy hair damp at the roots, he gripped the soft skin of her belly just once, as if he had the right, as if he had put life in there.

Chapter 43

*A*t first when Max didn't make the team, Toby Brooke was almost sick to his stomach. Everything about it was wrong. Max was at the very top of the age bracket for Travel B, and Toby Brooke was at the bottom. It was at Max's basket that Toby Brooke first learned to shoot, four years ago when all the Ameses had was a Fisher-Price plastic setup and Max had a regulation hoop. Being shorter, Max was going for point guard, and he was an awesome point guard, much better for point guard than Toby Brooke was for guard. Only there were two other kids, Dae Kwan Jones and Odel Spight, who were going for point guard too, and they were a little faster. Max said they got on the roster because they were black. But just as Toby Brooke was wondering whether to agree with Max in order to keep the friendship, Max got so jealous of him for making the team that he told the three biggest guys on it that Toby Ames had a girl heart. After that Toby Brooke wasn't sick to his stomach, but he was so mad that he made his mom promise that even if Max dropped dead tomorrow, he, Toby Brooke, would not have to get Max's heart sewn into his chest.

And so the yellow leaves fell and swirled on the facing driveways, only Toby Brooke shot alone at his hoop, and Max didn't come outside much. Of course Max didn't know that Toby Brooke was even going to need a new heart; no one did. Still the talk at school had gotten meaner. Fifth grade, Toby Brooke's dad had said, that's a tough one. And it was. Maybe, Toby Brooke thought, because there weren't girls around at all any more. They played on the other side of the schoolyard, their arms crossed over whatever was happening on their chests. Now and then they glanced at the boys, and when they smiled at Toby Brooke, he figured it was because they'd heard about the girl heart, and he looked away.

Even the girls knew a person had died, though. And even though none of the kids knew his arteries were hardening, when the boys got sick of teasing about the girl heart, they started making cross signs. They'd hold their fingers out like that, crossed, to ward him off when he passed in the hall. Watch out for Ames, they said, he'll rip your heart outta your chest and swallow it down. Hey Ames! they shouted. Your dad sell voodoo dolls in his shop or what?

The very first weekend his dad got his own apartment, Toby Brooke stayed overnight. They ate Weight Watchers chicken parmigiana—Toby got one, his dad had three—and he asked his dad what a voodoo doll was. "It's a superstitious thing," his dad said, pulling the plastic off the little tan-colored plate. "You make a doll of your enemy and stick pins in it, and where you stick pins, he's supposed to feel pain."

"If you stick a bunch of pins in the doll's heart, would it have a heart attack?"

"According to the superstition. But it's never happened. Why? Some-one got a voodoo doll of you, Tobe?"

"They were just talking about the teacher," Toby Brooke said, pick-ing at his chicken. He tried to eat it because he knew his dad got it for his arteries, just like he let his dad count out his meds even though he could do it all himself by now.

Next morning at his dad's shop Toby Brooke looked around, but he didn't see anything that looked like you could stick pins into it. Just Indian Army Lancers in perfect formation and Black Watch Highlanders positioned on a cardboard hill and several dioramas of Napoleonic guards. Toby Brooke had zero interest in what either of his parents did for work. What his mom did looked boring and difficult, and what his dad did looked babyish. But he loved the smells and sounds of the places where they worked. They made him feel safe, the benzene and alcohol of his mom's lab, Tomiko's squeaky voice, the tinkle over his dad's door, the throaty greetings of the old men who wandered in looking for antique sharpshooters. "I could just stay here all day tomorrow and help you," he offered. "We're not doing anything at school."

"You must be doing something."

"Not anything important. Well, math."

"Math is important."

Toby Brooke couldn't argue with that, except that they'd started giving him harder math, the way Linsey'd said they used to give Brooke. Numbers danced in his head. At practice he saw forty-degree backboard shots, figured the number of dribbles per minute, calculated rebound percentages. "I can do math by myself," he said.

"You can't give yourself grades," said his dad. He was touching up a kneeling British fusilier, his weapon perfectly parallel to the fake ground. Swiftly Toby Brooke counted: six fusiliers, nine and a half minutes to touch this one up, fifty-seven minutes for the group.

So he went and put up with the stupid comments about him being a vampire and him being a girl inside, and he aced the math tests and tried not to glance over at Max's house when he bicycled to basketball practice. Every morning he did fifty sit-ups and two hundred jumping jacks. Holding steady, Dr. Lieberman said, checking him just after Halloween. I hope you're not sick of that heart just yet. Not just yet, said Toby Brooke obediently, and Dr. Lieberman messed up his hair the way he always did. His mom said he could call Dr. Lieberman "Ben" outside the office, but Toby Brooke was sticking for now with Dr. Lieberman.

Funny, though—when the NBA season opened and his mom let him stay up late to watch the Heat beat the Mariners, he was like a different boy watching. The year before he'd still been stuck home, taking little walks to the end of the block and back, waiting to see what basketball card Max might drop by. He'd been, his mom kept reminding him, one sick puppy. But he'd watched the season opener then too—Knicks versus Wizards—and he'd pictured himself first as Sprewell, then as Camby, then as that draft pick the Wizards had got. Now he saw a bunch of athletes like he'd never be, doing incredible things with an orange ball. Having a good time? his mom asked when he jumped up on the couch. Yeah! he said, and he was. It was just different.

Then one day, when his dad came over to the house to talk about arrangements, Toby Brooke said he would walk Coal, and he slipped over the fence behind Max's back yard and through the woods to the hay field. They'd done the last baling for the season, and the bales stood round and yellow as peanut butter logs in the sloping meadow. Just the way he used to with Max, Toby Brooke climbed up onto a bale and stuck a long piece of hay between his teeth. Coal backed way up, then took a leap, and sat panting next to him. Sharp ends pricked their butts. The meadow ran down to the river where his dad jogged. In winter when Toby Brooke was little, before they found anything wrong with his heart, his mom would pull him in a sled over the snow here. The runners, he remembered, sang in the snow, and bits of old hay would poke up and make him think of his father's beard in the morning.

Toby Brooke sat the way Linsey had taught him, both feet poised on his thighs, wrists on his knees. He shut his mouth and eyes and breathed through his nose, one two three in, one two three four out. He tried not to think about Max or the kids who made vampire crosses with their fingers or that one girl in the other section who'd biked down his street and smiled but then sped up. He could smell apples rotting from the tree at the edge of the wood. He sat like a statue until something in the sharp wind tickled his nose, and his legs sprang undone while he sneezed.

Always they baled the hay while he was at school. The yellow combines came through and sliced down stalks that had been taller than he was. He used to imagine this was an arrangement his parents had made, in case he were to be playing among the tall hay and be cut down like that. Once Max had shown him the head of what he said was a rattlesnake cut by the mower. The mouth was open and you could see the slender fangs on each side, the oily scales stretched around the snout and over the bony frame of the dead pencil point eyes, the neat nostrils at the square tip. It was missing the tongue and looked the way Toby Brooke imagined he looked at the dentist. The blades must get mice, too, he and Max had agreed, and even slow rabbits, and the grasshoppers probably turned to green juice.

From the bale Toby Brooke could see the arc of the interstate against the mountains, the blue mist that gave them their name. When his parents drove him to Durham, they went over the ridge there, and his ears popped. From behind him, he could hear the roar of the arterial. If he turned around he'd see the Star just lighting up the mountain that they said lay in the heart of Roanoke. The stubbled hay lay across the meadow like yellow skin.

They just used the names, of course. Artery, heart, skin. The head of the path, the shoulder of the road. That stretch of road just before his neighborhood, what they called the neck.

He curled his toes in their sneakers, over the side of the bale. He was in the body of what he could see, like Brooke was in his body. Brooke, Toby, world. Brooke. Toby. World.

Suddenly, next to him, Coal barked and stood, batting his tail. Twisting around, Toby saw Max push out of the woods.

"Your mom said," said Max, hoisting himself up on the bale, "you'd headed back this way."

"I didn't think she saw me."

"What's your dad doing here?"

"I dunno."

"Aren't they getting divorced?"

Toby shrugged. "Maybe not. Linsey left."

He didn't think he wanted to mention Dr. Lieberman.

"I joined the swim team," said Max.

"Hey. That's good." Toby could feel his heart begin to beat faster. He didn't want to say too much.

"Sorry about that stuff I said."

"It's okay. It is a girl heart."

"You want to shoot some?"

"Maybe," said Toby. "In a minute." They sat on the bale. Coal licked Max's ear, and Max knocked him off. He scrambled up again and lay down behind Toby's back, his black coat warm in the afternoon sun. After a few minutes Toby said, "See that pine tree there?"

"The one that's all stripped at the bottom? Yeah."

"Say that's at a right angle to the meadow."

"The meadow slopes."

"That doesn't matter so long as the tree is at a right angle. Okay," Toby said, licking his dry lips, "say it's fifty feet tall, and the sun's shining on it at an angle of sixty degrees. How far is it from the base of the tree to the end of the shadow?"

Max shaded his eyes. "I dunno. A hundred feet?"

"More like eighty-seven. Well, not quite. But that's as close as I can figure in my head."

"I don't get it," said Max.

"You have to make up a bunch of triangles," said Toby, "until you get one where all the sides are fifty feet. Then you add and multiply them all together. It's like a jigsaw puzzle."

"I don't even get one triangle," said Max. "Can we go shoot now?"

"In a sec."

Toby took another stalk of hay and chewed it. Its sweetness went right down to his belly. Somewhere back in the neighborhood, a leaf blower started up. "I'm not going to be a pro basketball player," he said.

"Toby, I apologized already. You don't have to make me feel better."

"I'm not." Toby lay back against Coal, who had to scoot almost to the edge of the bale. The dog's fur felt cooked; underneath, his lungs went like bellows. Above them a few stray clouds scudded. The earth felt round. Circumference, Toby thought. Diameter. He was in the world, Brooke was in him. But like a memory. Not Toby Brooke anymore. "You can do a bunch of things with a transplanted heart," Toby said to the passing clouds. "But you can't be a pro athlete."

"You never know," protested Max.

"You know," said Toby, "a few things."

He sat up, then stood. Then leaped down from the bale at a forty-five degree angle. The bale six feet, length on the ground six feet, he'd jumped more than eight feet. He rolled three and stood up. Hay stuck to his shirt and pants. "Elephant," he said, "and I get to shoot first."

"Only if you reach the pole first," said Max.

Susannah and Nick, standing some distance apart on the back deck, watched them streak across the yard, Max ahead and pulling ahead farther. At the oak tree Toby leaped, swung, glanced back quickly at the distance he'd covered, then loped on, leaves showering his wake.

The letter from Linsey was waiting when Nick dropped him off from an afternoon at the shop. He and Susannah both waited until Toby had taken it into his room to read it. When he emerged, he left the torn envelope, as if by accident, on the piano. Then they each—one by one, without ever talking about it—took a turn. They read the loopy scrawl, the lines wavering on the unmarked bond paper, the captions on the back of the two photos Linsey had taken the day of the basketball tryouts.

One photo, they learned from reading, had been kept back from them.

Susannah returned the letter to Toby's desk, where it disappeared. The letter read:

> My dearest Toby Brooke (well, you are the only
> Toby Brooke I know, so you have to be my dearest),
> I wanted to say goodbye to you, but I was afraid you
> were already mad at me for some things and if
> you started to be mad again, I would stay and made a
> nuisance of myself. My son Charlie who you met invited
> me to come live a spell with him in Nashville. and I said
> OK. He needs me right now even more than you, and
> you know how we mamas like to be needed!
> Any how, I called your mom before I left. She told
> me you're doing great! She said you're probably going
> to get a new heart before spring is out. I think that is so
> good, and I hope you're lucky and get a nice healthy
> heart before those dumb old arteries slow you up too
> much. I am proud of you, and I know your mom and
> dad are proud of you too for being so brave about this

stuff. I told Charlie's friend Jermaine all about you, and he said you remind him of the Tin Man in The Wizard of Oz. You know, the one who supposedly doesn't have a heart, but he is the kindest of them all? (I thought he got a heart in the end, but Jermaine says no, he just gets a certificate. Which wouldn't be enough for you, but you see what Jermaine means. It's not the physical heart that counts so much as the idea of the heart.) (Jermaine had to explain all this to me.)

I know you're worried about the fact that when you get your new heart they will be taking Brooke's heart away, and it will stop beating forever. I had to stop writing here for a minute. Because it makes me sad. Sure it does. But not like you might think. I will miss Brooke's heart beating in you the way you miss anything that reminds you of a person. Like when my daddy died and I wanted his fishing boots, and my mama had thrown them away. I'd like to have killed her! But that's all it is. And you know what? I think whatever was reminding me of my daughter, which I called her heart, has just gone right into you now, Toby. Like blood into your veins. Which is why if you don't mind I will take you up on your offer and address you as Toby Brooke just between ourselves.

My son Charlie and I scattered Brooke's ashes over Carvin's Cove (near you) so whatever happens to her heart it will probably be near to what was left of the rest of her. Maybe you will go there from time to time and think about us. I enclose two pictures I took of you and one I took of Brooke a year and a half ago. You are right now just about the age that she will always be in my mind.

One more thing. I know it was for Brooke's sake that you did not blow a gasket at me those last few weeks I was in Roanoke. As time goes on and you get your new heart and you grow up, I expect you will not think too kindly of me. Because for a little time there I took your daddy away from your mama, or so it must seem. It must seem a poor way to treat people who welcomed me into their lives. It is not the way any of us are brought up. So if you have to get mad about it, then get mad. But know this: all I just wrote about Brooke and her heart, how she's really truly gone into memory, I knew all that before—I mean before all the grown-up stuff started happening. So what happened was really just about my feelings and your daddy's feelings (grownups can be mixed up too!) and nothing to do with you or Brooke.

I hope you never think I had a wicked heart. The doctors say all hearts are more or less the same. And I guess I want to say the same thing about the other kind of heart—they're kind of the same, not one more wicked or kind than another, and that includes people I've known in my life too.

If you want to write to me I will be at the address on this letter. I am weaving a lot and teaching classes, and Charlie showed me how to get a grant from the state to do some of the old designs. If I move, I will let you know. Always, unless you tell me not to. Today I did a Heart Sutra Meditation for you. You are a brave boy, and I hold you in my heart, and I want you to grow big and strong and wise, and I will always watch for you.

Your friend,
Linsey Hunter

Nerves of the Heart was designed and typeset on a Macintosh computer system using QuarkXPress software. The text is set in Janson and the chapter openings are set in Isadora. This book was designed by Cheryl Carrington, typeset by Kimberly Scarbreough, and manufactured by Thomson-Shore, Inc. The paper used in this book is designed for an effective life of at least three hundred years.